Marya

Marya

by
Elinore Keister

MOODY PRESS

CHICAGO

© 1982 by
THE MOODY BIBLE INSTITUTE
OF CHICAGO

Library of Congress Cataloging in Publication Data

Keister, Elinore, 1934—
  Marya.

  Summary: When a young woman makes Jesus a part of her
life all the uncertainties and heartaches of the past become
easier to bear.
  [1. Christian life—Fiction] I. Title.
PZ7.K2524Mar   [Fic]   82-3489
ISBN 0-8024-5199-3   AACR2

ISBN: 0-8024-5199-3

2 3 4 5 6 7 **Printing/LC/Year** 87 86 85 84 83

Printed in the United States of America

*To Ann, without whose travail in prayer
this story would not have been brought forth*

Part 1

1

The clatter of the day's business was winding up to its usual frenzied racket. The typewriters' staccato was punctured intermittently by the slam of a file cabinet drawer, while chair wheels squealed under their occupants' weight, and numerous phones on numerous desks jangled in unison.

If the silence started imperceptibly that morning, it ended pronouncedly. And the silence was more deafening than the noise. No head turned to see what caused the interruption; it was the Interruption that precipitated the head-turning.

The Interruption was a trifle over six feet tall, crowned with a luxuriant sea of blonde waves and illuminated by two penetrating beacons of steel-gray. As the glittering beams scanned the unfamiliar scene before him, a calculating, cynical half smile accentuated a deep cleft in the broad, square-set chin. On this occasion an avocado green suit was molded around the athletic frame, and the tie was a wild plaid ablaze with brilliant red. With long strides the Interruption turned down the corridor leading to the accounting department.

"Catch an eyeful of that!"

"There, Goldie, how about a go-around with that one!"

"Say, where did *he* come from?"

"Is there a ring on the third finger?"

The whispers joined a few faintly audible sighs, and slowly and reluctantly the clatter resumed in Central Typing.

Allyn Jespers managed to unearth from the bottom of her file drawer an all-but-forgotten memorandum that suddenly required immediate attention in the advertising department. Of course, in reaching Advertising with the memo, it was necessary for her to pass by the door into Accounting. There she observed that the newcomer had taken the desk vacated recently by the retirement of the chief accountant's assistant. Having deposited the memo on a puzzled young clerk's desk, Allyn made a circuitous path back to her typewriter. At each typewriter she passed, she paused in reply to eager queries to relay the scrap of information she had been able to ascertain.

It was only a few minutes until Martha Holliday, secretary to the office manager, hastily remembered a clipping from the newspaper that her boss had asked her several days before to carry into the advertising manager. She had misplaced it in the incoming mail, and it was only with some annoyance that she finally located it. Her observations on her way past the door into Accounting didn't reveal any more than had Allyn's. What a pity Advertising was the only department farther down the hall than Accounting. The girls in the main office couldn't think of any other reasons for going to Advertising or any reason for visiting Accounting.

It wasn't until the ten o'clock mail delivery that their golden opportunity dawned. The new girl from the mailroom was beginning her morning rounds. She would stop by each desk in the accounting department as part of her duties.

"Hey, Bonnie," Sue Ramsey called as the mail girl passed her desk with the morning's delivery. "When you get into Accounting, look to see if that blond Roman god in the green suit has a ring on his left hand."

Bonnie Lake registered some perplexity, for the mailroom was secluded from the main traffic through the office and she had not seen the new arrival. But she made a mental note that some sort of Roman god had shown up in Accounting and she must look for a ring on his left hand.

When Bonnie reached Accounting, she discovered it was break time for the accountants, and only two were at their desks. Of those, neither was wearing a green suit and she would never have mistaken Tom Robard and Hal Gregersen for Roman gods. Having been at Paramount Plastics for only three weeks, she did not yet know many of the other employees. She had, however, made the acquaintance of Tom and Hal. Tom's girth must be somewhere in the neighborhood of fifty inches, and if his hair had ever been blond there was no evidence of it now. In fact, there was precious little evidence of any hair at all. Roman god? She even laughed out loud.

Hal was a different matter. Although it would be difficult to imagine him commanding the thunder or riding a chariot across the sky, he at least wasn't half bad as far as looks were concerned. And he had been a most amiable companion on the one date he and she had shared the previous weekend. It had been nothing but a frivolous concert and a milkshake on the way home, but they had enjoyed each other's company. Bonnie had every reason to suspect it might not be their last date.

"Hi!" he beamed up at her as she dropped some mail into the basket on his desk. "How's the girl today? Aha! The scent of roses blooming in the cheeks." And with that, he lifted and slowly turned his head while inhaling a long breath as though to fully appreciate a delectable aroma.

"Thanks," she responded to the implied compliment. "I'm fine. A little behind in delivery. There was a pile of mail this morning."

"Good! Must mean business is picking up. How about keeping the weekend open?"

"Oh, uh—sure. I mean, check with me a little later in the week."

"Full calendar, hey? I hear there's to be another concert at the armory."

"I'll think about it," she called from the next desk where she was lifting the outgoing mail.

The other accountants were in little clusters by the windows overlooking the boulevard many floors below and the lazy Ohio River in the distance. Bonnie's quick glance in their direction spotted two green suits. As she couldn't appear to be just standing there staring and could not yet name all the men, she could not guess which one was supposed to be the god, let alone determine whether he was wearing a ring on his left hand. Even though she circled slowly among the desks in the room, she could learn nothing more.

When she returned to the main office, all the girls looked hopefully toward her for some sign that would indicate either negative or affirmative. Instead they received only a slight upward turn of her own empty palm to indicate she had observed nothing.

The remainder of the morning passed uneventfully and rather slowly in spite of the excessive amount of mail. Bonnie had time to muse over her new job. At first she had felt it would be rather boring to spend most of her time simply opening, sorting, and stamping outgoing mail in the little room off the main office with only the company of her immediate supervisor, Peggy Rosensweig. But as she became familiar with her delivery route through all the departments and suites that covered one floor of a new aluminum-clad steel skyscraper in Pittsburgh's Golden Triangle, she realized she was in the center of the action. She was the only person in the whole establishment who could move freely from

12

one department to another. If there were any news to be gleaned, she would be among the first to hear it.

She was even winning her battle with the teletype. One of the fastest typists among the 1958 graduates of Oakland High, she now found her hard-gained speed a detriment to the type of keyboard on which she was assigned to work. The teletype's mechanism would respond only so fast to her eager, nimble fingers, and she found herself constantly making mistakes and having to retype the telegrams sent to the Western Union office a few blocks up the street. But she was learning to adjust her pace to the machine's rhythm, and the two of them were becoming more efficient. She only hoped that when she was finally assigned to a regular desk job her speed would not have become so slowed she would have difficulty increasing it again.

She had acquired this job with the understanding that she would eventually work into a position in the main office. All new female employees of Paramount Plastics started in the mailroom, where they were expected to gain some overview of the operation of the entire office. As a position became open farther up the line, she would be moved into Central Typing, which in turn served as a pool for the selection of private secretaries as the positions became available. The opportunities were as great as her ambition and ability. Altogether, it was a job that offered possibilities for a new high school graduate. She knew some of her classmates had fared worse.

And then there was Hal. He was an interesting development that she hadn't initially anticipated. There was nothing about him that had caused her to single him out from the other strange faces in Accounting. But he had discovered her on her first round through the office. She remembered how his face had broken into a cute little grin as he looked up at her, whistled softly, and

13

exclaimed, "Say, who's the new *gal?*" It had taken him two weeks to summon the courage to suggest that one date. Now, he had requested another.

Her first impulse had been to say, "Sure, any night you name." But she couldn't sound that eager. Coolness was the name of the game.

She was beginning to think about which of her dresses would be suitable for the armory, when the teletype clattered for her attention. She rose from her seat at the mail table and went to sign it off as received when it immediately began another message. It was in the middle of the second that Peggy picked up her purse and announced that it was lunchtime and that Bonnie could join her and the other girls in the cafeteria several floors below.

"Sure. See you there," Bonnie answered and started again to position her fingers over the keys for sign-off receipt. The machine immediately started another message. By the time six more messages had clattered across the yellow roll of paper Bonnie was ready to believe that business really must be picking up. She also believed that it was probably too late to join the others for lunch. They may have found the cafeteria already full and gone to a nearby restaurant. Snatching her purse and hurrying for the elevator, she anticipated a lonely lunch. A brief glance in the cafeteria door confirmed her suspicion. The others were nowhere to be seen, and she could not guess where they might have gone. She might as well remain here.

As she had begun her lunch hour late to start with and the cafeteria was crowded when she arrived, nearly half of her allotted forty-five minutes were gone by the time she moved through the line and picked up her chicken salad sandwich and Bavarian cream pie. She ate as hastily as she could. But by the time she returned her tray, dashed to the powder room for a quick lipstick

14

touch-up, and then waited for the overburdened elevator, she was a few minutes late in returning to the mailroom.

"Sorry," apologized Peggy, "but when the cafeteria was full we couldn't wait for you. Had no idea how long you'd be. We went to the lunch bar in the five-and-ten. It tasted like dog food, though. We should have stayed here."

"Oh, my lunch was passable and—that's OK. I didn't think I was going to get out of here myself. Eight 'grams came in. Looks like business is booming for sure. Do I hear that thing running again?"

Indeed, she did. And after several more messages had rattled their way onto the paper, Bonnie had a number of them waiting to be sent out. She worked at the keyboard until it was time for the afternoon mail delivery. Picking up the correspondence Peggy had opened from the afternoon US delivery and some interoffice mail that had accumulated since the last trip, she started out.

The machines in the main office were all in high gear with the normal nerve-jangling racket. Even the girls who usually found it necessary to stop often and file a broken nail or pat a recalcitrant curl into place were intent on the paper before them. No one looked up when she passed. As she had spent her lunch hour alone and had talked to no one, she completely forgot about the events of the morning. Even Hal was some distance from her mind when she entered Accounting. And here, also, everyone was intently pursuing the business before him. A picture of great diligence and studied concentration greeted her eyes as she started down between the desks.

The man at the first desk was rummaging in the bottom drawer and never even noticed the pile of yellow sheets Bonnie dumped into his mail basket. At the second desk, its occupant was more intent on lighting a cigarette than on the afternoon mail. When she passed Hal's desk, she pretended not to notice him watching her approach out of the corner of his eye. He obviously had been waiting for her.

"Hi! Has the most weighty matter been granted any of your kind consideration?"

"Catch me later." And although she tried to sound hurried, she paused long enough to favor him with a mischievous grin.

Crossing to the other side of the room, she prepared to add the mail still addressed to "Mr. Witherow" to that for the desk next to the one recently vacated by that gentleman's retirement. But as she approached the once vacant desk, she observed it was now occupied. A blur of green passed before her consciousness, jarring a vague memory of the girls' conversation in the main office. What was it she was supposed to look for? Green—green god—oh, yes, ring on left hand.

Without being consciously aware of what she was doing, Bonnie leaned across the desk, attempting to determine whether there was a ring. She saw none, but she did suddenly realize how awkwardly she was staring at a person she had never seen before. She drew herself up in embarrassment and fumbled with Mr. Witherow's mail, hoping to deposit it quickly and move on. She wasn't quick enough.

As she raised her eyes from the basket, her attention was arrested by a glint of steel in this stranger's face. Unwillingly she felt compelled to focus on the origin of the gleam and found she was gazing into two huge pools of molten metal. A quizzical look danced out of their depths, while an amused smile played across full, sensuous lips and emphasized the cleft in the broad chin below.

Ah, yes, she had met the Roman god!

2

Bonnie kept the date with Hal, as she had known all along she would. It was a lovely end-of-June evening, with the scent of early summer flowers wafting from the landscaping around her apartment building. The air was clear, balmy, and refreshing. Gone was the haze from the steel mills that had obscured the golden streaks of the late evening sun. The huge corsage of American Beauty roses Hal had brought with him when he picked her up nestled in her ballerina length froth of white lace and ruffles. When they reached the armory, they discovered that her red and white effect beside his blue serge suit matched the streamers that twined up to the center ceiling, from which hung paper sprays resembling fireworks. They laughed as they realized they had inadvertently dressed patriotically, not remembering that the Fourth of July was within the coming week.

The evening was pleasant and ended too quickly. As the convertible wound its way back out to Oakland and parked before the entrance to the Shadyside Apartments, Hal stole one arm around Bonnie's shoulders and drew her to him. Little matter that the gorgeous roses received a slight crushing; the evening was over, and they had served their purpose well.

"Little girl," he began softly, "have I ever told you how much I like you? You're the kind of gal a fellow dreams of."

"Sure it's not a nightmare?" She never could resist some mischief, not even when the tone of voice and the setting showed promise of matters of the utmost gravity.

He twisted his face into a frown in mock reproof, but chose not to answer directly.

"Listen, you little imp, I can see you would be a trial to handle. Nevertheless, I'm asking you: Will you forget about the other guys and just keep the lines open for me? I mean, really, how about going steady?"

"Oh, uh, well—" She wasn't sure which would be the best choice of words. "Hal, you really are a neat guy and I do think a lot of you. But I'm just not quite ready yet to think about getting serious with anyone. I mean, I may even decide to go on to college. Mother and Dad would like for me to. I just don't know yet. It seems as though I've been in high school all my life, unable to breathe freely on my own, and now I want some time to simply coast along until I can decide what I really want to do. You do understand, don't you?"

"Sure, Bonnie, I understand. Had a couple years like that myself. Just kind of killed time until I could get it all together. But I'm twenty-three now and have decided it's about time to think about a little place out in the suburbs somewhere—somebody to come home to in the evenings— But, you'll still go on seeing me, anyway, I mean just on a friendly basis for a while until—"

"Oh, absolutely," she interrupted. "I don't mean not to see you, just none of that class ring hanging on a chain around the neck stuff. Just friends for the time being. OK?"

"Sure thing," Hal grinned. "In fact, next Saturday, same time, same place. Well, whaddaya know? Friday is the Fourth. Maybe a private little picnic in Schenley Park, concert in the bandstand in the evening, fireworks, the whole bit. Think you can throw a couple sandwiches together?"

18

"I'm the best sandwich-thrower-together there is. Chicken salad or ham on rye? Never mind, I'll make both."

"About four then? No, make it three. That way we'll have time for a longer stroll through the park."

"OK, but I'll see you Monday morning at work too, you know. And I've really got to go in now. The folks will be wondering where on earth. Maybe when you come by on Friday you could come in for a minute and meet them."

"Yeah, sure thing. Be glad to. Must be a couple of super parents to have a daughter like you. Here, I'll get the door." He hopped out, ran around the front of the car, made an exaggerated swing at opening the door, and swept into a deep, extravagant bow. Most of the effect was lost on her, though, because it was quite dark.

Unfortunately, when Friday dawned it appeared to be the beginning of the tropical monsoon season. When Bonnie awoke to leaden skies and a steady, relentless downpour, she at first hoped it would spend itself soon enough for the ground to dry out. By noon, however, the downpour was if anything even heavier than it had been. When the phone rang, she knew before answering it that Hal was calling to discuss some alternative way to spend the holiday.

"I'm not the museum kind, but at least the place has a roof overhead. Or maybe just dinner out," he suggested above a peal of thunder that crackled over the connection.

"Listen," she shouted over another ear-splitter, "why not just come over here for dinner? Then if it's still too wet to go somewhere later in the evening, we could play Monopoly or something. Third floor, apartment three-A."

Bonnie never had been very good at pie baking, but now was as good a time as any to practice. Mrs. Lake certainly would need some help in the kitchen after her daughter had invited company for dinner at this late hour. When the pie crust kept falling apart, Bonnie kneaded and rolled it out again and again until she knew it had to be tough. She momentarily thought of making a molded salad. But she did have presence of wit about her to realize that would be total disaster; it would never have time to set now. Between her and her mother they managed to assemble a meal that looked as if it had been planned beforehand. Her hair felt like it was in strings and she still had an apron over her jeans when the doorbell rang.

"You're drenched!" She greeted him. "Did you walk the whole way?"

"Not at all; I ran from the car into the building. There were just too many drops against this one drip. That's a real storm out there."

"Well, come on in, Drip, and dry. How many other cycles does your model come in?"

"Just one — spin, for fellows whose girls give them the run-around."

"Oh, dear! Just disconnect that one and let me hang up your jacket."

With the jacket duly hung from the pole lamp in the hall, she took his arm and steered him into the living room. Her father was enjoying his holiday on his favorite chair before the television set. Upon the entrance of the two young folks, he rose to greet them.

"Dad, meet Hal Gregersen," she introduced eagerly, hoping her father would find it in his heart to put the young man at ease.

"Glad to see you, Hal," her father responded warmly. "I remember the time I would come out in a deluge like this just to see a pretty girl. Now living color girls on the screen are more my speed."

Bonnie felt as though her starch had just been watered

down while inwardly groaning, *Dad, how could you?* But aloud she tried to recoup the situation. "Well, he surely knew a pretty girl when he met one. Just wait until you see my mother. Here, sit down and I'll call her."

She led Hal toward the sofa and left the room.

As Hal settled and stretched his long legs out over the flowered carpet, the rustle of a sports magazine drew his attention to a chair by the window. A rather small, cherubic face appeared, partly camouflaged by a mass of strawberry blonde curls. Their owner drew himself up all the way his slight build would reach, and he stepped toward the visitor.

"Oh, this is my son, Perry. His ball game got rained out, so he has to spend the day in the unstimulating company of his family. He hasn't even discovered girls yet."

"Hi, Perry," greeted Hal. "I follow the fortunes of the Pirates pretty closely myself," he said, choosing to ignore Mr. Lake's last remark. "Read everything printed about them in every sports magazine there was when I was your age. What position do you play?"

"Oh, I don't actually play. Got a couple friends who are going to make it to the Babe Ruth All-stars this season. I just hang around and watch them."

"Babe Ruth, huh? That must mean you're about fourteen. Right?

"Yeah. I'll be fifteen in September. I started out playing with the guys in the minor league when we were eight, but I only made it through one season. Most of the guys were a lot bigger than me."

Hal sympathized. Perry didn't look more than twelve even now.

"I had just the opposite kind of problem. I was always bigger than the other kids my age. That made everyone expect a little more of me, and I just simply couldn't deliver. I was turned down for Little League three times.

About the only thing I could come across in was swimming. I did make the swim team in high school, although I can't say I won any laurels for the old alma mater. I still paddle around the Y pool now and then, but a hundred yards is about all I can do in one stretch."

"If this rain keeps up, you may have to rely on your swimming skills to get you home," cut in Mr. Lake. "By the way, what are you driving?"

"Fifty-eight convertible. Eight cylinders, over three hundred horse power. You ought to see that sleek beauty—super chromed, white sidewalls. She'll do sixty in eight seconds."

"You drive like that in the city?" Mr. Lake asked incredulously.

"Never fear. I took her out on the turnpike once just to see what she really would do. Man, was that thing cruising. Laid that needle on the peg at one hundred twenty miles per hour. Purr like kitten and speed like cheetah. What are you driving?"

Mr. Lake didn't have a chance to answer. Bonnie, having remained in the kitchen to help a little more with the dinner, now returned. With her was a tall, very trim, and definitely handsome lady with soft, brunette hair neatly waved around an oval face. Her makeup reflected exquisite artistic skill with the brush and pencil and gave the lie to any possible tell-tale lines of approaching middle age that may have been lurking underneath. Although she wore a pair of casual slacks with a tailored blouse, she carried them with the dignity usually associated with a cocktail dress. And every movement was a deliberate study in grace.

Hal was instantly on his feet. His appraising eye took in every detail of her immaculate neatness, neatness in spite of the slacks. For ladies of any breeding to think of wearing "men's clothing" for any occupation other than berry picking, gardening, or window cleaning was a new style innovation. His own mother would rather be caught dead. Somehow it was very becoming to Bonnie's mother.

"Mom." Bonnie took Hal's arm. "Meet Hal."

"I'm so pleased to meet you, Hal," Avonelle Lake replied warmly in a low, musical voice. "It was rather kind of the weather to bring you two indoors today so we could meet you. I hope you have a pleasant evening."

"I'm sure I will. I feel right at home with your family already."

"Well, this family was never known for shyness. You can't remain a stranger for long around here. Perry especially is always happy to have another man around. He thinks he's stifled by too many women."

"Yeah, there ought to be another guy in the house," Perry agreed. "One about my age. But we can't even have a dog in this apartment."

Hal disguised a slight puzzlement. The male-female ratio looked pretty balanced to him, especially when the latter was represented by these two lovely creatures. He couldn't imagine how anyone could possibly feel stifled by them. But he thought it better to say nothing.

"Anyone for some lemonade?" asked Bonnie. "We need to give the roast a few more minutes."

She disappeared and returned immediately with a frosty pitcher and matching glasses. Mrs. Lake poured while Bonnie handed each of the men a tall, refreshing glass.

Hal sipped and smacked his lips. "Sweetened just the way I like it. Did you dip your little pinky into it?"

If she missed the meaning of his words, she didn't mistake the look in his eye. She returned his gaze levelly as she said, "You men can go on solving the world's problems while Mom and I finish dinner. We'll call you in just a jiffy."

When the two ladies had returned to the kitchen,

23

James Lake set his glass on the coffee table and turned his rocker away from the TV set.

"Have you been with Paramount Plastics ever since you got out of school? Or did you put in some time in college?"

"No and yes. I take night courses about every semester at Pitt—accounting, a little bit of management. I hope to reach the top some day—soon. Could have taken a whole four years on the GI bill, but I wanted to get right into the job and make some rungs on the way up. School can fit into my spare time.

"Paramount Plastics is a good place for a fast climb. It's a relatively new company, and there's plenty of room for expansion. I figure that as soon as they start opening branch offices in other cities I should be in line to step right into department manager somewhere. Maybe the south. Maybe New England. Who knows? Right now they're looking toward the south. The biggest market seems to be opening up down there. New England is running a close second, though. On the other hand, if they move some of the other guys out of here to take those positions, that means an open shot right here in home office. Shouldn't be too far then to vice president." He rubbed his hands together in anticipation.

"Sounds like pretty high aspirations for a young man your age. No doubt you'll make it, too. You say you could have gone to school on the GI bill? You weren't by any chance in the Korean Conflict, were you?"

"No, you've got me tagged a couple years ahead of my time. I was drafted just out of high school, but by the time I got through basic training and was ready to go to Korea, they called the whole thing off. Spent the rest of my time as a corpsman in the military hospital at Fort Sam Houston. I fell in love with the area down there and was tempted to stay. The folks wanted to see me come back home, though, and wrote to say this new company was opening up and probably offered some opportunities. I got off the train on a Thursday and was working Monday morning. I've been there three years now. But if they open up an office anywhere in southern Texas, I'll be at the head of the line trying to get there."

"Then you didn't see any real action in the service. I got in right at the beginning of World War Two. I was one of those who waded ashore at Normandy Beach and pushed across France and on into Germany, slaughtering Hitler's war machine all the way. I can tell you, I didn't see anything that would ever make me want to go back there. Bombed out shells of buildings, children roaming the streets looking for garbage to eat, fields rutted by tanks and heavy artillery, dogs running in wild packs, old folks sitting by the road side with a glazed look in their eyes, your buddies lying at your feet with arms and legs gone— Had a few close calls myself. Once a mine went off ten feet behind me. Blew my helmet off and tore the back out of my jacket, but somehow I didn't actually receive any wound. I guess my time just wasn't up."

"I've had some close ones myself," Hal answered. "Nothing I didn't ask for with my own recklessness, though."

James Lake raised one eyebrow in a knowing look and suppressed a little upcurling of the corners of his mouth as he remembered the 120 miles per hour on the turnpike.

"This way, please," Bonnie addressed all the men as she appeared, took Hal's arm, and led him through the door into the dining room.

Hal noticed this room reflected a little more color than the living room which, though neat and tasteful, was not outstanding for imagination in decorating. The dining room had a slight touch of pink in the neutral background of the wallpaper. An exquisite walnut dining suite with oval table occupied the center of the room directly under a simple but elegant crystal chandelier. The six chairs surrounding it had needlepoint seats in variegated shades of roses. Crystal candelabra, each holding two pink candles, graced the carved walnut buffet. And the centerpiece on the table was a vase of pink roses. Hal was about to exclaim on their beauty when he discovered on closer inspection that they were made of silk.

Mrs. Lake was directing him to a chair beside Bonnie on the side of the table next to the windows when Mr. Lake asked, "Where is Sylvia?" Perry, about to sit opposite Hal, released a low groan. Hal, having helped Bonnie into her seat, turned to pull out his own chair. As it slipped out from under the low-hanging Italian lace tablecloth, an elegant blue-point Siamese cat rose from the needlepoint cushion and leisurely stretched himself with a gaping yawn.

"If this is Sylvia, search no more," he laughed as the sleek, lithe body dropped to the floor, arched its way in a stately pacing across the room, and leaped onto a plant stand in front of the windows.

Now all four of the Lakes laughed.

"Sylvia's a *girl*," Perry explained with a pronounced show of contempt.

"That's Yang," ventured Mr. Lake, indicating the elegant Siamese.

"Sylvia is my younger sister," explained Bonnie. "Haven't I ever mentioned her?"

"She's always in her room, endlessly playing records," finished Mrs. Lake for her. "If I had a star for every time I've heard 'Catch a Falling Star and Put It in Your Pocket,' I'd have half the universe by now."

"You should have to share the room with her," added Bonnie. "I'll call her." She left the dining room but returned very shortly alone. "Said she has to get some makeup on. We might as well eat without her. The meal could be over before she finishes."

Hal rose from his chair, helped Bonnie once more into hers, and reseated himself. Mr. Lake lifted the platter of the most tempting standing rib roast that Hal had ever seen, and the meal began.

Yang, tempted by the tantalizing aromas wafting in his direction, leaped down from the plant stand and passed from one to another around the table, rubbing his neck on their ankles, arching his sleek back, and curling the dark tip at the end of his tail.

"Didn't you say, Perry, that you can't have a dog in this apartment?" asked the visitor. "Strange that they would permit cats if not dogs. Usually it is just 'no animals — period.' "

Mrs. Lake answered for Perry. "They don't notice if you have something that remains quietly inside the apartment. Please help yourself to the rolls, Hal. Pass the butter, Perry."

"We had a parakeet once," Perry garbled with his mouth too full.

"Guess who left the cage open?" Bonnie raised her eyebrows in Perry's direction.

"And guess who got the parakeet?" Perry finished.

"Oh, no," groaned Hal, as the culprit reached his ankles with his silken neck.

"Yes, guess who left the cage open." A new voice was heard in the doorway — a taunting, high, lilting voice. "I see we have a guest!"

"Telescopic vision!" twitted Perry.

"Come in and sit down, dear," invited her mother kindly, but unnecessarily, for the newcomer, having hovered in the doorway just long enough to command the entire stage, fairly floated to the table and seated herself in a manner more becoming Victoria at the opening of Parliament. She proceeded to accept the dishes offered her by her father in the same manner. The effect couldn't have been less lost on the visitor if she had been the venerable Queen herself.

Hal sat momentarily transfixed, thinking he had never seen a vision of such exotic beauty. Dark eyes flashed beneath silken lashes and widely-arched, thick brows. A ponytail contained the long, raven-hued, deep, curling waves of hair; but Hal could still see that they were thick and lustrous. Her complexion was the color of burnished copper, and Hal wondered whether that could be natural, as her hair was so dark, or whether she had a magnificent tan from long hours in the sun, then concluded it was probably both. A halter top, tied skimpily in front, revealed a tiny midriff, and a pair of the new, slim-fitting peddlepushers finished the picture of lithe youthfulness that had seated itself directly across the table from him.

"This is our daughter Sylvia," said Mrs. Lake after inviting her to the table. "Sylvia, I'm sure you knew Bonnie was entertaining a guest this evening. Say hello to Hal Gregersen."

"Hi!" replied Sylvia. "Sure, I knew Bonnie was entertaining this evening. I just didn't know it was Troy Donahue."

"How do you do, Sylvia?" returned Hal. "Neither did Bonnie tell me that her sister is Cleopatra."

He figured he might as well play her little game, although he knew perfectly well she had only given him a snow job. He couldn't be mistaken for Troy Donahue by a blind man during a midnight power failure.

"Are you enjoying your summer vacation?" Hal asked.

"Vacation!" snorted the raven-haired one, with a toss of the ponytail. "Who has time to take vacation? While sister spends her days toting mail to the handsome males at Paramount Plastics, and brother hangs around the sandlots, this gal is working for an honest living." She paused to savor the effect she knew that revelation would have on the newest victim of her charms.

"Working? Oh, yes, of course. Some little dears in the neighborhood have the most glamorous babysitter ever known in these parts. Right?"

"Wrong! I—"

"She sells seeds door to door," interrupted her ever-sarcastic brother.

"Perry!" exclaimed Bonnie reprovingly. "Actually Sylvia is a lifeguard out at the Northside Pool. She has always been an excellent swimmer. Swam like a porpoise when she was only four. She completed her Red Cross Senior Lifesaving last year, but had to wait until this year when she was sixteen before she could get a job."

Her father chuckled at those words. It was clear that all the family were very proud of their beautiful vivacious Sylvia.

"No," he said, "she isn't as delicate as appearances would have you believe. She packs a real wallop in those fragile little limbs of hers. Hauled two kids out of the deep end herself last week. Say, didn't you say you had been up on the swimming yourself? You probably noticed her picture in the paper last February when she was sent as Pittsburgh's representative to the state regional swim competition. And only a sophomore at that. She lost to a senior then, but just watch her next year!"

"Now that you mention it, I believe I remember about it. Of course, it was just a name to me then. Imagine having the honor of meeting the one and only Sylvia Lake in person!" He flashed a generous grin across the table, to which she replied with a slight tilt of the head and another toss of the ponytail.

To say her eyes flashed in reply would be an understatement. *Her* eyes never quit flashing. Neither did she pass an opportunity to exchange a glance with the visitor. She had long known her special charms could be worked on men, and she practiced on them every chance that came her way.

"What swimming was Dad referring to that you did?" she asked of Hal.

"Oh, I was the champ out in Mount Lebanon where I went to school, but that was a few years before your time. You must have been only somewhere in the grades. I got away from swimming in the army. Don't know if I could swim enough to save myself now. Say — that's a thought. Northside, did you say? I'll drop by, or rather, *in*, someday and see if you can rescue me."

" 'Twould be a pleasure." The ponytail swished once more.

"You must be ready for a coffee refill," Bonnie offered, as she started to rise from the table.

"Let me." Sylvia was up and to the buffet in less time than Bonnie could sit down again. *Funny*, Bonnie thought, *where was she when Mother and I worked all afternoon to get this meal ready? Oh, well, she might as well do what she will. That's little enough.*

Before long, the standing roast was reduced to nothing but the ribs. The last parsleyed potato had disappeared. Bonnie rose to clear the table, Mrs. Lake to serve the pie, and Sylvia to make the rounds with the coffee pot again. Yang had resettled himself on the plant stand with some African violets. And the rain continued in the same relentless pouring that had pounded away the entire day.

Although the evening was still young when the family gathered in the living room, the storm clouds gave the impression of a very late hour. Thick darkness gathered itself early over the sprawling city like a blanket snuffing out the long, golden rays of the late sun. The incessant pelting of drops muffled the usual sounds of the neighborhood, even of the low-flying jets making their approach to the airport, creating in the little parlor the impression of seclusion from the outside world. In the quiet contentment of the little group, the mood was anything but subdued. Sylvia, never one to be out of character, immediately lugged her record player from her room, and "Santa Catalina" and Debbie Reynolds's lovely rendition of "Tammy's in Love" spun among other current hits.

It was Bonnie who set up the card table and suggested a game of Scrabble. She placed a chair for Hal and seated herself on his right. Perry's attempt to place his chair on Hal's left was quickly discouraged with a slight shove on the shoulder by his raven-haired sister. Sylvia motioned for Perry to take the place opposite Hal, while she seated herself on his left. From that vantage point, she wasted no opportunity to catch Hal's eye. Should anyone have been observing, it would have appeared that opportunities abounded. But Hal showered no less attention on Sylvia's sister, and he obviously enjoyed his position and the attention he received from two charming ladies. Any undercurrent of rivalry between the two of them was well buried beneath the merriment of the game.

Wits were honed in the hours' excitement, and the game proceeded quickly. Even Perry was able to hold his own against the older opposition. The major boner of the evening was committed by none other than Sylvia when she insisted that "pisa" spelled pizza.

"P-i-s-a, dumb-dumb, spells a tower—the one that leans—remember?" Perry reminded her. "You can't spell 'pizza' any better than you can make it."

"Oh, you want to see?" she retaliated. "Just you wait until the game is over. I'll make the best pizza you ever ate, only you won't get any of it."

She repaired her damaged pride by carrying off the top score.

"There now, smarty pants. Maybe I did goof on one

word, but I won the game. And now if you all will excuse me, I'll show you I can also make a pizza."

If she was reluctant to leave her place beside Hal, Sylvia was more than compensated by her ambition to show him her one culinary skill, for she did consider herself rather competent in assembling pizzas. While she was so occupied in the kitchen, the remaining gamesters tried their hand at Chinese checkers. That particular game required some rearranging of positions. Bonnie and Perry exchanged chairs so that she would play opposite Hal, and Perry prevailed upon his father to play opposite him. James and Avonelle Lake had unobtrusively whiled away the evening watching television. But James willingly accepted the challenge to Chinese checkers while his wife watched.

The foursome played two games—both of which Bonnie won—in the time it took Sylvia to prepare the pizza for the oven. When she had popped it in, she reappeared. As usual, she couldn't just walk in and sit down quietly.

"Move over, Dad," she commanded. "No, you stay and play opposite Bonnie. Perry, you go on and wait this one out while I give poor Hal a chance to win. C'mon, Sis, let me play opposite Hal this game."

Obligingly her sister moved into Perry's chair. They soon tired of the game, and after one win by Mr. Lake, they were all relieved when Sylvia announced that the pizza was ready. She carried it triumphantly into the room and placed it on the coffee table, where she cut it with a flourish.

"Now I will have to say," Hal announced while reaching for a second piece, "it doesn't make any difference how you spell it so long as you can make it taste like this. It's really good."

"She just cleans out the refrigerator when she makes it," chided Perry. "You never know what leftovers you'll bite into next."

32

"Perry!" reprimanded his mother. "You know that isn't true."

When the last crumb of pizza had been devoured, Hal pulled his lanky frame up from the sofa, and surveying each of the family in turn, said, "I can't say how much I've totally enjoyed the evening with you all. You are just the greatest. I'm glad the rain did keep us all indoors or we would not have had such a lovely, entertaining time together. And to you, Mrs. Lake, and Bonnie—" he paused to pull her up beside him and slip an arm around her waist, "the meal was nothing if not superb. And permit me not to forget one magnificent pizza, Miss Sylvia." The wink that flashed her direction was answered by a flutter of the silken eyelashes. "And Perry, you and I will just have to see one of the Pirates' games together sometime. Perhaps Mr. Lake will join us. It was very pleasant to meet you, sir."

"The pleasure was all mine," James replied. "I suppose we'll be seeing more of you in the future."

"Yes, do come back, Hal. I'm glad you enjoyed the dinner. If the weather ever clears, perhaps we can make that picnic you and Bonnie had planned for the day a family affair."

Hal had started to walk toward the door, his arm still around Bonnie. Sylvia jumped to her feet and was at his other side in a moment, tugging at his free arm.

"You will come back, won't you?" she asked impulsively.

"Of course, you'll see me back here often." He bent to brush a light kiss across Bonnie's forehead. "You bet, as long as this gal is here."

Evidently Sylvia knew when she was beat and returned to her perch on the sofa. Hal and Bonnie proceeded on to the hall where she retrieved Hal's jacket from the pole lamp. "It appears, it has had time to dry," she observed, handing it to him.

"Ha! That will be short-lived. About from the building to the car."

At the door he enfolded her in both his arms, and that time the kiss was not fleeting. " 'Bye now, and see you soon."

He did not bother to ring for the elevator but took the stairs two at a time. At the outside door, he pulled his jacket tighter, lowered his head, and dashed for his car parked at the curb. In the time it took him to unlock the door he was soaked to the skin. "What matter," he said to himself as he revved up the motor. "I'll have to congratulate myself on being the one guy in the office to recognize a prize when the new mail girl was hired."

3

Bonnie was never quite sure how it had happened. It may have been the pulse-racing stimulation of the ill-concealed jealousy of the girls in the main office.

"How does it feel to be the sole recipient of the undivided attention of the Roman god?" Sue Ramsey asked with a disdainful arching of the eyebrows as Bonnie passed her desk on the morning round. Although they had long since learned the name was George Morrow, Sue still called the newcomer the Roman god.

"I wasn't aware I was," Bonnie replied, not certain whether she could commit herself to such an admission. It was, however, an intoxicating thought.

Goldie Klingensmith and Allyn Jespers were huddled over Karen King's desk as Bonnie strode through Central Typing.

". . . every day for the past two weeks," the latter overheard in a low voice. Just then Goldie caught sight of her, shot a warning glance toward the other two, and then in a much louder voice chirped, "It really was one of the most insipid books I have ever read. I don't recommend that you read it."

Bonnie attempted to smother an irrepressible giggle at what she knew was an abrupt change of subject for her benefit. She was tempted to ask which book that was, but knew it would only force the three girls into an awkward moment that wouldn't tell her anything more than they already had revealed. She wasn't sure which was greater, her annoyance with the gossip or her exhilaration at being the object of their envy because she had lunched with George Morrow every day for the past two weeks.

It wasn't that she had captured the attention of the Roman god immediately upon his arrival at Paramount Plastics. Other than his amusement at her interest in his left hand the first time he had seen her, he had scarcely noticed her twice daily transit through his department. He had applied himself with all diligence to his new job. A couple of times he had looked up to see who was the recipient of a friendly, whistled greeting, and then returned his attention to his work. He gave every evidence of being a diligent, productive, and promising young man. It was not long until he had earned the respect of the other accountants, some of whom had had many years' experience with other companies before coming to the fledgling Paramount Plastics. Each, of course, had his own reasons for leaving his former place of employment to join the new company, but once within the fold of Paramount Plastics, they formed a common bond of buoyant optimism for its ultimate success.

A young graduate of Carnegie Tech had been the first to see the possibilities in capitalizing on the by-products from the steel mills, which could be obtained for a low price, and processed into a salable product. He had embarked on his venture with a few thousand dollars from his mother's estate, and by producing cheap, colorful toys to be sold in supermarkets, drug stores, and any place frequented by the mainstream of humanity he soon had reaped his investment many hundredfold. He had then turned his attention to more profitable commodities. The Pittsburgh factory was then producing household products, such as dish drainers, soap dishes, and table utensils. With the water playland surrounding the south, his assembly soon concentrated on producing float rafts, beach balls, and even small flatboats for use on tranquil waters. Now he was toying with the idea of combining the readily available steel as an outside retaining wall with a plastic liner as a new kind of backyard swimming/wading pool.

In fact, there was no end to the possibilities presented by the field of plastics. The fever of expansion and financial gain was in the very air like a virus that affected each employee interested in a climb up the ladder of success. If the promise of a new and expanding business were not enough to lure and hold the energetic and imaginative, the guarantee of a handsome bonus for those who dropped successful ideas into the suggestion box attracted those who might not otherwise have an outlet for their creativity.

It was in this attitude of mutual growth for mutual gain that each man was rated by his colleagues, and George Morrow passed his initiation test. He had come from a large firm in McKeesport, and his flashing eyes, bold self-assured demeanor, and degree from Penn State assured him of ready acceptance among climbing aspirants.

He probably wouldn't have given the little brunette from the mailroom a second thought if the rain had stopped that Fourth of July weekend. But it hadn't. Saturday morning dawned with clear, bright skies, and the city resumed its normal bustling activity. Shoppers flooded the downtown streets, and children streamed to the playgrounds, hopping over and around the puddles. Family gatherings assembled with picnic baskets in the parks to make up for the preceding day's lost holiday. Here and there in the suburbs laundry hung hopefully on a backyard line. But clouds sent warnings by late forenoon, and by the middle of the afternoon, the deluge resumed. It poured then, steadily, for the remainder of that day, all night, and Sunday. The Allegheny River rose two feet, the parking wharf on the bank of the Monongahela was flooded by Sunday evening, and the Ohio churned through its channel as though the Great Lakes had suddenly emptied into it.

Monday dawned no better. When Bonnie left for work that morning, her mother handed her a shopping bag, asking that she exchange its contents on her lunch hour. "I just hate to ask you to go out in this if it is still raining at noon, but since you'll be in town anyway you can save me a trip by going up to Gimbel's and getting an evening slip about two inches shorter than this one. I thought this one would do for the gown that I'm going to wear to dinner tonight, but it is too long, and I just have to have a shorter one. So if you don't mind? Maybe with some plastic rain boots and an umbrella you can keep from drowning."

"I won't melt. Of course I'll exchange it. I'll bet you'll wish you had an excuse to get out of the apartment, though, since both Sylvia and Perry will have to spend the day shut up together at home."

"You may have a point there. 'Bye, dear. Have a good day."

At noon at the door of the Gateway Center office building, she paused to put up her umbrella. George Morrow greeted her on his way to lunch.

"Hi, there! Going my way?"

"Well, if you're going to Gimbel's, I guess I am. I wouldn't be going out in this dismal drizzle except that Mother asked me to make an exchange for her."

He took the umbrella from her hand and, taking her by the elbow, proceeded to propel her out the door and down the walk with the umbrella cozily over both their heads.

"I'm just going for a bite to eat, and I guess Gimbel's Cafeteria is as good a place as any. That is if you don't

38

mind sharing the umbrella. I don't want to lose my curls, you know."

"It doesn't look to me as though your problem in that respect is as great as mine. I would say your curls are set very permanently, while my permanent is very temporary. And subject to sudden rain squalls." Bonnie looked somewhat enviously at George's mass of golden waves.

"Well, that was quite a mouthful for a little gal like you. Do you come off with those bits of philosophy very often?"

"Not usually in the rain. It's a little brighter when the sun is shining."

They had reached the curb where a torrent was raging down the gutter over nearly half the street.

"If we walk around this rampage I'm afraid it will take a couple blocks to get to the end of it. I suggest that we just try to jump it." He tightened his grip on her elbow and together they sprang like children playing hopscotch. They landed a little short of the edge so that they made a considerable splash.

"We can hardly get much wetter than we already are anyway," Bonnie laughed as they giggled at their foolishness. "I guess most people had enough sense to just stay in today, so there aren't many to see us in our graceful glory."

"By the way, you are new to Paramount Plastics too, aren't you? I believe I heard someone say you had been there only a week or two before I arrived. Right?"

"Yes, you heard right. I just graduated from high school this year and got this job right away. I consider myself rather fortunate. I heard there aren't many jobs available for this year's graduates. And it is rather nice to be in a new company and in a nice new building. Do you think it is going to be satisfactory to you?"

"Oh, yes, I'm quite well satisfied. I had looked for some time until I found just the right setup to suit me.

Plenty of room for advancement—lots of room at the top. I don't suppose you have any idea, though, of making this place your permanent abode. Pretty girl like you will capture some fellow's heart, ride off on a white charger to Never Never Land, and leave the everyday work-a-day world behind."

Once more she caught that glint of steel, but this time it was warm, relaxed, accepting. She knew she was not considered to be any great beauty, but he was evidently not too critical in his evaluation. In fact, he made her feel rather comfortable, equal, not the driving accountant with the lowly mail carrier.

They had reached Gimbel's by this time, partly because they had not far to go, and partly because they were all but sprinting in their haste to escape the rain. They ducked, panting, inside the door.

"Look," George directed, "I'll go on up to the cafeteria and wait for you by the door. When you are finished with your errand, how about joining me there for lunch?"

"OK. It will only take me a moment, I'm sure. At least I won't have to wait long for a clerk; this place is nearly deserted. See you there."

He insisted on buying her lunch, and she dined much more elegantly than she would have had she been alone. With the first tasty mouthful she exclaimed over her delight, and picking up his cue, George leaned forward to ask intently,

"Say, now, how would you like to sample chow mein in San Francisco's Chinatown? Or Peking duck in the Imperial Palace?"

"Sounds scrumptious. I'd be tickled just to see San Francisco."

"Oh, but the best part of seeing the place is sampling the cuisine. You just wouldn't think of a weekend in New York without dining on game pie with truffles at

Delmonico's. Or perhaps Crapodeen partridge. And then you may make a selection from—"

"You have my mouth watering already," she interrupted wistfully. "It must be great to be able to eat like that."

"That's nothing," he dismissed her words with a wave of his napkin. "How do mussels in white wine at Labière's in Princeton strike you? Or perhaps frogs' legs Provençale at Kilvarook Inn at Litchfield, Connecticut? Oh, yes, one can always sample côtelettes de ris de veau at the Waldorf-Astoria."

"Pardon my ignorance, but when you order, how do you know what you are going to get?"

"It's the surprise when you see what you get that enhances the enjoyment. And then there is New Orleans. Ah, yes! That is where the good food is. The French Quarter, of course. Small omelet, veal in Creole sauce—that is at Brennan's Restaurant. Then there is Antoine's, Commander's Palace—"

"You've eaten at all those places?" she asked, somewhat skeptically.

"Uh-huh. Those and more."

"You must really get around."

"Oh, there are times I just fly to some distant city for the weekend. Say, do you know what it is to be hungry, I mean *really* hungry? So hungry that your sole passion in life is just to find a scrap of bread crust some place, so hungry that those pangs of emptiness in the pit of your stomach pervade all your waking hours, let you think of nothing else, pursue your dreams, that is if you're ever able to get to sleep with all that knawing ache, make you see visions of soup, potatoes, meat—real meat—all night long only to waken the next day and start it all over again? Too weak from starvation to stand on your feet, so thin you can count every rib. Have you ever been that hungry?"

"Well, I—I can't say that I have." She stumbled uncertainly with the answer, fearing that some dreadful revelation was about to ensnare her.

"Well, I have." The words were spoken with a pronounced bitterness, and the steel had been flickering with the intensity of a million synchronized fireflies on a balmy summer evening. Suddenly the eyes narrowed to thin slits, cutting the penetrating brilliance to one sharp shaft like that of a sword. His voice took on a note of determination that made their casual lunch seem like a life-and-death struggle. "And when I was that hungry, I made up my mind that if I ever got to the place where there was food to eat, and there was any possibility I could get it, I wouldn't only ward off starvation; I would eat the finest food there was in all the world—and all I wanted of it. And no one would stop me."

Once the determination had been pronounced, the air cleared somewhat. The ominous spell around her was broken, and she was able to say rather casually, "I should think you would. No doubt I would do the same. By the way, do you realize what time it is getting to be? You carried me away there in New Orleans, but I fear now it's time to head back to one little old plastics company in Pittsburgh. Thanks much for the luscious lunch."

"You are more than welcome. I wonder if it might have stopped raining."

It had not. The two of them retraced their steps in much the same way as they had come, he guiding her by the elbow and jumping the puddles, pulling her along with him. They didn't giggle so much, though. Somehow the humor had fled from soaked clothing and drenched bodies.

The rain let up somewhere along in the afternoon, and by dismissal time, some golden rays of sun had broken through. Bonnie even thought she caught the hint of a rainbow over the western hills as she headed home in the streetcar. A fresh breath of air was blowing, clean and purged with the long washing it had received.

Mrs. Lake found Bonnie had made a wise choice in the exchange of the slip, and it exactly suited her purpose. She adorned herself in her newest formal, a lovely swath of mint green chiffon, most becoming with her brown waves of hair, and went dining like some woodland nymph, bedecked in her emerald necklace and with makeup immaculate as usual. James Lake beamed at his vision of queenly elegance as she bent to brush his bald pate with a kiss on her way out the door. He wondered how he had come by the good fortune of having his household graced with a bevy of lovely ladies.

As for Sylvia and Bonnie, they vied with each other for the phone all evening. Hal had told Bonnie that day he would phone in the evening, but she soon realized it would be impossible for him to reach her. Sylvia would no sooner bid so-long to one young swain, then another would dial. Bonnie finally prevailed upon her to cut short one conversation in the hope that Hal would be able to get through before another call would come.

"You're just jealous because you have only one guy calling you, and I've got dozens of them," taunted Sylvia.

Bonnie felt a pang of regret that her sister should be cultivating such a vain attitude, but thought it best not to reply. Hal did soon call, and they spent half an hour catching each other up on the minor details of their lives since the previous Friday. And so the evening passed.

Unfortunately, when the next day dawned, the rain, which long ago had worn out any possible welcome, resumed its patter and cast its gloom over half the state. Thankfully there was no errand to take Bonnie out of the office building that day; but she once again had such a busy morning she could not leave her post when the lunch hour began. The sales department had left several very urgent messages for her to send over the wire, but the teletype was kept so busy with incoming messages she could not send hers out. And she did not dare leave for lunch without having it done. By the time she pecked out the last signoff, she had completely given up any hope of eating with the other girls and feared there would be no room left in the building cafeteria. She was right. Except that there was one seat left, and who should be sitting there at the same table as she hustled past with her tray but George.

"Hi, there! Hello again," he greeted cheerily. "I do believe the fates have decreed we should dine together again, although the young lady should have her choice." He rose to help her into her chair.

"Yes, thank you. You are so very right. I must say this meal is not as taste-tempting as the one we shared yesterday, but it sure beats hopping lagoons to reach it."

"Their lasagne here isn't too bad, but there is a little Italian place outside Ebensburg that makes lasagne you wouldn't believe had been created anywhere short of Italy. Ought to try it next time you're up that way."

"Up that way! Why, I never go near the place. That must be a hundred miles from here, and I have no reason to travel in that direction. May I ask what takes you out that way?"

"Food, of course. I'll go practically anywhere to get a good meal. That makes a nice little Saturday afternoon drive. Tell you what, maybe sometime when I get the urge to go, I'll just take you along. How about that?"

"Well, it might be rather nice." She remembered the pleasant evening she had spent with Hal the weekend before, but she really hadn't made any commitment to him. She had made it very clear that she intended to be able to see other men, also. This proposition sounded like an interesting excursion.

"Let me know when you get that urge sometime. By

44

the way, is the 'urge' for Italian food any different from the 'urge', say, for Chinese, or some other national cuisine?"

"Kiddo, when I get the urge for food, it doesn't matter what kind. I just go."

At that moment Hal's eye met hers from across the crowded cafeteria. She nodded, and he waved in reply. She could see he was seated with a group of men from his department. Talking business, no doubt. She always had lunch with the girls if she could get away from the teletype in time, and he evidently ate with his colleagues. Perhaps in time he would join her for lunch, and they would have that much more time together.

"I could show you some other good eateries, too, right around here for that matter," George was continuing. "Say, how about it? Since this seems to be getting to be a habit, I mean our lunching together, let's make it a date for tomorrow."

She glanced over at Hal. She could barely see his head above the masses of seated diners. It was a good thing he was tall. He seemed very much engrossed in the conversation at his table. That burning determination to get ahead. Well, she wouldn't interfere. More power to him.

"I'd love it. That is, if I can get away in time."

And she did. The rain stopped. The next time the sun's rays forced themselves through the gray dreariness, they drove it completely away. Hot summer weather returned to the area, and it was some time before it rained again. But the lunches with George continued.

He first took her to Stouffer's where she sampled their lobster Newburg. Then she began to understand what he meant about good food. She told herself that if she kept up that kind of eating, she would soon be too wide to get through the door. But she needn't have worried. The next day it was a little sandwich bar on a corner just a couple blocks up the street. The following day it was the lunch bar in Woolworth's. And then he found a little greasy spoon below street level up a side alley where few people traveled. It didn't have the atmosphere that the ritzy restaurants had, but then, it really was only a lunch hour from work, and the place *was* cozy. George seemed to be very relaxed there, and the food was edible, so she wouldn't be one to complain.

She continued to keep her weekend dates with Hal, and they enjoyed each other's company just as much as ever, but the lunch hour with George seemed to slide into a permanent habit. Hal was always intent on furthering his interests in the business aspects of his job, and his social considerations were motivated accordingly. On the other hand, George appeared to concentrate just as heavily over his work, but he evidently didn't feel the need to be with the other men as Hal did. In fact, it appeared that he withdrew more and more to himself.

And it didn't take long before all the girls in the office began to notice that their erstwhile companion in the cafeteria was now occupying herself elsewhere. Sue Ramsey permitted her jealousy to surface most obviously, for it was she who had set her sights on George the moment he strode so confidently into Paramount Plastics in June. But somehow he had never been more than vaguely aware other girls even worked in that office.

"How did you do it?" Sue asked enviously once as Bonnie went past her desk on her mail route.

"Do what?"

"Capture the Roman god."

"The w-what? Oh! That! I mean, *him*. Why, it was just the rain," she grinned mysteriously and continued on her way.

It *was* a nice feeling. No one noticed when she had a date with Hal, even though they occasionally saw another of the girls also on a date wherever they happened to be. And as for Hal, he was always courteous, attentive, steady, the charming companion. But perhaps he was too steady.

George was another matter. Bonnie never stopped being fascinated by those steel glinting eyes. She never knew whether he would be frivolous and the eyes would sparkle with warmth like the sand on a sun-kissed beach, or whether some petulance would suddenly surface by a chance remark or an unwelcome subject, with that sparkle suddenly narrowing to a penetrating blade that sent out warning flashes, or even flare in volcanic fury with ill-conceived vehement anger. Sometimes George's eyes reminded Bonnie of heavy artillery shells encasing explosive material.

In mid September in their sub-street level hideaway, she witnessed his most violent outburst. The lunch hour had begun as casually as any other with a pleasant early autumn stroll from Gateway Center. When they reached the bar, they saw campaign posters for the upcoming elections had been placed in conspicuous positions along the walls. They took a table directly under one bearing the likeness of a middle-aged, otherwise undistinguished looking gentleman with the name of Josef Morawski, with "for city commissioner" underneath.

"Looks like we're going to have a threesome today," Bonnie quipped.

"Oh, yeah," George responded with a nod in the direction of the poster. "Must be a cousin of mine."

"Really? You're not kidding?"

"No, I'm not kidding. Actually, the name is the same. My mother left Poland with that name. When some immigration official couldn't be bothered with writing the whole thing it came out in the shortened Americanized form."

"Well, I never would have taken you for Polish. Did you know that Sue Ramsey referred to you as a Roman god for some weeks after you came to Paramount Plastics? And I would have chalked you up as one of those blond, northern Italians. Or maybe even German. You know, that proud Aryan race that was going to conquer the whole world?"

"No!" He swore, spitting out profanity that she had never heard him use before.

"Well, OK. So you're Polish. Glad to know you. I'm completely unidentifiable myself," she once more attempted a lighter vein. "You say you came here with your mother? Do you have any brothers or sisters?"

"Not a one."

"What about your father?"

"I have no father!"

The explosive force with which his words came out caused her to recoil. Immediately myriads of questions flooded her mind. Was he cruel to you? Did he leave your mother? Suicide perhaps? But the set of his lip and the hard, untempered shaft of steel in the narrowed slit of his eye warned her not to voice any of them. She could only stammer, "I-I-I'm sorry."

"Save your pity," he snarled, but it was more of a threat than an amenity. And his menacing gaze warned her not to ever bring up the subject again.

At times she wondered what dark secrets he harbored beneath that flashing armor of hardened steel, but in his lighter moments he was so debonair, so chivalrous, humorous, and even gentle, that his more enigmatic characteristics only heightened her interest in him. She eventually found her dates with Hal too predictable. Hal was always correct, always punctual, always talked about the same things, always went the same places. On the other hand, even though George never asked her out except to lunch, she found his company stimulating. And she would catch herself during the morning mail trek, or while sitting over the teletype, wondering what challenge his mood would offer her that day. Furthermore, she enjoyed the ever-present, thinly veiled envy of several of the office girls. The choice between the two men became no longer difficult.

4

The trees on the Pennsylvania hills hinted their first signs of scarlet, gold, and rust. The air grew crisp and stimulating. The wind blew in stronger gusts than the limpid wisps that stirred the lazy summer days, and carried with it a foreboding of difficult months to come. Occasionally a flock of birds chirped or honked on their way to more southern climes. The azure blue of the afternoon skies would fade into long streaks that reflected from the surface of the three rivers like so many streams of liquid gold. Families scurried to the parks to absorb as much of the fleeting remains of summer as they could before storing the picnic baskets away for the winter. And it was time for the annual Fall Flower Show at the Phipps Conservatory.

"What do you say to grabbing a quick sandwich in the downstairs cafeteria today and then taking a lazy stroll down to the Point and watching a few river boats and soak up some autumn inspiration," George suggested when Bonnie paused at his desk on her morning mail route. She never tired of gazing into those pools of molten metal if they weren't flashing in scorn or fury.

"Can't think of anything more enticing at the moment. I've always loved October's bright blue weather. In fact, I believe it would be my favorite month if it weren't that its passing means winter is coming."

"It used to be mine. But I think I've changed that

50

preference to June now, since it was then that I first feasted my eyes on you."

"For a guy who knows what starvation is, I wouldn't think you'd settle for the likes of me as a feast."

"That wasn't the kind of feast I had in mind. See you at the door at twelve sharp. No overtime, now. Those telegrams will just have to wait."

She quickly touched up her lipstick, patted down a few hairs, straightened one seam in her hose, snatched up her purse, and met George just as he was leaving the accounting department. Fortunately, most of the other occupants of the building must have had similar ideas of absorbing October, for the cafeteria was nearly deserted and the couple went through the line in no time. They ate quickly and walked outdoors into one of the most glorious of autumn days either could ever remember. Bonnie drew in great breaths of the fresh, invigorating air, and exclaimed delightedly, "Isn't this just absolutely delicious?"

"Mm-huh," was the murmured reply. "And so is this." He placed an arm around her and drew her close. "Bonnie—" he paused, savoring the sound of her name, and checking the street for oncoming traffic, "I don't know how to say this, but the more I see of you, the better I like what I see. And the more of you I would like to see. I mean, like sometime besides just at work."

"Oh! I thought you'd never ask."

"I was thinking that since the fall show is at the conservatory, we might take it in on a Saturday. I expect to be tied up for this Saturday, but maybe we can arrange for next week. How about it?"

"By all means. I always go to it, and I can't think of any one I'd rather go with than you."

By this time they were standing right down at the water's edge, below the bustle of the traffic above them and quite isolated from any prying eyes. He drew her to himself and sought her lips with his own.

On the day agreed upon for the excursion to the conservatory, she looked for him all day. She had carefully chosen a sensible little suit that would do for all the climates represented in the giant greenhouse. When she was in the jungle room, she could remove the jacket and not feel uncomfortable in the humidity. And because Pennsylvania usually has a chilly sting in the air in late October, she would be quite comfortable otherwise indoors or out with just the suit jacket, and thereby eliminate carrying a coat around in the conservatory. She accented the ensemble with a dashing scarf tied with little butterfly scatter pins, chose her newest low-heeled walking loafers, and laid out gloves beside her purse. She felt passably neat and attractive, if not stunning, and settled herself by the front window to wait for George.

After the first ten minutes or so, she picked up a magazine and attempted to read a short story. But her mind refused to concentrate on the words, and she began to wonder whether he had lost his car keys, got caught in heavy traffic, or maybe had trouble finding her address. Or—most likely—had he been seized by his obsession for good food and taken off for some distant, fabulous restaurant—the Italian place in Ebensburg, without taking her as he had promised? But after half an hour her fury was moderated by concern, and she began to conjure up dreadful accidents that must have befallen him: A collision at a busy intersection, a run-in with a streetcar, a fall down the steps as he left his own place. However, she didn't know whether his place had any steps. He had said nothing about his living quarters; she didn't know whether he were still with his mother, had a singles apartment, shared with a roommate, cooked his own meals, or dined out *all* the time, in addition to his weekend jaunts to distant cities. In fact, now that she thought about it, she knew very little about him at all.

Their conversation at lunchtime was always impersonal, even distant.

After an hour's vigil, she removed her jacket and kicked off her shoes, then went to the kitchen for a cup of coffee. She might as well be comfortable while she waited. It wouldn't have been so bad if Sylvia had not been sitting at the kitchen table poring over her homework. She wanted to be sure to have it completed by evening as she would be having her usual Saturday night date. Sylvia was never without a date. It didn't matter so much who it was, either. Young men seemed to stand in line. And each dropout she would dismiss airily with a wave of the hand. "Nyeh! Men! There're plenty of fish in the sea. Might as well try them all and have my fling."

Bonnie plugged in the pot and reached in the cupboard for a cup.

"Well, for Pete's sake, sis!" Sylvia looked up from her book, "don't tell me you've been stood up! How's that for a double-crossing Grecian god, or whatever it was you said they called him down there in that chain gang of yours. Rotten luck! How about sharing one of the guys that keep my evenings busy?"

"No thanks, Sylvia; your kind are a little young for me, you know." Bonnie preferred to ignore the obvious insult.

"I wouldn't say that. In fact, you know I have always preferred older men." She accented each word, attempting a melodramatic effect. "Men my age are—well, in fact, they are not even men yet; they are just *boys!* You know very well I don't even look at anyone without some sophistication. And *experience!*" The last she punctuated with a broad sweep of her hand. "By the way, did you know Hal phoned me one night? About two or three weeks ago now. I told him I'd give it some thought if he would want to try again later."

Bonnie winced at the mention of Hal. He would not have left her high and dry for a planned date, at least without phoning an excuse. That was the least a person could do. She ached for the put-off Hal had received at the hands of her own sister. Sylvia had a lot of growing up to do. She had just turned seventeen, but in some ways she acted fourteen. Bonnie despaired of her ever developing a proper appreciation for the attentions she received from the opposite sex. She seemed to regard men as something to manipulate, a source of amusement.

Mercifully, Sylvia returned her attention to the lessons before her. Bonnie emptied her cup and returned to her vigil by the window. To be honest, she realized that even if George did come now, there wouldn't be enough of the afternoon left to see much of the conservatory. She might as well admit to being snubbed, change her clothes, and help her mother with a little dusting. She wondered how she should approach George on Monday. Chide him for not calling? Act as though nothing happened? Never speak to him again?

It was with some difficulty that she made her way into Accounting on Monday morning. But she figured that a head-on confrontation was in the long run best and least painful.

She put on her cheeriest smile, although with difficulty, as she paused by his desk.

"Hi, there!" came his usual greeting. "How is the fe-mail carrier?" She thought he appeared at least a trifle nonplussed, but she had never seen him in that condition so she wasn't sure.

"I'm fine. How are you?" She hoped her voice was steady as she resisted an urge to ask how his meal was Saturday.

"Heh, heh. Hale as ever." The eyes were not boring holes through hers this time; they seemed to be averted.

"Oh, uh, yeah—about Saturday. I know it was rotten of me. I really am terribly sorry. But something important came up. I just couldn't get away. I was sure you would understand. But, you know, the fall show is still on for another week. How about trying again next Saturday? I promise you, nothing will keep me away this time."

"You could at least have phoned me, you know," she attempted a faint reproof.

"I know, honey. Honest, I tried, but I couldn't find a phone." That was a likely story. "Look, I know I broke every rule in the book, but if you'll give me another chance, I promise you it won't happen again. Now if you'll just plan for next Saturday— How about it?"

"I'm not just sure right now. I have planned an out-of-town date. I'll have to let you know later. Check with me again toward the end of the week." It was slick how that just slid into her mind when she needed it. She hadn't thought herself capable of such a good on-the-spot lie and wondered whether she were unconsciously taking some lessons.

"Sure thing. But then it's still on for lunch today, right?" His eyes were playful again, bubbling, communicating. There was no way she could say no.

And she didn't say no when he approached her again on Thursday about the Saturday date. "Yes, if we are going to see the show, we'll have to go now. It will be over by next week. I postponed my other date." She knew she didn't fool him, but she might as well play the same game he did. At least, it was something he could understand.

But she had barely begun to dress again on Saturday, same little suit, same accessories, when the phone rang.

"Look, Baby, you don't know how sorry I am about this—honest, I really mean sorry, but I simply can't make it again this time. You will forgive me, won't you?"

"Well, at least, you did call. That is some help. I can't

imagine what important distractions they are, but they must be something."

"I give you my word, they are real biggies. Otherwise, nothing would keep me away from you."

James Lake looked up from his morning paper when she replaced the phone. "Must be some elusive bird you've got caught there on that limb. I've been waiting all this time to meet him, and he hasn't made an appearance yet."

"Dad, I can tell by the tone of his voice there really is something keeping him, but for the life of me I can't imagine what. I'll give him one more try."

"If he doesn't show the next time, I believe I'd try for that Hal fellow again. At least he never pulled that stunt."

Once more she winced at the mention of Hal. "I know, Daddy, but you wait and see. You'll find out how stimulating and interesting George is. When he gets this business—whatever it is—cleared away, he'll come around, and I just know you will like him."

"Uh-huh." James's attention focused again on the newspaper.

By the time George finally managed to honor the date, the fire was gone from the mountains and hillsides. In fact, about half the leaves had already fallen, and those remaining were wrinkled, brown ghosts of their departed glory. The squirrels in Highland Park were hard put to find any more acorns. The skies were no longer blue. The stark bleakness of the winter atmosphere was beginning to show itself in pale grays with long austere streaks of white cloud. The weather had taken its usual sudden drop in temperature, marking the end of Indian summer and the setting in of the cold. Bonnie decided the jacketed suit would no longer do. She would have to wear a heavy coat and be burdened with it as she walked the conservatory's lovely paths. What matter, anyway.

The excitement was rather dulled by now. In fact, the fall flower show was over. She chose just a simple pair of slacks with pullover sweater. To be truthful, she even dressed with one ear cocked toward the phone, half expecting it to ring again with George's stammered apology for breaking the date once more. But it didn't.

It was the doorbell that rang. And when she greeted him, and saw his broad shoulders pulled back so confidently, proudly, and of course the eyes—those eyes, soft and luminescent today—she forgot all about the frustration of the weeks before. As he swept her into the tightest embrace she had ever relished, she was aware of nothing but the exhilirating pressure of his lips on hers.

Strangely, after all the weeks her family had waited to meet him, they each had occasion to be out at the moment. Because there was no one to whom to introduce him but Yang, she locked the door behind her and they departed in silence. Words did not seem to be necessary. They found their voices again by the time they passed through the immense plate glass doors and down through the reception area of the conservatory.

"One good thing about coming here after the flower show is that we don't have to fight all those crowds," Bonnie exclaimed happily, her hand slipped ins' her companion's.

"No," he replied, "I doubt we'll have much trouble along that line. Everyone in three states who intended to come here has already done so. The place will be pretty well deserted now for a few weeks. Probably won't be much life around until about time for the spring show."

Bonnie felt a slight shudder at those words. "In a way, I wish it were time for the spring show. I don't relish the thought of those long winter months. Every year about this time I wish we could sleep through the bad weather, you know, like animals hibernating, and just emerge fresh and bushy-tailed with the return of spring."

"You're sounding poetic, my dear laureate."

"This place always makes me feel poetic—awakens some hidden creativity that always vanishes as soon as I leave it. Especially the Japanese Room. That's my favorite display. I'm anxious to see it again."

They had reached the Palm Court, which still reflected the aftermath of the special fall display. The organ, which always played continuously during the month-long shows, had not yet been removed, although of course no one was playing it. The large low-walled area in the court's center still contained a number of vases with withered fall chrysanthemums long past their glory. A few pieces of rough wood lay in some now indescribable shape with clusters of faded crepe paper streamers and bows strewn over them, evidently the supporting structure of a display for the show. Several orange crates were also left behind to grace the barren interior of the Palm Court, and the surrounding walks were littered with trampled bits of blossom and parts of dead plants. The sight was somewhat depressing. But the young couple wasn't about to let the scars of transition dampen their hilarity today.

"I believe that if we go out the far end of the court, and circle around to the left, we will come back in that entrance over there." George tightened his grip on Bonnie's hand and began to lead her through the central walk area when a family emerged from the far door where they were heading. The parents' eyes were drawn to the destruction that Bonnie and George had been surveying, but the little girl in her father's arms caught sight of George. She waved to him and flashed a dimpled smile, then pointed to him while trying to turn her father's head in George's direction with her other hand. The father appeared not to appreciate the attempted distraction, as he murmured something to his wife and made a sweeping motion of his hand in the direction of the rubble. But the child persisted in encouraging her father to acknowledge the obvious acquaintance. George stopped abruptly, his face blanched, and he tugged on Bonnie to turn around.

"Uh, listen," he stammered in a hushed voice, "on second thought I think it would be just as well if we went out at the left and circled around and returned by that door—you see, like those people are doing. I believe that is the proper way to do it."

Bonnie couldn't imagine how it made any difference, but being committed to no preferences, simply turned and followed him.

"Aren't you going to wave to them?" she asked. "They seem to know you."

"No, I never saw them before." But at that moment the man gave in to his daughter's attentions and raised his eyes to acknowledge George. The latter simply quickened his steps in the opposite direction, discovered a stone bench partially hidden under an immense palm fern, and stopped.

"You know what?" his voice sounded strained. "I realize I really should have made a trip to the restroom before we began this hike. Stupid of me—a grown man and all. Why don't you just sit here for a moment while I run along. I'll be right back." He was gone before he had finished speaking.

With no choice presenting itself, Bonnie did as bidden and proceeded to watch the little family. They stopped by the remnants of the deteriorated display, shook their heads at George's sudden exit, cast a curious scrutiny in her direction, and then turned their attention to the court. Although she was too far away to hear what they said, she guessed from their gestures and expressions they were reiterating what she and George had said about the rubble. Then they resumed their stroll and disappeared into the outer reception area. Bonnie continued to sit entirely alone in the vast Palm Court for some minutes. The stone bench was not at all comfortable, and there was little of interest in the spot where she found herself. The minutes dragged on, and she was tempted to rise and walk about. She was at first annoyed at the way this date, ill-fated from the very beginning, was turning out. Then she began to worry that all was not well with George. Surely if there were nothing wrong with him, he should be back by now. But then he hadn't seemed to be in anything but the highest of spirits when they had entered the conservatory. Except for looking very pale there for a moment or two— Maybe he really was sick. Her annoyance had nearly turned to sympathy when he finally reappeared, with jaunty confidence restored, and grinning broadly.

"Say, I can guess what you must think, but honest, would you believe I met an old college buddy in that restroom? Hadn't seen him in years. Says he's working now as air traffic control for Allegheny Airlines. Just had to take a minute to catch up on his past history. I knew you wouldn't mind. Shall we go on then?"

She was already on her feet. Enough of that hard bench. "I'm ready if you are."

"Let's go. Uh, where did those folks go? I'd hate to run into them again. Must have mistaken me for someone else. It would be rather embarrassing to have to convince them that, no, I'm not Joe Blow, or whoever."

"Relax! You'll never see them again in a million years. They left."

George did relax—obviously, for the time being at least. The path took them past a tropical area where little bananas were growing on trees amidst towering ferns and palmettos. That walk led into a larger area where orchids of many shades and sizes clung to dense jungle growth. Bonnie eyed them appreciatively, wondering how lovely it would be to live where you could just go out and pick them at will. She could envision herself lolling on an endless stretch of glistening beach with a necklace of orchids about her neck. Gentle waves would wash shells onto the sparkling sands, and she could feel the soft, caressing breezes—She awoke from her reverie to realize it was George's lips caressing the back of her neck. Lucky she had removed her coat and was lugging it on one arm. Otherwise, she would have missed that delight. Turning to acknowledge his affectionate gaze, she caught his quick glance behind them. She looked in the same direction, but could see nothing worthy of attention. It was on to the next area.

Ah! Her favorite room. Passing under the Torii Gate, she noted that nothing had been rearranged since she had been there last. In the corner just inside the door, a tall pagoda graced a grouping of Japanese cherry trees. Across the walk a bamboo tea house with hand-painted paper panels nestled among exotic flowers. The path wound up over a quaint, arched footbridge over a tiny stream in which darted several brilliant goldfish. The room's walls were lined with Norfolk Island pine trees. The whole effect was that of the airy grace for which the Japanese are justly famous. Bonnie had always thought this display to be the most romantic of spots she had ever seen and had dreamed of the day when a handsome young man would stand at her side on that rustic, fairyland bridge, slip an arm about her and pledge his eternal devotion. Her heart already fluttered in anticipation when she discovered to her dismay that a middleaged couple were already on the bridge. George and Bonnie had to step aside to permit them to pass as they approached the bridge. The magic moment was gone. The moment she had hoped to share in intimate bliss was shattered by the presence of other people. Well, there would be another.

George and Bonnie strolled appreciatively across the bridge, through the length of the Japanese Room, and retraced their steps. It was time to move on to the next area. When they reached the door, George stopped abruptly and looked out in all directions. Surely he was now checking to see whether they were alone so that he might make up for the moments of intimacy they had missed before. It was not too late to return to the bridge and absorb the romance of the atmosphere. But George merely led her on out and down the wall toward the Cactus Garden. Feeling slightly foolish, she chided herself for being disappointed; the hoped-for scene had been all in her own mind. It had probably never entered his at all.

They exclaimed over the great variety of shapes and sizes of cacti in the desert scene with the delight of two children discovering lollipops. Bonnie never ceased to marvel at the funny, rubbery plants, ranging from the giant saguaro to the tiniest of miniatures. Several species were sporting blossoms, adding a dash of color to an otherwise rather drab landscape. She was leaning over to sniff the fragrance of a vivid orange deep-throated beauty when she heard a sound like a small hard object dropping on the path behind them. George started like a rabbit in a field of clover at the sight of a dog, and whirled around, consternation on his face. When he saw nothing, he grinned and bantered, "Ha! Thought for a minute there we were being pursued by the phantom of the desert."

"Did you think those skulls over there by the sunken wagon wheel were coming to life?"

When they had traveled every walk and eventually found themselves reentering the Palm Court where they had originally planned to begin their tour, much time had slipped by. For the most part, the afternoon had been exceedingly pleasant, despite the evidence that the special showing had already ended. George helped her on with her coat as they made their way out of the reception hall.

"Look, dear heart, I know of a lovely restaurant out in New Stanton. We can easily make it there in time for dinner before starvation completely overcomes us. What do you say?"

"Lovely! When do we start?" She knew that they were at the height of the late afternoon rush hour and it would probably take forty-five minutes to an hour to reach New Stanton. But fortunately she was not famished at the moment and might even enjoy the little trip. It proved to be a pleasant drive, and the time again passed quickly.

At the restaurant they indulged themselves with filet mignon and South African lobster tails. The day had proved to be worth the long wait before the date could be kept. It wasn't until Bonnie was pinning up her hair before sinking contentedly onto her bed that she permitted herself to entertain any memory of the few awkward moments. And suddenly their true significance surfaced. The young family George swore he did not know, but who obviously recognized him; the constant lookout as though watching for someone. Someone who knew him, perhaps? Had he deliberately postponed the date until the flower show was over so that the least possible number of other people would be present? And she wondered for the first time whether an air traffic controller had really engaged him in conversation in the men's room. She remembered hearing somewhere that such professionals spent many years learning their skills, far too many for a peer of George to have completed.

Snuggling her face into the pillow, she refused to exchange her present happiness for misgivings. A few peculiarities could be tolerated in a man with George's divergent moods.

5

Winter descended early and furiously that year. The temperature dropped to ten degrees above zero and stayed there for days at a stretch. The snow put in its first real appearance just after Thanksgiving and was frozen over with a glistening crust. Every time the temperature managed to rise sufficiently, more flakes bombarded the last accumulation; and before any of it could melt, the temperature would drop and freeze a crust over it again. When the plows, manned by harried and weary street crews, attempted to clear away each successive layer, the drifts piled higher, until many streets were lined with snow banks nearly as high as the cars. In downtown Pittsburgh, the street crews hauled away as much of it as possible in trucks and dumped it into the rivers until their level began to rise.

The merchants, schools, and churches were hard pressed to keep their walks safe. All the shoveling in the world couldn't prevent the bitter cold from freezing a thin veneer of ice over the cement. The low temperature cancelled out the effects of salt, and ashes were hard to come by, for the city had proudly converted most of its energy consumption to gas in an effort to clean its polluted air.

People greeted one another in the streets with reminiscences of the great snow of 1950. It too had begun on the day after Thanksgiving. That year the cost of shovel-

stretching her budget, but then, a girl lives only once. And nothing could ever top this!

To be sure, the effect was all she hoped it would be when she entered the ballroom on the arm of her tall, handsome, blond god. She had assured him profusely that it was quite all right with her that he had arrived to pick her up a little later than the time he had specified. She didn't go on to explain it would give more people a chance to arrive ahead of them to view her triumphant entrance. She felt like Cinderella for the first time in her life. And for one who had had to live under the shadow of a voluptuously beautiful sister most of her life, she felt as though her moment of glory had at long last arrived. It seemed that everyone in Central Typing turned to look at them. How fortunate that Sue Ramsey was in her direct line of vision; she would have hated to miss that look of scorn and obvious sniff as Sue abruptly turned her head away.

Although she drank little herself, Bonnie noticed George made his way to the champagne table between each and every dance. And sometimes when he seemed more intent on the glass in his hand than on her, one of the other men would slip up and ask for the next dance. She enjoyed the attention that provided until she discovered that every time she found herself in another man's arms she observed George with one of the other girls. She would just have to guard her own property. And so it was that when Hal Gregersen approached her, she said, "I'd love to dance with you, thank you, but I believe I'll stay with my escort."

George seemed to be one to hold his drinks well for most of the evening. But the repeated trips to the bar finally took their toll. Not that he ever became embarrassing—he just slurred his words slightly, and the broad shoulders began to sag a little. However, he was able to make his way steadily up to the balcony when they decided it was time to sit for awhile. He found a secluded little wrought iron bench behind a potted fern at the entrance to the grand stairway, led her to it, and drew her to himself.

"Bonnie, my love," he began a trifle thickly, "I've tried to say something like this before, and I can't seem to get it out right. But I have just never met a girl like you. The more I see of you, the more I realize that unless your life is united with mine, I will only half live. I—I'm not quite ready yet for any definite plans; I'm afraid you'll have to give me a little time on that, but eventually, when I can see my way clear, I hope to change your name to Mrs. George Morrow. And what does my love have to offer in reply?"

"Oh, George, I'll wait as long as you need," she murmured in ecstasy.

Her heart sang all day Sunday, until her family began to ask her what had transpired the night before to put such a sparkle in her eyes. It was her father who finally laid it on the line, and there was no way she could convincingly deny it, not that she had meant to keep anything from her beloved family; she had just simply decided that she would say nothing until George could offer something more definite. She was still singing when she approached the Gateway Center building on Monday morning. Just before entering the huge plate glass door, she spied a tree, obviously growing in that spot, that she had never noticed before. It drew her attention now because huge colored metal balls had been placed on it for the festive season. Even they must have been there before this, for the street decorations had been up for a couple weeks, but she guessed she had never noticed them before because she was only now fully awake to all the beauty around her. The thought of a Christmas tree presented new excitement, because now she might even stand some chance of finding a sparkling diamond ring under her tree. How deliriously happy could a girl be before bursting at the seams?

As she took the elevator up to her floor, she wondered what remarks she would be hearing from the girls today. She would just play it cool for awhile, soak up all the envy she could, and let her surprise bide its time. When she could flash that sparkling dazzler on her left hand would be soon enough to let her exuberance spill over. In the meantime, she would act as if nothing had happened.

She need not have planned how she would behave before the girls that morning. The southern stores were making their purchases of summer water-play equipment, and the teletype was kept so busy she began to fear her lunch hour would be cut short. When at last the hour arrived, she breathed a sigh of relief to find that all typing was sent out and so far, none was incoming. Snatching her purse and coat, she darted out the door before the machine could start again.

Sue, Goldie, and Allyn passed right before her nose without so much as even glancing in her direction. But what did it matter? She could soon quit working and leave this den of petty rivalry. Then the other girls would be the typewriter slaves while she would be standing over a gleaming white range somewhere out in the suburbs cooking up a delicacy that would motivate George to say he had never in all his life tasted anything so fabulous, not in New York, New Orleans, Chicago, or even Paris or Milan.

"Hi, Baby," George greeted her at the door, eyes gleaming like headlights on a diesel engine. "Let's stroll up the street today and take in the display in Kaufmann's window. Then we could eat in their cafeteria."

She thrilled at the rare treat, for it was not often they dined anywhere but the little basement sandwich bar and grill.

Kaufmann's display aroused the child in her again, as it evidently did for many hundreds of people. For those whose childhood was just too far removed to recollect, the scenes before them could at least awaken nostalgia for a bygone era. George and Bonnie stood for half their allotted hour just gazing at the fascinating animation that stretched for the entire length of the huge department store facing on Smithfield Street. The scene was that of a miniature village with quaint little buildings from three to four feet high. Animals, sleighs, and parcel-carrying pedestrians traversed the snow covered streets, while here and there a group of carolers gathered around a lamp post singing spiritedly.

Most entrancing was the community life revealed behind curtained windows or open shutters, making preparations for Christmas. Grandmothers lifted golden brown turkeys and pies from ovens, a boy played carols on his trumpet, the post office buzzed with frenzied mail carriers, excited little boys hauled home trees on sleds while other trees were already being trimmed in parlors, and shoppers thronged the stores. But Bonnie's favorite scene was that of some mice in city hall's attic chewing up the town's decorations!

So engrossed had the two been that they hadn't noted the passing of time, nor had they reckoned on the extra crowds of Christmas shoppers that would delay them. Eating as hastily as possible, they left the store right at one o'clock.

Crossing Grant Street, they passed a jewelry store with its usual elegant display of watches and jewelry. A tiny Santa in flowing angel hair beard was holding out an open bag of brilliant gems.

"Let's stop for just a minute and look at these rings," Bonnie exclaimed. "We won't be the only ones to be late back to work."

She selected a set with one large, flashing solitaire on

an engraved band, with a matched wedding band. This set also included the engraved band for the groom.

"That one I like best. And it even has 'his' to match. Do you think you would like that design?"

"Uh, well, I — I don't wear — I mean I never was one much for rings of any kind. You just choose anything your little heart desires, and it will be as good as done. Only I doubt it is going to show up in Santa's bag just yet."

"Of course, dear one, there's plenty of time — "

She was cut short by the sound of a woman's voice calling, "George, George, hey there, George!" It was spoken in a foreign accent so heavy that at first she didn't recognize the name.

Bonnie turned to see a little lady approaching from across Grant Street, waving her hand to draw George's attention. She was wearing a gray cloth coat with an immense silver fox collar that showed signs of considerable wear. A close fitting gray suede hat concealed so much of her hair Bonnie couldn't tell whether it may also be gray. Her immediate impression, however, was that the hair was as gray as the clothing. It was nearly impossible to judge the woman's age, because her face was lined in a manner that Bonnie had never seen before. Furrows ran horizontally across the brow and then were crisscrossed with as many or more running vertically. The cheeks were deeply lined and gave breadth to the face. Bonnie couldn't tell whether the face was naturally broad or whether it was simply the effect of middle age on a face that might have been slimmer and faintly attractive in youth. It was the visage of one on whom much suffering has left an indelible mark. And Bonnie knew instinctively, in the brief moment that she was to observe it, that it was forever imprinted on her memory.

She did not have long to study it, however, for George snatched her hand and attempted to dart across Fifth

Avenue, ignoring her calling his name. He might have succeeded in eluding the woman were it not that in the time their attention had been drawn to her, another woman had slipped on a patch of ice as she stepped up to the curb directly behind them. The myriads of parcels and bundles with which her arms had been laden, and which no doubt kept her from steadying herself when she started to slide, had gone flying in every direction. She was evidently injured in the fall and unable to rise immediately, and a crowd of shoppers quickly gathered around her, picking up parcels and attempting aid. It was into this scurry of excitement that George plunged, and seeing his way of escape blocked, tried then just to melt into the crowd. But he wasn't fast enough. The older woman was upon him in the next instant, tugging possessively at his sleeve.

"George! I didn't expect to see you on the street at this hour! I've been trying and trying to reach you by phone, but Shirley tells me you're out a lot these evenings. Must have a lot of overtime at the office, huh? Well, anyway, I just wanted to tell you I'm expecting you all to come over for Christmas Day. And who might the young lady be?" Bonnie thought she wasn't going to notice her standing there. Could this be George's mother? She had been so anxious to meet her, and so desirous of winning her complete approval. She just wished she might have met her at a more opportune moment, one in which she was better groomed and could show herself in her best light.

"Oh, yeah," that beam of steel narrowed again into a piercing shaft. "She's just a young lady who works in the office. We were both going the same way for lunch, so we sort of found our way together. Listen, Mother, we really are late for reporting back and have got to go. But I'll be sure to call you first thing I get home this evening." And with that, he grasped Bonnie's elbow, jerking her arm painfully, even through her heavy winter coat, and propelled her through the crowd and back to the office.

Bonnie could scarcely believe what she had heard. The disappointment of not having been properly introduced to a prospective mother-in-law was stinging enough, but to be denied her relationship to the man she loved was the ultimate in humiliation and grief.

Why? she kept thinking all the way back to the Center. Her thoughts tumbled into one massive jumble, her temples began to throb, and she could scarcely see the way she was going. Several times her foot slipped under her on a slick spot on the walk, but George's strong grip on her arm kept her on her feet. She was hardly aware of being steered into the building, practically pushed onto the elevator, and then left standing alone in the reception area.

She numbly made her way to the mailroom, left her coat in a heap on the wide window sill, and sat at the teletype. Somehow through the haze she heard the clicking of incoming messages and managed to send off something in reply, but when she tried to send out the messages she had gathered on her morning round, she couldn't concentrate. She murmured to Peggy something about not feeling very well, made her way to the lounge, and took a couple aspirin tablets. Stretched out on a leather reclining chair, she attempted to make some sort of sense out of the confusion in her mind, but nothing could come through distinctly. She told herself that understanding would have to wait until the shock abated. For now it was sufficient to come to grips with the fact that George appeared so shadowy that it was unlikely anything meaningful could ever be between them.

After half an hour, she had regained sufficient calm that she could return to the mailroom and somehow finish the afternoon. She was thankful Peggy also appeared in a remote mood and did not press her for conversation.

If time is usually ruthless in its passage, occasionally it is merciful. And the day did finally come to an end. Bonnie stepped into the crisp cold evening air and found that the stimulation it brought to her head might help to clear her muddled thoughts. Perhaps if she just went up the streets and wandered about the stores before going home and facing her family, she might be able to sort out what she was feeling.

She really didn't know where she was going, nor did it make any difference. The tinsel and Christmas trees had lost all their excitement, the sparkle went out of the colored lights. Prospective gifts lay piled on top of one another on the counters, but her eyes were unseeing. She thought once she recognized the face of an old friend in the crowd but hurried on before having to stop and make conversation. Up Liberty Street, across Sixth Avenue, and on she plunged blindly. And finally, after a couple hours, she found her mind was cleared enough that she was able to piece together some clues she had before ignored.

First, it had been the young family in the conservatory. Then, alerted that others who knew him might be around also, he was constantly on guard to make sure he didn't run into any other acquaintances. That explained the choice of every place he ever took her, including the basement hideaway, where he was sure he would go undetected. The office Christmas party was safe enough, because there were only the usual crowd with whom he worked every day. So either he didn't want to be seen at all or he didn't want to be seen with her.

Lastly, his own mother. Surely he wouldn't be hiding from her! It must be that she, Bonnie, was the reason for the elusive behavior. Perhaps if she could recall just what his mother's words had been, she might reach the bottom of the riddle. Now the first thing she had said was, "I've been trying to reach you by phone, but—" *What* had she said? When she spoke with such a thick accent, recall was difficult. "But *Shirley*—" Wasn't that the name she had used? Shirley! The word couldn't have hit more forcefully if it had been wrapped in a cannonball that found its mark squarely between her eyes. She staggered for a moment and would have fallen except there seemed to be something solid beside her on which she could steady herself. So that was it. Shirley. How could she have been so blind as not to have seen it before? At least, now Bonnie knew what she must do.

6

Her resolve firmly established, Bonnie now was able to think about her present actions. She realized that she must have worried her beloved family. She had never been out this late before without telling them of her plans. She must by all means make her way home as soon as possible and allay their fears. But added to the hour's lateness was the early descent of darkness at that time of year. Fresh snow clouds obscured what light may have been reflected by the moon, and the falling flakes added to the dismal scene greeting her when she emerged from the store. Many late shoppers crowded the streetcars, and with her confusion not entirely cleared from her worn, numb brain, she was hardly aware that she followed a group of shoppers into the first car that stopped near her. She hadn't given a thought to which one it was. She was only thankful that it offered a place where she could find a seat and rest her weary body, if not her heart.

There she bowed her head, propped one elbow in her lap, and supported her chin with the palm of her hand without looking up, until some inner time mechanism suggested that she must be nearly home. It was then she discovered that nearly all the passengers had disembarked at the various stops, of which she had taken no note.

With sudden panic, she wondered where she might be

and frantically began to try to find some passing land-mark. However, no street looked familiar. It was difficult to make out anything in the nearly pitch darkness, but under the dim flicker from the streetlights it appeared that great spaces had been torn open here and there with the removal of whole blocks of buildings. Now new panic struck with greater intensity than that which she had already experienced, for it looked as though she must be completely out of town. Then as one saved from the brink of disaster she realized the car was passing in front of the Allegheny General Hospital, and she re-monstrated with herself for not remembering that the redevelopment of the North Side was responsible for the large-scale destruction she had just witnessed. She knew then that she had even crossed the Allegheny River. The car turned past the side of the hospital and con-tinued in a northerly direction — opposite the direction in which her home lay.

She knew it would avail her nothing to stay on the car for each moment took her farther from her destination. There was nothing to do but simply get off and fend for herself in this unfamiliar section of town in the black of a winter night. She alighted at the next corner into a bank of deep snow and started making her way down the walk. There was little hope of another car's coming her way again at that hour, especially one with connections that would carry her in the right direction. She realized with a slowly creeping, sickening fear that she was enter-ing a residential section. It was impossible to tell who might be lurking in the shadows behind some shrubbery or maybe at the rear of a parked car. Should she ap-proach a house, knock on the door, and ask to use the phone? That would be risky, she knew. But where would she find a phone out here so far from public buildings? Walk back to the hospital? It must be three or four blocks back, and she vaguely remembered the car's making several turns since she had passed the hospital.

Despair wracked her frayed nerves, and she wanted to cry as she had never cried since the time when as a child she had been separated from her mother for several terrifying minutes in the Highland Park Zoo and was surrounded by huge, ferocious beasts.

When all courage had been drained, Bonnie observed something large and well-lit at the far end of the block. Perhaps it was a restaurant.

The sidewalks had not been as well cleared here as they were downtown, and the new snow made travel extremely difficult, but she pressed toward the lights as fast as she could. She slipped and scraped one knee on a hard object in the snow. She had nearly reached the building when she realized it was a church.

A church open on a Monday night? She thought churches were open only on Sunday mornings. But surely a church would have a phone. She could at least step inside and inquire.

Once she was inside the door however two pleasant, smiling ushers came toward her. When she opened her mouth to voice her question, one of them greeted her with a "Welcome to our program tonight." He sounded genuine. The other offered his arm and asked, "Would you prefer the side or the middle?" And before she knew it, she had been propelled toward a choice seat in the sanctuary from which escape would be impossible without drawing more attention to herself. Being seated in the middle of whatever was going on had been embarrassing enough. She might as well resign herself to waiting it out. Surely this couldn't go on all night.

It was soon apparent that the proceedings involved children, dozens of them, it seemed. Only they didn't all appear together. Singly or in little groups they would mount the platform, girls bedecked in fancy little lace-ruffled velvet or chiffon dresses, and boys in oversized first time neckties, and lisp into a microphone some little rhythmic verses. When each would finish, the audience would "ooh" and "ah" and eagerly await the next pint-sized orator. And then, after several of these narrations, a large group of them would sing a song or two. At least, the songs conveyed some meaning. She recognized them as carols—everyone learned carols as children. And before she knew it, she was listening to the words of the little rhymes:

> The angels sang of peace on earth,
>   And the shepherds told of the new babe's birth.
> That tiny prince wore no crown of gold,
>   And for thirty pieces later was sold.
> On a cruel cross His life He did give,
>   That a sin-wrecked world might then live.

The next narration spoke also of the love of a God who reached down from heaven one dark night two thousand years ago and brought hope to a world that had lost all hope. And the next, and all following. In fact, that must be what the whole performance was about. Bonnie had never thought of Christmas in that light before. She knew people often put those funny little crude shacks with plaster of paris figurines under their trees, but that had carried no real relevance to the spirit of Christmas for her. She had been reared in a home in which the word "Christ" was only an expletive reserved for extreme frustration. Church was useful only for weddings and funerals. Christmas was merely the time of year when people renewed their feelings for the brotherhood of all humankind and more or less churned up enough goodwill toward others to last them until the next Christmas.

Bonnie found herself becoming more and more intrigued by this new interpretation. Perhaps there was more meaning to this season than she had discovered before. She felt badly when the last little cherub took her stand on the platform and, with a dainty little curtsey, blew a kiss toward the audience as she bid them all a blessed Christmas and a cheery good night.

She had forgotten the passage of time, how far she was from home, and that her parents had no idea where she was. Those memories began to rear their ugly heads and clamor for attention, when a middle-aged man strode to the platform, opened a large Bible and started to read:

> "And it came to pass in those days, that there went out a decree from Caesar Augustus, that all the world should be taxed. . . . And all went to be taxed, every one into his own city. And Joseph also went up . . . to be taxed with Mary his espoused wife. . . . And she brought forth her firstborn son . . . and laid him in a manger. . . . And the angel said . . . For unto you is born this day in the city of David a Saviour, which is Christ the Lord."

Bonnie slowly perceived he must be reading the story of the birth of this One they called the Savior. She had seen that word Savior before, but it had conveyed no meaning to her. Now as the man quit reading and began to make a little speech, she began to form some conception of how this Jesus had made a way of hope for a world that had lost its way. Surely she knew what that meant this evening. Did she ever need hope! And somehow this was all tied up with a very great love, so great that we mortals simply cannot measure it. She had just lost her first real love, and if ever a mortal had need of it, she did now. Only this man was speaking of a love on an entirely different plane from anything she had known from George, her parents, her brother and sister, and even the best of her friends. This was a love that was greater than all other loves and made even the most wretched of humans happy in its security and embrace.

"And this love is experienced when the Babe of Bethlehem resides within the human soul. Emmanuel," the kindly gentleman was saying, *"God with us.* In coming to earth He came to take up His abode in the hearts of mankind."

"As the darkness on the Judean hillside was illuminated by the brilliance of the angel choir, so the darkness of the human soul is dispelled by the Light of the World come in the person of that Babe, bringing peace in place of confusion, hope for despair, and love to conquer fear."

Bonnie lost herself again in the marvel of it all, until all too soon, the man whom she assumed to be the minister concluded with the same wish for a blessed Christmas season previously bestowed by the little girl. The audience stood to their feet and sang "Joy to the World" with an enthusiasm she had never heard before. The pastor pronounced the benediction, and the sickening thought returned that she must now without further delay make her way home.

She turned to look for the two ushers, thinking them to be the logical ones to ask the location of the phone, when a young woman who had been sitting in the pew next to her turned and said warmly, "I'm so glad you are here tonight. I don't believe I've seen you before, have I? My name is Barbara Courtney."

"I'm Bonnie Lake, and I haven't been here before, but I did enjoy it very much. Perhaps you can tell me— where can I find a phone? You see, actually, I'm sort of lost tonight, and I must call a taxi."

"Where is it that you need to go?" asked her new friend.

"I live out in Oakland. You see, I blindly took the wrong streetcar, and here I am, miles from home. If I could just phone for a taxi—"

"You'll do no such thing. I live out that way myself and would be glad to take you. As soon as I retrieve my daughter, we'll be on our way."

The retrieval proved to be very speedy, for the daughter was no less than the tiny moppet who had bid them all a good night; and at that moment she pushed her way through the crowd to her mother's side, grabbed her hand and chirped, "Mommie, how did I do?"

"Wonderful, darling. I was so proud of you. Too bad Daddy had to work tonight and couldn't see you himself." To Bonnie she said, "This is Lisa," and busied herself for a moment with pulling leggings over the tiny one's already white stockinged little legs, buttoning her fur-trimmed coat, and tying her bonnet.

"Come, Bonnie, this way."

Bonnie followed as though in a dream. Was this really happening? Did people honestly act like this in church? All she had ever heard of people's behavior in a church was the well-worn cliché that everyone therein is a hypocrite.

If this woman was a hypocrite, she certainly was a loveable one.

As the three made their way to Barbara's little sports car, they observed that although the snowfall had slackened considerably, the street bore a two-inch new covering not yet reached by the road crews. They were probably in for bad traveling.

"Never fear," Barbara assured her passenger, "you'll be amazed at how well this little buggy takes to snow. You'll be home in no time. By the way, where do you usually go to church?"

Never in her life had Bonnie felt any embarrassment in admitting she did not attend church. It was just a fact of life; either you were one of those who seemed to find it necessary because it was the "thing" to do or maybe you couldn't handle life without some kind of a crutch.

Or you were one who simply did not bother. Were explanations necessary? Now, however, she was suddenly uncomfortable in the presence of this caring, gentle lady. It seemed as if Barbara's sweet spirit somehow exposed her for somewhat less than she ought to be. She had the distinct but inscrutable impression that if she were to look any deeper into herself than just under the surface, she would discover something she would not like.

"I—" the answer was hesitant, mumbled, "I really don't go anywhere. It was by accident that I got there tonight, although as I said, I thought it was a lovely service." She hoped that the compliment would ease what might seem to be rudeness in that explanation for her evening's attendance.

"Well, then you just must absolutely come back again. If you think the children were charming tonight, wait until you have met our college and career group. You'll find them to be the greatest bunch of students and working gals you'll ever find anywhere. They meet on Thursday nights. My husband and I help lead the group. He hated to miss this evening, and he certainly doesn't make a habit of working evenings, but sometimes things come up he can't avoid. He's a dentist, and one of his patients was suffering from an abscess, so he had to treat him on an emergency basis. I was hoping he might be finished in time to come late, but he didn't make it. Maybe he was afraid to risk it in his car. His doesn't take the snow like mine does."

Bonnie had to agree that her car handled the treacherous streets very well. They had crossed the Allegheny and were on their way out the Boulevard of the Allies by this time with a minimum of trouble.

"I think you have yourself to compliment as well as the car. You are handling it—snow and all—very well."

"Well, I've been a Pittsburgh gal all my life. I know these streets like the back of my hand. Or at least, I did.

This redevelopment is beginning to get a little confusing. Sometimes you can look for a street that has always been here, and now suddenly you can't find it."

"I know," laughed Bonnie. "I've heard other people say the same thing. And apparently the worst—or best—is yet to come. There are a few more buildings to go up yet in the Gateway Center. That's where I work. And I guess there is to be considerable change over on the North Side."

"Yes, we're fortunate our church is far enough out that it won't be razed. Several churches just a few blocks down the street from us will have to go. I know one that is already being rebuilt in its new location. We love our old structure and would hate to lose it."

"I understand that quite a few people have had to find new homes also. But the city planners assure us it will all be lovely when it is completed. A lot of that ancient construction next to the river was long past time to be cleared out."

"You say you work in one of the new Gateway Center buildings? Did you come in from outside to find work, or are you a native daughter also?"

"Quite native. But I don't know where I was born. I hate to say it, but if you turn right at the next corner, you will be on my street. I mean, I hate to see this lovely ride come to an end. I can't thank you enough."

"Not at all. I've enjoyed it, too. I'm so glad you happened onto my pew following your—your accident! Look, Bonnie, how about letting us stop for you the next time we go over to youth meeting? We'll be driving over anyway, so we might as well come around and pick you up. Since Christmas is on Thursday, there won't be any meeting this week. Nor next, either, as it will be New Year's Day. But—just the perfect thing! We're having a New Year's Eve party on Wednesday. We plan on its being an all night affair, and a few hardy souls do manage

84

to prop open their eyelids and stick it out. But most of us peter out in the wee small hours and go home. We always have a barrel of fun, though. I can't think of a better chance for you to meet the gang. You will, won't you?"

The car had pulled to a stop in front of the Shadyside Apartments. Lisa had long since been asleep with her head resting on Bonnie's shoulder. She hated to disturb her.

The sight of her home and the knowledge that she must now pick up her burden and make some sort of an explanation to her parents crowded out any excitement she might have felt for the invitation. Her mood changed so abruptly that Barbara wondered fearfully whether she had caused some offense.

"It's very kind of you to ask—" Heaviness in her voice made Barbara sensitive to the severity of the "accident" she had suffered. "But at this point, I can't say what I might be doing a week from Wednesday." She wanted to say, "what I might be *feeling* a week from Wednesday," but judged better of it. "My phone is listed under James Lake. You could call later on, if you wish."

"Why, of course. I will be very glad to. And let me say again how tickled I am to have met you tonight."

"And I you. Thanks again loads." Bonnie was out of the car and into the elevator before the dread feeling hit again in its fullest force. Now her parents would be asking questions, and she wanted nothing better than to hide in the earth's farthest recesses. And on top of her devastation, she would even have to offer an apology.

Her hand was shaking when she reached for the knob. The lift she had felt as she sat in that church listening to the assurance of God's unfathomable love had vanished as surely as if she had dreamed it all. For that matter, she was beginning to wonder if she hadn't. Maybe it had all been one horrible, excruciating, gigantic nightmare. Maybe even George was only an illusion.

The relief on the faces of her parents as she stepped through the door brought her back to reality. Her mother's mouth opened in a cry of anguish, and her father's eyes spoke rebuke.

"I know I've worried you terribly," Bonnie began, barely fighting back the tears. "I'm awfully sorry, but— but, well, could I wait until later to explain? I simply can't talk about it now."

"That's all right, dear," her mother attempted to soothe. "So long as you are safe, that's all that really matters. Is there any way I can help you?"

If only there were! At least, her mother seemed to understand.

"I think I'll go right on to bed now. No—" she read her mother's thoughts "—I don't want anything to eat. I'll be quite all right. Good night, both of you."

"Good night. Sleep peacefully."

When Bonnie reached her room she wondered what chance there was for a peaceful sleep. It was at times like this she would prefer not to have a roommate. For there was Sylvia, like the keeper in the zoo, perched on the middle of her bed completely surrounded by stuffed animals. There were giraffes, frogs, elephants, dogs, a whole collection of teddy bears, a kangaroo with a little one peeping from its pouch, a family of raccoons, and a six-foot green plush snake stretched out across her pillow. It usually took Sylvia five minutes just to clear her bed before she could get under the covers, and as many more to replace them all in the morning. And her suitors kept lavishing more for birthdays, Christmas, proms, any and every excuse they could manufacture.

And then, of course, there were the endless phono records. Sometimes she didn't mind them—even listened herself. But this was the *last* night she would possibly wish to hear them again. This was no hidden recess in the bowels of the earth; it might as well have been

Grand Central Station.

"Kinda late, aren't you, sis?" Bonnie could scarcely hear her above the din.

"Yeah. Would you mind turning that down a little? Please."

"Sure. Anything you say."

She should have asked for a lot, because a little was all she received. At least it was better. Bonnie lost no time in falling into her bed. She didn't even remove her makeup. She had never known such utter exhaustion.

But merciful, obliterating sleep wouldn't come. She lay in one position until she ached. Changing position helped only for a short time. She hated to thrash too obviously for fear of arousing Sylvia's curiosity; hers were the last questions she wanted to answer at the moment. She would have liked to remind Sylvia that she should get to sleep so she would be able to get up and go to school the next morning, but, unfortunately, Sylvia's Christmas vacation had begun. Bonnie groaned when her sister turned all the records over and started again.

She tried to shut out any thoughts, thinking that a blank mind would be more conducive to slumber. But self-recrimination would not be silenced. Why hadn't she heeded the warning signals? She should have been suspicious in the very first place when George would take her nowhere to eat except a sleazy joint in a dingy basement. He never had been interested in meeting her family, nor did he make any effort to acquaint her with his. Oh, many were the signs—if she had only looked. How blinded must one be to stumble over the obvious?

What a laughing stock she would be now in the office if anyone should ever learn the truth! The object of the envy of half the girls in Central Typing wouldn't be able to face them, should they ever know.

And the pain! The excruciating, wrenching pain! For no matter how cruel, a first love dies slowly.

Bonnie didn't know what time Sylvia finally turned off the record player, for she eventually dozed into spells of fitful sleep. And then she dreamed that she was in the midst of a massive surge of movement, like the tumultuous, restless tide of the sea. She seemed to be pulled and shoved in every direction at once, with great waves of misery engulfing her.

Her face was hot and feeling flushed, although something cold was splattering against it. And she heard a woman's agonizing voice crying, "Marya . . . Marya . . . Marya. . . ."

She was still suffering the despair that flooded her spirit when the third cry awakened her. Shivering almost uncontrollably as reality crowded in upon her again, she realized she must simply have been reenacting her grief in her sleep. But she did not know anyone by the name of Marya.

7

Thankfully, there were only two days to work before Christmas. Perhaps she could make up for some lost sleep on Christmas Day. That wouldn't do her any good today, though, having awakened with her head feeling like a ton of cement, and her eyes swollen and purple. A couple aspirin tablets and some coffee might revive her sufficiently that she could somehow get through the day. But just getting through was not enough. For she had some business to transact on this day. Serious business. And she wanted as level a head as she could get cleared.

A new snow had fallen during the night, not heavy, but enough to make the walks even more treacherous. Shrubs and the bare tree limbs etched a delicate, lacy effect that hinted of a fairy wonderland. And the air was clear, sweet, and invigorating. In other circumstances it would have been a wonderful morning to be alive. The little brunette with the heavy heart trudged down the block to meet the streetcar feeling some lightening of the spirit. It was enough to help her more clearly plan her strategy for the moment when she would confront George, but not quite enough for complete lucidity in what she was doing. Her mind intent on the choice of words she would use when the time came, she plunged unseeing toward the track where the car was rapidly approaching. A wild screeching of metal on metal and a shower of sparks from the power line jolted her out of her mental vision of the encounter to come, and she felt the tug of a strong arm pulling her back, as the monstrous car skidded to a stop before her, so close she could feel it brushing her coat. She realized she must have walked directly into its path before the point at which it had intended to stop.

She barely saw the stranger who by some freak of happenstance was in the right place to avert a tragedy. Usually she was the only passenger to embark at this stop in the morning.

"Thanks," she murmured in embarrassment. "Stupid of me, wasn't it?"

"Not stupid. But you sure look like you're carrying the problems of the world on your shoulders. If you've got any profound answers, I'm sure Ike and the other boys in Washington would be mighty glad to hear them." He released a jolly, hearty laugh and guided her toward a seat. She hoped fervently that he wouldn't then sit beside her and try to make further conversation. But she needn't have worried, for he went back a couple more seats and engaged himself in the morning paper.

The morning passed uneventfully, except that mail was heavy and telegrams profuse. Strange that in the midst of the Christmas hustle and bustle there should be a work rush for summer items in resort areas! But she knew that stores would be stocking such merchandise immediately after dismantling Easter decorations. Perhaps it was good to keep very busy, for it kept her from dwelling on the lunch hour scene that was sure to come.

She had decided that the best approach would be to go along with George to the basement hideout the same as usual, with no hint of her suspicion. She could have just refused to see him ever again, but a sharp pain in the depths of her spirit cried out for a hearing, an urgent insistence that George be forced to make open admission and perhaps offer justification for what he had done. It was a trifle difficult to sound detached and lighthearted as she slipped and skidded up the street at his side, and she recoiled at having to place her hand in his, but she must not put him on guard before the time came.

When they were at last seated, he offered to take her coat as usual. She demurred with something lame about being a little chilly after the walk. And now she must waste no time, for this must be attended to before they were served.

Courage, girl, courage, she prodded herself as she swallowed a great gulp to quell the wild pounding in her chest. And suddenly all agitation left and she was as calm and collected as ever she had been.

Looking him steadily in the depths of those pools of liquid fire, her voice clear and firm, she said simply, "You're married, aren't you, George?"

The fire was instantly extinguished, and George Morrow dropped his gaze, looking like a small boy whose grandmother had caught him in the cookie jar. For several long, silent moments the two of them simply sat, she searching his expression to read any emotion that might be registered, and he with his eyes averted, a red flush creeping up around his collar, a hand flustering nervously with the salt shaker on the table.

"I—I was afraid it couldn't last." The regret sounded genuine. "Honestly, Bonnie, I didn't mean to let it happen like this. To say I'm sorry, I guess, would only add insult to injury. But to be perfectly truthful—" The eyes softened and met hers once more, "I was just drawn to you as a man is attracted to a girl who reminds him of his mother. I don't know what there is about you, but something—I can't, for the life of me, put my finger on it—something of my mother just comes through to me. I never meant to hurt my wife—Shirley is a wonderful girl and would be crushed about this—but as I was more and more attracted to you, I thought maybe in time I would be able to pull away from her, eventually get a divorce, provide plenty for her and the—"

Bonnie could listen to no more. Feeling nauseous, she drew herself up to her full height, leaned down for one long, last penetrating gaze, and reached for her purse to depart. For in that moment she loathed him with the same passion with which she had once loved him. She turned and walked out of his life.

It was with a liberating sense of relief that she climbed those dingy steps back up to street level. Thank goodness she wouldn't have to be buried down *there* again! But now where? She certainly didn't want to go back to the office and while away a lonely hour, nor did she care to find anything to eat. She might as well traverse the same streets she had covered the evening before without really observing them. Anyway, she still had a little Christmas shopping to do. She could decide on nothing at all for Sylvia, for there was one girl who lacked nothing. At least, she lacked nothing that she really wanted. For apart from men, her only interests lay in her swimming and her records. Bonnie certainly couldn't buy a pool for Christmas, and if she got any more records for her sister, she would be punishing herself. What a problem!

Bonnie found her steps taking her past a jewelry store. When memories rushed in, bringing a shudder with them, she turned her head quickly and darted across the street. It would probably be awhile before she could look at diamonds without a sinking feeling in the pit of her stomach. She headed into an alley and, realizing there would be no display windows there, looked for the nearest exit. Behind one small store she found an opening back out to the street, and turned left. It was a side street with which she was not familiar. Wondering whether she should retrace her steps back to Liberty

Street, or just keep on going, she was arrested by the sound of music floating in the crisp air high overhead. Angel choir? In the heart of Pittsburgh nearly two thousand years after that first one of which she had heard only last evening? No, just Tennessee Ernie Ford singing hymns. She would recognize that voice anywhere. Some store must be advertising over a public address system. But what were those strange words that she was hearing?

"Who at my door is standing,
  Patiently drawing near?
Entrance within demanding,
  Whose is the voice I hear?

"Lonely without He's staying,
  Lonely within am I;
While I am still delaying,
  I am condemned to die!

"Door of my heart, I hasten!
  Thee will I open wide;
Tho He rebuke and chasten,
  He shall with me abide.

"Sweetly the tones are falling:
  Open the door for me!
If thou wilt heed my calling,
  I will abide with thee."

"Who at my door is standing?" repeated Bonnie to herself. *Now what could that "patiently drawing nigh; Entrance within demanding. . . ." possibly mean?* The beautiful voice that Bonnie had loved for years was proclaiming a promise, even a commitment, that must be offered by the Lord God Himself. At any rate, it had seemed to her last evening that this was what the folks in that church had been trying to say. Somehow God could even take

up living with us. Interesting thought; she would have to look into it sometime. Never mind Sylvia—she would get the record for herself. It took her several moments to locate the building from which the music was amplified. Approaching a clerk, she asked, "Is this the store that is playing the records over the public address system?"

"Yes, I'm afraid it is," was the cross answer. "And you're not the first to complain about the disturbance."

"Oh, no, not at all. I would like to buy the one I just heard." Bonnie didn't know whether to laugh or weep at callous people who would complain because their Christmas bustle was soothed by Tennessee Ernie's soft, mellow voice.

"Basement, counter number four," barked the disinterested clerk.

A little Christmas spirit wouldn't hurt her any, Bonnie thought ruefully as she made her way to the basement.

The afternoon passed much as had the morning. The only difference from the usual routine was that both morning and afternoon Bonnie had timed her mail route as nearly as possible to coincide with the few minutes George took off for his break. It would be awhile before she could pick up and deliver at his desk without any feeling of revulsion.

It was with considerable relief that four-thirty arrived and Bonnie could take her leave for the day. And now she must face her next problem, how much to tell her family. She could just evade the fact of George's marriage and simply say it was all off between them. But she had never withheld anything from her folks, and she feared that if she said nothing now, eventually something might just slip out, and they would be hurt that she hadn't confided all, although it was difficult to imagine under what circumstances she would ever want to mention George's name again.

Around the dinner table that evening the usual family

prattle was tossed, especially between Sylvia and Perry. Their mother allowed once that she would be glad when vacation was over and the two of them could get back into school and out of each other's hair. Finally the verbal blows were spent, and one of their few calm moments ensued. Bonnie knew she would never have a better opportunity.

She struggled again for composure, but this time a quaver remained in her voice.

"I have decided not to see any more of George Morrow." She waited for that to sink in before offering any more.

"We rather suspected last evening you would be telling us as much. We're sorry, dear." Her mother's voice was soft, encouraging.

"You see, he—he—" If only she could get out those first awful words, the rest would probably come easy. "He's already married."

Exclamations arose from all present.

"Why that skunk," raged her usually placid father. "I'd like to get my hands around his rotten neck. What did he think he was doing anyway, leading my daughter on like that?"

"Well, actually, he said he didn't mean to just lead me on—" Bonnie's tongue was loosed in the loving security of her home, and she poured out the whole tale, not omitting all the little details that should have made her suspicious, but to which she had willfully been blinded. "I guess I loved him so much that I would not see it," she confessed in conclusion.

"I thought something was amiss when he kept standing you up for that first date," sympathized her father. "But don't go blaming yourself. What's done is done. We all go through that first love experience and for some of us it is more devastating that for others."

Bonnie appreciated his putting it in that light.

"Well, for Pete's sake, sis, you'll just go back to giving me some competition with Hal," snorted Sylvia.

Even though it was a rather crude attempt, Bonnie recognized that her sister was simply trying to remind her that this, too, would pass, and somehow there was still a future for her out there somewhere. In a way, it was touching of Syl to try to reach out and comfort her in her hour of pain.

They heard on the late news broadcast that night that a Mount Lebanon woman had been killed that day, slipping under the wheels of a streetcar on an icy street. With utter detachment, the thought flitted through Bonnie's mind that but for some almost unseen stranger, she might also have been killed. As she pulled the covers up over her head to block out Sylvia's lamplight and buried her head in the pillow to try to drown out the records, she wondered whether it made any difference that she hadn't been.

The next day passed in much the same manner as the previous one. Bonnie once again timed her transits to evade George, but how long could she keep that up? Peggy would soon catch on that she was interrupting the prescribed routine, and she would be forced to abide by the schedule. But as if that weren't already enough, a new problem began to surface. It happened while she was out on her lunch break. She knew that sooner or later the other girls were going to realize she was not eating with George anymore; probably she would eventually resume going with them to the downstairs cafeteria. But for the present, she would continue the illusion that she was going out with him; questions would be easier to answer if they were postponed until the pain was eased by time.

Anyway, there was still the matter of a gift for Sylvia. And this was none other than Christmas Eve. She could delay no longer. Kaufmann's would no doubt feature the most extensive display from which to make a selection, but she didn't feel up to seeing that animated village again. Not for this year, at least. And the Jenkins Arcade was closer anyway. Surely she could find something there.

She had barely started down the center mall when an array of silver charm bracelets caught her fancy. The perfect answer! Why hadn't she thought of that before? Very cleverly, she commended herself, she selected a three-quarter inch record and a miniature teddy bear. They didn't begin to fill the bracelet, but at the price of sterling silver, that was about all she could afford for this time. If only she hadn't done all that foolish splurging on her fancy outfit for last Saturday night! One thing was certain. At least that was one record she wouldn't have to listen to. Maybe Sylvia's young swains would be inspired in the future to present her with other silver animals, and Bonnie wouldn't be forced to move out of their bedroom to make way for more plush ones.

After a leisurely sandwich, she made her way back to the office. But at the elevator she had the misfortune to run into Sue Ramsey.

"Alone again!" her former rival exclaimed. "Don't tell me Santa's reindeer have charged off with your romance."

Bonnie's heart sank to stomach level. Perhaps a partial truth could salvage the situation.

"I had some last minute shopping to do. Let me show you what a darling little bracelet I found for my sister."

Sue ignored the attempted distraction. "But I saw you alone yesterday, also, at the five and dime. Lovers' quarrel, huh?"

Oh, that Tennessee Ernie record. Well, she couldn't deny it. But Sue had offered her an out. "Yeah," she attempted to sound casual. "Lovers' quarrel. They usually blow over, you know."

But now it was out. If she could only hold them off with that explanation, it wouldn't be as bad as being made a disgrace for dating a married man. And she was reasonably sure that George would never talk. Whatever he might be, he wasn't that big a fool.

But girls' gossip dies a slow death. Everywhere she went now on her rounds, heads were turned and whispers began behind her. And always there remained that devastating ache — much as she loathed the thought of George, an agonizing amount of attraction remained. She had heard it is possible to love and hate at the same time. Now she was experiencing its nasty ambivalence. And visions of his beautiful blond waves and fantastic eyes kept crowding unbidden into the secret chambers of her heart.

She was thankful when the company dismissed them all early in the true spirit of Christmas. To get out of the place would provide a welcome break from the strain.

The evening and Christmas Day, for that matter, passed quietly and uneventfully at the Lake household. Even Sylvia and Perry appeared to be touched by the peace and calm of the season, and not an insult passed between them. Bonnie spent some time in the kitchen helping her mother prepare a lovely Christmas dinner, and then gratefully repaired to her room. Sylvia had become taken up with the afternoon soap operas while on vacation, and for once Bonnie found peace and contentment in a solitary room. It was heavenly! She got out a novel that she had started to read several weeks before and lost herself in the triumphs and tribulations of an imaginary heroine until her eyes grew heavy. The sleep that followed was deep and healing. She awoke feeling more refreshed than she had in some days. After a light evening snack of sandwiches and left over pecan pie, she resumed her reading until once more sleep overtook her. That night she did not hear the endless grinding of the records.

The sense of physical well-being with which she awoke in the morning did not have long to last, however. All the old stresses were renewed when she walked through the plate glass doors. First, she had the misfortune to enter the same elevator with George. She had had a wild impulse to dart over to another one, but the door had begun to close and hastily departing would have betrayed a weakness she was determined would not be apparent. The strained embarrassment was alleviated somewhat by the continual stopping at successive floors as the heavy morning traffic entered and exited. On second thought, it may have been better to crack the ice in this manner, because she was going to have to get used to passing his desk. Deciding it would be less painful to make a frontal attack, she returned to her usual routine. But when she entered the door of the accounting department and caught sight of his handsome blond head, her heart involuntarily quickened its pace and some of the old exhilaration flooded over her. As hard as she tried to revive her revulsion for him, she had to acknowledge the agony that he who belonged to another was the object of her affections.

Impressions of his vivid eyes reflecting fluctuating moods kept intruding, unbidden, into her memory, and she strove to down them in torrents of self-recrimination. Those periods alternated with feelings of guilt and disgrace for having kept the company of a married man, although she knew she had done so innocently. Perhaps it was the abhorrence of her failure to detect that ignominy that increased the degree to which it overwhelmed her. When she tried to sort it all out she always came back to the same place, and that desolate place was pitiable confusion. If she had only had her own inner turmoil to contend with, that would have been more than sufficient. But there were always the other girls' continual whispers and the ever present fear that the secret would be discovered.

And while her mind went round and round in that dizzying jumble, she had to concentrate on her work. That became no less difficult. Occasionally the messages she attempted to type blurred behind a mist of tears.

George had at first ignored her altogether, whether in anger, humiliation, disdain, or pain akin to hers she could not guess. But all doubt was removed the day she felt the pressure of his electrifying gaze following her movements about his department, and discovered on his stricken face the most intense longing she had ever seen. She began to question whether she could remain in Paramount Plastics's employ.

When New Year's Eve arrived, she welcomed with the utmost gratitude the opportunity to escape for one more holiday the stress each day in the office heaped upon her. She had barely entered the sanctuary of her beloved home when the phone rang.

"Hello, Bonnie?" a strange voice replied when she answered. "This is Barbara. How are you? Did you have a nice Christmas?"

With a start Bonnie wondered how she could have been so completely immersed in her woes as to forget so lovely a new friend. She struggled frantically to remember what it was that Barbara had promised to phone about. And then she revived some hazy memory of a youth group and a party—why, of course, this was New Year's Eve!

"I'm fine, thank you. And we had a very relaxing, quiet Christmas at home. I wish I could have seen your little girl's eyes on Christmas morning!" Bonnie's mind was numb and her nerves jagged, but she was determined to repay courtesy for courtesy.

"She was a joy. We thank God for her every day. I'm

rather rushed for time as I still have to get some of the refreshments rounded up, but I'm calling for your answer. I do hope you have planned to go to our party tonight."

Now how was Bonnie going to say she had completely forgotten about it and didn't feel in the least inclined for a party, without really saying it? The worst of it was, her mind was too dull to think quickly. An awkward pause followed as she groped for some lame excuse.

"Bonnie—" that kind voice again, coming to her rescue, "something is troubling you, dear, isn't it?" Not prying, not intruding on personal territory, but genuinely concerned. Could these churchy people read other people's thoughts?

"Yes, Barbara, I am in the midst of a very trying time, and I don't feel up to a party tonight. I really appreciate the invitation, but hope you understand. Perhaps you will think of me again some time."

"You can be sure I will think of you, and I will be praying for you. Now I must run along. Sorry to have to rush off. 'Bye now."

Bonnie replaced the phone in amazement. Never before had anyone told her she would pray for her. Was this something more that those Christians did?

New Year's Day was, if anything, more leisurely than the previous holiday had been. Bonnie again sought a novel with which to lull herself to sleep after her annual pastime—watching the Tournament of Roses Parade. And all too soon the day was over. But now there was nothing to which Bonnie could look forward for relief from the agony at the office. At least, there was only one more day this week and then she could recoup herself a little over the weekend.

She stepped off the elevator the next morning with resignation and challenged herself to make an attempt to break her somber routine by joining the other girls for lunch. If they asked any questions, she was not compelled to give them a complete answer.

She was in the middle of sorting the postal service mail and running it through the opening machine when Peggy returned from a few minutes' absence and reported that Mr. Paczak wanted to see her in the manager's office. Puzzled, Bonnie smoothed her hair and tugged at her skirt. It surely couldn't be that she was to be transferred out of the mailroom. She knew of no one leaving or of any transfers up the line. Perhaps it was only a special message to be sent immediately. But he usually relayed those by his secretary. Still more baffled, she entered his private office.

"Miss Lake, please be seated." Mr. Paczak seemed extremely agitated. She fervently hoped she was not the sole cause of it.

"I have the misfortune to have to call to your attention the fact that you have misaddressed a shipment order to Wrightsville Beach, North Carolina. You apparently typed a 'D' instead of the 'C' in the abbreviation for the state, and an order for beachballs and snorkels was directed to North Dakota. To be truthful, we don't know where in the world it is. If the trucking company ever succeeds in tracking it down, we will have to stand the cost of transporting it back across the country. In the meantime—"

Bonnie lowered her gaze and shifted her feet. She clasped her hands together in her lap until the knuckles turned white.

"—the retail outlet in North Carolina has threatened to seek a more reliable company to fill their orders in the future. Now I needn't remind you that this is a young, struggling company. We need all the business we can get. You understand, of course, that this is the peak ordering season for summer merchandise, and mistakes such as this are extremely costly, and if I may put it so bluntly, inexcuseable. I must warn you that in the future if you don't give greater diligence to—"

An inaudible cry escaped her throat. She had been afraid she would make just such a mistake in her distress.

"I'm extremely sorry," she interrupted, not wishing to hear anything more that he had to say. "I will just leave your employ right now. I feel reasonably sure that Peggy can handle all the work in the mailroom until you can hire a replacement. If—"

"Oh, I didn't have that in mind at all." Mr. Paczak's tone changed to a softer pitch, but his agitation remained. "Actually your work has been of the highest quality, and you are well received by your colleagues. I was merely saying that in the future, you would do well to pay more heed to your work."

"I feel that it would be better for me personally if I were to just turn in my resignation. I will do so immediately if it meets with your approval."

Mr. Paczak shook his head. He clearly had not expected this development and might even have changed his tone to appeasement; however, his agitation spurred him to cancel out any change in his voice.

"If that is your final decision, you may stop in the payroll department and pick up your check before you leave today. But you may still reconsider, if you so choose."

"I feel it is in the best interest of everyone," (George included, she thought to herself), "if I abide by this decision. Perhaps I may not be asking too much for a reference?"

"No, no, not too much at all. I will give you only the best." He indicated by his manner that he preferred this interview to end.

Bonnie murmured a thank you and left Mr. Paczak's office as hastily as grace would permit. She nearly collided with two distinguished looking gentlemen seeking entrance to the office. They wore the usual severely tailored business suits and each carried a briefcase. She probably would have thought little about them, except that they also each wore some kind of a badge. Bonnie was too engrossed in this new complication to her own woes to give any more thought to them. But when she carried the mail through the office, she encountered them in various places throughout the day, looking into files, sorting through papers, and conferring with various department heads and executives.

By lunchtime, her resolve to eat with the girls had disappeared. With this abrupt twist to her fate, she would never have to listen to their gossip or answer any questions again. So she might as well remain aloof for one more day and just be done with it. She did, however, stroll through the Jenkins Arcade once more to take a last look at the merchandise on display and remove herself from the oppression the office forced upon her.

She thought that that afternoon was the longest she had ever endured, and despaired occasionally of its ever coming to an end. The hour hand finally stretched out toward the 4, and Bonnie knew that if she were to pick up her check, she should do so now rather than wait until the closing hour when the treasurer would be clearing his desk for the day. She could slip into the payroll department under the guise of a routine trip, but she knew some of the payroll people would know why they had made out her check on special instructions, and feared questions would soon be demanding answers. So she quietly slipped her coat over her arm, picked up her purse, hurriedly snatched her check, and managed to get clear past the reception desk and into an elevator with no more than a couple pairs of eyes raised along her route. It was only a dim impression she received of two uniformed men stationed by the door who scrutinized her leave.

Nineteen floors below she exited the elevator and hurried outside. As the big plate glass doors swung shut behind her for the last time, she released an enormous sigh of relief, for even though the job that had begun so promising had met a devastating and untimely end, and she didn't know where her path would lie next, she now had walked out of George Morrow's life forever.

The snow's many layers upon layers were by now showered with a thick dusting of black grime over which the long shadows of the late afternoon sun cast a depressing gloom. The most dismal time of all the year had arrived, when winter's bleakness would hold the whole world in its desolate grip until broken by the first stirrings of spring. Bonnie felt all nature itself reflected her bruised and bleeding spirit.

The little tree by the entrance to the Gateway Center building did not escape her notice as she passed, for someone had forgotten to remove its Christmas ornaments, and she observed several of the giant balls lying now broken on the ground and, like her heart, gaping open from great, hollow rents.

Falling into bed that night, depleted of all strength, once more she tossed and turned, dozed and awakened. Sylvia finally sensed her utter exhaustion and solicitously turned off the light. Still Bonnie agonized and thrashed.

When at last blessed relief overtook her in a deeper slumber, she again envisioned herself pummeled about in a great wave of movement. Her face felt damp in that strange mixture of warmth and cold, and frantically she was reaching and grasping, for what she knew not. Again she heard the frenzied cry of that strange voice calling, "Marya . . . Marya." Blackness completely engulfed her as she made one last desperate attempt to clutch the unknown, and her arm's thrashing awakened her.

In her twilight state of transition between sleep and

wakefulness, her conscious mind became aware that she had dreamed that same dream many times before. Had it always been in times of stress, she now wondered. The dream had never awakened her before these last two times, but neither had she ever met stress this severe.

And how could she now explain the sensation on her face? She had not recently been out walking in a snowstorm. The overall impression was that of moisture. Therefore, the heat and flushing could mean tears. But the cold — she was now aware of being cold all over, for she was shivering. But she had awakened herself with a wild thrashing of her arms, like a grasping motion. Was the cold a shower of sea spray? There had been that surging. She must have been engulfed in waves and clutching for a rope.

There now, with that settled she would try to get back to sleep. But there was something more. She suddenly realized that in her dream she was very, very small. She still had no idea who Marya was.

The next time she woke, broad daylight streamed through the window, and Yang was curled in a sleek gray ball at the foot of her bed. The apartment was strangely quiet. She judged it must be mid-morning, but she couldn't account for the stillness in their usually bustling home until she remembered that Perry had spent the night with a friend and her mother was doing the weekly shopping. Her father was probably occupied in some activity, and it was hard to tell where Sylvia might be. All the better; she didn't feel like stirring. She wished she could even go back to sleep and shut out painful reality. But she knew she had slept herself out, and more sleep would probably only bring with it some kind of nightmare. At the thought of dreaming, she remembered the strange dream that had awakened her. Funny, to know now that she had dreamed that dream all her life and had never been aware of it before waking. And puzzling over what it could possibly indicate, she almost felt herself again the victim of those overwhelming waves.

Oh, well, never mind dreams. She had to face real life, whether she wanted to or not. No matter how much she could sleep and drown out her misery, she would always awaken. And for the present at least, that meant she faced no love, no plans, and no job.

She wondered for a moment whether she should enroll in a college. The idea wasn't new, but she was still not certain into which field she would go if she did enroll. It would be better judgment just to look for another job. The folks had been simply marvelous last evening when she dropped inside the door (staggered would probably be more accurate) and unloaded the newest development. They had told her she needed a good, relaxing rest and should not think about working again for a few weeks at least. Perhaps even a vacation trip somewhere would not come amiss.

Now as she lounged in bed that Saturday morning, she knew the worst thing she could do would be to sit around unoccupied. There was no way she could unwind from this tremendous emotional upheaval save through the tried and true healing properties of time. And in that time she would aid the process by keeping her hands busy and her mind off—must she be forced to remember his name? She would just start out to find another job.

January was never the best month for a turnover in personnel. Probably her best bet would be to look in the newspaper's help wanted section.

She hopped out of bed and ran straight to the kitchen, where the paper was usually left. No paper. Passing on into the dining room and living room, she spied Sylvia curled in the chair before the big front window painting her nails.

"It's not quite time yet for lunch." Sylvia didn't look up.

Bonnie didn't know whether to interpret her remark as sarcasm, sympathy, or simple statement of fact. It really was none of Sylvia's concern when she got up.

"Where is the newspaper?"

Sylvia looked startled for an instant, but replied casually, "How would I know? I never read anything but Dear Abby and the comics."

Bonnie raised her eyebrows, nodding slightly in agreement, and retraced her steps through the rooms, looking under magazines, the mail, anything she could imagine might be concealing the paper, but to no avail.

Well, she told herself, I'll just borrow the one next door. Pulling a dressing robe over her nightie, she pushed the button by the door marked 3B.

"Are you by any chance finished with the morning paper? I'd like to borrow it a moment; seems like ours has disappeared."

Simple enough request. The neighbor granted it without any more than "A nice day, isn't it?"

Bonnie was thankful she had propped herself up comfortably in bed before unfolding the paper. For when she did so, there staring at her from the front page were those two penetrating steel-bullet eyes.

"George!" she cried aloud. The exclamation brought Sylvia to the door instantly.

"Where did you get that paper?" she demanded agitatedly. But Bonnie did not heed her. Her eyes were busy scanning the caption under the picture.

"North Hills man arrested for embezzlement," she read incredulously. *One of the ritzyest sections of town*, she thought to herself, as she read on. "George Morrow, twenty-six, was apprehended late yesterday afternoon at the Gateway Center offices of the Paramount Plastics Company. Morrow, an employee of the local firm since last June, will be charged in district court with fraudulent transfer of the company's funds. . . . discovered making bank deposits and falsifying reports."

Bonnie laid down the paper. There was more to the article, but her weary mind wasn't capable of absorbing anything else. So that was how he financed all those eating escapades in distant cities. And hard telling what else he did when he got there!

So George wasn't going to be an employee of Paramount Plastics anymore. If only she had waited one more day before hastily deciding to resign, she might still have had the job. And the flurry over the disclosure that George had been embezzling would effectively still the rustle over her sordid romance. In time, things would have returned to normal, and all would have been well.

Now she understood why the paper had been missing from the apartment. Her dear family had disposed of it to protect her from this last jolt. Could she ever repay them for the loving devotion they always showered upon her?

With the edge worn off the initial shock, she permitted her eyes to scan the remainder of the article. It was mostly legal terms, all meaningless to her. But the very last line arrested her attention as nothing else had done. "Morrow is the father of a ten-week-old daughter."

She could not have been more stunned. To think that a person could be so low as to keep the company of another woman when he was beginning a family—the time in life when a man should show the utmost devotion to those near to him. What kind of a husband would he have ever made if he had succeeded in his little plot to lead her on until he could arrange a divorce and take her in? Having pulled a trick like that once, the next time would be easier.

And she realized that with this news spread over the whole of Pittsburgh, it would not have been possible for her to remain in Paramount Plastics's employ. For everyone, absolutely everyone, now knew she had been dating a married man. Her reputation was disgraced for all eternity.

Her thoughts traveled to that poor, innocent bundle of a baby daughter. What chance in life could she have with a father like hers? Disgraced from the start, and only ten weeks old. Ten weeks old? Bonnie counted backward rapidly. December, November, October—it couldn't be! It wasn't for waiting until the flower show was over that George broke the first date. The first time that baby had probably been born, and the second time was possibly the very day he took the mother and newborn home from the hospital!

Barbara Courtney phoned the next afternoon.

"We had a great time last Wednesday night, Bonnie. We would have loved for you to be there. This is the first Lord's Day of the new year. How about starting the year off by going to the evening service with us tonight?" Barbara sounded breathless and enthusiastic as she had every time Bonnie had heard her voice.

Bonnie didn't have long to debate. She remembered the peculiar uplifted feeling she had received in that church before Christmas, and even if that were a special occasion, never to be repeated, what did she possibly have to lose?

"Why, yes, I believe I will."

"Wonderful! We'll pick you up about seven."

It was with no vanity that Bonnie looked in the mirror when she began to get herself ready. She hadn't done a thing with her hair since the last time she had gone to work. With all the tossing around on her pillow she had done since, her hair hung in strings. But maybe if she pinned here, coaxed there, and put a little artificial flower in it—no, that would only call attention to it. There were dark circles under her eyes, and her complexion was rather sallow, but a dab of makeup would help that. Well, maybe it would take more than a dab.

Dr. and Mrs. Courtney pulled up just when she reached the door. If she hadn't caught a glimpse of Barbara in the passenger seat, she would not have recognized them, for they hadn't driven the little sports car in which she had ridden home, but the most elegant, polished pale blue sedan she had ever seen. She caught her breath at the thought of riding in that, she who had spent most of her traveling in noisy, dirty streetcars.

"Good evening," the sharp-looking young dentist greeted her, as he hopped out to open the rear door. "Let me guess—I believe the name is Bonnie. I'm Dennis, and I'm happy to have the privilege of escorting you to Emmanuel Tabernacle tonight."

"I guess you spared me the introductions!" Barbara laughed as they got on their way. "Denny has been looking forward to meeting you, Bonnie."

"Thank you. I've also looked forward to meeting the doctor."

"Dennis, the name is," its owner instructed with mock severity. "We don't stand much on formality."

"No, you'll find that we are just one, big, happy family," agreed his wife. "And the best of it is, there is always room for one more at our church."

This was some of the strangest talk Bonnie had ever heard. Imagine people in a church calling themselves a family.

"This is the slow time of year, as you are well aware," she heard the doctor say, interrupting her thoughts. "But our gang always has something going. Right now we're planning a Valentine social, and we hope to put together an Easter cantata. We've looked at several samples, but the committee hasn't decided on one at this point."

"Sounds like a stimulating group." Bonnie couldn't think of anything more profound to offer in reply. "I'm looking forward to meeting them."

"And they will be just as delighted to meet you as we are to introduce you," assured Barbara.

How could Barbara tell what attitude the group would have? They may take one look at her and withdraw into their secure circle. The office girls' whispers echoed in her ears. Bonnie wasn't sure she was ready to tackle another group.

But she didn't have long to speculate on the problem. The distance from her home to the North Side must have suddenly been shortened, for the pleasant ride with her sparkling new friends ended too soon and it was time to enter the church.

At once Bonnie felt a loving, peaceful atmosphere, the kind that made one feel as though one had found a calm port after being tossed about on rough seas.

The congregation sang several numbers out of the hymn book, then a young lady introduced as Luanne Marks sang a pretty song about an anchor (just what Bonnie suspected of the place when she walked in, only this anchor seemed to be a Person). Soon that sweet, silver-haired gentleman got up again to speak. First he opened his huge Bible and read a strange story about a woman at a well of whom Jesus asked a drink. Custom decreed that Jesus, being a Jew, should not talk to that particular woman, who was a Samaritan, in the first place, but that was not the remarkable part of the story. Bonnie found herself as perplexed as that woman long ago when Jesus told her, "Whosoever drinketh of this water shall thirst again: But whosoever drinketh of the water that I shall give him shall never thirst; but the water that I shall give him shall be in him a well of water springing up into everlasting life." The pastor read all the way through to the end of the story, looked up, and began explaining the meaning of the Scripture.

When he had finished, he bowed his head and prayed

in a manner in which Bonnie didn't know people prayed, for he seemed only to be talking to someone. She lifted her head a little and tried to peek without being noticed, but she discovered no book from which he could be reading except that one huge Bible. And he was asking that the Lord would speak to hearts through His Word and lead some to repentance and into the knowledge of His Son Christ.

At the end of the prayer, the organist started playing quietly while a few people here and there slipped out of their seats and up to the altar around the front of the platform. Bonnie wondered just who was expected to follow that particular ritual, but when she looked to the Courtneys with an unvoiced question, they both had their eyes closed. A short time after the last person made his way to the front of the church, the pastor prayed again a short little prayer in which he asked for the Lord's blessing upon each and everyone as they returned to their homes and dismissed the congregation.

During the ride home, Bonnie's mind was swirling with the unfamiliar words she had heard that night. There were many, many questions she would have liked to ask of these new friends, but this short trip home didn't seem to be the time to begin what she felt would be a rather lengthy session. Besides, she wanted more time to sort things out on her own. She wasn't even sure what questions to ask. One thing she did know was that she would have to go back again and again to that little North Side church. If anyone could guide her through the morass she found her life to be at the moment, she felt sure it would be that congregation, that pastor, and these wonderful new friends. Promising to accompany them again next week, she slipped out of the beautiful automobile and up to her apartment.

"Is there a Bible around here anywhere?" she asked, when she stepped in the door.

"Don't tell me you got religion?" her father grinned good-naturedly from his seat in front of the television set.

"That pastor said some rather thoughtful things tonight, and I just wanted to check some of them for myself."

"Not that I know of," Mrs. Lake answered Bonnie's question slowly. "Unless—the only one I can think of is the white one my mother carried at her wedding. I had intended to carry it myself when I got married, so she gave it to me to keep. But your father and I sneaked off in the dead of night, and something to carry was the last thing on my mind." James's eyes twinkled at his wife's recollections. "Mother passed away before I ever returned it, and I believe it is still in the trunk at the foot of our bed. You may look, if you wish."

There was a weird collection in that trunk—an album of pictures of the children when quite small, a faded old-fashioned formal gown, a yellowed, lacy, once-white christening dress, one beautiful hand-pieced quilt, a tarnished set of sterling silver table service for eight, two pairs of hand-embroidered pillowcases, a fur muff, a pair of binoculars, a heart-shaped pillow covered with smocked velvet, a frayed tuxedo jacket, and various other bits of odds and ends. The deeper Bonnie looked, to no avail, the farther her heart sank. The very last box in the bottom of the trunk was much too large for a book, and she removed it despairingly. A string, blackened with age and wound several times around it, was tied in such unyielding knots she had to find a pair of scissors to cut it.

A heap of dried, crumbled flower petals greeted her curious gaze as she finally got the lid off. They had been colorless for so many years it was impossible to determine what kind they had been. Near them was a crushed bow of many loops of narrow ribbon. Whatever bouquet it had once graced, it must have been elegant. To Bonnie's delighted eyes a flash of light glittered from within the folds of a swathe of silk, rotting and yellowing with age. She drew out the sparkling object and discovered with growing excitement a diamond set in the clasp of a beautiful pearl necklace. Wondering what other treasures the box might hold, she carefully lifted out the ancient folds of silk and uncovered the object of her search—a small, perfectly white Bible.

Satisfied it was there, she next concerned herself with the silk. It proved to be a delicate, lace edged, hand sewn negligee. A sense of awe pervaded her soul, and near guilt for desecrating a legacy from the dead. What right had she to pry into these things that had been the most sacred personal treasures of another? The right of progeny might have granted some justification, but she realized with a pang that she who had laid these treasures away with such care and affection had not been her progenitor, for she, her brother, and sister were not her parents' natural children. They had been adopted when they were very young. She was suddenly seized with the desire for a sense of continuity, of belonging, to know who had been her natural ancestors.

She picked up the Bible and was gratified to see it was of exquisite quality onion skin paper with a lovely gilt edge. It showed no sign of age. It opened rather of its own accord to a heavier, glossy page somewhere past the middle, which Bonnie discovered to be entitled "Certificate of Marriage." The ink was badly faded and nearly illegible in spots, but she could make out the names Eliza Gilbert and Matthew Jefferson, and the date, July 19, 1916. She could not see clearly the town's name but she could decipher Jefferson County with some difficulty. A large scrawl was on the line for the officiating minister, and the names of two witnesses appeared underneath. She gave up trying to make them out. She turned the page and found the next one entitled "Births." The first recording was that of Alexander Jefferson, born August 21, 1917. She couldn't remember ever hearing of him, but the adjacent page, marked "Deaths," explained the silence. Alexander's name appeared with the date, November 15, 1917.

The second entry under the births was Avonelle Sarah Jefferson, born February 20, 1919. Written in between the lines directly under the name was, "Married to James Arthur Lake, August 6, 1938. And the third entry was, Jessica Elizabeth Jefferson, born December 18, 1920. As a child, Bonnie had seen her Aunt Jessie often, but Jessie had married at the age of thirty-five and moved to Detroit with her husband. She had seldom written since then. The names of two other sons appeared next, but they were also on the following page, one having lived two years and the other apparently dead at birth. *Poor Grandmother,* thought Bonnie, as she closed the Book, *giving birth to five children and rearing only the two daughters. But that was the way of life in those days.*

She left the clutter on the floor while carrying the necklace out to her mother.

"Oh!" exclaimed Avonelle, "I had completely forgotten that lovely thing was in that box. I believe the last time the box was ever opened was shortly after we returned from our wedding trip when I wrote James's name under mine. I probably assumed then I would be opening it again shortly to record the births of my own children. And by the time I knew that was not to be, I never remembered to open the box again to remove the necklace. We might as well leave it out now; I may wish to wear it some time. I'll just lay it in my jewelry chest."

Together they returned to the bedroom where Avonelle carefully laid out the necklace on a tray in her velvet-lined jewelry chest, and Bonnie refolded the ancient negligee and replaced all the contents of the trunk.

Then Bonnie took the little white Bible, bade her parents goodnight, and propped herself up on the pillows on her bed. For once she did not mind that Sylvia's light was on, for her own was also. And when Bonnie asked Sylvia to turn down her records, marvel of marvels, she did so.

Now to find the place where the minister had read that evening. Remembering that he said it was the book of John, she looked for a table of contents, found the page, and turned to the first chapter. Knowing nothing else about the passage's location, she started at the beginning—just as the book said: "In the beginning was the Word, and the Word was with God, and the Word was God!" That was incomprehensible to her. How much she would have to learn if she were really to go into this seriously! Verse 3 was a little more intelligible, for she was aware some people believed God had made all things, although she herself had been taught evolution in high school. As she read on she was amazed to find some of the things the minister had spoken about in that Christmas program—the idea of a Person as Light, lighting everyone in the world. Verse 14 read, "The Word was made flesh, and dwelt among us." Why, that was exactly what he had said, only he hadn't spoken of "the Word," he had simply said "Jesus." Could that be the key? She reread the chapter up to that point and every time she saw the word "Word" she substituted "Jesus." Now it was becoming a little more clear. With that encouragement, she read on and on.

She found other phrases that appeared to indicate the same Person: "The only begotten Son," "the Lamb of God," "the Son of God," "Rabbi," and "Master." This was getting exciting; she had never dreamed that reading the Bible could be so interesting.

Then she came to some little stories. She hadn't

known there were stories in the Bible; she had only a vague idea of the Bible being a collection of mystical proverbs that only the most profound mind could interpret. At least parts of this weren't mystical at all; and the more she grasped, the more she was able to see. All was going well until she reached some verses in chapter 3 about a second birth. It was getting far out again, but she could see that the gentleman to whom Jesus was talking was just as confused as she was. Jesus was patiently explaining to the man that this new birth had something to do with the Spirit. She remembered that in the sermon she had just heard, the pastor had read, "God is a Spirit: and they that worship him must worship him in spirit and in truth." Therefore this second birth must be a kind of uniting of our spirits with God. Well, she would just have to wait until someone could explain it all to her.

When she read further, she saw that whoever believes on this Son of God would not perish, but have eternal life. That also sounded like the sermon, for Jesus had told that woman at the well that she would get thirsty again if she drank only there; but Jesus was a well springing up into everlasting life (that Christmas talk again), and she felt that she was getting somewhere until she reached verse 17. And here she read, "but that the world through him might be saved." Now what could that mean? She remembered the darkness of that first Christmas night, and how the minister had related it to the darkness that enveloped the whole world, and she felt again the black hopelessness of despair that engulfed her; and in that moment she began to comprehend that whatever all those words meant, there must be a Light that could shine into the darkest corners of one's soul and dispel the shadows as the sun turns night into day, and in the process a new kind of life is offered, one that is satisfying enough that we don't "thirst" again. And as

118

she closed the little white Book and turned out her light, she determined that whatever it was all about, she would try to find it for herself. That night she slept better than she had in weeks.

8

Every muscle in Bonnie's body ached. She could have sworn she heard creaking from her joints with each weary move she made. And she vowed that this was the last time she would wear high heels while looking for a job.

Bonnie had scoured the want ads, made phone calls, and filled out application blanks until she was sick of the sight of them and thought that she couldn't write "Bonnie Lake" on the line one more time. She had sat through interviews answering the same questions over and over again until she had little inclination to face another uninterested prospective employer. When she had exhausted all the possibilities in the line of bookkeeping and typing, she then tried her luck at the stores, but none had any immediate need for a sales clerk. Neither did the telephone company have any vacancies in the ranks of switchboard operators. She lost count of the number of places where her application was placed on file. She wondered idly how many lifetimes of employment would result if they all called at once. For the present, she would be grateful for just one.

One more company looked as though it might hold some promise, and it had placed an ad only the previous day. She deliberately ignored that one until last, hoping that surely something would turn up before she was forced to try there. But nothing had materialized, and now she would have to bring herself to enter that Gateway Center building again. Knowing there was no danger she would encounter George again in that place made it a little easier, but she had no desire to re-enter it. Now she resolutely turned her weary steps in that direction, encouraging and cajoling herself along. Just pushing the elevator button required a deliberate effort, but somehow she succeeded in propelling herself into the office and was ushered into the presence of the manager.

"Good afternoon, er, Miss Lake. You look rather— rather familiar. Haven't I seen you on the elevators here?"

"Oh, yes, you probably have. I used to work up on the nineteenth floor." She was momentarily tempted to deny the connection, but knowing the falsehood would catch up with her, thought better of it. Now, however, Mr. Parker would demand an explanation for her resignation. Again she debated whether the truth or a fabrication would be more prudent. She didn't have long to consider.

"And what, may I ask, prompted your leaving?"

She might as well out with it; in the end the direct route would probably save another untruth.

"I had a rather unfortunate romance with another of the employees and thought it better to leave."

"Not by any chance that fellow they nabbed up there lining his own pockets with company funds?" The amused grin on his face told Bonnie he was not actually linking "that fellow" to her, but only wanted to bring up the subject, and she hoped the expression on her face wouldn't betray her. She soon surmised that George's misappropriation of funds was the talk of all the firms in the building.

"They say he left his last employer down in McKeesport because he had been trying the same thing there and feared he would soon be caught. When that company began their year-end audit and discovered what had been going on, they tipped off Paramount Plastics, although the tip wasn't really necessary. Clever as that fellow was, he wasn't clever enough. He hadn't reckoned on one thing. That sort of activity is harder to conceal in a small company.

"I will have to say, Paramount Plastics is the envy of all the other firms in Gateway Center. Most phenomenal growth rate of any around here. Must be accounted for by a saleable product—everybody wants to play these days. Now take our company, for instance. We're an old reliable manufacturer of bathroom and plumbing fixtures for over a hundred years. But if you market a product that has to be replaced every few years, you lose your reputation, and shall I say, your business also goes down the drain? Heh, heh!"

Bonnie had to struggle to keep from nodding. She had been weary enough when she walked in there! Before long she questioned whether she could possibly work in a place where a chatty boss might lull her to sleep on a regular basis. But then, if you were paid the same for sleeping as for working— It didn't appear the chances were so great for either. When he had finally spent himself, he added casually that they had had many applicants, would process the applications in due season, and would notify the fortunate one. So that was his bag! He probably knew who he would hire before she ever walked in there, he figured his working day was about over, and he would gas away the remainder of it—at her expense! She shuddered in disgust as she rose to leave.

She discovered with dismay that it was four thirty, dismissal time for Paramount Plastics. The man had detained her so long that now she stood the chance of running into some of the people from Paramount Plastics leaving the building, and they were among the last she would wish to greet at this moment. To her relief she shared the elevator with only a couple gentlemen she did not know, and prepared to duck for the outside door the second the car stopped.

She did, and ran smack into Hal Gregersen departing the adjacent elevator.

"Hey, there!" he exclaimed, throwing his arms about her before she could back away. "As a flower peeping through the winter snows is the sight of you to my work-worn heart today. How is it going with you?"

"Uh — uh, excuse me. Guess I wasn't watching where I was going. I'm fine. How are you?"

"Couldn't be better. Are you going my way? How about a cup of coffee, or maybe a coke?" He took her by the elbow and directed her out the door. "You have sure missed some excitement around here!"

"Yes, so I have learned."

"I believe the day they got that character was your last at Paramount Plastics, wasn't it?"

"Uh-huh. But I left early and missed the action."

"Too bad. You should have seen him. He got pretty fidgety as the day wore on with those inspectors nosing around. Probably knew they were going to close in on him. So he tried to make a bolt for it a few minutes before closing time. But they had expected that kind of move and had a couple policemen stationed by the door. Imagine the look on his pretty-boy face when they thwarted his getaway! The receptionist was sitting right in a front row seat and reported the show was hilarious!"

What George had done certainly was not right, but Bonnie was too numb to see much amusement in the scene.

"Say, then —" They had reached the corner snack shop. "Maybe you could find it in your sweet little heart to at least give me equal time." He stopped abruptly, waiting to see whether she was going to make any move before committing himself further. She couldn't blame him, although she knew he hadn't exactly just been pining away for her, either. She had picked up hints he had seen Goldie Klingensmith at least a few times during the weeks she was in George's company.

"I—I think that would be lovely, Hal," she spoke slowly, choosing her words with care. "Although I would appreciate a couple more weeks to—well, to just pull myself together. Why don't you just wait a little and then phone me?"

"Aha! The same put off I got from your sister, hey?"

"Sylvia? Heavens, no. You mustn't mind her. She doesn't know what she wants. I really mean I just need to think a little bit yet. Really, there are several things on my mind right now. But I believe that in just a short time I'll get squared away and then, I promise, I'll be tickled to hear from you." She patted his arm and returned his deep gaze to pledge her good faith.

"Weighty matters, huh? Be careful not to overburden that pretty little head of yours."

She did not feel this was the opportune moment to confide in him the midnight sessions she was holding with the little white Book and all the questions flooding her mind. Nor could she explain that the more she read, the more it held her in a strange, compelling grip as though beckoning, even requiring her to come to some personal persuasion concerning its message. She couldn't convey to him that she felt there was something to which she must attend before she could concern herself again with more mundane affairs. She couldn't even understand it herself.

"Yeah, real weighty." She didn't know whether her attempt to sound light-hearted was convincing.

"Thanks for the coke, Hal. I honestly am ready to drop on my feet. I just have to take the first car home that I can get. But you'd better believe I'll be expecting that phone to ring before long."

He escorted her out to the corner and waited with her until the first Oakland car appeared. As she stepped forward to board it, he lightly touched her lips with his, squeezed her hand, and helped her up.

That night she played the Tennessee Ernie record several times until the words were imprinted on her mind. His voice's rich resonance spoke unexplainable encouragement to her through the song's message. However, one phrase very strongly threatened doom in the midst of comfort. "I am condemned to die!" How on earth could that have any meaning? She took the little Bible out of the drawer in her night stand, more perplexed about its contents than ever. What was it that had tried to surface during her conversation with Hal, and yet she couldn't grasp it herself? What message tried to command her attention and place her in a position of responsibility to it? That was the secret: Somehow there was a responsibility implied. But what? Perhaps she had missed it on her first reading and should reread to attempt to discern it. She opened again to the first chapter of John.

The first few verses shed no more light than they had the first time. But when she came to the twelfth, she was suddenly arrested with some words that had previously escaped her notice. "But as many as received him, to them gave he power to become the sons of God, even to them that believe on his name." Did that mean anyone could become a son of God? Anyone in addition to that one Son that was always spelled with a capital S? And just what all was involved in "believing"? She flipped over to the third chapter and read again, "He that believeth on him is not condemned: but he that believeth not is condemned already"—that same idea that seemed so peculiar in the second verse of Tennessee Ernie's song—"because he hath not believed in the name of the only begotten Son of God." Now that clearly said to believe on the name of the Son of God, but how was one to believe on a name? And what condemnation was one under if one did not? She turned back to the first chapter again. "Which were born, not of blood, nor of the will of the flesh, nor of the will of man, but of God." There was that idea of a birth again. And she reread the third to thirteenth verses of the third chapter. *Born not of flesh, but of spirit,* she mused to herself. Well, it was only two days until Sunday again. Maybe she could begin to receive some answers then.

Just before she closed the Book in nearly as much confusion as that in which she had opened it, her eyes fell on the last verse of the third chapter. "He that believeth on the Son hath everlasting life: and he that believeth not the Son shall not see life; but the wrath of God abideth on him." Those certainly were strong words! If you don't believe on the Son, you don't even have life. That couldn't be natural life; obviously she had that whether she had asked for it or not. This must mean that other kind of life she was beginning to glimpse on these pages. A special kind. And without that, a person had God's wrath on him. She remembered when as a little girl she had gotten into Aunt Jessie's purse, "borrowed" lipstick, and emerged with the evidence all over Sylvia's face and her own. When she denied it, Aunt Jessie had told her God would strike her dead with lightning if she told lies like that again. It was foolishness to her now; but nevertheless she had retained some vague impression of a God who retaliated with a bolt of lightning if one told fibs. She knew it wasn't true, but here it plainly stated that some degree of wrath was upon the one who refused to believe. Just how severe was that wrath? A sense of fear and dread came over her, and her sleep was not as peaceful that night as it had been of late.

It hadn't altogether left her by the time she woke the next morning. She busied herself diligently with the dust cloth and sweeper, thinking to still that nagging little voice. But it persisted all that day and into the next. She watched several television shows, but found it difficult to follow the action. When she tried to read a story in a magazine, her eyes couldn't seem to focus on the words. She tried to dismiss it partly as restlessness from the insecurity of having no job. But when she attempted to turn her thoughts directly to that problem, the phrase "Ye must be born again" would crowd in unbidden, and she would be forced to reckon with it again.

By Sunday afternoon she was so desirous of getting back to that little church to find some of the answers that she couldn't wait to see whether Barbara would call her. Looking in the phone book, she found the number for Courtney, Dennis, D.M.D., and made arrangements for the good doctor and his wife to pick her up once more. Barbara was delighted to hear her voice and assured her repeatedly that she was more than welcome to ride with them across the river.

The congregation sang only a couple verses of the first song, and then the pastor asked whether anyone had a word of testimony. Was she really in a courtroom instead of a church? Bonnie wondered whether there was to be some sort of a trial and half expected an attorney to step forward. But a young man near her age stood to his feet and, in a clear, ringing voice, declared,

"I'm glad to be able to say I'm a Christian. I met the Lord only two years ago, but I can honestly say that in that time I've found out how to live and am so thankful I can trust Him for direction throughout the years ahead. I'm thankful He turned my life around when I was headed in the wrong direction. I ran with the wrong crowd, did things I knew I shouldn't be doing. And in the place of all those old things, He has given me peace and purpose. Hallelujah!"

A very ancient, white haired gentleman right up in the front of the auditorium rose unsteadily, and with his hand raised heavenward made an effort to be heard in spite of his quavering voice: "The good Lord saved me nearly seventy-five years ago when I was but a very young lad, and I can truthfully say I've never regretted it for one day. All has not been rosy; I've buried two fine Christian wives, God bless them. There have been times when things were hard, but the Lord always saw me through. And now I'm expecting Him soon to take me home. Praise His holy Name!"

He had half turned around as he finished his little speech, and the radiance on his face alone would have testified to the expectation he cherished. Bonnie had never seen such a look, nor heard anyone speak of dying as though it were an experience to welcome joyfully. And there was that strange expression of being "saved" again.

Her puzzlement changed to delight when the minister, opening that huge Bible, began in his deep, resonant voice, "And now to continue our studies in the gospel of John, please turn in your Bibles to the third chapter." The very place where she had so many questions! "In verse seven, 'Marvel not that I said unto thee, Ye must be born again.' And then again in the ninth verse, Nicodemus answered and said unto Him, 'How can these things be?' Now you may ask the very same questions, 'What do you mean, Jesus, when you say you must be born again?' And 'How in the world can a person ever be born twice? I thought Christians didn't believe in reincarnation.' But don't lose sight of that sixth verse. 'That which is born of the flesh is flesh; and that which is born of the Spirit is spirit.' In our finite minds we can only comprehend the physical, the material things about us. Birth to us is a physical event when a red-faced, probably squalling little kicking bundle enters a home and becomes part of a family. You have a mother, father, possibly already some older sisters and brothers. You are given the family name, and from that time and forever after, you are known as one of the Joneses, or the Smiths, or whatever. You are endowed by virtue of your heredity to take on that family's characteristics. Be they tall, short, handsome or homely, by all probabilities you will bear close enough resemblance that you may be identified with your family by physical characteristics alone.

"But what we are speaking of here is a spiritual family, and just as you were born into your earthly family, you also become a member of the family of God by birth, but a spiritual birth. And you take on the family name, so you become Christian, for Christ is head of the family. And by all means you should take on some of the characteristics of your new family. Just as brother Dave testified tonight, old things drop away. Your new life brings new activities, a whole new set of friends who become your brothers and sisters in Christ. 'Old things are cast away; behold, all things become new.'

"And now you say, 'How do I go through this birth process? I had no choice in my physical birth, that was all determined for me. But now I must make a conscious decision to experience this new birth. What is it that I must do?' Well, let me tell you, you aren't the first one to ask that question. Nearly two thousand years ago, the apostle Paul and Silas were thrown into a Philippian jail upon false accusation. And while they were hunched there in their chains, praying and singing praises, mind you, a great earthquake shook open the prison doors and even rattled off their handcuffs. The warden, knowing his life was in danger if his prisoners made the slip, figured he might as well end his life himself before the magistrates got hold of him. He had his sword aimed at his chest. But Paul, peering out from the dark recesses of that dank hole in the ground, called out to him, 'Don't do it; we're here, just where you left us.' Then the warden, in great fear and trembling, asked, 'What must I do to be saved?' And what did those intrepid missionaries tell him in the dead of that dark night so long ago: 'Believe on the Lord Jesus Christ, and thou shalt be saved.' Now you may say, 'sure I believe that God had a Son named Jesus, I believe He was born of the virgin Mary, I believe He was crucified by some Roman soldiers, and I even believe that He rose again from the grave. Is that all there is to it?' That's a giant step. But you are only believing *about* Him, and this Bible tells you to believe *on* Him. Romans ten, nine and ten says: 'That if thou shalt confess with thy mouth the Lord Jesus, and shalt believe in thine heart that God hath raised him from the dead, thou shalt be saved. For with the heart man believeth unto righteousness; and with the mouth confession is made unto salvation.' This implies more than just a belief; this man is saved when that belief reaches into the heart and confession is made by the mouth. God expects His children to make verbal confession of salvation."

There were many other things that fell from the minister's lips that night, but Bonnie found it impossible to grasp them all. If she could understand one step at a time, she would be doing well. When he had finished and closed his big Book, he looked out over the audience, seemingly to each one personally, and said, "And now, if you wish to make the confession of which Paul and Silas told the Philippian jailer, I invite you to kneel at this altar of prayer and settle it now with God." The organ played softly, and a couple people accepted the invitation. Bonnie felt a tugging on her heart stranger than the fear of wrath she had received during her reading the other night. Something seemed to pull her feet toward the front of the church; but somehow she felt as though she still didn't understand what it was she would be doing. She would have to have the rest of her questions answered first.

The service was dismissed, and the worshipers again began to file out. But Bonnie felt cement in the soles of her shoes. How could she go back to her little room with Sylvia's records blaring in her ears, nearly drowning out her thoughts, and try again to discover for herself how it all tied together when she had already spent hours poring over those strange words and couldn't make it out? She was going to have to have someone explain it to her.

Barbara had reached for her coat, but seeing the expression on Bonnie's face, seemed to sense her new friend was not ready yet to leave.

"Is there any way I can help you?" she asked kindly.

"Why, yes. Yes, there is. I mean, there are so many things I would like to ask. Perhaps you could arrange an interview with the pastor for me? I would so like to know some of those things he was talking about."

"I'm sure he'll be glad to talk to you right now."

"Oh, I couldn't keep you and Dennis waiting. You've done so much for me already."

"Not at all. We'll gladly wait all night, if necessary."

Leaving the dentist with tiny Lisa stretched out on the seat asleep beside him, the two made their way to the front of the church.

"Pastor Thomas," Barbara said, "I want you to meet my new friend, Bonnie Lake. She first came here during the children's Christmas program and has come back a couple times since. She would like to talk to you if you have a little time now."

"Of course, Barbara, and—Bonnie. I'm so glad to meet you." He offered his hand. "Why don't you step into my office where we can be undistracted? Right this way, please."

Barbara turned to go back to join her little family, and Bonnie soon found herself in a comfortable chair in a little room just off the platform.

"And now, Bonnie, what is it you have in mind?"

"Well, there is that word, 'saved,' to begin with. What do you mean when you say you are or can be saved?"

"Bonnie, you understand that the Christian walk is a life. A life separate from the life the world knows. It isn't just a matter of forsaking the things that are not in keeping with the behavior of a child of God. It is also a life of service and devotion to Him. We like to emphasize a positive religion. Not just don't do this, don't do that. It is do this, do that. Do acknowledge God and His leading in your life, knowing that He is ever by you, actually within you in the Person of His Spirit. Do remember to praise Him. As the psalmist says, 'I will be glad and rejoice in thee: I will sing praise to thy name, O thou most High.' Do talk to Him daily, as a child talks to his father, do read His Word, hide it away in your heart and live by its precepts. Now when you determine to do these things and live in the way God wants you to live, you receive life that is eternal, from which you never die. And you have left behind those things that would hinder us in this new Christian walk. We are not only *saved* from the eternal consequences of sin and assured of spending eternity with God, but we are also saved from the consequences of sin in this life. Sin has no more hold over us. We are alive unto God. And Jesus became our Savior by bearing the consequences of our sin on His cross."

A memory of the stranger snatching her from the front of the streetcar crossed her mind. Just as he had saved her from death, was this Jesus saving her from the consequences of sin?

"Are you telling me then, that sin is to be taken

seriously? I always thought of it as just a way to express, well, you know, when you're having some kind of fun you know society doesn't approve of. You know how they say everything fun that isn't fattening or illegal is sin. I thought that was just an expression."

"No, Bonnie, sin is a very serious matter, so serious that when Jesus was hanging on the cross His own Father had to hide His face to keep from looking on it, for God simply cannot tolerate sin. And it doesn't have to be any out-and-out gross type of sins. You see, we are born as sinners, and our spirit is severed from God because of it. If we don't confess our sins and believe on the Savior, we are condemned already."

"Oh, so that is what that verse means! Now it is beginning to come through a little. You mean if I don't make this—this confession, I am already condemned to the eternal consequences of sin?"

"Yes, Bonnie, We speak of it as repentance, not so much in the sense that you are sorry for having sinned, but as a turning around. A change of direction. As Jesus told the woman taken in adultery, 'Go and sin no more.' "

"But if we are just naturally sinners, and we are born right in it, how can we keep from continuing to sin?"

"We can't in our own strength. But when we receive this new life within, the Lord's Spirit moves right into our very beings, and He gives us the power to keep from sinning, gives us new desires so that we no longer want to sin. He takes over the job for us."

"Is that what I read in the first chapter of John where it says, 'to them gave he power to become the sons of God?' "

"Yes, Bonnie, so it is. I believe you are ready to make such a commitment yourself. Would you care to ask the Lord to do this kind of work for you and turn your life around right now?"

"Oh, yes, I would. But must I go out there and kneel at that altar?"

"Why, no, absolutely not. God can be found anywhere at all; wherever you look for Him. You may pray right here and ask Jesus to save you and make a new person of you. And while you're asking Him to do something for you, you make a promise to Him and to yourself to walk from this time forth in all the light that you have—that is, with all the understanding you have to do what is right and follow Him."

Having never uttered a prayer before in her life, Bonnie felt rather hesitant, and her voice trembled as she breathed, barely audibly, "God, I can see that I've sinned and I ask you to save me. Please give me this new life and help me not to sin anymore. Amen."

It was with tears in her eyes and a joy in her heart she hadn't known existed that she left the office and rejoined the Courtneys.

"I—I—well, I guess I am supposed to say, I've been saved," she greeted Barbara. Barbara wrapped her in her arms and with tears on her own face, breathed fervently, "Well, praise the Lord, Bonnie. You don't know how overjoyed I am to hear that."

Bonnie floated out of the car when it stopped in front of her apartment and felt as though she didn't need the elevator to carry her upstairs. When she burst in the door, she found her parents in their habitual places before the television set.

"Mother, Dad," she exclaimed radiantly, "I've been saved. That is, I've become a Christian, I guess, is the way you put it."

"Aren't we all?" Her mother scarcely glanced at her.

"Well, this is different, I mean, you aren't a Christian just automatically. I hardly know how to say it, but I've committed my life to the Lord Jesus Christ, and His Spirit has come into my heart. And it is—"

She was interrupted in mid-sentence. "Is this something like confirmation? Or some new kind of sacrament? If you had told us you were going to— Why didn't you get a new outfit for the occasion? That little dress must be a couple years old."

9

If Bonnie began the week floating on air with the
elation of her new-found experience with the Lord, she
ended it nearly dragging in the doldrums for the discouragement of finding no job. Each day she flew to the
phone upon the first ring, only to add to her disappointment when it proved to be no place of business
saying she was their choice among all their applicants.
She ventured out a couple times for interviews when
there was a new ad in the paper, but no prospective
employer ever offered anything but prospects. They all
had more applicants than positions.

However, when the day brought discouragement, the
nighttime offered solace and a sense of security, for taking her little white Bible out of the drawer in the night
stand and hungrily absorbing the things she read had
now become a habit. One night her Book opened unbidden to a book called Peter, and her eyes fell on the
words, "As newborn babes, desire the sincere milk of the
word, that ye may grow thereby."

That is I, she thought to herself, *a new baby born into
the family of God, who is to grow in this new kind of life by
the words of this Book.* Then one night during her reading
time, Sylvia was playing a record popular some months
before, one she had heard many times without giving it a
thought. Now, suddenly, it came in upon her heart with
exciting reality. It was the voice of a young boy singing,

"He's Got the Whole World in His Hands." When the record, scratchy from its many repetitions, came to the verse, "He's got the little bitty baby in His hands," her heart responded as flower petals open to the sweet rain. Was she not that tiny baby in her Father's hands? And would He not look after His child and provide for her necessities—even a job?

She so thrilled to her new revelations that night that she read late. Sylvia actually turned out her light before she did, and those records along with it. Several minutes later, a rather cross, sleepy voice drifted across the room to her: "Come on, sis, couldn't you turn off that light so a body can get some sleep?"

A fine switch that is, Bonnie thought to herself. But never mind, she could still pray in the dark. And pray she did, for when the pastor had told her she was to talk to her new Father, she had begun uncertainly, feeling it wasn't anywhere nearly as good as those fancy prayers written in books. But the more she made the attempt, the more comfortable she became with it, until she genuinely began to feel that both she and her prayers were accepted just as offered. While reading in John, she discovered the promise, "Whatsoever ye shall ask the Father in my name, he will give it to you." How fantastic it was to think that she, Bonnie Lake, could ask and receive of God! And the more she asked and conversed with Him, the more her heart bubbled in praise to Him.

It was near the end of the week that she met Bill from apartment 3B on the elevator.

"Why so glum, chum? I haven't seen that perky smile for quite awhile."

"Just deep in thought, I guess. To be truthful, I'm looking for a job. I've run down absolutely every lead I've come upon, and there is just nothing to be had in this city. The old story, you know—we'll call you, only they're not doing it."

"Well, I know a one-girl office without a girl. Just came from there. They do the mechanical work on my car. They give good service, if you get the right mechanic. But they don't seem to keep girls for long. Don't know if they don't pay or what. But you might give them a call and see. Vito's Auto Repair, over on Pecan Street."

She winced at the thought of a repair shop while conjuring visions of bolts, spark plugs, and grease. But a one-girl office sounded good at a time when she could profit by a respite from group pressure. And when the elevator stopped, she pushed the button and descended again. There was no streetcar near the shop, but six blocks was not too far to walk. She mentally noted she could hike there in less time than it had taken to ride to Gateway Center.

It was a large shop that she entered through overhead doors. Not immediately seeing any sign of an office, she hesitated, wondering whether to approach the owner of the backside that was all that was visible by a raised hood, or the other end of the body from which feet protruded under a truck chassis. Her dilemma was short-lived, for a stocky, dark-haired man strode toward her with a crooked grin that revealed a couple of missing teeth.

" 'Afternoon, ma'am." He tipped the visor of the greasy cap with which he tried to protect his hair. "You're not by any chance looking for a nice office job, are you? I see you haven't brought a car in for mendin', so chances are you're the gal I'm looking for."

"I understand you are in need of one, Mr. — "

"Vito's the name, miss. I didn't catch your name the first time."

"Bonnie Lake. I live in Shadyside Apartments over on Oak Street. I believe I can type somewhere in the neighborhood of sixty words per — "

"Never mind the typing. Mostly what you do here is bookkeeping and ordering parts. The boys here, they take some keeping in line, also." A short, wiry little fellow, also of dark complexion, straightened up from under the hood. Vito raised his voice. "I say, there, Miss Bonnie, the boys here, they need a little keeping in line. Now this Nino here, I had to fire the last six girls I had because Nino lost his rivets every time one of 'em walked past. Tried to put carburetors where the generators belong and never could get the spark plugs tuned up right. People kept bringing their vehicles back sayin' they lurched like jack rabbits."

Nino wiped a drizzle of tobacco juice from his chin. "Pay no mind to what that Vito says. Actually, all them girls quit because Vito couldn't remember who was what around here. Handed the keys to a doctor's Caddy to some joker what cleans out Joe's Bar after hours, and tried to pawn a pre-war model Nash off onto the doc. Does tricks like that all the time. Blames the girls for not keeping the slips right, but he's got his eyes on the girls instead of the slips. So the gal, she gives *him* the slip."

"As I said, they take some handling, these boys." Vito was unperturbed. "Now then this way, Bonnie, and I'll show you where you'll be located."

Somewhat dubiously, she followed him up the lone step into the little cubicle that contained one completely cluttered desk, a dilapidated file cabinet, a couple of fifty-gallon drums, and a candy bar dispenser.

"Now this here," he said indicating a slip taped to the window of the door they entered, "is your 'wanted list.' Whatever you see here you order from those parts catalogs over there on the, well, somewhere under this rubble. . . . There now, no, this must be it; aw, well somewhere in here, you see there's some parts catalogs. And then there's the—"

He was interrupted by a phone jangling from under

the litter. "Vito's Auto Repair. . . . Yeah, tomorrow 'bout two o'clock. We got into a little more trouble than we expected. But it will be ready at two, for sure." He replaced the receiver. "As I said, there's the phone to answer. And you make one trip to the bank every day just before it closes. Anything that comes in after that goes in the file cabinet until the next day. Now there's the matter of getting to the bank. We got our own pickup here that you run over there in. You drive, don't you?"

"Why, no, I'm afraid I don't."

"Never mind. One of the boys here will teach you. Just you have your permit by the time you come in on Monday. Now if there aren't any questions, I'll expect you at eight thirty Monday morning."

"Y-yes, sir. I mean, Vito." She wasn't positive this was the job she had had in mind. And she was half way home before she realized her salary had never been mentioned. She barely had time to catch the nearest streetcar and make it into the court house to apply for a learner's permit before closing time.

A new, albeit light, snow had fallen early Monday morning, which added slippery footing to the trepidation with which Bonnie began her hike to the shop. She hadn't reckoned on the extra time the difficult walking would require, and now she feared she might be late. A fine way to begin a new job!

But late or not, she was greeted heartily by her new employer when she stepped through the overhead doors.

" 'Mornin', there! Just step in and set to." A broad wave of the hand indicated the office of which she was to take possession.

"G'morning, Miss." Nino's round, dark face turned up from behind a tail light.

"Good morning, Nino," she responded, not a little gaily. These friendly, breezy guys might be all right, after all.

"This here's the fella you haven't met yet," Vito nodded toward a slender black man who had entered the huge doors behind her. She judged him to be somewhere in middle age. Oh, yes, the one with the feet, she recollected from her previous encounter. A wide grin spread across his pleasant face as Vito continued, "He's the one what's hard to catch. He's a good mechanic, though. Well, we're all good here. Got the best reputation in Oakland, all the whole city, for that matter. But you take this one here," indicating the black man again, "ain't nothing he can't figger out what's wrong about a car the first thing he hears it run."

"And sometimes he don't hear it run," shot up from the other tail light. "They don't allus run when they come in here, y'know."

"I'm sure you are excellent," Bonnie greeted him, "but I haven't gotten your name yet."

"Jeb, Miz Bonnie, jes' call me Jeb." He offered a big hand which she was relieved to know hadn't begun its day's work. The other men already had hands black with grease. She wondered how long it would be until she looked like them.

"I'm glad to meet you, Jeb. I know now who to call if I ever get a car and it quits running." Then to all three men in general, "Guess I'd better be getting on with it." And she hurried into the office and shut the door, thinking to keep out the cold. She discovered to her dismay when she removed her coat that there wasn't any heat in her little cubicle. She opened the door again and put her coat back on. There wasn't a good place to lay it, anyway. *But how does one do desk work,* she wondered, *with a heavy coat on?*

She pulled out the creaky chair by the desk and, sitting down, kicked something with her toe. Peering into the kneehole she discovered a wastebasket running over with grimey papers and, in the far corner of the recess, a tiny electric heater. Well, the first task was easily determined. Scooping up all the litter from the floor and cramming it down into the basket as well as she could, she carried the overflowing wastebasket out into the shop. Sure enough, there was a small door in the rear and, going outside, she found a couple trash cans against the outside wall of the building. Having emptied the wastebasket, she could turn her attention to the heater. Some poking around finally revealed an outlet behind the file cabinet, and she soon heard the steady hum of the coils. Placing the heater by her feet, she "set to" as per instructions. It took about forty-five minutes of studying the assortment of vouchers, invoices, receipts, and various and sundry memoranda scattered over the desk before she could begin to sort and file them. The phone rang twice in the process. Both were people wanting to know when their vehicles would be finished. As she made the second trek out to the shop to ask, she realized she would have to develop her own system for keeping track of the comings and going of the vehicles. That probably even involved learning all the makes and models! She had up to then felt it sufficient to identify cars by color.

When she finally found the top of the desk, she looked into every desk and file drawer without locating the ledger book. There could be only one more possible hiding place, and for that she would have to ask for the safe's combination. Returning to the shop, she asked Nino how the safe was to be opened. He replied that only the boss knew the combination, and he had stepped out for a minute—always went up the street for coffee for them all at that hour.

That was nice, she thought, but now what was she to do until he returned? And she wondered whether she couldn't get a little coffee pot and make the coffee herself in the office. Her mother never lacked for coffee at their house; she probably had an extra pot around somewhere that she could bring.

Feeling somewhat grimey herself by this time, she decided to look up a lavatory and wash her hands. It was a little door that opened from the shop to a cubbyhole behind the office wall. She would never be able to enter it without the men observing. Well, hopefully they would be too busy to notice. She flipped the switch and closed the door behind her. Yeech! The commode was full of cigarette butts, and looked as though it hadn't been flushed for a week. The seat was grease-smeared and the sink chipped and rusted. There was a can for cleanser in a corner, but it had been empty for who knew how long. Perhaps some naphtha on the floor would take off the first layer of crud. She would have to ask Vito for some kind of overhead allowance for a new wastebasket and some cleanser for starters. And she would bring some old clothes tomorrow to don at the end of the day for the major assault on the lavatory. At least there was ordinary, clean water in the faucet, and she rinsed her fingers (ice cold!) and flipped them dry.

The phone had started an incessant clanging while she was washing her hands, and by the time she reached it, it had rung several times. Just as she lifted the receiver she heard Nino's voice from under a station wagon, "Hey! Where's da dame?" She would have to take it off the hook after this when she was in the lavatory.

"Vito's Au—"

"Why don't you people answer your phone down there? I rang for quarter of an hour." There wasn't any question about the impatience in his voice. "Get that tow truck over to 78th and Maple immediately. Some fool ran into the side of my car." And the receiver banged in Bonnie's ear. Now, had he said Maple or Stapleton?

Vito arrived with the coffee.

"Sure, the book is in the safe," he replied to her question. "Combination is simple—one turn to the left, six to the right—There, m'lady."

She was cold enough by now that she thought a cup of good hot coffee had never been more relished. And while she sipped, she proposed the allowance for the cleaning materials and a can of coffee. "I'll make it right here in the office, if that meets with your approval."

"Good girl. Looks like you've got yourself another job. Of course, I'll miss my chitchat with the boys in the coffee shop, but that way I can pay more attention to business here in the morning."

A client arrived to pick up his auto. When he handed her payment in cash, she realized with momentary panic that she hadn't discovered any receipt books while tidying up the desk.

"I've mislaid my receipt book," she fabricated. "Perhaps this envelope will do." On the front, she started to write, "received from—" and paused, hoping he would volunteer his name.

"C. V. McCartney, young lady. They all know me down here. But seeing as how you're new, just remember me the next time."

Whew! she sighed under her breath. *I hope they're not all like this.* And she added "receipt book" to her shopping list.

But when she attempted to enter the receipt in the journal, that proved to be another matter. Whoever had been keeping—or not keeping—the books apparently knew nothing of the correct procedure. She could make neither head nor tail out of the jumble of figures splattered over the columns. She never would be able to figure out what was going on until she pulled out the old receipts, invoices, and credit vouchers and sorted through the confusion. With a heavier sigh, she pulled open the file drawers and began.

The little space heater barely made a dent in the chill. Her legs began to feel slightly toasted while the rest of her body was tolerably warm only while she wore her coat. But the sleeves kept brushing the slips of paper off onto the floor. When she removed the coat, she shivered so violently, she had to put it back on. Attempting to type addresses on some envelopes, her fingers were so cold they were stiff. She wondered how the men could remove bolts and screws if their fingers were as cold as hers. Curious about the heat in the shop, she sauntered out to explore and discovered a little wood-burning stove in one corner. That explained the pile of firewood she had seen while emptying the trash. And it also meant she had to contend with the cold in the office as well as she could. Maybe several layers of sweaters would give more flexibility for working. She would ask Vito if he minded her wearing blue jeans instead of skirts in his office. That would also save on hosiery. She had already snagged both of hers today.

"You wouldn't cover up them purty legs of yours in a pair of blue jeans, wouldja?" was his reply. But she knew by the twinkle in his eye it was not a denial.

She hadn't known whether it was better to carry a sandwich with her or go out for lunch, so to be on the safe side she had one in her purse. But by noon she thought how welcome a warm little sandwich shop would feel to her frozen bones and, wrapping her coat more tightly around her, she set out down the street. She hadn't far to go. It wasn't much of a place. But it *was* warm. She ate as slowly as possible so as to spend all of her lunch hour basking in its comfort. With some reluctance, she braved the chill while making her way back to her private ice box.

She scarcely had begun to unravel the tangle in the ledger book when it was time for the trip to the bank.

The work had been hampered by the phone, but she had at least dispatched the tow truck to the correct street intersection.

Promptly at two thirty, Jeb appeared in the little doorway. "Miz Bonnie, the boss tells me it's my duty to take you out for your drivin' lesson today. Now if you has your permit ready and git all bundled up tight, we'll jes' set out, you and me. The jalopy is ovah this way."

He twirled some keys on a ring while heading toward the far corner of the shop. Bonnie rose to gather up the day's receipts and follow him, but the going was difficult with watery knees. Was she really expected to drive a pickup truck when she had never touched a steering wheel before?

Jeb led her to the driver's side and opened the door for her, then ran around and swung himself in beside her.

"Now you jes' turn the key in this ignition while pumping on the gas pedal at the same time you let out the clutch. Slowly now so's you get 'em both going together, only reversed. One goes in while th' other goes out. There now, you feel them engage in there somewhere?"

She didn't. A couple more attempts brought a measure of success, and upon the fourth a steady putt-putt rose from the throat of the machine.

"Now you put that clutch back in again while you shove dis stick up a couple inches and then down. Easy now, like so. Now, that's—"

His words were almost broken off against the windshield. The truck gave a violent lurch and stopped dead. Bonnie caught sight of Nino scurrying across the shop, evidently looking for cover, and Vito had removed his hat to run his fingers through his hair.

Bonnie was ready to resign on the spot, but determination superceded her trepidation, and she gamely attempted to start the motor again. This time it came a little more smoothly.

"Easy, now. Jes' take it easy on the clutch while you push down on the—" Another lurch and jolting stop.

"Ah think another time will do it now, Miz Bonnie." Jeb sounded less ruffled than she felt. But she wondered how long his patience would hold out. Her next attempt was successful. At least the truck started moving with a minimum of jerking. Nino sprang out of hiding to open an overhead door, and the truck careened toward the hole in the wall. Bonnie feared the open space wasn't wide enough. But somehow they managed to miss scraping the side as they headed across the walk and into the street.

"Start turning now, Miz Bonnie, sharp. Sharp!"

The front tires touched the pavement and were turned up the street, but she didn't straighten the wheel quickly enough and the front end hit the curb while the back skidded upon hitting the snowy pavement. The truck was thrown slightly sideways into the path of an oncoming car. Its driver swerved to the right to avoid collision, but succeeded in going into a skid himself. Bonnie was sure his hair stood on end as he slid past her, but he managed to right the car before disaster hit. Bonnie was so unnerved that she forgot to synchronize the gears and clutch, and the truck lurched once more to a dead stop.

"Bonnie, I'm afeared we ain't goin' to git to the bank afore it closes at dis rate. I suggest that for today you jes' let me drive you to the bank. Tomorrow we kin try the lessons agin." Bonnie was so grateful to hear those words that she jumped down from the driver's seat and ran around to the other side before Jeb could get his door open to move himself.

It was a rather red-faced young woman who was escorted back from the bank. She fervently hoped that Vito and Nino hadn't been watching when she had started out. And she offered no contradiction when Jeb announced, "She done jes' fine, jes' fine."

With a sinking heart she returned to the muddled bookkeeping. For as much as she worked on it, she hadn't clarified enough to make her own entries without further confusing the columns. By five o'clock, her brain felt as muddled as the pages, and figures swam in circles before her eyes. Wearily she twirled the little safe's knob, unplugged the miniature heater, and ventured down the street. The sun was casting long shadows to announce its soon departure for another winter day; and having never felt comfortably warm while she was in the office, she froze nearly to the bone on the way home. Her walk seemed much longer on the return trip than it had in the morning.

She headed straight for the bathtub, filled it with water as hot as she could stand, and relaxed in its comforting warmth.

Hal phoned later that evening.

"Hi, little girl. Anything new? Did you get a job yet? Boy, I sure miss you around Paramount Plastics. You ought to see the charmer they got to replace you on the mail route. Crossed eyes, nose like a hawk's beak, bowlegged. And I doubt she can make a knowledgeable distinction between the outgoing and the incoming baskets. Now, how is it?"

"You don't give a person a whole lot of a chance to say. But now you mention it, I did start work today." And she regaled him with a recital of the day's activities, ending with, "Now, if it isn't bad enough that I should have to learn to drive on a pickup truck, it's slippery streets yet. You should have seen that fellow in the car. I'll bet he's home right now telling his wife about this dumb brunette in the pickup coming at him like an idiot. Can you just picture what we must have looked like? It's hilarious now that I'm safe at home and comfortable, but it wasn't funny then."

"It probably isn't going to be tomorrow when you have

to try it again, either. Although I did hear that warmer weather is forecast, so the snow may melt. I'll tell you what, I'll come by tomorrow evening and pick you up while there's still a little daylight. And *I'll* teach you. My car has automatic transmission, so that should take some of the load off until you get so you can maneuver about the streets in the right lane. We'll just go out of town where we can get a clear shot at the highway, and maybe you can learn to steer in your first lesson."

"Now if that isn't a rope thrown to a drowning man! You bet I'll be looking for you."

Bonnie left not a drawer unopened the next morning searching for sweaters to layer one upon the other. Finding an old pair of knee socks, she concealed them under a pair of blue jeans and borrowed her mother's fur-lined boots. Now, if it were only possible to work in gloves, she might ward off freezing! As she tried to get her coat buttoned over all that bulk, she discovered it was already smudged with grease.

Tucking under her arm the old coffee pot she had unearthed the evening before from the back of the cupboard, she set out, stopping at a little corner grocery to make the necessary purchases; a bar of hand soap, paper towels, cleanser, coffee, sugar cubes, powdered cream, paper cups, and a wastebasket if they had one. With the bulk in which she had already smothered herself, it was with some difficulty that she lugged her sack of purchases the remaining blocks to the shop. At least the weather had warmed and cleared most of the treacherous underfooting from the walks. She hoped fervently the worst of winter's fury was past.

She hurried into the office to relieve herself of her load before greeting the men in the shop. Then from the doorway she called as cheerily as she could muster: "Good morning, you all out there, in, under, and over your duties." To Nino, who was under an auto on the overhead hoist, she teased: "Now that is what I call shouldering your responsibilities.

He responded, "Yeah, and I'd shore like to see you get down to business like this here is going to." He reached for the button to lower the hoist, and the station wagon he was working on slowly descended to floor level.

"Really buckles down on the job, he does," Vito yelled from the top of a ladder propped against the parts shelves. "Glad to see you show up again, Bonnie. Half afraid we froze you out yesterday."

"I came prepared today; but wouldn't you know, it's going to be a little warmer, anyway."

"Won't last. Winter never gave in this easily."

In reply to her initial greeting, a foot had wiggled from under the station wagon. Was that Jeb's favorite haunt, or was it merely a very long job?

Turning back into the office, she removed her coat and promptly put it on again. Still chilly. Clearing a spot on top of the file cabinets, she laid out some paper towels and opened the can of coffee. No place to fill the pot except in that cruddy lavatory. Being careful not to touch the sink with the pot, she discovered the pot would not fit under the faucet. It was back to the office for a paper cup with which to fill it. Having measured out the coffee, she was feeling rather satisfied with her accomplishments as she plugged in the pot. Then she plugged in the little heater and turned her thoughts to that ledger book again. A volley of shouts rose from the shop.

"Hey, what happened to the lights?"

"That air compressor stopped again!"

"Somebody get another fuse."

It was to be either coffee or heat, not both. Reluctantly she unplugged the heater and hoped that the pot perked quickly.

She struggled with the books until time for the bank

trip. Fortunately there had been few interruptions from the phone and no one came to pick up or leave a vehicle. If things could continue slowly for a few more days, she might begin to get the hang of the place. Once when she needed to stretch her legs and get her chilled blood circulating again, she had gone into the shop, sought out Jeb from under a hood, and asked him the make and model of each vehicle there. He looked perplexed for a second, cleared his face, and replaced the look with amusement. "You women," he shook his head, and the bangs and clanging from the shop activity drowned out the rest of his words. Bonnie felt it was just as well, for she didn't need to be told how foolish she was not to know. When Vito ceased the racket he was making with an air chisel, Jeb graciously supplied the information she had requested. But the amusement still twinkled in his eyes. Now if she could just remember those models, she would ascertain each one in the future as it came in. She had looked stupid for the last time!

The moment she dreaded arrived much earlier, she thought, than it had the day before. Removing the keys from their nail beside the door, she tremulously forced some noise from her throat that she hoped Jeb would interpret as, "I believe it's time for our little jaunt."

"Why, sho' thing, Miz Bonnie. You jes' say the word and we're off." Again he opened the door on the driver's side of the pickup and seated himself beside her. She looked for signs of uneasiness, but once more he was calm. Vito's choice of instructor had obviously been made with a knowledge of the metal of which his men were made.

This time she started the motor on the second attempt. And she even got the contraption into the street without bouncing off the curb. Staying in the right lane proved to be a little more difficult than it looked when someone else was doing it, but with the good luck of meeting little traffic, she was able to keep the wheel all the way to the bank. It was only the parking that posed a near catastrophe. She entered the lot beside the bank and nosed in toward the building.

"Let that clutch in easy, Miz Bonnie, while you set down on the brake and shift gear."

For once she did exactly as instructed. Very easily she let in the clutch. The building loomed closer and closer. While Jeb covered his eyes with his hands, she forgot the clutch and the gears and shoved on the brake. The truck lurched to an abrupt halt inches from the cement block foundation of the bank.

Peering from behind one hand, Jeb speculated, "Well, Miz Bonnie, you shore is an apt pupil. When ah sez stop, Miz Bonnie stops."

The return trip was made without a hitch. Bonnie was beginning to feel really proud of herself. This probably wasn't going to be the impossibility she had feared. All went well, that is, until she turned across the walk to enter the shop. The gentleman who had been promised his car that afternoon at two was only then arriving— just in time to be entering the shop when the truck plunged wickedly right in his direction. He jumped straight up and managed to propel himself sideways while still in midair. As the pickup charged past him, barely missing his flapping overcoat, Jeb, looking straight ahead with a totally stolid expression, observed in a flat voice, "Miz Bonnie, that ain't recommended as a successful business procedure."

A little light began to filter through on the books by the time the figures again swam before her weary eyes. Perhaps with one more good day's work, she would have things in respectable order. For the time being, she was grateful for a respite from the columns of numbers even though it was only to scrub that filthy lavatory. Good humoredly she gathered up her new cleaning materials and removed all but one sweater, the sleeves of which she pushed to her elbows. It was now or never.

Using some old newspapers soaked with naphtha, she removed streak after streak of grease from the floor, thinking surely there must be an easier way. But with the diligence of the proverbial elbow grease, she made some encouraging headway. The commode was another problem. She would have to leave some cleanser in it overnight in hope of loosening its yellowed film. She scoured the sink until nothing else could be removed. If it weren't exactly gleaming porcelain, at least what remained was only scratches and corrosion.

A horn blaring from outside the big doors promptly at five signaled her time to hastily flop the hair from her eyes and dab a little lipstick. With "See you in the morning" tossed over her shoulder to the men removing their coveralls, she was beside Hal in his smart convertible in a flash.

"And how's the little grease monkey?" Hal's appraising glance didn't miss an inch. She suspected she should check for telltale smudges. The mirror in her compact confirmed her suspicions. The dim light in the lavatory just hadn't revealed the two black finger streaks across one cheek.

"Bet you couldn't guess what else I did today," she challenged, while trying to erase the streaks with a tissue.

"How many guesses?"

"First one doesn't count."

"Then I wouldn't venture you plowed that pickup through the rear wall of one certain auto repair shop."

"Better than that. I nearly made a grease spot of one of the customers."

"Uh-huh!"

She wasn't sure whether that meant he was preoccupied at the moment with the traffic they had entered, or whether the admission was no less than he had expected. She knew she hadn't painted the picture very clearly and couldn't expect replies any more intelligible than those she was receiving. And as Hal seemed more intent on the rush hour traffic, she fell silent until they finally wended their way through the heaviest congestion and headed out of town.

They were still in a steady stream pouring in one direction, but it was moving. And they had left the red lights and intersections. Hal leaned back and relaxed.

"Had a rather rough day myself. We're still trying to break in the new guy they got to take George's place. And I must say, he doesn't pick it up like that old goat did. Has to be shown the same thing over and over. It's tough on the rest of the department when one person has to be replaced without being there himself to train his successor. No one else fully knows his job. We have to piece it together bit by bit from around what we are doing.

"I hear the old buzzard's bail was set high enough he couldn't make it, so he's sitting over there in the county jail awaiting trial."

If Hal had considered what Bonnie's reaction to his words would be, he never would have dreamed she suddenly and for no explicable reason remembered the suffering-etched face of the little gray-haired lady she had seen on the street, so anxious for the company of her son on Christmas Day. She ached for the mother, if not for the son!

Bonnie wished to pursue neither subject that Hal had broached, but for lack of an inspiration for changing them, returned to the former. "It must be some place down there now with a mail girl who doesn't know one basket from the other, and an accountant who doesn't know what to put into them anyway." They both chuckled.

"Have you given any thought to maybe going back and trying to get hired on again? You know, after all, you resigned; they didn't fire you. Could be the door is still open."

"No, thanks. At least, nor for the near future. And I haven't really given much thought to anything. Except for—" She was on the verge of sharing with him the joy she had found in her new spiritual experience. If he was to renew his acquaintance with her, and perhaps deepen it, then it was only right that he should be introduced to the new "her." But he was looking for a place to pull over. When the opportunity presented itself, he switched off the ignition, slid over to the middle of the seat, and said, "C'mon, over you go."

Reading his intentions, she attempted a kind of slithering over him and found herself caught in his arms and pinned on his lap while he planted a kiss squarely on her lips.

"Right in broad daylight!" she scolded when her lips were freed.

"It isn't so broad. We'll have to get on with the lesson if you're going to get any driving in before it gets dark. Now on this limousine, all you do is turn the key while pressing on the accelerator. There, see—that wasn't so difficult, was it? Now pull toward you on the gear shift, move it to the 'D' and take off."

She thrilled to the ease with which the big automobile responded to her gentle manipulations. Driving would be no problem if she only had something like this instead of a pickup truck with stick shift to work on. For forty-five minutes they skimmed along, saying little except Hal's instructions for driving. Even she was able to shed some of her tension and almost relax to the point of enjoying her newly developing skill. But dusk crept up on them before either welcomed it, and Hal took the wheel to return to the city. They laughed and conversed about old times together until the time between the old and the present seemed to be erased, and she began to feel that life was good after all.

When the big car pulled up to the apartment, Hal reached for Bonnie's hand. "Little girl, at the rate you're going, it won't be any time at all until you'll be ready for that driver's test. Please don't learn too fast—we'll need an excuse for going out every night to practice."

"Do we really need an excuse for going out?"

"No more of an excuse than this." He enfolded her in his arms and kissed her again.

The remainder of the week passed more or less uneventfully. The capers on the way to and from the bank became less frequent and fraught with peril, although also less interesting. Bonnie never ceased to marvel at Jeb's composure. She also observed he never used the kind of language she occasionally heard from Nino and Vito, and that he silently bowed his head for a few moments before opening his lunch box. She would just have to ask him some time if he knew the Lord Jesus as she was beginning to know Him, but she doubted she really needed to ask.

The books finally almost balanced—close enough that Vito told her to never mind one or two deposits in the book for which there were no records of receipt from customers. At least it was an error on the credit side. On the whole, he was delighted with the order she had made of his muddled ledger, and secretly told himself he would have to keep giving her raises so as not to lose a good girl now that he finally had one.

By the end of the week Bonnie surveyed her domain with considerable satisfaction. Everything was in order both in and on the desk and in the file cabinet. The office and lavatory sparkled as much as old scarred furnishing, fixtures, and flooring would permit, and she had even developed her coffee-making to perfection, although she still couldn't use the heater while the pot was plugged in.

Unfortunately, the weather had taken another turn for worse, and she didn't seem to have enough layers of clothing to pile on to keep the icicles out of her blood. But Hal's car was comfortably warm every evening, and she was spared the long freezing walk home while her driving skills improved at the same time.

But there was the matter of her clothes. All the lovely little dresses and suits into which she had put most of her salary from Paramount Plastics now hung uselessly in her closet. In the repair shop, her prime clothing concern was how to get the grease out of her blue jeans every night and whether she could pile on enough sweaters. She had already ruined three of them. But she felt well compensated when she saw the check Vito gave her on payday.

10

Lighting out on the count of three, Bonnie remembered half way to the pile of shoes in the middle of the ring that she had not noticed what color Hal was wearing. Turning to go back to look, she collided with Luanne Marks. Luanne's lovely singing voice registered a squeal, but she was not to be hindered in pursuit of Ron Walker's shoe. Hal in his chair in the circle hiked his pant leg and kicked his shoe-covered foot in Bonnie's direction. *Brown,* she noted frantically and dove into the scramble of girls with arms flailing wildly, each hopeful of being the first to retrieve the shoe that matched the one her date still had on one foot. Because Dave Fisher was wearing black and white oxfords, Lucy Arnold had no difficulty claiming the prize. She was awarded a tiny heart-shaped box of chocolates while the others smoothed disheveled hair and nursed a few scratches. Not to be completely outdone, each girl dutifully searched for her partner's missing shoe until all were restored.

Bonnie had never enjoyed such simple good fun at a party. It wasn't so much the corny activities as it was the fellowship of the other young people. Bonnie had soon discovered the truth in Barbara's words when she had first told her about the college and career group at the church. These people were sharp, vibrant, aware, and caring.

And they truly were united in a bond as strong as kinship. "We are just one, big, happy family," Barbara had told her. When Bonnie began to comprehend the relationship of believers as brothers and sisters in the great family of God and saw genuine love evident among the members, she thrilled to the joy and acceptance she found among them.

Some of the gang were delightful case studies in personality. The Walker brothers—namely, Ron, Royle, and Reginald—but better known as Readin', Ritin', and 'Ritmetic, were a case in point. The studious one of the three, Ron, was the original inspiration for the nickname when he was always seen with a book in his hand. Royle, a talented artist, had painted a lovely young couple standing hand in hand on a large heart as a backdrop for this particular evening's decorations. His "writing" he did with paint brush.

Reginald just as easily acquired his own moniker. An accomplished pianist, he had once attempted to explain to Dominic Pizzuti that the rhythm and harmonization of music are basically mathematical. Poor Dominic, chubby and good-natured, lacked inherent musicianship. The hilarious argument that had ensued upon Reginald's startling pronouncement drew the attention of the others, and Reg was forever after dubbed " 'Ritmetic."

Merideth McMaster was the first to whom Barbara had introduced Bonnie when she began to attend the Thursday youth affairs. Merideth, with her steady, mature, and gracious demeanor, had taken Bonnie under her solicitude and insured that none of the others remained a stranger. She appeared to be waiting for her each time Bonnie entered the church and proferred friendship while asking no favors. She had seldom left her side until this evening, when Bonnie had persuaded Hal to escort her to the Valentine party.

Hal had been somewhat reluctant to attend any church function, but brightened considerably when Bonnie led him into the circle of revelers.

"Believe I know you from Mount Lebanon High," Dave Fisher greeted him upon introduction. "Aren't you the Hal Gregersen of swim team fame?"

"Swim team, yes; fame, no. You say your name is Fisher? Dave Fisher." He repeated it slowly, trying desperately to revive some faded memory. Oh, yes, now he remembered. The quiet fellow who usually escaped notice. Odd sort, always carrying a Bible among his textbooks. The other kids often called him "Parson," out of derision rather than respect. "Sure, now I remember. Good to see you again. Several years now. Where you been keeping yourself?"

"X-ray technician at Allegheny General Hospital. Where have you been hiding out?"

"Paramount Plastics at the moment. Served a stint with the United States Army but never saw any action outside San Antonio."

"Yeah? I enlisted myself, hoping to get some free training in the medics. I was honorably discharged in six weeks after they discovered I'm a sleepwalker. About all I got out of the venture was the shiniest shoes in boot camp."

"Rotten luck, I would say. I hoped to see some action, maybe some of the world, although it most likely would have been Korea at the time, and all I got out of it was the medics. Well, that's the army for you."

"What do you do at the plastics company? President, or are you still only the veep?"

"Accountant."

"This fellow here's in accounting. Only he's still a student. Actually, he hails from some little place outside Harrisburg. Comes to church here during the college term. Drew, how about meeting Hal Gregersen?" The young man to whom Dave was referring turned at the sound of his name, flashed a congenial grin, and offered his hand.

"Hal, meet Drew Anderson," Dave continued. And to Drew, "Old friend of mine from high school days. Hal's an accountant with Paramount Plastics. Maybe he can teach you how to add a column of figures."

"I doubt that. Nobody else ever succeeded. Here, meet my date, Ruth Konevich."

Ruth bore strong resemblance to Sylvia Lake, and it was difficult for anyone not to appreciate dark, striking beauty. Ruth was considerably taller than Sylvia, a statuesque model of grace and charm.

"How do you do, Hal?" she responded. "I'm so glad to see you here with Bonnie tonight. You know we are all learning to really love her. We're—"

"So am I," Hal interjected, and drew Bonnie closer. She had been standing silently by his side as the two fellows conversed.

"Of course"—Ruth chuckled before continuing—"we're awfully glad she has become a part of our group. And I do hope that you will too."

"Yeah, thanks." Hal sounded unenthusiastic. "Maybe sometime."

The first of the games was announced, and the four seated themselves in the circle of chairs. Bonnie noticed that Hal entered into the exuberance of the revelry and could have enjoyed himself thoroughly except, he told her, for not feeling free to indulge himself with a cigarette. No one else was smoking, and the atmosphere suggested that such activity would not be welcome. "This is a strange bunch," he whispered. "Just what we always thought of Dave Fisher."

When the last of the games had been spent, Dr. Dennis rose to his feet, read a short portion of Scripture, and asked whether anyone had a very up-to-date testimony.

Lucy Arnold jumped to her feet and reported she had been given definite guidance in a matter that had given her some concern, but which she did not wish to share with the group. Pia Erasmus said she had been praying for some time about a difficult situation where she worked. An older woman who had not taken to her had been discreetly moved from her department. Dave Fisher's sister Irene, a timid, wispy little blonde, fairly bubbled at having received the boldness to witness to a classmate in business college.

On and on the narrations went. It seemed each one had some exciting experience to share with the others.

Bonnie listened, nearly spellbound. She had not dreamed her Father had so much concern over the mundane, trivial affairs that affected His children. The biggies, yes. Nearly everyone has some concept of God's controlling major events in our lives. But directing a person to the location of a lost set of car keys? It was nearly more than she could grasp. Once or twice she stole a look in Hal's direction. But his expression was noncommittal. She could not tell whether he was skeptical, bored, or impressed.

When the last praise was given, Dennis asked for those who had prayer concerns to share them with the fellowship. Again their confessions came from their innermost hearts. Several were burdened with the lost state of their families. A couple desired prayer support as they witnessed to their fellow workers on the job, and three expressed physical needs. Then all joined hands in the circle while several of them prayed a simple, unaffected petition for God's intervening in the situations surrounding each request.

Bonnie thrilled to the uplift she experienced as she joined her newfound faith to that of her brothers and sisters. Remembering Barbara's promise to pray for her several weeks before, she now began to comprehend the concern for others that would have motivated that prayer, and to grasp the enormous power behind prayer when several people of like concerns joined faith in presenting needs before their Lord. It had certainly been as a newborn babe that she had made that first faltering venture a short time ago, and she was only beginning to see the vast scope of spiritual adventure on which she had embarked. She had heard Pastor Thomas once use the term "abundant life." It had been perplexing at the time, but now it was becoming exciting. If this wasn't abundant living, she didn't know what would be.

Glancing once more at Hal, she was at a complete loss to read his expression. It actually looked more blank than anything else. Could it be he was simply not comprehending what transpired around him? Was a person spiritually dead in his sinful condition not able to grasp what one could perceive with the eyes of faith? She felt a shudder somewhere in the depths of her being. How much he was missing! And she began to long for him to know the same joy she was gaining in greater intensity each passing day.

Then she remembered her own family. Several of her new friends had requested prayer for their unsaved families, and the others were right now praying for them as naturally as one would carry an aspirin to another with a headache. She knew then that she would not be content to keep her new joy to herself and not share it with her loved ones. They also needed salvation. Perhaps next meeting she would have the courage to speak out and ask the others to remember her folks also.

Hal seemed somewhat relieved when the last good-bye echoed through the fellowship hall, amidst several requests for him to join them all again. The big convertible would have headed for the Sixth Street bridge in silence, except that Bonnie was bubbling over with elation and found it difficult to share his mood.

"I'm so glad you came with me tonight. I do hope you had fun too, although I'm not positive you are returning with the same shoe you arrived in."

"You know what they say, 'If the shoe fits, wear it.' I'm wearing it, so at least it fits. And if I recall while there was still light to see by, it was somewhere near the proper color."

"I have wanted to tell you, but didn't quite know how to go about it—in fact, I'm not sure yet. I had an experience about a month ago in which I learned for the first time that I am a sinner in need of salvation and—"

"Ha! You a sinner! I guess that makes me a reprobate. So where do we go with that new evaluation of ourselves?"

"Well—the best place to go is straight to Jesus, because He forgives us for it and we don't need to consider ourselves sinners any more, but new—new, well new babes in Christ's family, because it is a new life that He gives us. We—"

"I liked you just the way you were. Now let's leave it at that, and none of this sinner talk. I thought that went out with Freud."

Bonnie sighed inwardly. But then, she hadn't understood it all at first either. She would give him time—and pray for him.

Sylvia was brushing her long magnificent locks when Bonnie slipped into their little room that night. Bonnie had often wondered about Sylvia's parentage. Could she have been Jewish with those dark, sensuous, enigmatic eyes and lustrous hair? Somehow the features didn't bespeak a Jewess. Italian? The nose was definitely not patrician. Maybe Spanish. But try as she would, Bonnie could not visualize a lace mantilla sitting high atop the proud little head. Nor would Sylvia ever bother to flutter those silken lashes from behind a fan. For her the direct approach was more effective. However she had come by it, Sylvia was just one of the blessed.

Bonnie herself was only thankful that it was currently fashionable to cut the hair quite short and try to coax a little reluctant curl into the edges. With her straggles of fine brown wisps, she could only think of a wet mouse when she looked in the mirror. With a sigh, she reached for the thousandth time for the bobby pins to attempt to pin-curl the straightness out of it.

"Have a good time tonight, Sis?" Sylvia was never reluctant to hear about a date.

"Did I ever! We played some of the most hilarious games—"

"What! Games! Was it a children's party?"

"In a way, yes. Some of us are only babies, and then others have had a little more growth, but I think you could safely say we are all children."

Sylvia gave Bonnie a long thoughtful look before saying disdainfully, "Well, I spent the evening more maturely. I do prefer a more adult type of entertainment, especially for Valentine's Day. By the way, did you see the fabulous corsage Paul gave me when you opened the fridge?"

"I didn't open it. There were lots of refreshments at the party, and I wasn't hungry when I got home. We really had a good time. Why don't you plan to go along next time?"

"College and career group, you say it is? Well, you know, I always did prefer older men. How are the pickin's?"

"Don't get your hopes up. They are all pretty well paired off already, although I guess there is a single here and there. But that wasn't the point. I mean, there's more to it than just games and guys. You wouldn't believe what those kids said was happening in their lives in answer to prayer, and how they then prayed for each others' needs. It's all one happy family of loving, caring people. It's like nothing you ever saw."

"For Pete's sake, Bonnie, what's all this about prayer and caring people? I look out for one person, and I'm going to see that she gets what she wants. If I don't, who in the world will?"

"Well, Sylvia, I haven't really been able to put it into the right kind of words, but I've been wanting to tell you about the new kind of life I'm finding over there. I mean, actually, it isn't that it's just there. You find this kind of life when you know Jesus Christ. You see" — Sylvia had turned to scrutinize her in depth with a quizzical expression on her own face. — "I learned a few weeks ago that we are separated from God in our natural state and only when we find Him again in the Spirit can we ever truly live. You just sort of turn your life over to Him and become like a child being led by its Father, and something becomes alive inside you. You can have joy no matter what happens in your life. It's the most wonderful thing that ever happened to me."

"You've completely flipped. You don't expect me to go along with this religion jag, do you?"

"Sylvia, I wish you'd try to understand. It is hard for me to put it in the right words, since it's all so new to me. But if you'd go along with me over there, they'd be able to put it all together for you, and you could come to understand it as I've done."

"Of all things. My own sister turned into some sort of religious nut!"

Bonnie could see that further pursuit of the subject was useless. Her pin curls were all up, and she would just take her little white Bible and commence her nightly reading. And Sylvia switched on the record player, a trifle louder than usual.

Bonnie began the following week in what she later came to consider the proper manner. In response to Barbara's invitation at the Valentine party, she had arisen on Sunday morning and accompanied the dentist and his wife to Sunday school and morning worship service for the first time. She was delighted to find a class composed primarily of the same great gang that met on Thursday evenings. Pastor Thomas's sweet, gracious wife was the teacher. Bonnie sat spellbound as she elucidated on the social customs and physical environment in which Jesus had grown up and later ministered. She had not thought much of Jesus' humanity, and found that seeing Him in the light of a humble Galilean who worked with His hands in a carpenter shop and—as boys of all ages have done—went fishing over in the lake with His friends, helped her better to visualize some of those stories and parables that she was reading. And as she and Meredith entered the sanctuary for the worship service, her heart welled in gratitude to a gracious God who had favored her with permitting her to become acquainted with this Son who was both human and divine.

Her father was already off to his Sunday afternoon bowling by the time she arrived home. Following a late, leisurely brunch, Sylvia had repaired to their room with the everlasting records, and Perry was in his room trying to get his homework out of the way before a three o'clock activity with the fellows. Bonnie was pleased to find her mother had reserved her own lunch to share with her upon her return. The two of them sat down to tuna salad, tomato aspic, and Boston cream pie.

"I'm happy to see a smile on your face again after the dreadful experience you had a couple months ago, dear." Her mother's soft musical voice conveyed loving concern. "And may I say I'm happy to see Hal around here again. I liked that boy the first time I met him. Did anyone ever tell you how nice you two look together?"

"No, they haven't. But, Mother, I've been wanting to tell you—it isn't Hal's presence that makes me so happy. It's knowing the Lord Jesus as my Savior. I've found in

Him a happiness you don't find with other people. And I would probably not have gotten over the shock of my experience with George if it were not for the peace I've found in Christ."

Avonelle's eyes narrowed thoughtfully. "Yes, Sylvia was telling me that you said some peculiar things about a new kind of life. I must say she was a little concerned about you."

"Concerned? But I've just found out the only real meaning in life. You have no real purpose until you become a Christian."

"*Become* a Christian? If you 'become' a Christian, what do you do that is any different from what you always did? Now I always did say that in order to be a real Christian you have to be broad-minded and accept the fact that everybody has his own way to reach heaven. Everyone is going to the same place, and you should respect everyone's religion. And I just bend over backward to do so. You know the Red Cross serves everyone alike, regardless of color, race, or creed. And you can't tell me the time I devote to that worthy cause isn't going to carry some merit when the time comes."

"Mother," Bonnie began faltering, the Bible says that, as you say, 'when the time comes,' all that is going to matter is what we did about Jesus Christ. Our good works will be burned up, and we will have no merit except what Christ gave us when He died for us. If we don't accept that—"

Avonelle interrupted, her tone condescending, almost rebuking. "Now, darling, I know that it has been devastating to you to have your romance with George break up, but really I think it's left you a little bit—" she twirled her finger in a circular motion by her temple. "You know, you'll straighten out after a while; you'll get your bearings again and be able to see things in their proper prospective. Time will heal, and someday you'll get completely over this. In the meantime, please don't take it too seriously.

"Did I ever tell you about that other James I dated before I met your father? Jim, people called him. And I made sure to refer to your father as 'James' to make a distinction when I finally met him. Well, Jim and I had the date set, and would you believe, another girl in town claimed he was the father of her unborn child! A thing that just wasn't done in those days. Being the gentleman he was, he married her for decency's sake, but if you don't think I was in complete shock for months afterward! I got over it and now look at the marvelous man I've been privileged to share life with. And then there was your Aunt Jessie. Did you ever wonder why she never married sooner? Well, this fellow she was seeing—"

Bonnie recognized the deliberate attempt to turn the subject away from spiritual things. And with it she glimpsed some of the pitiful density with which her mother viewed the subject. Feeling painfully that it would be a long while before she would ever be able to reach her with the truth of the message she was trying to share with her, a mist gathered over her eyes, and one tear managed to overflow down her cheek.

Seeing it, her mother hastened to say, "There now, dear, you know that all turned out well after all, and even though it was a long wait, she is deliriously happy now with her Sam. I fear perhaps you are just a bit too emotional."

Avonelle solicitously patted her daughter's hand.

Knowing that any further words would avail nothing, her daughter simply replied, "Perhaps I am."

11

Spring arrived early in Pittsburgh that year, and Bonnie had never welcomed it more fervently. Try as she had to force away winter's bitter memories, they occasionally crept in unbidden with a shudder more convulsive than the cold precipitated. When she had watched the leaves turn scarlet and golden, then wither and drop, foretelling the bleakness of the months that lay ahead, she could have in no way anticipated just how deep would be the despair into which she was to plunge. Now, as she gleefully greeted each bold little crocus and delighted in the first shooting of the daffodils, she felt a lift and newness of the spirit that seemed to erase the clouded memories of the dismal past.

Under Jeb's patient tutelage with the old pickup, she mastered the stick shift, guided the jalopy skillfully into and out of the shop, threaded her way through traffic, and even managed to park uneventfully at the bank each day. And when she drove away from the police station bearing a brand new license, she wasn't sure whether it was she or dear Jeb who was the proudest.

She had quickly learned the names of the vehicles brought into the shop, and soon she was major traffic director, keeping accurate account of their comings and goings, seeing that no customer was disgruntled with making futile trips when his vehicle was not ready. Vito was lavish in his appreciation of the way she handled the business side of his affairs, although he was careful to keep her efficiency a secret in the presence of other businessmen who called. In addition, he systematically increased her salary to discourage anyone from luring her away from his service.

If there was a dark spot on her bright cloud of happiness at the moment, it was Hal's reluctance to share her enthusiasm for the life of the church and the joy found in serving the Lord Jesus. He had accompanied her to Sunday evening service once or twice, but Bonnie felt it was only to spend the time with her. The more she applied herself to her spiritual development and increased in knowledge of the Word and her Savior, the more removed from her companionship he seemed to be. He did not complain when she insisted on keeping Sunday and Thursday nights free to attend services, but neither did he share her enthusiasm for them. She feared a rift was insidiously developing between them.

Sylvia never ceased the late-night racket with the records. If anything, the collection grew as each recording star cut a new one. On occasion Bonnie had tried to speak to her again of spiritual matters, but she was always rebuffed. It was plain that Sylvia was bent on having a good time and enjoying her youth to the fullest. Perhaps her exquisite beauty was a detriment, considering the awful truth that youth and appearance fade and eternity goes on forever. And the steady stream of suitors never diminished. Bonnie suspected there must be a lineup across town, each waiting for the one ahead of him to encounter her disdain, while she went on to new amusements. Each evidently hoped he would have the magical key to hold her attention for more than a couple of dates. It seemed the only flaw on Sylvia's slate was losing the regional swim meet that spring. No one from her school placed above fifth in the competition, and there was rumor the coach would be replaced the next year.

Bonnie had not meant to directly confront her mother with her need of a Savior, thinking it better to live her own testimony quietly before her until Avonelle could see evidence of a new birth in her daughter. So it came as some surprise to her when her mother brought up the subject on a Saturday afternoon late in April. Bonnie had decided to try her luck with a new cookie recipe while her mother was spring cleaning the cupboards in the kitchen.

"There, now," Bonnie said, proudly sampling the first batch to come out of the oven. "Pretty good, if I do say so myself. Why don't you warm up the coffee and take a little break, Mother?"

"That sounds like a refreshing idea. I would like to get off my feet for a minute. Seven down and four to go. I always did hate this job. I find so many old things stashed away in the corners that I hate to throw out but never use, either. If you ever set up housekeeping, I believe I could outfit your kitchen with doubles of everything I have around here. Then my shelves could quit groaning under all that weight.

"I'm working on it," Bonnie laughed lightly. "But I am a little worried, though. You see, the more I become involved in the activity of the church, the more distant it seems Hal becomes. He doesn't complain, but we just aren't seeing eye to eye, if you know what I mean. I feel as though I'm being pulled in two directions. One draws me to Hal, and the other draws me Godward, and somehow I feel as though the two of them aren't compatible. I mean, in order for Hal and me to really communicate, we would have to be on the same wavelength, and we—we just aren't."

"Honestly, Bonnie." Her mother seated herself opposite her at the table, placing a cup of coffee before each of them. "I think I told you once that you should be coming down off that high, or whatever it is you are on since your breakup with George. I have kept looking for some return to normal, but it isn't coming. I really do wonder what has become of you. As if that isn't enough, Sylvia tells me you say these peculiar things to her also. She is getting rather worried about you. You should know that your family is concerned about you, and we will certainly stick by you, but I should think it has been about long enough—"

"But, Mother! It isn't something that you get over. I have entered a new life and have found it the most rewarding I have ever known. You see, I received Jesus Christ as my Savior and I was changed from the old me into a new creature. That's what the Bible says it is that happens when we confess our sins and believe on Him."

"Confess your *what*? What kind of talk is this now? Honestly, Bonnie, I must say, I really wonder—"

"I said confess sins. You see, we're all born in sin, or rather, under its power, and we can't be free from its hold on us until we receive forgiveness through the atonement that Christ made on the cross. We—"

"Well if that doesn't beat all! What sin are you talking about? You haven't been pulling the same pranks that George fellow was with Paramount Plastics, have you? Or what on earth is it you are trying to tell me?"

"Mother," Bonnie lowered her voice and looked her mother steadily in the eye. "The Bible says that all have sinned and come short of the glory of God. 'Coming short' simply means that you miss being all that God intended for us to be."

"But how can sin keep you from it when you don't do anything that bad?"

"We all sin all the time. Just failure to acknowledge God in our lives is sin. You don't have to do anything big—like robbing banks or committing adultery or murder. We just are all in sin because that is the natural human condition."

Avonelle put down her coffee cup with a shaking hand. She placed both hands on the edge of the table and leveled her gaze to Bonnie's. In a husky voice, which she struggled to keep from rising, she asked evenly, "Are you telling me that *I'm* a sinner?"

Bonnie felt pressure closing in on her from all sides. Something in her mother's attitude indicated she had somehow gone too far. But there was no turning back now. Sending up a quick prayer for guidance, she chose her words carefully and attempted to demonstrate her love for her mother by her expression.

"Mother, *I* didn't say it originally. In fact, I would not have known it at all except that the Bible says, yes, we are all sinners."

Avonelle pushed back her chair and pulled herself up to the extent of her dignified height. Her face blanched as she struggled to maintain control.

"Do you mean to tell me—do you actually mean to say that I am a sinner? I—who took you from a dismal, dingy orphanage in Reims, France, rescued you from who knows what miserable existence, nursed you back to health, gave you everything I had to give, brought you up as my own daughter, and tried to provide a comfortable and meaningful life, and you are telling me that I am a sinner? What kind of gratitude is that?"

Bonnie felt an icy hand squeeze her throat until the breath was cut off. Her head reeled, and she had to grasp the edge of the chair to steady herself. She longed for the earth to open and swallow her, or for complete darkness to engulf her so that she wouldn't have to face the wrath of her beloved mother—or the horrible reality of her unknown past. She had assumed she was merely the offspring of a promiscuous young woman of American heritage. Now what she was hearing—was it reality, or was her mother simply being carried away in anger? And then through the haze she heard her mother continuing.

"You should have seen the condition you were in when your father brought you home with him at the end of the war. He had looked in every orphanage and foundling home in France and finally found you, a pitiful little creature staring at him with huge, sunken eyes from a dirty crib in a drab hovel, who cried in fear when he approached. He had a time just trying to get you through all the red tape and get passage for you across the Atlantic. He couldn't take you on the troop ship returning the American heroes, so he had to book passage at his own expense on one of the displaced persons vessels. It was so crowded he had to hang onto you all the way over for fear of losing you in the mob. And when we got you here, I could count every rib in your body, and your hair was a matted fright. Your father tried to wash and brush out the snarls in the hotel before boarding ship, but you screamed so shrilly he feared the other guests would think he was beating you. Then he understood why the overworked, probably harried attendants in the orphanage had permitted you to acquire that condition. There were black circles around those haunted eyes, and you cried all day for two months."

Avonelle stopped abruptly and peered intently into Bonnie's face, seeming to study every feature individually. "Do you know why we named you 'Bonnie'?" Not pausing for any more than a bewildered shaking of her daughter's head, she continued, "I had meant to use something elegant like Melissa, or Stephanie, but when I looked at that pitiful little sight, I had to see you for what I hoped you would become, not as you were. So we named you Bonnie — 'beautiful.'

"Well, then, after crying for two months, you suddenly shut up and wouldn't open your mouth again. Since you didn't talk, no one could tell for sure what nationality you were, but we thought you had been with a group of refugees that came out of Hungary. When the rest of your party had found haven or passage to America, you were left behind—completely abandoned. And do you know, you rocked back and forth and sucked your thumb for a solid year! The pediatrician X-rayed your wrist and looked at your teeth and said you must be about six years old, but we couldn't put you into school until the emotional scars healed. That's why you were older than most when you graduated. We thought that the companionship of another child would be helpful, so we adopted Sylvia when she was three. Perry followed soon after, already walking and trying to say a few words."

Bonnie, in spite of her extreme shock, had to smile at the thought that the picturesque Sylvia, with her magnificent raven curls, would have been the one to provide companionship for her with her plain little peaked face and mousey hair. She could imagine the comparative attention the two of them would have received from others!

"Why," her mother was continuing, "we don't even know when your birthday is. We celebrate it on June 21st, because that is the day you joined our family, but we have absolutely no way of knowing when it really is, or exactly how old you are, for that matter. When I saw the plight of children like you and others who came out of the horrors of war, I decided to donate some of my time to the Red Cross to try to repair some of the tragedies caused by the destruction. And now you are telling me I'm a sinner in need of forgiveness. My very own daughter!"

Bonnie was smitten speechless for what seemed like long minutes. The wretchedness she had known in her experience with George was nothing compared with this. The world seemed to close in on her and then fade away beyond the point of grasping. She felt as though she had entered a vast black void from which there could be no return. But still the darkness did not mercifully swallow her up and blot out her consciousness. At last she was able to regain her speech, and she looked levelly at her distraught mother, as she spoke in a quiet, gentle voice.

"I'm sorry, Mother. I had no intention of sounding ungrateful. If I had all eternity, I don't believe I would be able to fully say how deep is my appreciation, nor how much I have loved you and Daddy. I will try in the future to make it up to you if that is at all possible. And I'll— I'll keep right on praying for you."

"Humph! I should think you might better pray for yourself!"

Bonnie remained long enough to remove the last sheet of cookies from the oven before fleeing to her room. How thankful she was that Sylvia was not in it! Flinging herself face downward on her bed, the hot tears gushed forth like fountains of the deep, broken up by convulsive earthquakes. For many long moments she permitted all the shock, grief, and agony to break forth uncontrolled. Her soul seemed wrenched and torn, fiber from fiber, until she stood naked and stripped of all semblance to the girl she had understood to be Bonnie Lake. For, in fact, now she did not know who she was. A victim of war, abandoned by those who had sheltered her, left nameless and forgotten in a dingy French foundling home. Had she ever had any personal identity? The void into which she had glimpsed a short time before widened and enfolded her in its murky depths. And she wandered alone, in the blackness of despair, feeling that she would never find herself again.

After several hours of soul torment, she dozed into a semiconscious state from which she awakened later, somewhat recovered from the shattering shock she had experienced. Reaching into the stand beside her bed, she drew out the little white Bible. Obeying the urging of some hidden voice, she turned to the Book of Psalms and began flipping over the pages. Suddenly the word "mother" arrested her wandering eyes, and she paused to read the entire verse. "When my father and my mother forsake me, then the Lord will take me up." One of the first things Barbara had told her about that little church was that they were all one big family. Now a new comprehension of that term came in with the quiet confidence that having been born into the family of God, she would never be left Fatherless or without a large company of blood-bought sisters and brothers eager to extend the bond of spiritual relationship. There are no orphans among God's children!

Finding comfort on the spiritual plane and slowly coming to grips with her lack of identity on the physical level, she turned her attention to the problem immediately confronting her with her mother. Had she spoken rashly? Had she rushed in with too much zeal when she should have been more attuned to the Spirit's leading in her choice of words? Was she never to know how to witness to another in such a way that the Spirit of the Lord could use her faltering testimony to convict another of his need? And when she could be so completely swept over by hearing the information she had just heard, did she have any security in her relationship to the Lord that she could tell others about? It was all too much for her to sort out. Maybe sometime when her mind was cleared and she had recovered from the stunning blow, if indeed she ever did, she would be able to reason her way through the morass and be able to cope with it.

Relinquishing the struggle for the time being, she closed her eyes and gratefully gave in to the sleep that threatened to overtake her. And she did not rouse when Sylvia entered the room later to prepare for the night. At first, she tossed fitfully; then as the pain and numbness gave way to the healing balm of sleep, she became lost in oblivion.

That night she dreamed the dream again. All the while she was being tossed to and fro by the surging, pulsating waves, the frenzied voice screaming "Marya" in heart-wrenching sobs seemed to crescendo and then recede. Crescendo and recede, with each crescendo becoming fainter until with the last receding she was left all alone. Desolately alone. And when the emptiness threatened to swallow her completely, she awakened in a cold sweat.

12

It was only three or four weeks until Bonnie's decision was finalized. Not that her mother ever for one moment asked her to leave and seek her own residence. It was just that, considering all things together, it seemed to be the preferable option.

Bonnie very carefully avoided any reference to the Saturday afternoon conversation between them, and to anything concerning her faith. She assumed duties about the home in an attempt to lighten her mother's work load and permit her more leisure to pursue activities of interest to her. Bonnie soon discovered, however, that her ministrations were not always appreciated; Avonelle evidently was happiest when feeling she was needed by her family. Bonnie then turned her attention to a gift for Mother's Day, which she hoped would convey her love and appreciation. The selection was extremely difficult, as her mother was in need of nothing and James freely supplied her wants. At last, she settled on a bracelet to match the emerald necklace. The price tag was beyond the range her budget could accommodate without strain. However, she felt any price she could possibly manage would not be too great if the gift would demonstrate her desire to heal the breach. But when she presented it proudly, waiting breathlessly for Avonelle's reaction, a new pain gripped her heart as she realized her mother looked on it as a peace offering, almost so base as a bribe to placate her wounded feelings.

"Why, darling, you know you didn't have to do that. I love you all the same, no matter what comes between us. You really shouldn't have been so extravagant on your limited means." But the voice in which she said it, usually so soft and lilting, carried the sting of wounded pride. Avonelle, in spite of her words and outward actions, nursed an air of aggrievance in her communication with her older daughter. Bonnie began to feel that her presence in the home was a source of perpetual discomfort to her and that it would perhaps be better for them both if she removed the thorn from her mother's flesh.

Sharing a room with Sylvia was another matter. The little room seemed to be constantly shrinking as Sylvia's animal collection increased. The amusement Bonnie once saw in the imagined threat of her having to move out to make way for the stuffed menagerie looked as though it might change to necessity. The plush population was beginning to take over the dresser and night stands. But it was the records that caused Bonnie the greatest grief. As she became absorbed in her nightly devotional time, it became increasingly difficult to concentrate with the ceaseless renditions of the recording stars. Bonnie attempted to find another corner of the house, but the apartment was so small that upon leaving her room, she could not escape the sound from the television that her parents always enjoyed at that hour. She next tried to change her devotional time to early morning, before she left for work. Sylvia immediately complained that the light disturbed her. It was increasingly clear that not only the little room, but also the whole apartment was not spacious enough to accommodate the Lake family any longer.

Emboldened perhaps by her mother's injured feelings, Sylvia was not entirely above a snide remark on occasion. It was on another of the evening hair-dressing rituals that Sylvia turned to her, brush poised in midair, lowered the silken lashes to aim a cool direct gaze, and chided,

"Well, sis, I guess the grateful one has lavished gracias for her family's unselfish devotion. I tried to tell you that you were getting some awfully kooky ideas, but her royal Head-in-the-Clouds couldn't listen."

"Now, Syl" — Bonnie removed the bobby pin from her mouth to speak more distinctly. "I don't believe you really think I deliberately intended to hurt Mother. You know very well that I love her as much as you do. In fact, if I didn't love her, I wouldn't have any concern that she should find the same joy in knowing Jesus that I have found."

"And so for starters, you're letting us all know that the happiness we have here together as a family isn't enough for you."

"Sylvia, our happiness as a family does not supply the inner peace I have, knowing that my sins are forgiven and I belong to a family whose Father is the almighty God."

Sylvia twisted her locks into a bun and covered it with a shower cap.

"There you go again, Bonnie. All that our folks here have provided isn't enough for you. And you some little waif that was left over when the smoke cleared from the battlefield!"

The hurt and anger began to rise in Bonnie's voice. "After all, Sylvia, you were a castoff yourself before the authorities found you in the basement of that scroungy tenement, starved and practically naked. You might have known who your natural mother was, but for all that she would care for you, I can't see you were any better off than I was."

"You're precisely right. Someone did know who I was.

And *I* know when I showed up on this earth. You don't even know when you were born."

Bonnie laid down the comb and turned to look directly into the glittering black eyes. Compassion replaced the anger in her voice, and her words were low and gentle.

"Sylvia, I don't know when I was born. That is true. Nor do I know where. But this I do know. I know when I was born again, and in the final analysis, that is all that really counts."

Sylvia threw her hands, palm upward, into the air with a shrug. With eyes rolled heavenward, she headed for the shower.

Bonnie had long since found the courage to request prayer for the salvation of her family at the Thursday gatherings of the college and career group. Several among them assured her on repeated occasions that they were continuing to lift up the Lakes in their private devotions. And the fellowship that she shared with them formed a strong tie that sustained her in the increasing alienation she felt from her family.

And so it became perfectly natural for her to share her concerns with her spiritual family. In the meeting following Sylvia's outburst, Bonnie stated simply she thought it best to find her own place and asked for prayer for guidance in acquiring something suitable.

On the way home that evening, Barbara Courtney voiced her concern as her husband turned onto the bridge.

"Bonnie, are you sure you have ruled out wanting a place of your own just so you won't have to listen to the ridicule you receive from your family? You know, sometimes we meet with misunderstanding, and we find it a little hard just to stand there and take it. The easy thing is to run away from it. But maybe God is saying, 'Stay there and continue to witness.' "

"I really have given that some honest consideration. And I believe I was ready to admit that may be the problem. I have told the Lord I will stay if that is His choice for me. But I don't really feel peace about staying. I believe He would have me in a place where I can find quiet solitude to read the Bible and try to learn what He has to say to me. And I feel that for the present, at least, my presence at home is too much of a contention for me to be able to witness anyway. I fear I am hurting more than helping."

"Well, then, I think I may know a good place for you. Before I was married, I worked with Child Evangelism Fellowship teaching Good News Clubs. Housewives gathered groups of neighborhood children in their homes after school, and I taught them Bible stories and the way of salvation. I stopped when Lisa was born, but I like to keep in touch with them. They have a regional office over on Arch Street that was once a doctor's residence. Miss Travis, the directress, and a couple of workers live and have their offices on the first floor, and they rent the two upper floors."

"Did you say on Arch Street?"

"Yes, Arch. It is only a few blocks from the church, you know. You could walk over in daylight if you wished, but naturally we will always be available to drive you home after dark."

"I wonder if I would have any problem getting back over to Oakland to work. I'm sure I could take a streetcar most of the way, but I would probably still have to walk the last few blocks as I do now."

"I'm quite certain you could make some kind of connections."

"Now that I can drive, I'm sort of hoping I'll be able to get my own car before too long. Although with living on my own, I'm afraid such a purchase will have to be put off for a while. I guess with the buses and streetcars, I don't really need my own."

"It's always nice to have your own car. Gives you more of a feeling of independence. As for the CEF headquarters, I'm not certain whether they have an available room right now, but it seems to me one of their tenants left recently. I'll phone them tomorrow and find out. Then if they have a room I'll come by at the garage and take you over to see it after work."

Barbara was waiting for her at the curb the next evening at five. With some difficulty they threaded their way through the heavy traffic back across the river to the North Side. But turning left off Sixth Street and making one right, they suddenly left the mainstream and found themselves on a quiet, tree-lined avenue. The houses were darkened with age and air pollution, but proudly bore traces of a former glory. Barbara pulled up before a three-story structure with a wide front porch. Bonnie later learned that the house was narrow, but very long. And even though it was sandwiched closely between its neighbors, the leaded beveled glass in the broad door promised a faded elegance within. Miss Travis opened it herself in response to Barbara's ring. Bonnie found herself confronted by an older version of her mother's immaculate grooming, grace, and dignity. The silver hair was swept into a framing halo about a lovely, aristocratic face that had not lost a beauty only few possess in youth. Bonnie immediately discerned a warm, compassionate nature.

"So nice to see you again, Barbara," Miss Travis greeted, with an affectionate clasp of her hand. "And this is the young lady of whom you spoke."

"Yes, this is Bonnie Lake," Barbara replied.

"How do you do?" Bonnie felt already she could gladly be a part of this household.

"We'll be very happy to show you our establishment here, and you are more than welcome to one of the rooms. Actually, two are unoccupied at the time." Miss Travis led the way into a long hall. To the left was a paneled wall not part of the original design. An opening in it with a counter top inset indicated that some sort of business was probably transacted there. Behind it a young woman sat at a desk typing. Looking through the opening, Miss Travis said, "This is Myra Hayes. She does our bookkeeping. We also have a teacher living here who is out in classes at the moment."

"Hello, Bonnie." Myra looked up from the typewriter.

"Hi!" greeted Bonnie in return. Peering into the room where Myra sat, she observed a magnificent tile-inlaid fireplace on the opposite wall, a heavily draped large front window, and several pieces of Victorian furniture. Gold leaf ornamented the molding around a high ceiling from which hung an elegant crystal chandelier.

Miss Travis next began to mount a very long stairway. Following her, Bonnie noticed a large doorway across the hall with heavy oak sliding doors that were open to reveal an immense canopied bed. Evidently all, or most, of the staff lived on the first floor. Reaching the second, Miss Travis sorted out one key from a large ring and unlocked the door at the head of the stairs. It was immediately evident that the opulence of the old mansion was restricted to the first floor. Other than the high ceiling and a large bay window on the outside wall of the room, there was no indication that this could be any other than an ordinary room, slightly drab and scarcely inviting. A worn carpet of a nondescript color didn't cover quite all of the floor, the walls had long since witnessed the fading of the last color in the blossoms on the paper, and the furniture may have been scrounged from a Salvation Army donation.

"Now the kitchen facilities are here," Miss Travis was saying, as she opened a large closet in the hallway adjacent to the room. Bonnie observed an old-fashioned sink and very small gas cook stove surrounded by a few rough shelves.

"And directly over this on the next floor is the other room. If you will come this way—" Miss Travis led the way down the narrow hall parallel with the stairway and guarded by a wooden railing, and began to ascend to the next floor. Bonnie was glad she did not have to comment on the room before she was shown the other.

At the top of the second flight of stairs, she discovered the same floor plan. Another hallway ran parallel to that stairway and disappeared around a corner toward the front of the house. The room she was shown seemed to be in the back of the house and across its entire width. Gratefully Bonnie observed that this room looked somewhat more inviting than the former one had. Though nearly colorless, there was more of a hint of browns and beige rather than absolutely no color. The dresser seemed large and spacious, the drapes hanging by the bay window were flowered with at least a hint of color, and the sofa that would open out into the bed was covered with a scarlet throw. One easy chair, a platform rocker, a floor lamp, and small desk completed the furnishings.

"And here is the kitchenette for this room." Miss Travis had produced yet another key. Bonnie saw little difference from the second floor closet, but decided it was at least functional. "Now the bathroom is down the hall and around that corner. A young couple with a small child live in the front end of the house. He is out most of the time to work, and we hear or see very little of them. But you must share the bathroom with them. This room is thirty dollars per month and the one downstairs is forty. You may take your choice of either one."

Bonnie hoped relief wasn't written all over her face. The room she preferred was the one with lower rent. It would be a tiring hike all the way to the third floor, up those long flights of stairs after a day's work, but the upper room was considerably more inviting, and definitely kinder to the purse.

"I believe I'll take this one. It looks rather comfortable."

"We will be so glad to have you, and you must feel welcome to trot downstairs and visit with us at any time. We always enjoy having other Christians in our rooms, although we don't require it. It just happens our tenants are usually Christians because mostly Christians know about us and recommend us. Barbara is pretty good at that. She brings us girls from time to time, but they always marry and leave us."

Barbara, who had remained silent throughout the tour, added, "Yes, occasionally Dennis has patients in his office who are career girls, and when they mention they are looking for apartments or rooms, he always directs them to me. I suppose you might say we help to keep the place in business."

Miss Travis smiled with her. "We surely did hate to lose you in our work, Barbara. You were a fine teacher for our youngsters. We still hear from many of the children, although most are nearly grown by now. A few have gone into some form of a ministry themselves. You know, if you reach a child for the Lord Jesus, his whole life is saved as well as his soul. You might consider this type of work yourself, Bonnie, although to be sure it is the Master Himself who calls laborers into His vineyard. I can only suggest."

"It is worthy of consideration, but at the present time I am such a new Christian myself that I feel the need to be taught, rather than being the one to teach."

The party had reached the first floor.

"I'll give you the keys now and then you may move in whenever you like."

"I think I'll be able to make it by the beginning of next week."

"So long until then. I hope you will be very comfortable with us."

The little sports car was on its way back up the Boulevard of the Allies when Bonnie said, "I think I will really be happy there, although I have always wanted to live in a place with a lot of color. It seems that Mother always decorated our home in very subdued hues, and although she used good taste and created a very pleasant atmosphere, I just long for bright colors around me. If I ever have a home of my own, I think I will have every room a different color, with plenty of contrast. But for the time being, I think I can live with those browns over there. At least it will be peaceful.

"I'm sure you will be content there. And you never know what the Lord may have for you next. It could be that you won't be there very long before He will say, 'I've got something better for you.' "

"Oh, really! I have yet to learn that I can *expect* His guidance in my life."

"You've come a long way, Bonnie. I'm thrilled to watch you growing. You know, if Lisa didn't need a larger size in clothing each season, I would be terribly distressed, even though it gets expensive to keep buying her a new wardrobe. I want to see her grow even though I know my baby will be slipping away from me in time. And it's the same in our spiritual life. I'm thrilled to see you making progress almost day by day as you learn to walk with the Lord.

"While I think about it, did anyone ever tell you that our college and career group goes to a little campground up in the mountains every summer for a week long retreat? We'll begin to make announcement of it soon. It is an interdenominational group that brings in speakers who know and understand young people. They usually have a missionary or two and good music. We stay in little cabins and swim in the mountain stream. We have a wonderful time, and we all come home with a blessing too huge to carry in the luggage."

"Sounds great. I don't know whether my boss will let me have any time off, though. You know, I haven't been there a year, and I don't know whether in a little place like that he will require a year's employment before I get a vacation or not. But I'll see."

"Bonnie, are you completely satisfied with that job? I've been wondering, Dennis doesn't need a receptionist right now, but he may know of another dentist who does. If you wish, he could probably look around for you. You might be able to quit that job in time to go to retreat and begin a new one when you return."

"I hadn't given a thought to leaving there. To be perfectly honest, Vito is very good to me, and the work isn't hard. I'll just wait and see how things turn out. Speaking of turning out, looks like the end of the line for me, and I'll be turning out—of the car, that is. Thanks again for the ride and for—for all that you have done for me. I don't know how I can ever repay you."

"You know what I said about Lisa growing out of her clothes, although I wouldn't have you thinking it costs me anything for the little I do for you, because it doesn't. 'Bye now. See you Sunday."

Hal promised to pull up to the apartment in Oakland at six on Monday evening to carry Bonnie's possessions to her new home in his car. She had packed everything she could call her own, for she felt a deep conviction that, leaving her parents' home, she would never return except to visit. Her mother was generous in the provisions from her own kitchen, as she had promised on the fateful day she had cleaned the cupboards. She had even removed a picture from the dining room wall and told her daughter to use it to make her own place more inviting. Bonnie was touched by her mother's consideration and sensed that Avonelle experienced some sadness at the first of her fledglings' leaving her nest. Bonnie longed to reach out and make emotional contact with her, but Avonelle remained politely aloof.

The phone rang soon after Bonnie arrived at work on Monday morning, but it was not a customer. Hal sounded strained and slightly shaken.

"Bonnie, listen. I was just turning onto Thirty-seventh from Monroe when a car shot through the red light and hit me broadside. I'm not hurt, but I think the car is a total loss. I got it towed off the street and caught a taxi to work. But now I won't be able to get you moved this evening. I'm terribly sorry."

"You needn't apologize to me. You've got problems enough yourself. I hope you have insurance to cover it."

"Of course, I have insurance. I certainly hope that nut does too! Usually you find that kind doesn't, though."

"I think my father will move my things. I believe he was trying to offer the other day, but I just told him you were going to do it. I'm sure he will when I tell him you can't. Now don't you worry about it. And I hope you'll find something else soon so you aren't left without a car."

"I was sort of looking over the market anyway. Maybe this is a lucky break. With the insurance settlement I can probably get a good down payment on a brand new car. Have any preference what color I should look for?"

"How about purple?"

"Remind me not to ask you again. I guess I'd better get to work. I can't even find my desk. So long."

Avonelle kissed her daughter as Bonnie hurried to the elevator. "Call often, darling. I'll always be glad to hear from you. And do come back and see us." They had loaded her father's car to the back seat windows after the trunk was filled. Bonnie had had no idea that she possessed so extensive an outfit.

"Now, Bonnie, honey." Her father relaxed at the wheel as they skimmed down the boulevard. "I want you to know that I think it is just fine for you to go in for this Christian stuff. You have awakened some long dead memories in me. You see, my mother had been the kind of Christian you talk about. She took me and my younger brother, Perry, to Sunday school when we were kids. We heard those stories about Jesus' healing and going around doing good deeds. Yeah—" James stopped speaking and mused for a moment. "That little boy who gave his lunch to Jesus, too. I always liked that one. But then we got older, as boys do, and figured we were too old for that kind of stuff. I married your mother, and we settled down to make our own life. Then the war came and interrupted everything. When Perry and I both went off to fight, and he didn't come back, it killed my mother. She lived long enough to see me again, but a heart attack took her soon after. I have always wondered whether my life would have been any different if she had lived. But knowing how adamant your mother is against Christianity, I doubt it. She just thinks that by doing the best she can, she'll make it. Now, honey, I just wanted to say I am happy for you when you are happy, but take it a little easy on your mother. You know?"

"Yes, Daddy, I do. I don't mean to preach at her or any of you, for that matter. I think you believe that; I just long for you all to know the deep contentment you have with yourself when you are at peace with God."

"Well, don't worry about me. I know I'm a sinner, but a man can't be a man and not sin a little." He chuckled with a sly wink. "I'll take care of myself. And I'm quite sure your mother will do the same. Uh—what I really want to say is, please don't let this be the end. You are still our little girl, and you are welcome at home any time. You will come back often, won't you? And bring that young man around, too. Come to think of it, I haven't been seeing as much of him as we did there for a while. Nothing happened between you, did it?"

"No, maybe it's just that we don't spend as much time in the house. And he phones often." Bonnie did not wish to bring up the subject of the growing estrangement between herself and Hal. Her father's understanding and acceptance were too precious to push too far.

"Daddy, I will be forever grateful to you for all that you and Mother have done for me. You don't think for a minute I could ever forget it was you who found a terrified waif in Europe and gave her all the blessings of life in this country and provided so much love I never missed having a natural set of parents. I hope someday you'll be real proud of me."

"I am already, honey." The car had pulled up before the faded mansion, and James' hand was free to reach over and grasp his daughter's for one wonderful moment.

Miss Travis was at the door to greet them.

"I'm so happy to have your daughter join our household here at the CEF headquarters," she said to James after the introductions. "She is a very lovely girl."

James pulled his shoulders back a trifle farther. "Thank you. Her mother and I heartily agree. We are going to miss her, although the two left at home do a mighty good job of filling up our apartment."

"Now you just make yourself at home and be sure to let us know down here if you need anything, Bonnie."

"Will do, Miss Travis. Now I think we had better get busy toting all that stuff up the stairs."

The stairs began to get longer. James and Bonnie both carried as much in each trip as they possibly could, but they found that repeated hikes to the third floor of that tall building approached being mountainous. Finally, the last box found its way to the little closet in the corner, and it was time for James to leave. Bonnie followed him to the door and watched as he prepared to descend the stairs for the last time. Turning to face her, he gazed long and tenderly into her face. She knew intuitively that he was seeing a tiny, wretched form crouched in a dirty crib in a half-bombed-out foundling home in Reims, France. And he was witnessing the product of his love and attention leave the sheltering protection he had provided for nearly fifteen years. She understood he was leaving a part of himself in that little room on the third floor of an old mansion. Stepping quickly to him, she threw her arms about him and, choking back the unbidden tears, said as clearly as she could, "I love you, Daddy. Thanks again." He returned her embrace silently, turned quickly, and strode down the stairs.

She watched as the dear figure, shoulders rather drooping now, disappeared around the bannister on the second floor. Resolutely she took the couple of steps back into the room and closed the door behind her. She immediately found herself enveloped in the most desolate loneliness she had known in her waking hours. Only in the dream had she experienced anything that approached the emotion of this moment.

"Father." She looked upward. "Help me now." She felt compelled to find her little white Bible. It took several seconds to remember where in her luggage she had packed it. But finally locating it, she seated herself by the lamp, laid the Bible in her lap, and opened it randomly. Looking down, her eyes fell on the words, "And every one that hath forsaken houses, or brethren, or sisters, or father, or mother, or wife, or children, or lands, for my name's sake, shall receive an hundredfold, and shall inherit everlasting life."

"Thank you, Father," she breathed fervently. Wiping

the tears from her eyes, she looked for her nightie. That night she went to sleep with the most profound sense of peace she had known yet.

Since the night Bonnie had first found the little white Bible in the bottom of the trunk, she had been possessed with a desire to learn her natural parents' identity. She had so completely become part of the Lake family as a child that she wasn't really aware of the meaning in her mother's words when she told friends her family was adopted. But after that eventful discovery, she found she increasingly desired to find her "real" family. Were they still living? Was her natural mother pretty? Did she herself resemble her father? What was their station in life? If by some miracle she could ever locate them, would they accept her as their own flesh and blood? Or having once given her up for adoption, would they disclaim her forever? And why had they ever relinquished their relationship to her?

She had alternated for weeks between feeling bitter grief, thinking her natural mother must not have loved her, and remorse, believing she had been loved but given up because her mother was not able for one reason or another to keep her. What pain had her mother known when she had made the agonizing decision, and what had been the circumstances surrounding that event? Knowing adoption records were sealed forever, she agonized many hours over the certainty that her questions would never be answered.

Then had come the dreadful disclosure on that April Saturday. She had staggered under the crushing blow for days. A war orphan? A refugee from Hungary? Was she to be totally nameless forever? One more statistic from the most horrible brutalities the world had ever known? One more slip of flotsam cast up on the beach of wretched humanity from a seething whirlpool of devastation and carnage?

When she eventually recovered from her initial shock, Bonnie was at last able to perceive the situation more objectively. No doubt her entire family had met death at the bloody hands of the Nazis. They could well be lying in unmarked graves in some forgotten field now behind the Iron Curtain. Perhaps their bodies had never been recovered from beneath the rubble of their little cottage, or some magnificent structure in the lovely city of Budapest. Yet there was the remotest, breath-taking chance that her family lived and searched for her. She scarcely dared to permit herself so dizzying a thought.

Bonnie became consumed with trying to piece together the events that probably surrounded her early years. Avonelle told her she was about six years old when the war ended. That meant she had experienced most or all of the hostilities. In what sort of a nation had her family been living, and what possible fate would have befallen them? When she expended her utmost effort, she could remember absolutely nothing.

She was gratified to learn that the Carnegie Library was near her new residence. She walked over one evening and checked out several books on Hungarian history from the period directly preceding and through the duration of the war. They evoked not the slightest stirrings of a memory. She began to spend Saturday afternoons in the library perusing every book she could find on the war period in Europe. If she could remember nothing of Hungary, surely there must be some faint recollection of France. But nothing on the pages spoke to her of the countryside or any urban settings anywhere. With considerable effort, she was at last able to resurrect some image of a gray, enclosed space with shadowy figures moving about and occasionally coming close enough to take on a semblance of real, though unfamiliar, humanity. That must have been the orphanage, although she realized now she had suppressed any memory she might have retained of it. Would that grayness lingering in her shrouded memory also account for her present longing for vibrant, bright colors?

She spent many a balmy, summer evening walking the tree-shaded streets of the North Side. On one such hike, she discovered a little out-of-the-way park that covered only about half a block, somewhere in the vicinity of the planetarium. It contained little but a few shrubs, a drinking fountain, a bird bath, and a flower plot. There were benches to sit on and relax and grass underfoot. Bonnie thought of it as an oasis in the heart of an active community and loved to sit and commune with her Lord. She soon began to stop along the way and purchase bags of popcorn and peanuts to feed to the pigeons that shared her delight in the little park. And here as she gathered a little flock around her, she would try again to dredge her memory's depths for any clue to her early years. As she encouraged her memory to serve her, the picture of the orphanage gradually took more definite shape. However, she never could recall anything but the inside walls, and before that period of her life, nothing. She couldn't even remember her passage to the United States with the man who was to become her beloved father.

It was on her return from one of her evening strolls that she stopped on the first floor to talk with Miss Travis and the girls of the staff.

"This is a pleasant evening after the heat of the afternoon," Miss Travis greeted her.

"It certainly is. The auto shop gets pretty hot, and I do enjoy getting out when the sun is going down. On a day like this, it is good to be alive."

"Bonnie, you know I told you once I have no intention of pressuring you in any way, but we do have urgent need of another teacher up in Beaver County, and I'm going to ask you to give it prayerful consideration. A young lady with your love for the Lord surely could find some place in His vineyard. Please ask Him what He would have you to do."

"I promise you I will, although I certainly never thought of myself as being a teacher. I—I just don't know what the Lord may have in mind—" she lowered her eyes as she spoke, and they fell upon an open magazine lying on a table. The words "War Refugees" leaped out at her from part of a title, and she immediately began to scan the page. "Do you mind if I just take this up with me and read this article?"

"Why, of course not. You're welcome to it."

She scarcely waited for the reply. Flying up the stairs, she settled herself by the little lamp and witnessed her world change before her eyes. For in the article, she learned that the Red Cross had been instrumental in reuniting hundreds of families separated by the ravages of the war. She need only enter her personal record with the thousands upon thousands of those already recorded, and the greater chances were that in time she could learn the location of her natural parents, or at least be assured they had not survived. Knowing the worst was infinitely better than knowing nothing. A tremendous surge of hope flooded her, and overwhelming excitement rose within as she realized for the first time that hundreds of others shared her plight, yet still realized their dreams. Could it really be possible? She scarcely permitted herself to hope.

She sat up late that night planning her course of action. The first problem she would encounter would be that of approaching the Red Cross for help without Avonelle's knowledge, for the latter spent many hours every week working for the organization. Bonnie could vividly imagine the pain and grief her mother would display if she ever learned her daughter was searching for her natural mother. Avonelle would consider that the ultimate insult.

"It wasn't enough that you don't even appreciate all the sacrifices we have made for you," Bonnie could imagine her mother saying. "Now you have to go and find your 'real' mother! What do you think I am, some kind of imposter?"

Bonnie's heart ached to even think of Avonelle's reaction. Her mother would never understand, no matter how desperately she would try to explain. There was nothing to do except file what little she knew of her personal history without Avonelle's knowledge. And that could prove rather difficult. For everyone at the Red Cross headquarters knew Mrs. Lake, and anyone receiving Bonnie's inquiry would immediately inform Avonelle that her daughter had placed it with them. She toyed with asking them to swear to secrecy, but dismissed it immediately. That would cast suspicion that could never be explained away. There would be nothing to do but go to another town and fill out the necessary papers. New Castle was perhaps far enough away that there would be no communication between the two offices. A few moments' reflection, however, discouraged that approach. With Pittsburgh's being the largest Red Cross headquarters in that area of the state, she could reasonably assume that any such inquiries would pass through that office. It might or might not be so; in any event, she could not take the chance. There was but one course of action left.

Assuming that an agency that offered a particular type of service would probably know of others offering the same, she would phone the Red Cross anonymously and ask. When she finally turned out the light at nearly one o'clock, she found herself unable to sleep. So great were her anticipation and excitement that the first streak of dawn was breaking through the draperies before she finally quit tossing and could sink into a light slumber.

Her heart skipped that day when she phoned from the shop and learned that the Salvation Army too was engaged in the same task with approximately the same degree of success. All she would have to do would be to stop at their Citadel on the Boulevard of the Allies and write out her advertisement, which they would then include in their publication, the *War Cry*. It would only cost a dollar. She had had no idea it would be so easy. She would ask Vito if she could leave an hour early that very afternoon to be sure to be there before the office closed.

"And this is all that you know of your past?" the officer for the Missing Persons Bureau asked. "Do you have absolutely no recollection what your name might have been?"

"None whatsoever."

"You realize, of course, that usually we have at least a surname to go on. It will be extremely difficult to try to trace the identity of a person on only the sex and approximate age. There would naturally be hundreds of little girls in Europe during those years. And you are not even sure of your age?"

Bonnie felt again that sinking feeling of being positively no one but a nameless, even faceless, blob rising to the surface of the scum of castoff humanity.

"No, ma'am," she replied weakly. "My adoptive mother believes I was about six _in_ 1945. That would mean I must have been born somewhere around 1939 or 40. But that is all I know of my past."

"I see. That means you probably lived throughout the entire action of the war. It is hard to tell how early you may have been separated from your family." The interrogator stopped abruptly and looked at Bonnie with a fleeting expression of pain. "I hesitate to tell you this, but I think it only fair to you to remind you that we have many cases of youngsters who were the result of rape by

200

the plundering soldiers. Their mothers were simple village girls who abandoned their babies immediately upon birth, not wishing to be reminded of the ignominy they had experienced at the hands of Nazis. And the babies—never were even given a name." She had lowered her voice, knowing the sickening impact her words would have on the young girl before her. Waiting a moment until Bonnie could adjust to this new painful possibility, she continued, "I'm sorry to have to paint such a disparaging picture. But I think it better that you be aware of the odds against your success in this search, rather than have you leave with an unrealistic expectation. I assure you the Salvation Army will do everything possible to try to locate any news of your people. But do not expect instant results. It sometimes takes years. And if the first inquiry is fruitless, we'll try again. But you can be sure we will contact you immediately when we learn anything concrete."

"Thank you very much." The spring was missing from Bonnie's step as she turned to leave the building. Her excitement had certainly been short-lived.

13

"Her name is Nancy Luck," Barbara was saying one night on the way home from youth meeting. "She is a friend of a cousin of mine, and lives in Butler. She graduated from nurses' training at Presbyterian Hospital last year and has been working at the Allegheny Hospital ever since. She goes home on her days off, but lives in the nurses' residence while on duty. The other nurses are fine people, of course, but Nancy misses fellowship with other Christians and is looking for another place to stay in the city. My cousin asked if I would know of anything suitable. Naturally I thought of the CEF headquarters. I'm going to bring her around on Saturday to look at that other room on the second floor. That is, unless they have it rented by now."

"No, it's been empty ever since I moved in. Be sure to come up and fetch me while you are there. Hal and I had planned to drive up to McConnells Mill in the afternoon, but I'll be sure to be here when you come."

"We'll make it morning then, before you get started."

Bonnie liked Nancy immediately. She thought she was the cutest little redhead she had ever seen when she appeared at her door with Barbara. Bonnie first looked straight over the mop of bouncy curls before realizing she would have to lower her gaze to avoid missing all of Nancy's four feet eleven inches. But what size Nancy could muster was solidly packed with vivacity. Her giggle was infectious, and if there was nothing at hand to laugh at, she could improvise instantly.

Nancy, with her own floral patterned drapes and spreads, was not the least daunted by the second floor room's lack of color. She took it on sight, and the three young women proceeded to the nurses' residence to load Nancy's luggage into Barbara's little sports car. They laughed their way up to the room until the last load had been deposited in front of the creaky dresser. At least they had only half as far as Bonnie had had to carry it.

"And one and a half times as many people to do the lugging," Bonnie finished in comparing the two tasks.

"I'm the half," Nancy declared, pulling herself up to her full height.

"Since you seem to be beside yourself with joy, there is enough of you to make one whole," Barbara smiled. She too had only just met Nancy. "You will have to join our college and career group at the church when you're not on duty. Bonnie has been with us only a few months, and I'm sure will verify that we have a wonderful bunch of young folks and a marvelous time together."

"Let's go up to my room to get a cup of tea while we talk about it," offered Bonnie.

Once on the next floor, Bonnie observed it was time for lunch and soon had put together some ham and swiss cheese sandwiches. Nancy declared that a campaign was not necessary to convince her their youth group was the place for her. She would be only too happy to worship with her new friends. The little party soon broke up by Hal's arrival.

In the days ahead, Bonnie learned more than ever before about the Lord's promise to replace her family with His own. Nancy became closer to her than her own sister ever had been. They were soon shopping together, sharing devotions occasionally, and taking all their meals together when they were both there. When

Nancy worked the seven to four shift, she was able to have the evening meal prepared by the time Bonnie got home from the garage. And Bonnie returned the favor with a hot meal when Nancy was relieved from the four to eleven shift.

Nancy had grown up in a Christian home and possessed what Bonnie felt was a knowledge of spiritual things far superior to hers. Furthermore, she proved to be a capable teacher, and Bonnie blossomed under the privilege of having someone close at hand to explain difficult passages with obscure meanings from the Bible. Nancy also was familiar with various books that were helps to reading the Bible. Bonnie purchased them upon her suggestions and delighted in her increasing understanding.

And when their more serious moments ended, Nancy's zany wit precluded any possible boredom. Bonnie was soon calling her "Plucky Lucky," a name she believed far more befitting a pint-sized dynamo. Bonnie had not even thought to ask her what department she worked in until the night she came home nearly rolling in laughter.

"You'd never guess what happened today, Bonnie. A woman who has seven daughters finally delivered a boy. When she was told she had a son, she replied, "But I can't afford a boy!""

From that time on, Nancy regaled Bonnie with anecdotes from her duty in the delivery room. If an experience wasn't especially hilarious, she always managed to make it sound humorous enough to be interesting. And Bonnie could only marvel at a person who was always able to lift the trivial things of life from the mundane and change an occupation into an exciting adventure.

They both regretted that Nancy was not free to attend the Thursday evening meetings of the youth group except once every three weeks, due to her shift work. But she was an immediate hit with the group and a most welcome addition when she was there. The very first time she attended she confided later to Bonnie that Dave Fisher had asked for a date.

"With you?" Bonnie asked in surprise. "I understood he was more or less spoken for by Luanne."

"It must be less then, because he certainly did ask. Of course, I told him I'm not free to accept because of Gilbert. I'm expecting him to ask the question any time now, and I know what I'm going to say. I hope he comes here soon so you can meet him, but it's hard for him to get away from the church in Butler. I'm rather confined to seeing him only when I go home."

"I know you told me, but I can't remember: Is he the pastor there or the assistant?"

"The assistant for now. Of course, after he's had some experience he hopes to have his own church before long. And he will be a very fine pastor."

"And you will be a fine pastor's wife. I'm so glad for you."

"What about you, Bonnie? Have you given any more thought to the request Miss Travis made of you? I mean about the teaching?"

"Yes, I have, and I can't say I feel any inclination that way at all for the present. I just don't know yet what I expect to do with myself. I still feel so very new in the Christian life. For the time being I need to do some more growing right in my own little garden."

The excitement in the college and career group was nearing feverish pitch by midsummer. All the talk was of the forthcoming retreat at Pineridge Camp. Those who had summer jobs with no vacation were going for the weekend, and those who were free were planning the lists of occupants for each carload, and purchasing new sleeping bags and athletic gear. Nancy had a week of vacation allotted to her, but chose to spend it at home in

Butler to be near Gil. Bonnie asked Vito if she could have the week off, only to be told that he was taking two weeks of vacation himself over that time and her presence was necessary in the shop in his absence. Her heart plunged until she remembered that Barbara had suggested that her husband query some other dentists concerning the possibility of employment as a receptionist.

"You're sure this is what you really want to do?" Dennis asked on the way home from the next Thursday night meeting. "The chances are you would not receive the same salary as you do at the shop."

"I believe that a move to a nice, clean, and quiet little office would be a welcome change from the grease and racket of the garage. With the streetcar tracks being removed by the redevelopment plans, it is becoming harder to make connections clear out to that garage in the far end of Oakland. Soon I won't be able to make connections at all. I just don't know for sure what I'm going to do then. The buses don't seem to be any more convenient than the cars."

"I'll be looking around. Maybe I'll be able to turn up something."

But he was unsuccessful. Several dentists ventured to suggest they might be looking for a girl before winter, but nothing was available at the moment. To her deep regret, Bonnie realized she would not be able to attend the retreat for any but the weekends.

The middle of August found her motoring with the Courtneys to the secluded little pine grove south of Connelsville, in the southwest corner of the state. The day had been hot, humid, and depressing in the city, and the three of them longed for the cool refreshing air of the mountains. Now as they skimmed along, they felt uplifted in spirit as the clear air of the forested areas cheered them.

Bonnie thrilled to feel pine needles underfoot as they made their way down the path to the meeting hall. If she hadn't had the direction of those familiar with the camp, she could have found the hall, anyway, for upon her arrival she was greeted with lusty, rousing singing from the gathering. And she had only to follow the joyous sound to find herself among the fortunate scores who had spent the entire week feasting on the exposition of the Word and the other campers' fellowship. When the singing ended, a young man stood to his feet to expound again on the new birth and the Christian's walk with God. Bonnie alternated between losing herself in the joy of a splendid sermon and feeling somewhat envious of those who had sat many times under the man and the truths that fell from his lips.

When the service ended, Meredith hurried through the crowd to find her and lead her to the bonfire. A different crew every night was engaged to have a monstrous roaring conflagration awaiting the campers at the day's end to ward off the evening chill and provide a setting for song and testimony. The bonfire always proved to be the highlight of the day's activities, as many related the blessings they had received during the day and new decisions made. Bonnie listened rapturously as several told of hearing the "call" to enter the ministry. Two volunteered that the Lord desired them on a foreign field of service. Among those whom she knew from her own church, Reginald Walker, better known as 'Ritmetic, said he felt led to enter the field of music evangelism. And Dominic Pizzuti sparkled with an inner joy as he vowed to live the best Christian life before his neighbors and friends that he possibly could with the help of his Savior.

The elation of the sharing time around the fire evaporated as Bonnie laid her head on the little cot in her cabin. The young people who had spoken so boldly of their intention to follow the Lord in Christian service had declared that they had received a "call." And she began to understand that those who followed Him in a specific occupation designed to reach others with the gospel did so rightly only when they had received a divine commission. It was only then that she comprehended why she had felt no interest in the offer by Miss Travis to teach Good News Clubs. And she understood why Miss Travis herself had not attempted persuasion. One did not attempt any kind of ministry unless he or she was persuaded of the Lord, and she had not received any kind of "call" in that respect.

What of those who had made testimony to the effect they had? How did one go about receiving a "call"? Did you have to be a super-super Christian? Did you have to have a special inside track with the Almighty? Or specific talents to begin with? What kind of people were those whom the Master called to work for Him? The troubling questions did not leave her as she arose the next morning with the first streaks of dawn, bathed in cold mountain stream water, relished a hearty breakfast, and made her way to the early chapel service.

The speaker that morning was a missionary from the Congo. Bonnie had never seen a genuine missionary before and was pleased to learn that the lady looked just like any other middle-aged matron. Nothing but the burning passion in the missionary's heart would have distinguished her from the other ladies Bonnie passed on the street. But as she talked of her work on the remote little mission station in the interior of Africa, Bonnie sensed she had no other purpose in living than to glorify her Lord among those who had never had the chance to hear of His redemption. And as she spoke, Bonnie began to yearn for the opportunity to reach others with the message of the Savior's love as she had heard it and to tell them that Christ had died for them also. She listened with head bowed and soul intent on the needs in other lands among those who had never heard, earnestly desiring that she might be among the company of those who were "called." But when others on the rough-hewn wooden benches around her made their way to the front of the hall to signify their intention to obey the voice of the Master, Bonnie knew that His voice had not spoken to her.

Perhaps she was not living closely enough to Him. Maybe He was trying to speak to her and she was unable to hear. Possibly she just was not possessed of the talents necessary to a laborer in the Kingdom. Her thoughts plagued her all day, through the afternoon's volleyball game, the Bible hour, the evening Singspiration and salvation message, and lastly the bonfire time of sharing. She was beginning to rejoice again in the testimonies of the others who seemed to glow with the joy of their spiritual victories, apart from the flicker of the campfire reflected on their fresh faces. And then one bashful girl said she had thought for some time the Lord wanted her in service for Him, but she had come to understand that He wanted her more than anything else to be the best housewife she possibly could and raise a little family to love and honor Him. Bonnie's heart leaped at her candid words. Could it be that that was what the Lord had in mind for her? Was Hal included in God's plan for her future? She felt a thorn pricking somewhere in her spirit as she thought of Hal. She had asked, even begged him to accompany her on this weekend retreat, but he — far from showing any interest — had even demonstrated some disgust.

"I just wish you would quit asking me to those affairs of yours at that church. Now if you want to go and spend your time with them several times a week, that is quite all right with me. But don't expect me to accompany you. I'm afraid that's where our ways part. I've seen too many people who look so pious on Sunday morning all dressed up like the Easter parade, but just watch them and see what they do the other six days of the week. Until I see some proof there is something to all they claim it to be, I'm not about to waste my time on it. I've got plenty more interesting things to do."

Tears had clouded her eyes as she had kissed him good-bye. Now she wondered whether he might be her mission field. Perhaps if she married him, she could show him "it's what they claim it to be," as he desired to be shown. Maybe that was the very thing God had in mind for her. She would just go home and accept his proposal as she was sure it would come in time, show him God's love as she ministered to him as his wife, and soon he would come to love her Savior as she did. She contented herself with that thought until the next morning's chapel service for women.

The speaker on that occasion was another lady, although not a missionary. As a businesswoman her call was to full commitment to the Lord, regardless of the occupation in which one found oneself. The salesgirl behind the counter, she said, is as much a witness for Him in her occupation as those who give everything they have to go out in His name.

"If those who claim the name of Christ do not exemplify Him before their fellowmen, there is no reason for the unsaved to believe the message that is preached to them by those who are in full-time service," she stated emphatically.

And then she began to talk of the hindrances that people permit to keep them from holy living. Bonnie already had become persuaded that there are places of amusement the Christian should avoid and some activities that do not glorify the risen Christ. But she was unprepared for the speaker's next statement.

"I have known of too many young women who

genuinely desired to follow Jesus in every detail of their lives until a young man came along. Did you know the Bible says we are not to be unequally yoked? If you can picture for a moment two oxen yoked together to plow a field. One desires a drink from the stream at the right of the field, and the other wishes to nibble a little straw to the left. Would either one reach the object of his desire? Or to put it differently, 'Can two walk together unless they be agreed?' Do not be deceived into thinking you will be able to lead him to salvation after you are married, for if he won't serve your Christ before marriage, he certainly won't feel it necessary to bother after he marries you."

The glorious weekend that had begun in such high anticipation for Bonnie now ended in perplexity. As if it weren't enough to have no direction for her future, she now realized her relationship with Hal must come to an end. Her mind clouded, worrying about how she was to tell him.

The first project that faced her upon her return was to break with Hal as gently as she could. The opportunity presented itself the first evening she was home. She answered a knock at her door to see Myra Hayes standing there, rather winded from the climb up the stairs.

"It's that young man who calls for you. He's down in the reception hall. Said he'd wait a moment until you get ready to go out, or I'm to report to him if you don't want to."

"Oh! Well, tell him—tell him I'll be right down. Thank you, Myra."

Hal didn't often call without phoning first, and it was a development she had not anticipated. It would have been so much easier to break the news over the phone where she didn't have to face him. But there was nothing else to do but to get on with it unless she wished to postpone her speech and lead him on for the time being.

She changed into a clean blouse and hurried down the stairs.

"Hi, there, little girl! That mountain air must have done wonders for you."

"Sure thing. You really should have been along, if for nothing else than to get out of the stuffy city for a breather. That is a fantastic place down there. Gorgeous scenery. I believe I'll go every year until I no longer qualify as a young person. Maybe then I can go as a counsellor."

"My dear, you will always be young. Or, if not, then let me grow old with you."

This was not the right moment. He shouldn't have brought that up so soon. She chuckled as he opened the door for her, and they started for his new green convertible. "I suppose our growing old will take place soon enough."

"Tell me, girl o' mine, when your locks are silver gray, are you going to turn them blue as I've seen some women doing?"

She laughed outright. "No bluer than I'll feel for leaving my youth behind. But what a morbid subject. Surely you did something interesting over the weekend. Come on, level with me."

"Watched a couple ball games on television. Washed the car. Ogled the pretty girls on the boulevard." He paused for the effect. She merely raised her eyebrows and grinned mischievously.

"That really does sound exciting. So what else is new?"

"You're impossible. Say, what do you say to a drive up through Riverview Park?"

"Sounds OK to me. I just hope it's cooler out there."

They had strolled hand in hand over the paths as she told him the highlights of the weekend, and finally found a park bench next to a fountain. Bonnie kicked off her dusty sandals and nestled back in Hal's arm. It was beginning to grow dark. They would have to be finding their way back home for the evening, and time was getting on. Somehow she was going to have to find the words to say what she had to say before the evening ended. If only Hal hadn't called for her tonight! Telling him over the phone would have been infinitely easier. He had been so sweet as they had strolled through the park that she was pained at the thought of bringing him grief. Yet she understood he would know greater grief if she were to marry him and take a stand for the Lord that he could not or would not share. It was now or never, for it would only be harder later. Sending up a silent prayer for guidance, she waited for the proper opening. And suddenly she received illumination concerning the course she was to pursue.

"Hal, you know I've been telling you how marvelous a time we had at Pineridge Camp. It would be great if you would join us next summer and get in on some of the blessing yourself. You just can't imagine how thrilling it is to hear those stirring messages, sing with a couple hundred other young folks, and gather around the campfire for a time of sharing the things the Lord has done for us."

"Sounds like the ultimate drag to me." Hal stretched out his long legs, recrossed them, and settled his elbows over the back of the bench. Bonnie was glad he had removed his arm from around her because if she must go on with her speech as she believed it would develop, it would be easier that way.

"It wouldn't be a drag if you could only know the joy you find in it. Living the Christian life is something you just don't comprehend if you don't try it. Let's say it's like—well, I know this is a crude illustration, but if a bird could talk to a snail, just imagine how hard a time he would have trying to explain to the snail how exhilirating it is to fly over the fields and flowers, light in a tree, and see about him for many yards, perhaps miles, and be absolutely free to go anywhere his heart desired. Do you think a snail could comprehend that unless he could come out of his shell, sprout some wings and take flight himself? We are told in the book of Pslams to taste and see that the Lord is good. In other words, you don't know until you have nibbled for yourself."

"Now, look, Bonnie, I thought I made myself clear before when I said that if that's the way you want it, you just go ahead. But count me out. I've got better things to do on a Sunday morning than sit in some stuffy, pious assembly of eggheads and fill my mind with dreaming. I've got to live down on earth where it counts, you know, the rat race and all. It's tough enough getting ahead in this world without being mystical about it. I'll make it on my own wit and hard work. In fact, it looks as though a promotion is in the offing for me right now. I hadn't told you about that yet. Saved it for the right moment. It may bring our future together a little closer." He attempted to reach his arm around her again as he gazed down into her eyes.

But she moved away from him and, taking his hand, lowered his arm into his lap. "Then I'm afraid that this is the point at which I will have to say there won't be any future for us—not together, at any rate. It hurts me to have to say this, but I know now that we simply could not make it together with me going one direction and you another. I have repeatedly tried to get you to accompany me to church and to share in the joy I find in knowing the Lord. But if your final word is that you will not, then I must make my final word no, also. I am truly sorry, Hal, but I don't see any way it can work."

"Oh, so you're telling me I'm not good enough for you now that you have these exalted ideas in your head? I've known many cases where the wife dutifully trotted off to church on a Sunday morning while the old man snoozed, and their marriages weren't any worse than any other." He paused for a moment, then continued, "Maybe that's because she wasn't preaching at him all the time."

"I am really sorry, Hal, but I don't believe there's anything more to say. I want you to know I appreciate all the good times we have had together, and I will certainly think nothing of you but the best. But I believe it is better if we don't see each other anymore."

"Very well, then. Have it your way." Hal shook his head detachedly as he arose from the bench.

In retrospect, Bonnie recognized that her first problem had been resolved far more painlessly than she realized at the time, for having stated her position and ending all contact with Hal, she found a release of her spirit that indicated she had been more burdened by her relationship with him than she had realized. She now felt a sense of freedom as though some new vista were about to open.

When she went to the first meeting of the youth upon their return from the retreat, others gave testimony to God's call upon their lives. Ron Walker, otherwise known as Readin', said he at last had peace concerning his life's direction. He was now sure the Lord would have him to be a professor in a Bible college.

And Reg Walker caused considerable ripple when he rose to his feet, pulling Luanne Marks with him. Standing with her hand in his, he said, "I believe some of you already heard me say I am to enter a ministry of music evangelism. I would like to declare before you all that Luanne has also heard the commission to use her magnificent voice for the Lord, and we feel that since we are both going in the same direction, we by all rights ought to go together."

A chorus of "oh's" and "ah's" rose from their friends as Luanne stood by Reg's side blushing, and he slipped an arm around her to receive the chorus of congratulations that came from several.

"You sure pulled a fast one on us that time, old buddy," exclaimed Keith Holcomb, who had had some designs on Luanne himself.

"Let's have a party to celebrate," rose from Ruth Konevich and Lucy Arnold simultaneously.

"Do you think Royle, you can paint your own brother for one of those gorgeous backdrops that you do for that kind of affair?" asked Dominic.

"Why, I'll just paint myself and see if *I* can pull that one off."

"Fat chance," rebuffed his proud brother.

Amidst much mirth, the group finally grew serious again and returned to the business at hand. Lucy Arnold rose to say her employment had kept her from the blessings of the retreat, but that the Lord had made up the lack to her by leading her into a deeper trust in His workings in her life.

"I began to understand," she was saying, "what is meant by that verse that says, 'In all thy ways acknowledge Him, and He shall direct thy paths.' We so often fail to see Him in the trivial things of life, and especially the hard things. We think if He were really in those, He would eliminate them. But that is not His way. He goes through them with us and makes smooth the path for our feet. Then as we recognize He is in the shadows as much as in the light, only then He is released to work out more of His will in us. It is a glorious thought when you really begin to grasp it, but unfortunately it takes an awful long time for some of us to get it."

The meeting ended on a joyous note, and Bonnie's heart wanted to sing. But her burden only grew heavier. Did the Lord have nothing for her but a greasy little car repair shop on a back street in Oakland? Had she no talents at all? Was there no place in this wide world where she could labor for Him?

She stopped on the first floor one evening after work to seek out Miss Travis.

"I have given much consideration to the possibility of my being a teacher for Child Evangelism. I want you to know that I would be most happy in such work if I could feel it was the Lord's choice for me. But I'm sure now it is not, and you must be free to look elsewhere for someone to fill the post."

"Thank you for speaking to me about it." Miss Travis never looked more kindly nor dignified. "Dear—don't give up. I'm sure He has something in mind for you."

Now why had she said that? Bonnie had not confided anything to her of the turmoil in her heart. Sometimes other Christians just seemed to be too astute.

But she still was not satisfied. When was she ever going to find what was to be required of her? There was only one thing to do. Pastor Thomas had answered her muddled questions so fully and lovingly at the time of her conversion that he surely would be able to help now. She would just go to see him on the next Saturday afternoon.

"I'm sure this sounds very elementary, Pastor Thomas," she began as they seated themselves comfortably on the leather upholstered furnishings of his study, "but I would like to know how it is one receives what you term a 'call' to the service of the Lord. So many of our group are now entering some type of active ministry, or maybe just going off to Bible school, with the expectation that something will develop later. I have searched my heart and hoped for some light to dawn for me, but it just isn't coming. Is it that I'm not in the place where I could hear His voice if He spoke, or is there nothing for me? Just how do you get this 'call'?"

"Now in the first place, Bonnie, for the child of God, there is no possibility that there is nothing for him or her, for God has a definite plan for each life. It may be nothing spectacular as others see it, but our times are in His hands. If you are specifically looking for God's will in your life, the best thing to do is to stay put until you feel definite leading. Usually when we become Christians our lives' outward circumstances don't change drastically. Where we live, what we do for occupation, and so forth remain the same. We may ask whether He has anything better for us and begin to knock on a few doors to see whether any of them open.

"Now, as far as a specific call is concerned, it says in First Corinthians twelve that He gives to each of us as He wills, which means the calling is His prerogative; we are only servants to do His bidding. And He alone chooses the servants. Without His Spirit's enabling us, we are not capable to carry on His work. In many, many cases the work is trying and outright discouraging. If we didn't have that assurance of His call, we wouldn't have the courage to continue.

"There is no sorrier spectacle in all the Kingdom than the young man or woman who goes out on his own steam to engage in some form of ministry, because personally generated steam, no matter how zealous, doesn't replace the genuine anointing of God's spirit."

"I see." Bonnie was relieved. "You mean then, that I really don't need to be worried about it, because if He wanted to lead me in any specific direction, He would make it known to me apart from my pestering Him about it?"

"Exactly. Many people have found that His call came at a time when they were already profitably or comfortably occupied, before they had given much thought to any claim He might have upon their lives. The main thing is to be ready if and when He does call. In the meantime, stand by. Here, let me read further in that chapter in First Corinthians."

Pastor Thomas reached for his Bible and quickly flipped some pages to the twelfth chapter, verse 28: " 'And God hath set some in the church, first apostles, secondarily prophets, thirdly teachers, after that miracles, then gifts of healings, helps, governments, diversities of tongues.' Did you notice, Sister Bonnie, that list of gifts includes the little work 'helps'? Now that is something each and every child of God can do, right where he is at any time. And even without a specific call. If we look about us, we can always find someone we can help, maybe offer a simple word of encouragement or even just a smile when others are feeling low. This Kingdom is based on love. If you don't show some of that to your fellowman, there is no gospel message to preach to them anyway. Remember, Christ has no hands on earth but ours through which to show His love."

The word "love" met a ready response in Bonnie's heart. For she well remembered it was through recognizing that same great love that she herself found the Lord Jesus Christ. Naturally, there was no other way to reach people with the gospel message. Love is the one principle unique to Christianity, setting it above every religion on earth.

"I'm so grateful for your patiently trying to get something into my dull head," she began hesitantly.

"Not at all," he interjected quickly.

"I'll certainly take this seriously. And by the Lord's grace and with His help I'll try to show His love to anyone and on every occasion in any way I possibly can."

"That's fine. Very fine. And now could we have a word of prayer before you go?" Pastor Thomas laid a hand upon her shoulder and, lifting his voice heavenward, pronounced what seemed to her a benediction upon her life.

"Our most loving Father, You have seen and heard the declaration of Your servant, Bonnie. And now we ask Thee to seal this testimony forever upon her life and use her in any way You may see fit, to further the cause of Your Kingdom and demonstrate the power of Your love here on earth. Amen."

14

With extreme reluctance Bonnie watched the flowers fade and the days become shorter, knowing that time could not be turned back. For although she was determined not to let the memories of the past winter haunt her, she still never welcomed the thought of an oncoming winter, especially when she faced the prospect of long, icy walks to reach the auto shop and hours perched atop the little heater that blew fuses when the coffee pot was plugged in. She hoped this year's weather would be more gentle than last year.

But there was no future in merely hoping. Remembering that Pastor Thomas had told her we can seek the Lord's will by looking for opportunities to improve our circumstances, she turned her thoughts once more to a better job. She shrank at the thought of pavement-pounding for interviews again, and determined that the best place to begin was merely to ask Dennis whether any of his fellow dentists were looking for a receptionist.

"Sure thing," he responded over the phone. "A friend just let me in on it a couple days ago, and I meant to pass it on next time I saw you. He's only a few blocks from you. You should be able to walk it without any difficulty. Name's Gardner, on Federal Street. I'll tell him you're coming by to talk to him."

"Great! I surely do hope it works out."

And work out it did. Dr. Gardner was a congenial

man, young enough to be abreast of new developments in his field, and not old enough that she feared the job would not be permanent. The office was small and quiet. However, the salary was not handsome. At least, it would pay rent and supply some choice morsels for the meals she shared with Nancy. Furthermore, she could save carfare, and for now she could postpone her ambition to own an auto of her own. For the time being, she was learning to live one day at a time, depending on her heavenly Father for guidance and to supply all her needs. One unexpected bonus was that she could still wear all those lovely little suits and dresses she had purchased the year before while she was still with Paramount Plastics. The styles had taken their drastic turn a couple years before when the fitted waistlines and wide long skirts had gone out, so although her wardrobe was not the very latest, it still reflected current trends. And joy of all joys, the little office would be comfortably heated in the winter!

Vito's face reflected a collage of mild anger, regret, and despair when Bonnie informed him she was soon to leave his employ. But she hastened to assure him she was looking for more comfortable working conditions and never expected to find an employer who would treat her more justly than he had. She was also prepared to propose for his consideration as a possible replacement for her Eloise Baldwin. Eloise was a new high school graduate who lived in the vicinity of the garage and was a member of the youth group. Vito was only too happy to interview Eloise, and she quickly found herself absorbed into the position as unceremoniously as Bonnie had been.

Training Eloise was a pleasure, and fortunately she had come equipped with a ready-made driver's license! Bonnie would have regretted seeing poor Jeb have to teach another. She never did divulge some of the hairy moments to which she herself had subjected him in her lessons. Those were secrets to be locked between them forever.

Of the three men, Jeb was the one Bonnie would miss most. On her last day, he shyly brought a lovely cake his wife had baked for the occasion and treated all to cokes. Tears sparkled from both his and Bonnie's eyes as he shook her hand to wish her a pleasant road ahead. And she in turn thanked him for all the kindness he had shown her. Then she bade farewell to Vito and Nino and hastened down the street, not trusting herself to a backward glance.

Bonnie enjoyed meeting and exchanging casual chitchat with the varied array of patients who patronized her new office. They kept her from being lonely at her post behind the little window. And some who made more frequent appearances began to seem like personal friends.

At home in the evenings she felt as though she could communicate more understandably with Nancy, who also worked with patients. They began to exchange more anecdotes concerning the pathetic as well as the humorous side to the patients they saw each day.

The news on the home front when Bonnie made her usual Sunday afternoon visits was that a new swim coach had been hired at Oakland High, and Sylvia was floating on air as well as on water. For it appeared that in addition to being just out of college, he was extremely handsome. Though he was not large in stature, everything was put in the correct place, right down to the last rippling muscles over his broad chest. His hair also rippled, in black waves that insisted on constantly falling in a recalcitrant ringlet over one eye. The sardonic grin played about the corners of his sensuous mouth, and a gleam sparkled from jet eyes and reflected from the deep dimples in his cheeks. Bonnie suspected that if Sylvia had been honest with herself, she would have had to admit she secretly feared she would not place in the competition again this year. To be a winner, one had to concentrate on the swimming rather than on the coach. The best was that the new chap, Dewey McMillen by name, also seemed to realize Sylvia was more than a good swimmer. As an instructor, he feared to make any overt moves toward a young student, but his manner with her indicated she would not always be his student. Sylvia could only dream and hope. And hope she did.

Elsewhere, the return of the school term meant other changes. Some faces disappeared from the youth group, but new ones replaced them. Ron Walker, forever the Readin' member of the debonair trio, was now enrolled in seminary in a distant state. Ruth Konevich had gone to Florida to a school for airline hostesses. And Dominic found employment as a custodian in a state institution some miles away. Of the three, it appeared Dominic would be the most missed. His radiant smile simply could not be replaced.

Among the students new to the city who found their way to Emmanuel Temple, the one who attracted the most curiosity showed up on a Thursday evening with Drew Anderson. Drew lost no time in introducing him all around as Buz Rockwell, a high school friend from back home in Harrisburg who was transferring to Carnegie Tech for his graduate study. A twitter followed them behind their backs, particularly among the younger girls, as Drew led the way through the group. Buz's crewcut tended to give him added height, but it still was not enough to make him appear even average. His most prominent feature was a crooked scar remaining from a poor reconstruction job of a harelip. When he spoke, his voice resonated with a nasal quality that revealed the cleft palate.

Bonnie heard the snide remarks even before she met

Buz, and she was determined to go out of her way to extend to the newcomer the hand of fellowship.

"I want you to meet my pal, here, Bonnie." Drew soon told her. "Buz, this is Bonnie Lake."

"I'm so glad you will be a part of our group." Bonnie extended her warmest greeting. "I haven't been here long myself, but I can assure you each person who ventures within this fold is immediately one of the flock. I hope you feel at home with us."

The crooked mouth flashed into a wide, boyish grin. "Thanks a lot. I'm sure I will if you are an average specimen of the breed."

"Let me introduce my almost-roommate. Nancy—" Bonnie turned to attract Nancy's attention. "Nancy, this is Buz—what did you say your last name is?"

"Rockwell. Well, if it isn't rock, it sure is hard." The four laughed giddily.

"I wouldn't say that was so hard; it should be easy now. I love your name," replied Nancy. "Sounds so romantic. You're not related to the great artist by any chance, are you?"

"Not that I know of. He would certainly never admit it if I were."

"You never can be sure," Bonnie demurred. "Come talk to us again after you've met everyone."

"Thanks. I will."

But the service began before Drew and Buz had completed the rounds. And when it was over, the Courtneys needed to make a hurried departure so Bonnie and Nancy, in order to have a ride home from the church, did not speak to Buz again that evening.

The next Thursday was designated for the social of the month. Plans were made to celebrate the engagement of Reg and Luanne. Luanne had taken the job of church secretary to wait out Reg's final semester of his graduate course in music, and they planned a Christmas Eve wedding.

"We used to celebrate the birthdays every month," Meredith explained on one of her frequent visits to Bonnie's and Nancy's apartments. "But as the group grew, the birthdays became too numerous. It took half the evening just to read the list of names. Well—almost. So we narrowed it down to just engagements and goings away. But just wait until one of the gang gets married and see what a bash we stage for the occasion! We send 'em off in fine style."

Bonnie eagerly awaited the opportunity to observe such a "bash," and even though there were four months until the grand happening, she was now to witness the preliminaries. She understood that such an event was little more than honorable mention and an appropriately inscribed cake with fancy napkins at the usual monthly social; however if there were time, Ritin' of the Walker three would paint the large, nearly life-size picture of a couple, resembling the genuine pair as nearly as possible, and using a suitable background. The painting would then be hung again at the wedding reception.

Luanne had eagerly corraled her future brother-in-law with detailed instructions for her design. The couple were to be posed before a silver bell, befitting the Christmas season, golden notes of music were to adorn the bell, and the girl's gown was to be cranberry red. With considerable difficulty, Royle resisted the urge to paint himself in the position of the bridegroom-to-be, and the features more nearly represented his older brother. With Luanne's natural beauty, her likeness was a pleasure to paint. And the lovely sight that greeted the gang upon arrival at the social was proclaimed by all around to be Royle's masterpiece.

Bonnie and Nancy were giving it an appreciative look when Drew and Buz approached.

"Hi!" they all greeted one another.

"It's great to see you back." Bonnie beamed at Buz.

She still felt the sting of some of the others' cruel words.

"Thank you, my lovely lady," Buz bowed ceremoniously if somewhat stiffly toward the picture.

Bonnie nudged his elbow. "Here. Here I am, you short-sighted nut. None but a hoot owl in broad daylight could make a mistake like that."

"Mistaken yourself, my fair one. Whatever my other disabilities may be, short-sightedness isn't one of them."

Oh, no, she groaned to herself, *he must think I'm trying to call attention to his harelip.* Aloud she said as sweetly as she could, "You don't impress me as being disabled in any manner. I presume you have licked many a fire-belching dragon in your brilliant career."

"Ah, yes. If you will be so kind as to visit the punch table with me, I will divulge some of my more remarkable feats for your approval."

Bonnie turned to make a courteous break from Nancy, discovering that Drew had already made himself lost, and caught a wicked gleam dancing from the corner of Nancy's eye. Then with one lifted brow, Nancy turned unobtrusively and faded into the crowd.

"Now, then, let's take canoeing for starters. Been practicing on the old Susquehanna since I was a stripling. It's pretty wild in some places. I figure I'm about in shape to try my hand at rubber rafting some white waters. Did you know there are a number of such sites about this fair and diverse state of ours?"

"Why, no, I didn't. But then, I've barely begun to explore our lovely land. I haven't been much farther out of Pittsburgh than to the summer retreat at Pineridge Camp."

"That place down near Connellsville? Drew was telling me about it. That area is one excellent location for white water."

"Now that I think of it, I did notice the stream that ran by the camp was pretty rough."

"I should say. It isn't too far from there that you sign out upon leaving and they go searching for the remains if you don't come back soon."

"You don't mean it! I didn't realize it was really that serious."

"I think there must be a lot of living that you have yet to experience outside of this city. I'll have to make it my personal project to see that you receive the proper initiation. And now then, for the second dragon. By the way, what would you do if you encountered a real dragon?"

"I'd finish reading the story."

He shook his head as though it were an impossible situation.

"Well, I've done a little stock car racing," he finally continued, "although I was younger then—when I was more foolhardy. I look on that type of activity now as irresponsibility, to our Maker, that is. Irresponsible for the fine physical equipment He has given us. And lack of regard for the gift of life."

Buz drained his first glass of punch and poured himself another. Bonnie had scarcely touched hers, so he led her away from the table without offering to refill it. Pulling two chairs to a spot near the coat rack, he motioned for her to sit down. But he had not seated himself before someone began singing, "Congratulations to You," to the happy birthday tune. He remained standing as Bonnie stood to join the others in song. Reg stepped forward with Luanne's hand in his to acknowledge his appreciation, and then gazed deeply at her as his friends sang to her "Best Wishes to You."

Amidst the applause that followed were cries of "speech, speech." Hesitating only a moment, Reg cleared his throat and began,

"Ladies and gentlemen, brothers and sisters all, I believe that Luanne and I have already declared our most solemn intentions before you. There is nothing to add except to reiterate that we feel honored to serve our Lord together in any way He sees fit."

"How about a song, Luanne?" someone called from the group.

"Yeah, how about it?" from another.

Seeing that resistance was useless, the two honorees conferred a moment and made their way toward the piano. In her clear, lyric soprano Luanne lifted her voice, trembling only momentarily, in the fine old gospel song, "Where He Leads Me I Will Follow." On the second verse, Reg amazed everyone by joining her in harmony, and together they changed the singular pronoun to the plural. By the time they reached the end of the touching rendition, scarcely an eye was dry in the little fellowship hall.

Dr. Dennis Courtney stepped forward and declared, "I think that following a testimony such as that, it is only fitting that a dedicatory prayer be lifted on their behalf. May we bow every head, please.

"Our Father, who is in heaven and here in our midst, we thank Thee for the talents with which You have blessed Your servants, Luanne and Reg. We ask that through them multitudes of others will also be blessed, and may many souls be born into Your Kingdom through their testimony as they minister for You. Direct every event and detail of their lives as we commit them to You for Your service. In the name of Jesus. Amen."

An echoing "Amen" rose from the assembled young folks, and the solemnity of the moment resolved into resumed merriment.

"I don't know when I've heard such a beautiful duet," Buz murmured as he and Bonnie seated themselves in the chairs he had arranged.

"No, I don't, either. And to think Reg didn't even disclose the secret that he can also sing until just now. He has always shone primarily as a pianist."

"I guess maybe it's falling in love that makes a guy want to sing. I may try it myself sometime."

"I surely hope your opportunity will come," Bonnie replied fervently.

"It may come sooner than you expect." The quick response and the intent look he gave her made her want to change the subject abruptly.

"Is Buz is your real name? If not, what is it?"

"Well, a bee got into the delivery room on that morning back in 1937, and the attendants thought my mother, in her groggy, weakened state, was trying to tell them the new baby's name. So that is what went on the records."

"Now, Mr. Rockwell, I'm beginning to think I may never know when I can believe a thing you say. But that story certainly tops any Nancy comes home with. Now what is the truth?"

"OK, I give. My true name is Nathaniel Gibson Rockwell. Nathaniel from father's father, Gibson from mother's father. Why do they call me 'Buz'? Well, it seems that I had quite a time of it to learn to talk so that I could be understood. The other kids, neighbors, cousins, et cetera, just dubbed me Buz to describe the way I sounded to them. Right? Right!"

Oh, I've really done it now, Bonnie reprimanded herself, wishing desperately she could take back the cruel question.

"Sorry I asked. It was very rude of me."

"Not at all. In fact, it's quite all right. Some people have one type of imperfection, everyone else another. It just happens that mine is more obvious than some. But I've learned to accept it as God's choice for me. Perhaps I need it to keep me humble." He finished with that broad grin playing about the corners of his mouth.

"I can't believe you need it to keep you humble. But it's wonderful that you accept it as part of God's plan for your life."

"Is there any other way to look at it?"

"No, I guess not. For a trusting Christian. Look, they're serving the cake now. You stay right here, and I'll bring you a piece."

Buz sought her at each of the next few meetings to sit and talk with her. Soon the gang began to plan their October social, traditionally one of the highlights of the year. It was set on a Saturday rather than Thursday and was planned to coincide with the long weekend that many college students took at mid-semester. It offered them a breather after their grueling studies and gave the others the opportunity to enjoy their fellowship again.

The decorations rivaled the fall show at the conservatory. A large shock of corn was brought in from a farm out in the country to grace the corner by the fireplace, and pumpkins, squashes, and fall fruits and flowers adorned the floor, tables, mantle, and any other convenient spot. The refreshment committee had no trouble deciding what to serve, as cider and doughnuts were always in order. The committee's only problem was securing enough to last the evening!

Bonnie found herself unable to engage unreservedly in the planning for this occasion, for she became quite certain that Buz would request a bona fide date for it. She had only intended to redeem the attitude of some of the group toward him, but it appeared he had misconstrued her friendliness for genuine interest. How innocently she had got herself into this! Refusing him now would add to the others' reservations.

Bonnie did not actually have anything against Buz, but she knew that if a few of the girls had voiced their opinions of him, there would surely be others who agreed with them, though silently. Did she wish to risk the ridicule she feared she would incur by accepting? Perhaps there would even be those who suggested she would accept Buz's offer because no one else would ask her.

As she was walking home after work one evening, Bonnie was suddenly arrested by the memory of her experience with George. It was partially the heady feeling of being the object of the other girls' envy that had influenced her to fall so ignominiously. Oh, how she loathed her recollection of herself at that time! How could she have acted so debasely? She was momentarily overwhelmed with shame. If those girls had asked her to sell her soul, she probably would have blindly done so.

But she was not the same person she had been then. She had read in the book of Isaiah that we are to "look unto the rock whence ye are hewn, and to the hole of the pit whence ye are digged." And she was looking. She was not in the pit anymore. She had put off the former life-style, which was corrupt, as it stated in Ephesians, and had been renewed. Her entire being had changed. She had "put on the new man, which after God is created in righteousness and true holiness." She need no longer loathe the person she had once been, for that was forgiven, cleansed away in the blood of Jesus. And she need not worry any longer about what others would say. The freedom she had found in the Lord would enable her to follow her own conscience regardless of others' opinions. She would accept or refuse Buz solely on the basis of her own desire.

With that new attitude and sense of her own worth, Bonnie strangely found herself wanting to accept.

When the evening finally arrived, it was lovely, though giving evidence of the early signs of winter's chill. Bonnie flew down the stairs when the bell rang.

"Here, I've brought you something," Buz greeted simply as he shyly offered an enormous, bronze mum.

"How lovely!" Bonnie's voice betrayed her amazement. "I didn't know corsages were in order for the evening."

"Perhaps they are only for you." Buz's serious gaze caused Bonnie to blush as she fastened the flower to her coat. Somewhat nonplussed, she took his arm as he led her out to his car.

When they reached the fellowship hall, she thought she had never seen such a display of hugging and backslapping as old friends greeted each other and the evening's merriment began. Everyone seemed especially pleased to see Dominic Pizzuit, who happily had also made his way home for the weekend.

It was difficult, if not impossible, to gain everyone's attention in the midst of the hilarity. But Dave Fisher, who had been selected as master of ceremonies, flicked the light switch on and off a couple times, and when the last girl's scream had died away, silence reigned.

"Our first game for this evening," Dave began, "is one we haven't tried before. I guess you could call it 'Chew your way out of this one,' or some such. And it goes like this: Everyone will be given one three-by-five card— here Dominic, start passing, please—and as many as you wish up to five sticks of chewing gum. You are to chew the gum until it's pliable, roll it into string—remember what you did on the back of the hymnal when you were four years old?—and arrange the strings on the card in a picture."

A chorus of groans arose, but it soon resolved into muffled giggling as Dave continued. "Prizes will be awarded for the most humorous, the prettiest, and the most imaginative. There will be no time limit, as creative genius cannot flourish under pressure."

The giggles erupted into several pronounced snorts as a flurry of chewing began. Dominic circulated among the budding artists, passing out additional sticks of gum as the contenders chewed and rolled vigorously.

"Oh, my sticky hands," squealed one unidentified feminine voice.

233

"Chew it a little longer and you'll be able to pry it loose," replied a male voice from somewhere in the hubbub.

"After it's plastered over my hands?"

"Here, Dominic, let me have another stick. This creature needs a tail."

As the creations neared completion, the glee turned to outright guffaws as friends showed others their masterpieces.

"This one should win a prize," was heard on all sides, until the committee designated to do the judging despaired of finding any more notable than the others.

Bonnie struggled to produce a willowy tree, thinking that its flowing branches and leaves would lend themselves to thin strands of rubbery goo. When completed to her satisfaction, she shyly turned to show it to Buz, fully expecting the same amusement with which the others were greeted. But to her amazement she discovered Buz reaching for his fifth stick, totally engrossed in the project before him. A look of deep concentration blazed from his eyes as he deftly rolled the gum into the minutest of strands and applied them to the delicate tracery that adorned his creation. And, following the movements of his large hands, Bonnie caught her voice in stifled awe. For there on Buz's card was the most magnificent Gothic cathedral she had ever seen in picture. It was executed in perfect proportion and perspective, in spite of the ridiculous medium, its graceful spires reaching upward in sublime grandeur.

"It's—it's beautiful," she breathed almost inaudibly. "How did you—"

"It's nothing." Buz sounded offhand and stuck the remainder of his wad onto the corner of the card. "Nothing at all. Listen, Bonnie, would you mind if we just left this party? I'm sure no one here would miss us. Could we just go out walking? Just down the street if there isn't any place in particular to go—"

"No, I don't mind at all. But surely you'll wait for your prize. None will be more creative than yours."

"No, I don't care for the prize. I'd just like to walk." He had risen to his feet and, taking her by the elbow, led her through the rows of revelers beside him. Pausing by the coat rack for their jackets, he threw his card into a wastebasket. She wanted to retrieve it, but better judgment warned her not to.

"I know of a place for walking," she volunteered on their way out the door. "It's only a very few blocks from here, over behind the planetarium. I walked there often in the summer. You are really secluded from the bustle of the city while being rather close to the heart of it. You turn this way."

Slipping an arm through hers, he guided her across the streets and down the walks she indicated.

"Now 'fess up, Buz Rockwell," she teased, "is you is or is you ain't an artist? I mean by profession. Obviously you are one. But just what is it you are doing with all that talent?"

He laughed a trifle self-consciously. "Actually, I planned once on being an artist. I've done sketches ever since I can remember. Won a couple prizes in high school for my drawings. But art is a very hard field to get into profitably. I thought it best to turn my attention to matters more concrete. Something that would give functional expression to my dreams. Say, like—well, if you put a little brick, wood and stone, perhaps some structural steel into it along with the concrete—if you mix those ingredients together in a pleasingly aesthetic and functional form and season with a little landscaping in a natural setting, you come up with—architecture."

"Oh!" she gasped. "I was afraid you were going to come up with some monstrosity of modern sculpture. You know, maybe one of those things you can climb over and even get lost in."

"Oh, no. Modern, maybe, but not monstrous. For modern architecture, far from being hideous as some believe it to be, is really ingenious. Many people are simply culturally accustomed to more traditional styles and have not yet developed an appreciation of that which our modern technology makes possible."

They crossed the last street before entering the little park, and Buz fell silent as he guided her through the traffic. At last, they left the sidewalk and turned down the little gravel path that led through the tiny patch of shrubbery.

"Did you know, Bonnie," he finally continued, "architecture is called the mother of the arts. For, although drawing on the walls of caves is the oldest of the arts to come down to us, architecture has sheltered and nurtured all the other fine arts. And did you realize that man's first reach into space was not through painting, music or sculpture, not even through modern rocketry; but through architecture? Although it was wickedly conceived and ill-fated from the start, the tower of Babel was man's first attempt to make something bigger than himself. His first real attempt to stretch up high enough to find gods.

"Later, after man understood the true nature of the God he was attempting to find, he expressed his reach toward God in magnificent cathedrals, the masterpieces of architecture of all ages. Man has poured the deepest longings of his heart into the pursuit of the Almighty."

Bonnie thought again of the little chewing-gum sketch tossed into the wastebasket and understood why the sight of it had so stirred her. This man by her side had poured something of himself into its creation. And that something permitted but the smallest glimpse into his creative soul.

"When I was a kid and first aware of those cathedrals

and monasteries," his voice nudged her out of her reverie, "I used to think their era would have been the most glorious time in which to live. I used to picture myself as a small boy playing along the banks of a stream winding under the brow of a hill crested with the mighty spires and domes of a Saint Paul's, Notre Dame, Chartres. Then as I got into high school and learned of the superstitions, fears, plagues, and poverty that stalked the Middle Ages, I wondered how men of those times had the fortitude to climb to the soaring heights that they reached in spirit as reflected in their buildings."

"You know—" He stopped for a moment and pursed his lips pensively. "—it just occurs to me now that maybe that is the reason they reached their zenith in such structures. Desperation drove them to put everything they had into it. Perhaps those old relics are testimonials to man's longing to acquire that dimension of the spirit to which Christ had already given them access through His death. But unfortunately, what they sought was locked within dank monastic walls and kept from the sight of common people. Yes, now it comes to me that some of that grandiose architecture was nothing but a burial vault, securing God's holy Word from the hands of people who lived in misery for want of it." His eyes squinted as he gazed into a distant past.

They kicked the dry leaves about exaggeratedly to make more rustle as they crossed the park. The pipe on the fountain looked somewhat rusty where it emerged from the stone wall, but the spigot responded readily, and they took a long draught of the clear, cold water. They stood for several minutes, silently looking into the last rays of the vanishing sun. Buz sought out a secluded bench and pulled her down beside him.

"Now, as I was saying before I got off on that side track," he continued, "the more I studied history, the more I came to believe that our nation's own early period was the time to be a builder. For one thing, there certainly was considerable demand for building! The people who came over here from the Old World came with new dreams burning in their breasts. Otherwise they would not have bothered to make such a move. They were inspired by idealism, a newfound freedom, a reborn democracy, unlimited opportunity. You would think it would have a direct influence on the course their architecture developed. But the more I learned, the more I realized all of that design we think so magnificent—such as the resplendent colonial mansions, the pillared facades of banks and libraries, the soaring beauty of many of the old universities—all of those were copies of ancient classics, merely revised and reworked to suit the materials and economy and climate of this new country. There was no innovation. The only originality that came through was in variations, like taking a theme from Mozart and improvising your own music. Even old Tom Jefferson, with all his inventiveness, was not able to come up with a purely American design."

Bonnie interjected on occasional "Uh-huh" to let Buz know she was still listening. But she was absolutely mute beside this flow of history.

"I thought for quite some time, also, that traditional architecture was where it was all at," Buz continued. "You know, the symmetrical, totally controlled dimensions, bound by tradition, shaped by necessity and convention. I revelled in the grandeur of those southern mansions. Took a trip the summer after my first year of college to see some of them. I was completely awestruck with the carrara marble mantels, the immense mirrors framed in rococo, the ornate brass chandeliers handcrafted in France, the magnificent spiral stairways, the broad, pillared verandas, the ornate, massive columns supporting the triangular roof structures. And then I began to realize those structures reflected a certain rigidity and represented a way of life incompatible with our thinking today. And in a very real way, they are incompatible with our life-style as well, for those structures were built on the principle of a stratified society. At the top were the wealthy, the freemen; the large class in the middle was composed of the masses of common working people, and at the bottom were slaves. But now we all are free. Just as it is in the Christian life. The Bible tells us there is no Jew or Greek, no one bonded or free. We all stand before God, stripped of all pretension, excuse or privilege, and on the sole merit of the blood of Jesus Christ."

Bonnie looked at this gentle stranger by her side, breathlessly unaware that some of his words did not come through distinctly because of his defect. She saw and heard only the beauty of a noble, creative spirit that had found peace with itself and its God. In listening, she was transported out of herself into a dimension of the spirit she had not known existed. She began to feel she could find tranquility at this man's side forever.

"And then," he was saying, "I began to understand that much of the architecture of the bygone periods was dictated by necessity. That is, the long hallways leading straight through the structures with doors at either end and the high ceilings were for ventilation. The thick, brick walls provided insulation. Those ornate fireplaces were the sole source of heat, especially in northern areas, to ward off the chill of severe winters. And all of it was constructed by hand. It remained for our present technology and new materials to free designers of those dictates, just as Christ's atonement on the cross freed men from the dictates of sin and enabled us to rise in newness of spirit, partaking daily in the power of His resurrection life.

"Can you think, for instance, what a Sir Christopher Wren might have done with the possibilities afforded by our technology? It remained for a Frank Lloyd Wright to pave the way. You know it was he who first incorporated freedom into his design. The idea of space for simple, relaxed living, the use of color to vitalize surroundings."

"I can relate to that," exclaimed Bonnie. "I never could endure drabness."

"With your personality, I'm sure you could not. Did you know, Frank Lloyd Wright also concentrated on using natural woods with stone? He always sought to integrate his structures with the natural environment." He hesitated for some time before continuing. "I've been thinking you and I together have the perfect materials for a 'Wright' structure, if you'll pardon the pun. Your name has the Lake, mine has the Rock. Perhaps if we combined them, we'd have a beautiful creation in a natural setting."

The look he gave her under the dim light of the street lamp made her distrust herself to say anything for a moment or two. But she recovered soon enough to chirp, "Yes, and with the well in your name, there would be plenty of natural water supply both for consumption and for recreation."

"Great! I can see you would make an excellent wife for an architect with your understanding of the artistry of his profession."

She was so sure she must have blushed that she was glad it had grown dark so he couldn't see it. But he reached for her hand.

"The more I learn of what Wright accomplished in his lifetime, the more I see that he blazed the trail for what I wish to become as an architect. It is my dream to take up just where he left off. Of course, I realize that must reflect considerable vanity and probably a gross over-evaluation of my abilities, but a man can always dream, can't he?"

"You would be a pitiful specimen if you ever dimmed

your vision. And I can't think how you could be any more qualified to dream creatively than you already are."

"I hope never to make any two designs alike. When I run out of new ideas, I'm finished. Even God Himself doesn't make copies. Each individual that comes from His hand is an unique creation—no two of us ever exactly alike. And the most unfathomable part of it is that He then respects that individuality that He created. He deals with each one of us in a manner suiting our personalities. And paradoxically, the more we are filled with His Spirit and become like Him, the truer our own individuality shows through."

"You would wonder that He ever bothers with some of us."

"I guess the fact that He does remains one of the deepest mysteries of our faith."

They sat silently for a few moments, contemplating the enormity of the subject. Here and there the stillness was broken by a distant car horn and the whir of an occasional plane making its entrance to the airport runway.

"I'm going to start with a dream home of my own," Buz said after a bit. "It's going to be on some wooded, natural setting that I can integrate with my design just as Frank Lloyd Wright would prescribe. I hope to find a lot with a nice little stream trickling through or around it. And I envision it to be a somewhat wandering, possibly pentangular structure with vertical California redwood siding. It will enclose a central, landscaped court that can be entered by a glass door in each room. There will be a bench similar to this one where we can sit, on into our old age." He encircled her in one great arm and drew her close.

New excitement invigorated his voice as he made a sweeping motion higher than his head with his free arm. "There will be two stories over only the living area. A

241

balustraded balcony will overhang the living room under high arched beams. Skylights in shades of rose and amber will light the balcony, where we'll arrange potted palms and other greens around some lounge furniture. The master bedroom will be on that level. Of course, there will be several smaller bedrooms extending around the court for — smaller people. Several of them. And the nursery will have to be in the vicinity of the master bedroom. The kitchen will be a chef's delight, with absolutely every modern labor-saving device available. How does it sound so far?"

"Unbelievable! When you said dream house, dream house is what you meant."

"But it is not to remain in the land of dreams. You see, actually it is a solid business venture. An architect can use such a showpiece to advertise his talent. When enough people drive by and stretch their necks, you don't lack for clients. Now, then, for some more dreaming. What would you say to a slight Spanish influence? I don't mean screaming Mediterranean. But just enough of a hint to give it character. And I'm not one to adorn the coffee tables with alabaster or onyx bulls, either. I prefer my art to be a little more refined."

"I should think you could paint your own scenes of medieval palaces and cathedrals to hang on the walls."

"I don't paint, my dear, only sketch. But it wouldn't be the first sketched cathedral to grace (or disgrace, as the case may be) someone's wall. My mother has had just such a — ahem — masterpiece since I was about twelve."

"I would love to see it. And would you please quit disparaging your work? It's simply magnificent."

"Perhaps you shall see it soon. Now, as for color, you can splash to your little heart's content. This will be no tomb to be enshrouded in gloom."

Bonnie was increasingly awestruck by the boldness

with which he referred to her presence in the home, as though it were a foregone conclusion. But she was unprepared for the suddenness of his next statement.

"I'm not sure yet where this is to take shape. It all depends on the location in which I expect to find the greatest market for my ideas. I doubt I will return to Harrisburg. And I don't think this area will afford the opportunity for free expression I am looking for. I may have to completely leave the state. I have the remainder of this term yet to make up my mind. You—you wouldn't mind leaving Pittsburgh, would you?"

Chills crept up Bonnie's spine. She blinked hard a couple of times, making herself once again thankful the street light was some yards distant. Could she really have heard what her ears were telling her? Perhaps that was all a dream like the unbelievable house. If she opened her mouth, she was sure to say the wrong thing, because she must have misinterpreted his intention. The silence was becoming awkward. She would have to say something before he began to think he had offended her.

"I—I will have to have some time to think about it," she stammered. But she knew as the words were falling out that she would need to do no more thinking than she had already done.

Suddenly his lips ravishingly explored hers, and she didn't remember that they were not the most beautiful lips in all the world.

15

The early winter months of late 1959 flew by, as time does when two are in love. If the snow was deep as Bonnie made her way to work, she skimmed over the top of it, scarcely noticing. When patients were unable to keep appointments, and the hours dragged by in the office, she welcomed the precious moments to think of Buz.

The ugly taste in her mouth left from her memories of a year ago had been completely erased with her new elation. However, from time to time she found it impossible not to compare the two seasons. Whereas George had been conspicuously absent the previous year on Thanksgiving Day, Buz was more than delighted to accept an invitation to the Lake home for dinner. He had too much work on campus to make the trip to Harrisburg for the weekend, and he would not see the holiday's passing without partaking of the traditional feast around a happy family table. If that wasn't blessing enough, the object of his profound affection would share that table with him.

The day passed pleasantly enough, although the pumpkin pies were not thoroughly set. In her nervousness over helping to prepare her first meal for her beloved, Bonnie put too much milk in the custard mixture. Never mind, next year when they had been man and wife for some months, she would turn out perfect pumpkin pies!

James and Perry had accepted the newcomer on first sight, much to Bonnie's gratification. But the appraisal Buz had received from Avonelle was somewhat less than satisfactory, if Bonnie read the signals correctly. Avonelle's eyes told her that at least for looks, Bonnie would have done much better with Hal. Perhaps that was so, if one looked no deeper than the skin. Bonnie was extremely anxious for her mother to recognize Buz's sterling qualities, but feared that in her unsaved state she might not be able to do so. At least Mrs. Lake was civil and did not make the visitor feel unwelcome.

Bonnie noted with considerable satisfaction that for once Sylvia kept herself inconspicuous in the presence of her sister's date. Sylvia was attracted more by appearance than by the maturity that she vowed was her first consideration. Bonnie smiled to realize here was one man for whom her little sister would give no competition.

Sylvia did well enough for herself anyway. The chatter about the swim coach, better known as "Mac," seemed never to end.

"Mac said that my back crawl is the finest in western Pennsylvania." Or, "Oh, those divine eyes. All the girls are ga-ga over him, but would you believe, he doesn't notice any of them but me." "I date any good opportunity I get, but those young guys are a bore compared with Mac. I'm really only killing time until I graduate, for I'm sure that then Mac will come out from behind his admiring glances and materialize into the knight who carries me off on a charger. Of course, I'll be very reluctant to mount at first; then he will swoop me up, plant me squarely behind the bridle, and leap up behind me to dash off into never never land." Then Sylvia would clasp her hands and roll her eyes sensuously.

If Sylvia seemed uninterested in commanding Buz's attention, he exhibited no more in attracting hers. He looked on her more or less as another little sister in the home, perhaps older and more sophisticated than his own, but a little sister nonetheless.

He talked somewhat of his family, describing his father as a hard-working engineer on the Pennsylvania Railroad, his mother as an excellent baker and preserver of the finest jellies, jams, and pickles in the truest tradition of the Pennsylvania Dutch, and of his own little sister, Gwen, a ten-year-old, flaxen-haired tomboy. He regaled Perry with accounts of his own boyhood antics canoeing on the Susquehanna, swinging from the rafters, and plunging into a haymow in his cousin's huge barn, and an occasional thrilling adventure in the cab of his father's engine.

The Christmas season proved to be more exciting to Bonnie than the previous one had been. Contrary to what she had feared, she dared to exuberate in the exciting dazzle that flashed from the street decorations, the trees, the vast array of gifts offered for selection in the stores, and beautiful renditions of the fine old carols. It was she this year who kept her record player revolving while in her room, for the carols held new meaning for her. She rejoiced in the knowledge the story reiterated in them and in her own life's change that the knowledge had wrought.

She made it a special point to attend the children's program at the church, for she wanted to savor every blessed moment of it with her man by her side, reminiscing on the program into which she had accidentally stumbled that changed her whole life. She grasped Buz's hand throughout, half fearing that he was a figment of an idealistic dream, soon to vanish.

They missed Luanne and Reg's wedding, for, having spent the first holiday of the season with Bonnie, Buz declared she was then to accompany him to Harrisburg for Christmas. "You know, Luanne and Reg will be able to tie the knot without our cheering them on." Upon their return they heard that the wedding had been one of the most magnificent yet to grace Emmanuel Tabernacle's sanctuary. The eight bridesmaids, all chosen from the gang, wore cranberry red velvet and carried candlelit lanterns nestled in arrangements of poinsettias. The bride herself wore pearl-studded ivory velvet with a breathtaking cathedral length mantilla of Brussels lace worn by all the brides in her family since the turn of the century. And for the final touch of poignancy, the bride and groom sang to each other as they stood before their friends to solemnize their vows.

"I can just hear us singing to each other," Bonnie laughed ironically when told about it.

"Why not?" returned Buz. "After all, making a joyous *noise* is all the Bible tells us to do. It doesn't have to rival the angels." She thought it best to drop the subject before he seriously considered singing.

They had set out for Harrisburg at the stroke of noon, following the gray of a winter morning.

"I always like to make the trip home in the afternoon," explained Buz as they headed for the Pennsylvania Turnpike, "because when you travel directly east, the sun hits you squarely in the eyes. Then you reverse it and make sure you come back in the morning. But the trip takes so long you can't escape it all. You might as well settle back and prepare for a long, hard trip."

The first fifty to seventy-five miles passed rather uneventfully through rugged rural areas interspersed with small industrial towns and occasional wooded sections. As they neared the state's center, Bonnie exclaimed at the beauty of the lower hills that rose into majestic mountains.

Soon they were snow-capped and rolled on and on as far as the eye could see. An occasional broad, tranquil valley wedged its way between them. Remembering the lush beauty of the area in which she had visited at the retreat she tried to visualize the splendor of these magnificent peaks during the height of autumn color.

"We'll make a trip out here next October just so you can see how gorgeous it all is," Buz assured her. "I've only begun to acquaint you with the beauties of Pennsylvania. Some think it is the most beautiful state in the Union."

They stopped in the late afternoon at a mountaintop restaurant from which the panoramic view was breathtaking. Mile after mile of snow-covered mountains stretched from one ridge to the next. The first amber streaks of the setting sun reflected off the peaks to the west, and about them the air was crisp, cold, and clear. If there were any particular spot in which to look for peace on earth this was it, thought the enchanted girl who slipped her arm through that of the young man at her side. Reluctantly they returned to the little auto and, turning their backs on the setting sun, headed toward the night.

Bonnie had been through the tunnels in Pittsburgh on occasion, but she was unprepared for those they encountered on the eastern lap of their journey. They seemed to go on and on forever. How could men have burrowed like moles under enormous mountains for such tremendous distances? She was nearly claustrophobic with just riding through them. But they always came out on the other side. And each time it seemed a little darker.

Night had settled in with finality by the time Buz pulled up to the small shingled bungalow on the outskirts of the city. But the warm light that glowed from within was sufficient to reveal the three forms assembled by the open door. Buz's mother, with her hair pulled back into braids wound about her head, rushed toward her son with open arms. His pleasant, round-faced father had donned his Sunday best to shake his boy's hand and say gruffly, "Welcome home, son."

And Gwen was nearly lost in a sloppy, floppy sweater trailing down over blue jeans. But she leaped into Buz's arms with agility that spoke of much practice, threw her ams about his neck, and squealed, "You've brought me a new sister, haven't you?"

"Not quite, but almost. And here she is. I want you all to meet Bonnie, the love of my life."

"We're so delighted to meet you, my dear," Mrs. Rockwell embraced her warmly, and her husband cordially accepted Bonnie's proffered hand. "We're awfully glad you could make this trip with Buz," Mrs. Rockwell was continuing. "We hope you'll enjoy your stay with us."

"I know already I'm going to."

Gwen puckered her tiny rosebud lips into a trace of a pout and staunchly declared to her brother, "I don't know if I'm going to share you with her."

"That's already been decided," he replied, laughing. "But just remember, you won't lose your brother; you'll only gain a sister. And I can tell in my bones you and she will get along wonderfully."

"Come this way," invited Mrs. Rockwell, leading them to the kitchen. "I'm sure you two could stand a little warming up after a long ride in the cold. Coffee is ready and you may choose any or all of the sweets."

Bonnie's eyes fairly bulged at the sight of the table. It groaned under the most extensive assortment of pies, delicate rolls, fancy breads, kuchen, tarts, and strudels she had ever seen assembled in one place. Since it wouldn't be proper to take one bite out of each, she decided that choosing one or two posed the greatest dilemma she had ever faced. But she observed that this family was no stranger to good eating, and she felt no embarrassment in sampling a few additional mouthwatering delights.

That tantalizing array, however, was only a dim foretaste of the feast to be spread on the great dining room table for Christmas Day. Buz's Pennsylvania Dutch aunt, uncle, and cousins had been invited for the festivities, and Aunt Rebekah brought along the most sumptuous dishes of corn relish, schmierkase, country cheeses, smoked sausages, roasted duckling, chowchow, pickled vegetables, country cured ham, a variety of canned fruits and berries, and freshly made applesauce that could be imagined. There was even a corn pie. When it was all added to the roast chicken with chestnut stuffing that Mrs. Rockwell had prepared, along with deviled eggs, steamed suet pudding, baked squash, and candied yams and topped off with whole cranberry sauce, cranberry relish, and cranberry jelly, Bonnie's sides began to ache with just thinking how she would feel if she tried to eat it all. She would probably also have to set the button over on her skirt's waistband.

When they were finally all seated around the enormous table, with every course served together according to the preference of the "plain folk," and Mrs. Rockwell and Aunt Rebekah had removed their aprons Mr. Rockwell folded his hands and thanked God for the bounteous supplying of their needs. *Plus some abundant luxuries!* Bonnie added to herself. She made a solemn vow never to question Buz's love for her; for anyone to have grown up at a table spread such as this and then be willing to spend the rest of his life with her humble cooking, it had to be love!

The next day, a pleasant Saturday, Buz took Bonnie for a drive to see the battlefield at Valley Forge. With the traces of the last snow lying yet on the ground, it was difficult to make out the panorama except the vastness of the area broken only by row upon row of crosses. Remembering that George Washington had knelt there in snow much deeper and more bitter than the thin carpet covering the now well-kept lawns to ask for the aid of the Almighty in the conflict confronting him, Bonnie could only weep at the visible evidence of the thousands who made the supreme sacrifice in order that there might be a free nation to welcome the earth's destitute and homeless, such as she herself had once been.

Wishing to give their guest a sampling of true "plain folk" worship, the family motored to Lancaster on Sunday to attend meetin' with Aunt Rebekah and Uncle Zeke. Bonnie was amazed to find herself entering a whitewashed structure more nearly resembling a smaller version of their trim, well-kept barns. Inside they assembled themselves along plain wooden benches with high, stiff backs. There were no musical instruments; the talented services of the new Mr. and Mrs. Reginald Walker certainly would not be required here. But as the congregation lifted their voices in lusty praises to God, Bonnie understood that the sentiment from the hearts of these simple people was more meaningful than the loftiest brilliance of trained artists. However, when the lay preacher took his place behind the plain wooden desk, spread the Bible before him, and expounded on the Scriptures, she began to comprehend the type of metal from which these faithful were molded. If Buz had been exposed to this manner of teaching throughout his life, it was only to be expected that his spiritual life would reflect a soundness and depth far beyond his years. How rich these beloved people were in the midst of an outward display of simplicity! And what she had missed in her own developing years! She scarcely noticed that the service continued for more than two hours.

With genuine regret Bonnie watched the days hasten by, and the glorious vacation draw to a close. She began to hope Buz might find it to be advantageous to settle in that area to begin his career, although better judgment told her there probably would not be as much demand for his creativity there as elsewhere. There was only one reason she would be glad to return to her own little room on the third floor of the old mansion on Arch Street. In the Rockwell's tiny bungalow that housed the family she had learned to love as her own flesh and blood, there was no guest room. And she had learned that Gwen thrashed wildly in her sleep. Bonnie looked forward to getting one good night's rest.

But loathsomely summoning all the self-discipline they could muster, the two arose with the roosters that crowed in Aunt Rebekah and Uncle Zeke's barnyard and turned the little auto westward with the first golden streaks of dawn breaking the leaden sky behind them.

Bidding a fond adieu to the gently rolling low-lying farmlands of the east, they made their way once more through the spectacular mountains and eventually pulled up to the Shadyside Apartments in Oakland.

Mrs. Lake was about to put the finishing touches on the evening meal as the door opened and her older daughter stepped in. Avonelle hastened to lay two more places and ask for a detailed account of the vacation. Bonnie had always considered her mother's cooking to be among the best; now, however, she caught herself stealing sidelong glances in Buz's direction to detect whether he displayed any disdain for the simple roast beef and mashed potatoes. She need not have worried. He obviously relished every morsel he lifted to his lips. That was fortunate, she noted with relief. There was probably no chance she would ever learn the culinary arts of the plain folk in the east.

When the meal was finished, down to the last crumb of red velvet cake, the Lake family exchanged belated Christmas gifts with their daughter and future son-in-law, a striking onyx desk set which rested in a block of jade for Buz, a delicate perfume and frilly lingerie for Bonnie to secretly tuck away for her honeymoon, and a gilt-framed photograph for which Bonnie and Buz had sat secretly for her parents. The couple produced a baseball almanac for Perry and a pair of plainly dressed dolls, in gray with the traditional bonnet and beard, which Bonnie had found for Sylvia in a little gift shop outside Lancaster. She hoped they might find a spot among the array of stuffed animals in and around Sylvia's bed. Sylvia, however, was much more absorbed in her own private phone, which she had asked for and received, installed in her room. "Now I can talk to my heart's content without bothering the folks," she explained, adding cagily, "Did you know that Hal still calls every now and then? In fact, I was out with him a couple weeks ago."

"How nice," her sister answered noncommittally. "What about Mac?"

"Oh, I'm still waiting. I'm just not letting any grass grow under my feet while sitting it out. You know me."

"I certainly do."

Weary from the long journey, the young couple left early to make their way to their respective rooms.

"I know my mother mentioned to you a couple times just how happy she and Dad are to welcome you into the family," Buz reiterated as he left Bonnie at the beveled glass door of the old mansion. "But I thought you would be interested to know that she took me aside once and told me that you are just the type of girl she has been praying for, ever since I was born, to share my life some-day. Perhaps that is one reason I recognized as soon as I met you that you are the one for me."

"All the world filled with books could not express the joy you have given me, Buz—including me in your life and your family. I hope I can make you happy and proud that I am by your side."

She slipped away and up the darkened stairway before she could trust herself to say more. But as she buried her head in the pillow that night, her heart overflowed until she felt she could contain no more. Reaching for the little white Bible, she opened it to Psalm 68, and her eyes fell on the words: "God setteth the solitary in families." How true that was! She was to be blessed with two families. One had accepted her in all her misery and destitution and made her their own, not yet knowing who that poor bruised little waif was to be. And now another was flinging wide its arms of loving welcome, fully knowing and accepting her just as she was. She thought herself to be the richest person on earth!

Part 2

16

"I believe this is someone you know," Miss Travis's eyes twinkled as she handed Bonnie the newspaper upon her return from work one evening. "Isn't that a face I've seen somewhere about these premises?"

"Why—why—" Bonnie clutched at her chest. The memory of George Morrow's picture staring out from the front page threatened to suffocate her. Did she have to endure another heart-wrenching trauma? What could possibly have happened this time? Surely not her beloved Buz would commit any crime that would prompt the spreading of his visage across the city's most prominent newspaper!

The hand that reached for the paper shook, and the eyes blurred until it was difficult to make out the caption's bold black lettering. "Wins," she managed to decipher. With a breath of relief she was able to discern the entire line. "Local Student Wins National Architecture Contest."

"Well, of all things," she finally blurted in a voice still slightly shaken. "He didn't say a word to me about even entering a contest." *That would be just like him,* she thought. *He probably considered it of so little consequence that he wouldn't deem it worth mentioning.*

A hasty scan of the article revealed that Nathaniel Rockwell had submitted a winning design to a national contest in the dwelling category. The thumbnail sketch of the dwelling given in the text indicated the design was the one he intended to build for himself—*For ourselves*, she corrected herself. The unbelievable dream house that was to sprawl around a central enclosed court on a lovely, wooded lot with a stream gurgling through it. Yes, that very one he had submitted, probably never even giving it another thought.

And not only was he smiling back at her from the front page of the newspaper, but his picture, along with the other division winners, appeared on the pages of every building and trade magazine in the country. The mail began to flood in. It was not long before Buz lost count of the architectural firms that wrote to offer him partnerships. Letters came from nearly every major city and from as far away as Honolulu. And by the score banks, hotels, schools, churches, libraries, town halls, the new shopping malls, and prospective home builders poured in requests for his services.

First, he mimeographed a polite, but firm letter of refusal, which he would send to every would-be client but one. However, quick to size up opportunities, he then obtained a large map of the United States and, using a red marker, checked every location from where he had received an offer. Then with the aid of an encyclopedia he checked the climate, geographical conditions, populations, and cost of living index of each location with the highest numbers of check marks. Placing the map on the wall above his desk, he began to compile a list of the ten most desirable and feasible locations, and as the weeks flew past, made calculated judgments concerning the order of preference as a place in which to locate.

The correspondence from the Pittsburgh and surrounding areas he carefully filed according to type of structure desired. He would not consider any of the multitude of commissions for a dwelling copying the one he intended to construct for himself. Having promised that home to Bonnie, he did not intend to present her with a copy of one first possessed by another; if there were copies to be made, hers was to be the original and every other a copy.

From the volume of other offers, he selected the most challenging, contacted the prospective client, and began working out a design. The project was that of relocating a major church in the redeveloping section of the North Side. The church was to be rebuilt not far from its original location, and would occupy a prominent corner in the heart of the new development. Buz understood from previous contacts that this particular denomination favored the Southern Colonial style of architecture and that his freedom in creativity would be radically restricted. However, the project was expected to involve a figure in the vicinity of a million dollars for a sanctuary large enough to seat one thousand worshipers. The challenge was irresistible. A structure of such vast proportions on so prominent a location with his name upon it was not a commission to be lightly dismissed. Many novices would trade their souls for such a testimony to their talents.

Buz spent many evenings with the building committee reviewing photos of like edifices, and on more than one Saturday he journeyed to a neighboring community with members of the committee to inspect a new structure of similar design. None, however, was of the proportions his project was to be. The design may be borrowed, but the dimensions would be his own. And he thrilled at the opportunity to apply his T-square to the drawing board across which his exciting structure slowly took shape.

The final design was that of a simple red brick building with plain Colonial windows in small panes, with a triple entrance within a columned Grecian portico. A white hexagonal steeple, stark in its simplicity, would sit atop a mounting of arched pillars tiered above an enormous white brick square. The interior, reflecting light and grace, would include white furnishings over scarlet carpeting. And the lighting would glimmer through elegant early American brass chandeliers. Buz's excitement grew daily as he longed to view the completed reality, already visible in his mind's eye.

Bonnie at times was tempted to feel slighted when Buz worked long into the night sketching, discarding, and re-sketching, taking only enough time from the drafting table for a hurried phone call. She longed to be in his company every possible moment. But she understood his need to establish himself in his career and reasoned that soon she would be able to sit by his side as he worked. In the meantime, she made diligent effort to obey the pastor's admonition to show the love of Christ on every opportunity. Dr. Gardner's patients soon came to recognize a quality in his receptionist that inspired their confidence. Some ventured to divulge a problem, and in doing so found a measure of relief just in having someone to listen. Others were cheered by the pleasant smile greeting them from inside the little window. And Bonnie was always alert to any opprtunity to serve in tangible ways, such as phoning for cabs for elderly patients or providing coloring books for the youngsters of patients not blessed with babysitters. She rejoiced in discovering that each time she gave of herself, it was returned to her a hundredfold, knowing she had extended Christ's hand to someone who otherwise may never have experienced His care.

The winter months passed quickly. February especially glided by with the rapidity only happy events and joyous anticipation can hasten. For Valentine's Day proved to be the epitome of delight to Bonnie, her sister, and her "almost" roommate.

Nancy had been planning her wedding since she returned from Butler at Christmastime with a lovely diamond. And now she was taking a job in the Butler Hospital and also as the wife of the assistant pastor of the little church on Mercer Street. She and Bonnie both regretted that their beloved gang at Emmanuel Tabernacle would not be available to "send the couple off in fine style," since the nuptials were to be solemnized in Butler. Royle did consent, however, to paint his traditional couple for the reception. Using a red heart for the background, the bride-to-be requested a white gown for the lady of the design. Forgetting to warn Royle that her bridegroom was rather broader than long, she was a trifle dismayed to discover a tall, thin gentleman pictured by her side.

"Oh, well," she consoled herself, "he needed to go on a diet, anyway."

Bonnie and Meredith were to be bridesmaids, along with three girls from the Butler church. It was an excited party that motored out Route 28 with Buz at the wheel on that crisp, sunny Saturday, ready for the ceremony the following day. For wishing always to celebrate her anniversary on the fourteenth, Nancy found it necessary to have a Sunday afternoon wedding in 1960.

This wedding party was likewise gowned in red, in keeping with the holiday theme, as the last had been; and the bridesmaids carried heart-shaped arrangements of simple stephanotis. Bonnie loved the simplicity of the wedding party and determined that her own wedding would reflect the same rather than the elaborate opulence of Luanne's.

Bonnie was delighted to discover that Nancy's Gilbert, in spite of being of somewhat broader stature than the lean gentleman of Royle's creation, was nonetheless very handsome. And the bridal couple made a striking pair under the flower-entwined arch before the altar.

261

And standing not far away, she also observed the tears of joy which the petite bride struggled to blink away as her groom proudly offered his arm to lead his new wife back up the aisle.

Bonnie was to miss the bubbling company she had found so edifying in her little third floor apartment. It was not much longer that she was to be in the old mansion alone. Upon their return to the city the evening following the wedding and having escorted Meredith to her door, Buz paused under the gilded chandelier in the foyer of the grand old house on Arch Street to slip a ring upon Bonnie's finger. It was a delicate design with two smaller diamonds set in white gold hearts flanking the large center diamond.

She caught her breath with its beauty.

"This one will do for now." He sounded somewhat apologetic. "But just wait until I've made my mark as a famous architect. I'll replace it with another so huge you'll need a wheelbarrow to carry it around."

"You'll do no such thing, Nathaniel Rockwell. This is my engagement ring and will always remain so. I'll cherish it alone for the sentiment it represents. None in all the world could replace it, no matter how spectacular another may appear."

"All right. We won't argue about that right now. My primary concern at the moment is how soon you can be prepared to receive its mate. I hate to press you into setting a date, but as soon as I graduate I'll be under no obligation to postpone it any longer. And I can assure you I am very anxious to carry off my bride, ne'er to leave her side again."

"Very well, then. Graduation it shall be. The same day or the next?"

"The same. Why drag out the agony of waiting?"

"I hope you still feel that way after you've eaten my cooking for a while. You may begin to think the agony

262

followed the wedding, rather than preceded it!"

Bonnie made it a point to hurry out to her home the very next evening to display her lovely ring and share her happiness with her family.

"I would like to come home to have my wedding, Mother, if that will meet with your approval."

"Of course, you may come home for your wedding." Avonelle beamed her genuine anticipation. "That is exactly what I want you to do—now that you have found someone—suitable." But her inflection on the final adjective implied Bonnie had not been as discriminating as she herself would have been. *Never mind,* Bonnie consoled the hurt, *in time you will come to see the wisdom of my choice.*

It was Sylvia who was more exuberant in her elation than Bonnie. For on the eve of the day for lovers, the doorbell had rung at the hand of a delivery boy. And there Sylvia had received two beautifully wrapped packages. The large flat one was easily identifiable as a heart-shaped box of chocolates. Curiosity led her to open the other first. She squealed in glee as she unwrapped the tissue which swathed a plush stuffed skunk. He was standing upright with his huge fluffy tail curled upward behind his back. A snowy white stripe stood out in sharp contrast to the sleek black of his body. And in his forepaw Sylvia discovered a tiny slip of paper folded over many times. Opening it out, she could not contain her joy as she read in a masculine scrawl, "Yours until you have graduated and I will be free to make a more positive commitment. Mac." Sylvia's feet had not touched earth since that hour. So great was her elation that her final success in capturing first place in the state regional swim meet scarcely merited a second thought. She knew it was impossible to state definitively whether her success was due to superior ability or a momentum born of very special attention on the part of the coach!

As the weeks wore on, Bonnie saw even less of Buz than she had since he had accepted the church commission. For not only was he pressing unreservedly to produce on his contract, but he now also had final exams to contend with. The one redeeming feature of the enforced separation was that he often needed a break from the pressure and used the excuse to phone her. She never knew when the ring would be prompted by a patient wishing to make an appointment or complain about the bill, or whether Buz would only be saying, "Hi! Just wanted to hear your adorable voice again. You're still there, aren't you? Just checkin'." And the constant contact by voice was almost as good as it would have been to see him more often.

She was also much occupied with her wedding plans. Sylvia, Meredith, her mother, and she had spent more than one shopping trip trying to find the exactly right gowns for the bridal party in keeping with the simplicity upon which she had already decided. A midafternoon wedding following Buz's morning commencement was an appropriate hour and would not dictate the fuss and encumbrance of a bridal train. And so she chose a simple little ballerina-length creation in silk organza over taffeta, with a high, broad v-shaped neckline, currently termed Bateau, inset with Venice lace and long, fitted sleeves. A circular, shoulder-length veil would fall from a miniature pearl crown. Of course, it was a foregone conclusion she would carry nothing except the little white Bible that had been her mainstay for so many months and that had been carried by her grandmother before her.

The bridesmaids were outfitted in street-length dresses of crystalette, in keeping with the current styles. Sylvia, as maid of honor, and little Gwen, the junior bridesmaid, would both wear dresses of a peach shade, and Meredith and Nancy chose a contrasting mint green.

Buz had chosen Drew Anderson and another boyhood chum from Harrisburg to serve as groomsmen. His best man was to be Steve Cameron, a fellow student of architecture at the university.

Happily, Reg and Luanne Walker, having completed an evangelistic tour taking them through points in Ohio and Indiana, were returned to the city for a break and graciously consented to provide nuptial music. And Royle obligingly combined the peach and green color theme in the lovely painting for which he used a cathedral for a background. When Bonnie had approached him with her request, he consented on the assumption that she merely wished it to appear as though the couple were emerging from the edifice following their wedding. And he was never the wiser, for the deep sentiment with which she linked her beloved with a cathedral was too sacred to divulge to another living soul.

"Who is this minister at your church who will perform the ceremony?" Avonelle asked in the midst of the preparations.

"Pastor Thomas. Dr. W. Everett Thomas," replied Bonnie, working over the list of invitations.

"You don't mean Waldy Thomas! From Fox Chapel? Is he about my age? I wonder if he's the Waldy Thomas I knew in school?" Avonelle had thrown her hands up in mock horror. "He was the terror of Fox Chapel High. When any mischief was done, the principal just looked for him. And now you say he's a—a minister?"

"Mother, remember how you told me once that you named me 'Bonnie' for what you hoped I would become, rather than for what I already was? Well, it's the same way with God. He calls His servants on the basis of what He intends to make of them, not for what they already are."

In time the photographer was engaged, the invitations printed, and the flowers ordered. The decoration of the fellowship hall for the reception would be undertaken by the beloved gang. At last Bonnie would witness the fine style of the group's send off.

With wedding plans completed, there was one task she felt yet constrained to perform, one that caused her anguish to contemplate for she could not guess how it was to be received. But how could she conscientiously present herself to a gentleman so fine as Nathaniel Rockwell as a nonentity, a no one, nameless, of totally unknown parentage, without his knowledge? Buz did not know she was not the offspring of Avonelle and James Lake. But before she summoned the courage to tell him, she would try once more to learn whether there was any word she so longed to hear.

She phoned the Salvation Army only a week before the scheduled date of her wedding.

"Miss Lake, you say? I don't recall that any information has come through on that name, but if you give me a moment I'll have someone check. It will take about fifteen minutes to go through the files, so if you will just please call back."

Bonnie didn't know whether to entertain discouragement or hope as she replaced the receiver. The fact that the receptionist did not have any information was not necessarily ominous. However, she believed that anything so startling as coming across something pertinent should be cause for rejoicing throughout the whole staff. On second thought, perhaps none of them was as anxious as she. If you were possessed of two natural parents and knew your family history, you probably couldn't conceive of the gnawing restlessness that vexes those who do not. The more she thought about it, the more anxious she became.

Hoping to occupy her mind until the fifteen minutes were up, she turned her attention to preparing the monthly statements. A couple of patients were so far in arrears that she decided it was time to speak to Dr. Gardner about them.

Finally, after a seeming eternity, the minutes passed and she reached for the phone. It was a shaking finger that finally found its mark on the dial.

"Yes, Miss Lake, we have opened your file"—(did she dare hope the "yes" meant good news?)—"and are sorry to have to report there has been absolutely no reply to the ads we have printed. And we placed them in every foreign publication we have. I can assure you, however, every possible attempt will continue to be made, and we will notify you the moment anything concrete is disclosed."

As the receiver landed in its cradle, Bonnie's heart plunged to her feet. Nothing! Nothing at all. Maybe Buz wouldn't even want her anymore.

What if there had been some dreadful hereditary disease that stalked her family and would appear in some of her children—hers and Buz's? Maybe something that couldn't be identified in time to prevent dire consequences. Her family could all have been lunatics, for all she knew. One thing was certain, she would have to let Buz know what he was letting himself in for. And if he then reconsidered, that was a chance she would simply have to take.

She told him as soon as he arrived for her that very evening.

"As if it isn't enough that I'm not the child of the Lakes, as you would suppose, I must admit I have no idea who I am. They tell me I was abandoned by some Hungarians in France. Maybe I'm even a gypsy! I don't know whether I was ever even given a name before the Lakes adopted me. If you wish—"

Amazement lit his irregular features. He leaned backward to gain a more level vantage point as he sought her eyes with his own. His voice sounded somewhat shrill, disbelieving what he had heard.

"You don't think that could possibly make the slightest bit of difference! I love you for being you. I'm taking unto myself a flesh-and-blood girl, as warm and genuine as any other who walks this fair globe — to have and to hold from this day forward. And if the name makes any difference to you, you will soon be Mrs. Nathaniel G. Rockwell, a name that will be wholly, legally yours as honestly and honorably as though you had been born with a string of European titles. And now don't ever let me hear a word about it again."

She felt such gratitude in her heart toward him that she could almost feel it made no more difference to her.

Sylvia's graduation was the first event to mark the end of the school term. Spotting her in the long line of fresh-faced youngsters pacing proudly to the majestic strains of *Aida* posed no difficulty, for the raven locks cascading from her aristocratic head were a stark contrast to the white robe and mortarboard that she modeled with elegant grace.

"There's one bridesmaid-to-be who will no doubt steal the show," whispered her sister to her mother, watching proudly from the audience. *And what a radiant bride she will make herself when her own time comes,* Bonnie added to herself.

Commencement at Carnegie Tech followed quickly. This time the object of Bonnie's search was not nearly so evident. In fact, the little architect might have been completely lost in the procession were it not that all the other graduates towered at least half a head above him. That is, until the diplomas were distributed. For when Nathaniel Gibson Rockwell, *magna cum laude*, was announced, the applause of the enormous crowd was thunderous. The moisture in Bonnie's eyes at least afforded a means of overflow; otherwise, she felt that if she had tried to contain all that pride, something would have burst. Even her mother and father appeared to be beaming. Perhaps her mother now would begin to understand. Bonnie stole a glance to her other side, for the reactions of Buz's parents were ones she could not afford to miss. How thrilled she was to note his father's firm squeeze of his mother's hand as they each flicked away a tear.

Bonnie had been most eager to see the Rockwells again. And she had wept at their warm embrace when they arrived for the double events. By the time they had presented her with a family heirloom, a golden locket set with a cluster of brilliant sapphires, she feared her eyes would appear red and swollen under her bridal veil.

This touching gift, however, presented a problem. For the night before, Avonelle had given Bonnie the pearl necklace she had found secreted away with the little white Bible in the bottom of the trunk. Now the bride-to-be was in a dilemma, for both necklaces could not be worn at once. Should she wear her maternal grandmother's when that lady had never really been her grandmother? Or should she wear the locket in deference to the fact that she was to join a family with blood ties and, by right of marriage, she would inherit genuine ancestors? The decision came quickly. She *could* wear them both if she wound the pearls around her wrist a couple times as a bracelet. The delicate strand lent itself surprisingly well to the modification. Symbolically, she would blend her adoption with her husband's natural bloodline.

Following the commencement exercises, there was no time to be maudlin, for haste must be made in preparing for the wedding. The Rockwells departed to their hotel room, and the Lake family made their way to Shadyside Apartments. Bonnie had already moved her possessions into the little apartment she was to share with Buz out in Squirrel Hill, and it was in her old room with Sylvia that she made her final preparations for her marriage. The bridesmaids assembled to assist with the blue garter and final adjustments. The locket she carried with her to be clasped at the last moment by Mrs. Rockwell. And finally, with the little white Bible securely in her hands, Bonnie left her childhood home to take her place beside the man she loved more than anyone else in the world.

Buz's eyes blissfully followed her every move as she made her way down the aisle on the arm of her beloved father. And as the radiant couple knelt at the altar, Luanne's magnificent voice sang the prayer of dedication. She had set Frances Ridley Havergal's, "Take My Life, and Let It Be Consecrated, Lord, to Thee," to a lyrical melody and changed the singular pronouns to plural. Not another sound was to be heard in the sanctuary until the last beautiful strain had died away and the new Mr. and Mrs. Rockwell embraced tenderly and rose to hurry back up the aisle and out to their reception.

The gang had exceeded themselves on this one, with sprays of fresh flowers hanging from the chandeliers, fireside baskets adorning the hearth, streamers and wedding bells cascading from every corner, and Royle's lovely painting occupying a prominent place just behind the seats for the bride and groom. It was a reception to be remembered forever.

But as the bridal couple dashed to their waiting car amidst the showers of rice and confetti, they had yet to learn all that Meredith had meant when she said the group sent newlyweds off in fine style, for tied to the back bumper was the longest line of battered old buckets Bonnie had ever imagined, and strapped to the roof was an old white chamber pot, upright with a motley bouquet of flowers!

They stopped to remove the evidence before entering the turnpike, and then settled themselves for the long drive back across the state Bonnie had loved in December. Their honeymoon destination was in the beautiful Pocono Mountains of the east. Bonnie thrilled to view the majestic mountains and rolling farmlands clothed in their luxuriant green, for they were ever so much more striking then than they had been in the starkness of winter.

Having settled themselves in the little hotel room overlooking a breathtaking view of a valley, and about to embark on their union as husband and wife, Bonnie took time for one last ritual, as sacred as any that had preceded it on this day. Out of her luggage she produced the little white Bible, now showing signs of much wear. And with a shaking hand, guided by that of her new husband, Bonnie wrote on the now dulled pages in the middle: "Bonnie Lake and Nathaniel G. Rockwell, Pittsburgh, Pa., June 3, 1960."

17

Two weeks later found the happy newlyweds back in the city. Buz had become so absorbed in the plans for the North Side church that leaving the project was difficult. Furthermore, he had accepted the offer of apprentice to the firm of Cohen Associates, Inc., established in a downtown office. Having weighed the alternatives, he had elected to remain in Pittsburgh. At the conclusion of their apprenticeship, he and his college buddy, Steve Cameron, planned to establish their own firm.

Mike DeSantis was to be the third member of the anticipated firm. Mike had graduated one semester ahead of Buz and Steve, and had already attracted a considerable clientele with a model displayed in the utilities office of East McKeesport. Using tiny panels of glass for the upper half of the one-story edifice and pebbles to represent the stone masonry of the lower half, he had created a scale model of his proposed design that drew prospective clients from many miles to scrutinize. Mike's career was assured. Full of confidence, he was striking out on his own for the time being.

Two floors above the offices of Cohen Associates, Inc., Buz's friend from Harrisburg had no difficulty securing employment with an old, well-established financial consulting firm. Considering Pittsburgh to be more economically progressive than his native community, Drew Anderson had also chosen to remain in the city. Within one building, the three friends settled themselves in anticipation of a secure future, making their mark on a rapidly changing world.

Meanwhile, Bonnie excitedly prepared to polish her skills as a housewife. The apartment they had found in Squirrel Hill for the time being was spacious and airy. The light beige carpeting permitted all the experimentation with color her heart desired. As excitedly as a child with new toys for Christmas, she had scurried to the paint store to secure myriads of samples. And after long deliberation she made careful selections of just the exactly right hues and nuances. The living room was to reflect several shades of green, all of them light and coolly relaxing. In keeping with her long-held opinion that one should dine in the cheeriest and most stimulating environment, she chose a rich rose for the dining room. And regardless of how one slept, one should awaken to a feeling of vibrancy. Undecided between royal blue or brilliant red, she chose to combine the hues in shades of orchid and magenta. The lighter shades would make suitable selection for the walls, and the more vivid solely for accent. After all, she did not wish to keep Buz awake!

Not considering herself too deft with the paintbrush and roller, she was nevertheless undaunted in her enthusiasm and plied the tools with exuberance. And with each stroke she thrilled to the new life she was instilling into her new home. At the end of her first day of labor, she painted a large heart with "Love ya, Buz," enclosed within on a wall that remained yet to be done. And, cleaning her implements for the next attack, she prepared a meal worthy of the object of her affections for his return from the office.

Having sat hand-in-hand on their little outdoor balcony in the cool of the evening, watching the streaks left from the jets plying their way toward the airport and listening to the last cooing of the doves as they roosted for the night under the eaves, the contented couple likewise prepared to end their day.

"I hope every day is as idyllic as this one has been," sighed the dreamy-eyed bride.

"You wouldn't want to paint every day, would you?"

"Well, no. At least not walls. Landscapes, maybe. And I hope Mr. Twineham doesn't give you a hard time again as he did today."

"Never fear. I believe we got him straightened out on that foyer that he's been—" The phone interrupted before he could finish.

"I'll get it." Bonnie was beginning to grow sleepy and hoped that it was a matter that could be dispensed with quickly.

"Bonnie?" Her mother's voice sounded somewhat agitated. "Is Sylvia there? At your place? Have you seen her?"

"Why, no, she isn't here. I haven't seen anything of her. Why?"

"She didn't come home this afternoon when it was time for the pool to close. We ate dinner without her, thinking she might have been held up somewhere and would surely come later. But she has not shown up. It just isn't like her not to let us know where she is. She at least phones if she has a change of plans. Surely if anything had happened at the pool—"

"Oh, yes," Bonnie tried to sound reassuring. "You would know if there had been any accident or anything. She must have met some friends and gone off with them. Maybe she even tried to call and there was no one home to answer. Were you at the Red Cross today?"

"Yes, but I came home at noon. She would surely have known she could reach me there if she tried. Once home I never left again. And the phone didn't ring all day."

"What about Perry? Was he there when you weren't?"

"No, he went to that new car wash down on Chestnut Street to try to get a job. Some of his buddies told him they were hiring high school kids for the summer, so he spent the morning going down there."

"Did he get the job?" Bonnie was a little incredulous at the idea of her brother's doing any work.

"No," and irritation was now more evident than agitation in Mrs. Lake's voice. "He was too late. They had already taken on all they need."

"Well, then, if Dad doesn't know anything about her, I can't imagine where she would be."

"Your father doesn't know any more than the rest of us. He came home at the usual time and wondered where she was. I thought I would try you first, and now I'll try to think of some friends she might be with. Can you think of anyone?"

Now that was a problem, thought Bonnie. Sylvia didn't have many girl friends. She had always found the male gender to be more stimulating as companions.

Aloud she suggested, "Have you looked in her room? Maybe she left a note or something. How about on the refrigerator?"

"There is no note anywhere in the kitchen, but I didn't think to check her room. Just hold the phone a minute while I look."

Bonnie shifted her position on the phone bench and figured she might as well make herself comfortable. Something nagging in the inner recesses of her mind told her this might be a long session. Then she reached for the phone book. She was leafing aimlessly through it, trying to summon some clue where Sylvia might be when she heard her mother's voice again, shrill with alarm.

"Bonnie, Bonnie, she did—a note, I mean—oh, would you believe," and a pitiful little wail escaped along with her torrent of words. Then she deliberately stopped as though to gain control of her voice and, after a moment's hesitation, began again slowly, each syllable enunciated distinctly but with great effort. "Bonnie, she left her stuffed skunk on top of her pillow alone—the rest of the animals were thrown in a heap in one corner of her bed. And pinned to the skunk's tail was a tiny slip of paper that says, 'Be back soon; don't worry.' Don't worry, she says. *Don't worry!*" And Mrs. Lake's voice again started to rise to a high, agitated pitch. "Whatever does she mean by this?"

"The skunk," repeated Bonnie, a blend of wonder and humor in her voice. "Why doesn't that sound exactly like something Sylvia would do? Honestly, Mother, I would have to laugh if it were not so serious a matter. Of course, if Sylvia had every animal there is in the zoo stuffed on her bed, and wanted to leave a note on one of them, she would choose the skunk. And the tail yet— Mother, isn't that just the silliest—" Suddenly the humor was gone. A pause followed. She was serious once more. Pensive. "Isn't that the skunk Mac gave her for Valentine's Day? Do you suppose she is trying to tell us something?"

"Oh, I never thought of that. Now let me see; Sylvia has disappeared, and it has something to do with that swim instructor. He must be the first person to try to find. What did she say his whole name is? McMillen, Dewey McMillen. Isn't that it?"

"Yes, I believe that's it." Bonnie finally had something to look for in the phone directory. "Just a minute while I see if I can find it. Let me see, Mac, MacMillen, Donald, Henry, James, Robert," and her eyes quickly skimmed the list of "Macs." "There isn't a Dewey here. It must be spelled 'M-c.' Yes, I believe that is the way it is." And she flipped over a couple of pages. Once more her eyes scanned every McMillen on the page, only to find no Dewey. "Mother, there is no Dewey McMillen in the phone book. Maybe his number is unlisted. You hang up and I'll call the operator to see whether she has anything for him."

A weary voice answered when Bonnie dialed "0" and it seemed to Bonnie that she waited forever for an answer. But finally the weary one returned to announce there was no Dewey McMillian listed anywhere in Pittsburgh.

When she had redialed her mother to convey this discouraging information, her mind started spinning, searching for some means by which she might be able to locate him.

"Mother, do you remember the name of the principal in that school? I know it was Mr. Sawyer when I was there, but I think they had a different one last year. Mancini, I think the name was. Let's see now," and again she flipped the pages in the directory. "Mancini, Anthony, Carmen, Frank, Joseph, R. S. — they called him Tony, didn't they? All right, it must be this Anthony. I hate to bother someone like that at this hour of night, but I don't know anything else to do."

"Just give me the number," her mother interrupted. "I'll bother him. It won't bother me at all. I've simply got to find out where that girl is."

"All right. The number is EL-four, four, one, two, four. While you are trying that, I'll try to think of some other places Sylvia might be. After all, we're not sure Dewey McMillen knows where she is, either. And now, listen, Mother, before we go any farther with this, I would like just to stop right now and commit Sylvia to the Lord for His protection, and trust Him to bring her back home."

"Commit — commit her to the *Lord?*" The voice this time was not only anxious, but verging on hysterical. "You mean that here it is, ten o'clock at night, Sylvia has not shown up all day, we are frantic trying to locate

277

her, and you sit there calmly and just say, 'Commit her to the Lord.' What does He have to do with it?"

"That's just it, Mother. He knows where she is, and He will take care of her if we just leave her in His hands."

"Oh, little Miss Prophet, where do you get your authority to say a thing like that?" The old friction was setting off sparks again. Bonnie knew she was treading on emotional ground, but surely in the face of Sylvia's disappearance there was nothing else to lose.

"It says in the Book of Proverbs, 'Commit thy way unto the Lord; trust also in Him; and He shall bring it to pass.'"

"Bring what to pass?"

"Her safe return. Look at it this way, Mother. Remember how when you adopted her, the state committed her to you, trusting you to be a mother to her and rear her with the best of care that you could give her. In a sense they just turned her over to you and never interfered again. They trusted you to do the job you had committed yourself to do. Now if you can only reverse that and turn her over to the Lord, would you believe that as a heavenly Father, He has more concern for her than you do, and He will see to it that she has the care she needs for whatever situation she is in right now."

Bonnie was more than a little surprised at the boldness with which she had spoken once more of such matters to her mother. She had no wish to antagonize; but she felt keenly the need to seek the Lord at this moment on Sylvia's behalf. There was no telling where that girl could be or what danger she might be in. Bonnie waited breathlessly for her mother's reaction to her words.

It was slow in coming. Apparently Mrs. Lake was allowing a little time for at least some of Bonnie's words to sink in. Finally, she responded in a low murmur.

"Well, then, that makes more sense than some of the

other things you've said. If that's the way you feel about it, you go ahead and 'commit,' or whatever it is you mean to do. As for me, if I don't hear from her by tomorrow, I'll call the police and trust them to find her. Now you see if you can think of anyone to call, and I'll get busy on that number. Ring me back as soon as you find out anything."

Bonnie replaced the receiver in a daze. Sylvia must really be actually gone. It was by now nearing ten-thirty at night, and the last anyone had seen of her had been that morning before her mother left for the Red Cross office. Or, at least, any one of the family. It occurred to Bonnie to try to find out whether Sylvia had ever reported on duty at the pool today. There was no use phoning there at this hour. Even the city offices that administered the recreational projects would be closed now.

When Avonelle Lake dialed the number of Principal Tony Mancini, she received a gruff "Good evening" from the other end of the line.

"Mr. Mancini?" she asked, hesitantly.

"Mancini here," was the reply.

"Mr. Mancini, I'm terribly sorry to bother you at this hour of night, but I have an urgent message for Dewey McMillen. It is my understanding he is a member of the faculty in the school of which you are principal. Is that right?"

"Yes, of course, that's right. What can I do for you?"

"I need to contact him about a very important matter, and I wondered whether you could give me his phone number. I really am very sorry about this intrusion, but you do have his number, don't you?"

"Why, yes, I have it, but it is unlisted, and I just simply cannot give it out on the phone like this." The voice sounded as though it were gaining impatience.

Its owner could just slam down the receiver at any

moment. Avonelle knew she was going to have to talk fast—and convincingly.

"But, Mr. Mancini, this is his cousin in Detroit, and since I'm calling from so far, I hate to have to make too many calls. You see, his aunt, my mother, just passed away this afternoon, and I wish to give him the news. Isn't there any way you can help me?" She knew it sounded rather limp, but if that didn't work, nothing else would either.

"Well," the voice slowed down a little, but the impatience was still there. "If it is his aunt who passed away, I should think you would also wish to contact his parents in Sewickley. Perhaps they would appreciate the news also, and they can tell you where he can be reached, if they wish. Good night." And then she heard the inevitable bang of the receiver.

Once more the information operator was dialed.

"I want a number in Sewickley," Mrs. Lake began, "but I'm not sure of the name and I have no address at all. I'm looking for a man by the name of McMillen. I believe that is spelled with M-c. Do you have a Dewey McMillen listed?"

Once more it seemed that the reply was never coming. Mrs. Lake was by now growing sufficiently frantic that even a moment seemed like ten minutes. But finally the operator returned with a negative answer.

"There is no Dewey McMillen listed in Sewickley."

"Well, will you tell me what McMillens you do have? Surely one of them can tell me where I can reach him."

"There are ten of them listed. Do you want them all?"

"Yes, every one. Please."

She scribbled hastily as the operator dictated, thanked her, and broke the connection. Each one of these calls would be long distance and have some charge, although not great. But no charge would be too great if it would only mean that she could learn where Sylvia was.

She took the list of numbers and started through them in the order in which she had received them. The first one rang a number of times before she gave up, hoped that wasn't the one she wanted, and dialed the next. On the second number, it was answered quickly enough, but proved to be as frustrating as everything else she had tried that evening. A gentleman answered, listened to Mrs. Lake inquire whether he knew Dewey McMillen, and replied,

"Oh, yeah, sure, I know 'im. Belongs to that bunch over in Edgeworth and we don't have nothing to do with them." He hung up before she could ask any further.

It occurred to her after trying four of the numbers that if Bonnie had unearthed anything, she would not have been able to call back to tell her so, since she herself had kept the line busy continuously. So it seemed wiser to phone Bonnie to ask before she went any further.

"Bonnie, have you heard anything?"

"No, Mother, I haven't." Bonnie sounded very weary. "I did call a couple girls she often mentioned as classmates, but they didn't know anything. I tried to call you to ask if you know who she is working with this summer, but couldn't get your line. Has she said anything at all about the other lifeguards? You know, we don't even know whether she went to work today."

"I didn't think of that. But I can't think of the other guards' names. She hasn't talked much since this summer started. Just stays in her room and plays those endless records. She has been terribly quiet, now that I think of it. Not her usual bouncy self. I wonder whether something has been bothering her and she has gone and done something terrible!" Mrs. Lake's voice quavered now to the point where it was a strain just to keep attempting to talk. She fell silent for a moment, long enough for the tears to start. An invisible hand squeezed her throat, and she began to slump over the chair. James, having sat nearby for the entire deluge of phone calls, listening to every word from his wife and guessing at those on the other end of the line, rushed to steady her with his arm. He took the phone from her hand and spoke.

"Bonnie, do you know anything about this McMillen fellow? You know, he told her he would be seeing her as soon as graduation was over. Hasn't done anything so far but call her on the phone. But now that she's graduated— If this is his idea of a date, I'll break every bone in his body."

"I don't know anything at all about him, Dad. Just the things Sylvia said. You heard those yourself. But, really, I think you and Mother should get hold of yourselves. There may be a perfectly logical explanation for all this. Why don't you two just go on to bed for tonight and see what develops tomorrow. Your being all worked up isn't going to bring her back, anyway."

"I don't believe that your mother is going to get any sleep no matter where she spends the night. But I'll let you go. You may as well get a little yourself. Good night, dear."

Having had time to pull herself together a little, Mrs. Lake took the phone when her husband replaced it. "I'll try one more time," she announced.

She was now on the fifth number on the list. When she asked the man who answered the ring whether he knew Dewey McMillen, he replied, "Dewey? Yeah, sure. That's my nephew. Just came home from his house a few minutes ago. The young folks have some kind of a party going on. He's got his girl over there. Cute little thing, she is."

Avonelle's heart leaped into her throat. Girl? Must be none other than Sylvia. But for a total stranger to be that talkative, the beverage at the party must be stronger than soda pop. That made matters even worse. Breathlessly she asked for Dewey's number. Scanning the list hurriedly, she found it was number nine on the list. At least she would be spared two useless calls. Her search must surely be over. Her finger trembled so badly that she couldn't find the right digits on the dial. She pointed to the number written on the list and James dialed. As he did so, she jabbered nearly incoherently about it's being Dewey's number and his uncle had said his girl was with him.

"I'll kill him," vowed Mr. Lake through clenched teeth. His hand trembled, and even he had to begin dialing again.

A young man's voice said, "Hello."

"Please," Avonelle began, "am I speaking to Dewey McMillen?"

"Yes, ma'am, you are."

"This is Avonelle Lake, Sylvia's mother. Will you please tell me whether Sylvia is there with you?" With the moment of truth at hand, Avonelle was so overcome with agitation that every nerve in her body tingled.

A very long, awkward pause greeted her. She was so anxious to hear that her daughter was safe and sound, even though under these circumstances, that she had to restrain herself to keep from shouting at him to hurry with the answer. Finally, a very stiff, cool voice said, slowly and distinctly, "Mrs. Lake, I told Sylvia two weeks before graduation that I have decided to marry my childhood sweetheart. No, Sylvia is not here. Good night."

The clock had just reached midnight.

Somehow the phone slid out of Avonelle's hand and found its way into the cradle. The blanching of her face told James all he needed to know, but she spoke the words anyway. "She isn't there. The girl was somebody else."

283

The words fell like a life sentence just handed down in a hushed courtroom. The two of them sat in stunned silence for several seconds, trying to absorb their full impact. As if it weren't bad enough that Sylvia might have been spirited away by a relatively unknown gentleman, it was even worse that she hadn't been. Because now there was no clue where she might be. No matter how bad the known may be, the unknown is always worse.

"I—I'll call Bonnie," Mrs. Lake said weakly.

A very drowsy sounding Buz answered. "Bonnie? Just a minute. She's been sleeping. Here."

"Yes, Mother." Bonnie was, if possible, sleepier than her husband.

"Bonnie!" her mother fairly shrieked. "How could you? Here your sister is missing, and you went to *sleep!* I finally found that McMillen's home, and Sylvia isn't there. Now I've no idea where she is."

"Why yes, Mother, I told you I was going to commit Sylvia to the Lord, and then I went to sleep."

"It is midnight, and you just commit—" Avonelle stumbled over the word itself as she stumbled over grasping its meaning. "What kind of a religion is this that teaches you to not care what happens to your own sister?"

"My 'religion,' as you call it, teaches me that Jesus cares more for Sylvia than even you or I do, and He will look after her, if we trust Him to do so."

"If He cares all that much for her, why did He let this happen to her?"

Bonnie was much too weary to take on any major theological arguments at this hour of night. She wanted nothing more than to roll back over under the covers and allow her body to refresh itself from the long, difficult day she had just spent.

"Mother, you know there isn't anything you can do

right now. Why don't you at least wait until morning? I think you and Daddy had better just go off to bed now and get a little rest. You may need your strength tomorrow. Good-night, Mom."

Although her father hadn't heard her words, he voiced her sentiment as Avonelle hung up. "Come on, dear, there is absolutely nothing more you can do right now. Sylvia will return from wherever it is she has gone whenever she is good and ready."

"Why, James Lake," his wife snapped, "as if it isn't enough that your other daughter just goes off to bed in such an emergency, you want to do so yourself. I wouldn't have believed the cold heartlessness of this family."

"But, dear, what do you think you can accomplish by sitting here stewing?"

"Well, I can phone the police, for one thing."

James sighed wearily. "Avonelle—" he paused "—they will not do anything tonight. I simply have to go and get some rest. If you aren't going with me, I'm going anyway." And he got up and left the room.

Avonelle watched him cross the hall and enter the bedroom. Then she sat staring blankly for a few moments. She had never felt more numb and exhausted in all her life. And yet she knew that sleep would be a long time in coming. Something somewhere in her body called for activity. She got up and walked out to the kitchen and put the coffee pot on. While it perked, she picked up the day's newspaper, or rather the paper from yesterday it was now, and attempted to read. Her eyes blurred so badly she could scarcely see the print.

When the coffee was done, she poured a cup and sat at the table for a long while drinking it. Then she poured another. After the third cup, she rose and walked into the living room. She went over to the window and pulled back the curtain. An overcast sky shut out any ray of light there may have been from the moon and stars. Only the street lights cast their weird shadows over the world below.

If she hadn't been so numb all over, she would have become conscious of extreme weariness just from standing motionless for so long. It was her subconscious rather than her legs that finally signalled to her to break the vigil at the window, for the longer she watched to no avail, the more pronounced was the finality that absolutely nothing was moving on the street. With a desperate sigh, she turned and walked back to the kitchen.

The first pot of coffee was now cold, and she prepared another. A shiver went up her spine as she reached for her next cup of coffee. Her hand trembled so badly she spilled some cream. But she managed to down a couple more cups. Then it occurred to her she might somehow feel nearer to Sylvia if she were in her room. Perhaps by some miracle she could feel her daughter's presence there and gain some assurance she was in no danger. It was then past three-thirty.

A little unsteadily she made her way down the hall, turned the knob and groped in the dark for the switch on the night stand lamp. Soft shadows played invitingly across the room, and she sank wearily onto the bed. Momentarily relieved, she looked about, and as human nature is, a satirical thought crept into her mind. "If she *had* to go off somewhere, this daughter of mine whose room usually looks a shambles, at least this time she has left the bed made. Yes, she has at least done that much. She who usually leaves her clothes strewn all over the place . . . yes, the clothes . . ." But the room was uncharacteristically tidy. There were no clothes in sight. Suddenly Avonelle jumped up and ran to the closet. It was usually packed. It didn't look quite so full now. Avonelle wracked her muddled brain to remember what should be in it but was missing. A white pique suit, a plaid jacket, surely there had been more skirts than these. Dizzily she made her way to a drawer in the dresser. Half empty. Now where did she keep her luggage? Oh, yes, she herself had given Sylvia luggage as a graduation gift. Could that have been only a couple weeks ago? It seemed now like an eon. In the boxes. Sylvia hadn't even taken them out of the boxes yet. They were lined up along the wall. Right over there. Woodenly Avonelle followed her own directions as though she had been given them by someone else. She shook the box of the small overnight case. It was heavy. Not that one, at least. The cosmetic case was next. She didn't even need to look in it. One shake told her it was empty. When her hand settled on the box for the large pullman, it nearly toppled over. No need to look in it, either. Avonelle's hand pressed to her forehead, trying to steady her reeling thoughts. She staggered back to the bed and sank full length onto it. Should she rouse James and give him this final blow? Surely she couldn't just let him sleep and ignore the awful truth. But no, he wouldn't do anything about it anyway. In fact, what *could* he do? She might as well let him get what sleep he could. Mercifully, her body was going to treat her the same, for her subconscious took over, and she fell into exhausted sleep.

The next thing of which she was aware was a faint rattling from the other side of the wall. But the alarm clock registered no more than an annoyance, and her weary body cried out for a return to oblivion. That was not to be. She was brought fully to her senses by her husband's voice as he burst into the room anxiously calling,

"Avonelle, Avonelle, where are—oh! You frightened me half to death when I awoke and you weren't there. Did you get any sleep in here?"

Avonelle strained with all the energy she could muster to pull herself upright, as her husband sat down on Sylvia's bed beside her. Her voice sounded strained and as far away as the alarm clock had a few moments before.

"Why, I—uh, yes, I slept a little—I guess. Although it seems like only a few minutes ago that I came in here. Look." And she gestured toward the empty luggage boxes.

James followed her hand with his eyes, but some boxes lined up by the wall registered nothing to him.

"Empty," she said dully.

He reached beyond her to tip the shade of the lamp on the night stand which had been burning since she had fallen asleep three hours before. As its beams fell over the boxes, he could make out the trade name of the luggage. Then illumination struck him also.

"She's—she's really gone." He spoke slowly, wonderingly, as the meaning of it fully settled in. "I wouldn't have thought she was all that unhappy. I mean, I've heard of kids running away from home, but usually they didn't have a home worth staying in. Did she seem to you as though anything were troubling her?"

"Well, she has always had her moments when she just shut herself in her room and played her records, but now as I think of it, I believe she has spent more time in her room lately than she used to. But for the life of me, I really can't explain a sudden departure with obvious intentions of staying awhile. Nearly half her clothes are gone. I believe I'm going to have to have some coffee."

Lifting herself off the bed seemed to require more effort than she could muster. Her husband slipped an arm around her to steady her as she rose, and arm in arm the two made their way to the kitchen, lonely, bewildered, and thoroughly worried.

Avonelle plugged in the pot and sat down at the table opposite her husband. He sat with his elbows on the table, hands clasped, and chin resting on his hands, looking pensive. Her eyes wandered past him and found their way to the calendar hanging on the wall. She hadn't let Bonnie's birthday creep up without being aware of it; she had simply momentarily forgotten it in the trauma of the last few hours. Now it stood out on the calendar sheet as though it were the only number there.

"James, dear," she reached over and took one of his hands in hers. "Do you know what day this is? Bonnie's birthday. At least it is the day she entered our lives. We gained one daughter and lost another on the same date."

"Now, dear, perhaps we didn't lose her at all. I think that in view of the fact that she obviously planned this escapade, whatever it is, she is probably safe enough and will let us know before long where she is. You just pour some coffee and pull yourself together. After all, she is a grown girl now. Remember, she is a high school graduate, and many young folks leave home for good at that age, fully capable of looking after themselves." He patted his wife's hand as though to punctuate his words.

There he goes again, she thought. *He wouldn't worry if a tidal wave swept them all away.* "The young folks you are speaking of let someone else know where they are."

"Not always." He went to the refrigerator for the cream, while Avonelle got some cups and poured the coffee.

"I've been thinking," she began slowly after a few sips of the steaming hot brew, "if we begin knocking on doors around this apartment to ask if anyone has seen Sylvia, they'll all know she has gone off somewhere without telling us. We simply can't have that. We are respectable people and only lower class people do such things. We can't have the neighbors know our daughter would do such a thing."

Avonelle rose to pour again. "Just the same, I'm going to phone the pool when it opens and find out whether she was there yesterday. Then I'll call the police. It surely can't hurt any to have them looking for her. It's time for you to leave if you are going to work. You surely aren't going today, are you? Not until we learn something about Sylvia?"

"No, of course not. I'll at least stay until we learn something."

They lapsed into silence, broken only by an occasional sip from a cup. Their private reveries were shattered many minutes later by the jangling of the phone. Her nerves frayed like broken twine, Avonelle was startled into spilling her coffee down the blouse into which she had changed the previous afternoon upon returning from the Red Cross. As she rose to answer the phone, she was aware for the first time of the sight she must present. Her slacks were crumpled, her hair was matted into snarls, and surely her makeup would be smudged and streaked from the tears. What matter, she thought, when the beautiful one was missing. There would be time later to put herself in order. This call may be what they were waiting for. It was a very trembling hand that reached for the receiver.

"Hello." The voice quavered and waited breathlessly for the reply. "Good morning, Bonnie. Happy birthday, dear." Another pause. "No, we haven't heard a thing. But we did discover she has packed a number of articles of clothing in the new luggage she received for graduation. She evidently planned to be gone for a time. I'll be sure to let you know as soon as we hear anything. Don't work too hard today, dear. Remember, it's your birthday and you should relax and treat yourself well."

"Now, Mother," her daughter replied, "you know there is only one chance in three hundred sixty-five that today is my birthday. No, three sixty-six this year. But I appreciate your thought. However, there is too much work to do around here to do any relaxing. It's fortunate we don't have any furniture to speak of. That would only be that much more to have to move to paint around.

Call as soon as you hear anything. 'Bye now."

As Avonelle replaced the receiver there was a shuffling sound from the doorway of Perry's room. The strawberry curls flopped at all angles over the frowning forehead, a couple fingers swiped at the corners of his eyes, and the boy had not stopped to put a robe over his pajamas.

"Can't a guy get any sleep around here?" he growled. "That phone has done nothing but ring all night long. I finally got a little snooze in, only to have it start all over again this morning."

His mother caught his arm on his way past her and accompanied him to the kitchen.

"Here, son, sit down and have a cup of coffee. I suppose the ringing of the phone did bother you; but while you were trying to get some sleep, we were trying to find your sister. You might as well know, she has packed a good many of her things and is really gone—"

"Humph! We may have some peace around here now. I bet whoever took her will bring her right back now that it's daylight and he can get a good look. No, thanks, I'll have a bowl of cereal instead of coffee. I'm going back to bed."

Mrs. Lake opened her mouth with a reproving look on her face, but her husband intercepted the intended speech.

"Now, Avonelle, don't raise your blood pressure over brotherly nonsense. I think I have something to say to the young man myself. Uh, Perry, what do you intend to do with yourself today—while your friends busy themselves in gainful employment?"

Perry shifted his eyes under his father's gaze.

"Oh, I don't know—go over to the carwash and just hang around, I guess. Maybe one of the fellows won't show up and they might give me the job yet."

"Slim chance. You blew it that time, young man.

Now, there was a 'Help Wanted' sign in the window of the service station on Thirteenth Street the other day. I suggest you get yourself over there and check that out. That is, if you're not too late there already."

"Yeah." The grunt was anything but enthusiastic.

"If you don't step around, the summer will be gone before you get started. It's past the middle of June now."

"Sure, Dad, I'll get on it."

Perry put his emptied cereal bowl in the sink and started down the hall, back to his bed.

Mr. and Mrs. Lake sat in silence for what seemed to be an eternity. There was nothing else to say, and no more ideas as to Sylvia's whereabouts were forthcoming. The optimism with which James had greeted the sunshine appeared to increase with time, not with any tangible reason for it, but perhaps an unconscious acknowledgment that no news was good news. Surely if something dreadful had happened to Sylvia, they would have received some information by now.

Avonelle was neither optimistic nor despairing. A dull numbness had taken the edge off her earlier panic, and she simply sat, staring into nothing, expecting something but she knew not what. Every noise elicited a reflex in her muscles, tense from the anticipation that some sound eventually would signal the advent of news. A door slammed on the floor above them, a delivery truck rattled to a halt before the apartment building door, some young people called to each other on the street below.

Avonelle welcomed a "Meow" from Yang as he leaped from his perch on the dining room window, sauntered into the kitchen, and indicated he wanted some attention. Rising and pouring milk into his dish offered meaningful activity to his grateful mistress. Finding that movement relieved some of the tension, she observed it might be profitable to shower and change the clothes she had been wearing since the previous afternoon. Before she left for the shower, she emptied the coffee grounds, rinsed the pot, and plugged in a fresh brew.

She chose fresh slacks and a cool casual blouse, as the day gave promise of becoming very warm, tied up her hair in a knot, and stepped into the shower. It proved to be refreshing enough that she delayed ending it until she was saturated with its stimulating effects. Then she reached in the medicine chest for some aspirin, thinking it would help chase the remaining cobwebs from her head. Feeling considerably better, she emerged from the bathroom and went straight to the kitchen for another cup of coffee.

"It's nearly ten o'clock," she observed. "I'm sure there will be someone at the pool now preparing to open. I believe the number is right here on the kitchen memo."

"North Side Pool."

"This is Avonelle Lake, Sylvia's mother. Will you please tell me whether Sylvia was at work yesterday, and if she was, what time did she leave?"

"Sylvia? Oh, yes. Sorry, Mrs. Lake. She never showed and didn't call in, either. Needless to say, the boss didn't take too kindly to that. We had to delay opening the pool until a replacement could be called in."

"Was — was there — had she said anything the day before about where she planned to go yesterday?"

"No, ma'am, nothing. She just simply didn't show up."

"I understand. Thank you." The weariness threatened to overwhelm Avonelle again, but she fought it off, realizing that she was better off not to give in to it.

"She wasn't there," Avonelle turned to her husband, simply. "I do believe it's time to call the police."

"Now, Avonelle, I don't know what you think they — look, Sylvia had been in full command of herself just the day before she disappeared and the chances are, she was when she left also. This appears to have been fully planned and executed with forethought. She wouldn't have been spirited away against her will when she had time to pack up her belongings. And the phone was in working order, so she could have called for some kind of help if she had chosen to. She simply did not choose to. I suggest that you wait a little longer, and surely something will develop."

Avonelle usually deferred to her husband's wishes, partly out of a sense of wifely duty and partly because he always made sense. In spite of his generally unflappable disposition, he usually thought with a level head. This time, however, her agitation superseded her better judgment, and she picked up the phone once more, anyway.

Gratefully she recognized the voice of the officer, Nick Cvetovich. His wife Rose had gone through high school with her, spent time occasionally on various Red Cross projects, and remained one of her closest friends. He surely would see that everything possible was done to locate Sylvia.

"Nick," she began, "this is Avonelle Lake. Listen, Nick—" She groped for words, reluctant to make such an admission to a friend. "Sylvia has disappeared. She was gone when I came home yesterday from the Red Cross. Luggage, everything. She left just a note saying she would see us soon. Do you—have you received any reports of accidents or—I mean, is there any way—"

"You say she took some luggage and there is no indication of any foul play? What was she wearing?"

"I've no idea what she was wearing. But she could be in anything now. She took a lot with her. You could set up an investigation or something—"

"Mrs. Lake, I'm sorry, but the police department won't do anything until she has been gone three days. And in the case of deliberately packing some luggage and leaving a note and no evidence of any struggle, we have reports of people going off like that all the time. Usually they are heard from soon. Now if you wait three days and there is still no word—"

"Oh, I see, yes, thank you, Nick. But you will have the patrol cars on the lookout for her, won't you?"

"We'll do what we can, Mrs. Lake. Now you just buck up. Sylvia will probably turn up any minute."

Avonelle wished she could be as optimistic. But there was to be no help there. It was evident there was nothing to do but wait it out.

Perry emerged from his room again, dressed and slightly less dishevelled.

"Couldn't get back to sleep, so I figured I might as well give it up."

"I should think you might," replied his father. "And I should think you also had better pound the pavement over to that service station."

"I'm on my way." The door closed behind him.

Avonelle poured another cup of coffee and opened the refrigerator to refill the cream pitcher. She settled herself once more at the table, with an air of resignation, expecting to resume the long and silent vigil. Her husband, having seen Perry out the door, turned into the bedroom, intending to get dressed. She hadn't long to sit. Once more the jangling of the phone pierced the stillness of the little apartment and jolted Avonelle upright in her chair.

It must be Bonnie again, she thought. *Probably wondering whether we have heard something and didn't think to tell her. Maybe she has heard something*—Aloud she said, "Hello."

"Mother? Guess what? I'm—"

The words fuzzed over in Avonelle's ears. Was she really hearing Sylvia's voice?

"—married, Mother. Hal and I. Hal Gregersen. We—"

It couldn't be. The strain of the past twelve hours was taking its toll. Now she knew she had slipped a little too far.

"— are in Hagerstown, Maryland, and are on our way down to Washington, D.C., for a little honeymoon. Mother? Are you there?"

The breathless torrent was momentarily stilled as Sylvia sensed something of the stunning blow her words dealt her mother.

It was several seconds before Avonelle could speak. She wanted to discredit her own ears, but somehow she must face the possibility Sylvia was never more serious.

"You say you are married? To Hal?" She repeated the words as though making an effort to comprehend their meaning.

"Yes, Mother. We stopped yesterday afternoon at a Justice of the Peace in Cumberland to tie the knot. I told you not to worry."

"But w-why did you do it? I mean, couldn't you have had a decent wedding here at home? You didn't even *tell* us!"

"Now, Mother, you eloped yourself. Remember?"

"But in those days that was the thing to do. People couldn't afford all those elaborate weddings. They just had to go off somewhere — at least, their parents knew what they were up to. You could have had any kind of wedding you wanted, but here you —"

"I did," interrupted Sylvia. "I had just what I wanted. Now are you going to wish me well, or aren't you? Say 'Hi!' to Daddy for me. We'll be home in a few days. Now we have to call Hal's folks and tell them. Oh, Mom, will you call the pool for me and say I'll be in sometime, maybe the week after next? 'Bye now."

A click signaled that that was the end of that. Just that simple, as though it were something one did every day.

James had appeared in the doorway on the first ring of the phone. His wife's side of the conversation had given him sufficient information.

"Well, I'll be!—Hal? So it's been Hal Gregersen all along. A sly one that Hal is. Knew he'd do all right with either one of our daughters. I kind of figured he wouldn't give up 'til he got one of them. He'll go a long way someday. Then we'll be proud of our son-in-law."

Avonelle stared at her husband in dumb amazement. "But what will people *say?*" It was more of a wail than a question.

"Say? Why, they will say, 'Congratulations!' That's always in order for newlyweds." There was a mischievous gleam in his eye. Clearly he was relaxed and not a little pleased with the outcome of the long hours of worry.

"But, but to just go off and—"

"I believe I'd better get started shaving," James interrupted his wife.

An unspoken question worked its way through the hurt look in Avonelle's eyes. James answered it as he continued: "It's early yet. I may as well go on to work. Being father of the bride isn't on the list of legitimate absences." With a wink he was off down the hall, Avonelle staring numbly after him.

When he had closed the bathroom door, she still remained motionless except for a slow, sad shaking of her head. Suddenly she started with the dawn of a returning memory. Bonnie! She must be given the news. Woodenly, Avonelle reached once more for the phone.

"There's—there's news, Bonnie. She called. Sylvia—" Avonelle paused, struggling to find the right words. "She's married. To Hal. In Maryland. They're on their way to—"

Bonnie interrupted. "Oh, Mother—" And then there was silence. Both women wrestled with their own counsel, trying to absorb the full significance of what it meant to each of them, to Sylvia, to Hal, to the whole family. Bonnie stretched as far as she could reach and replaced the lid on the paint can and laid the trim brush across the top of it. Fortunately, she hadn't been working too far from the phone. She anchored the roller on the edge of the pan and hoped the paint wouldn't dry in it while she was on the phone.

Finally, after several moments of reflection, pieces seemed to fit together in some semblance of coherence. At length she spoke.

"Sylvia always did like older men. Then along came Mac and she flipped over him. He led her on for most of a year while she waited in hope. But never entirely discouraging Hal, either. Just when she thought her dreams would be realized, Mac completely shattered them by the announcement of his coming marriage to someone else. Right?"

"Yes, I guess that's the picture," her mother agreed wearily, her voice sounding as though it came from the next county. "And you think that's the reason—"

"I'm sure of it. Sylvia just turned to the next most likely prospect and Hal wasn't averse to being agreeable. He always did have an eye out for her. I just hope— Really, if Sylvia were going to elope with somebody, she couldn't have chosen any better than Hal. And she certainly has known him long enough. Really, Mother, once you get over the shock, it doesn't seem so bad after all."

"How can you say it isn't so bad? Lower class people elope. Respectable ones have decent weddings as you did."

At that Bonnie laughed. "Mom, you don't really think I'm any more married than Sylvia is, do you?"

"Well, yes, it seems so—so *right* to get married properly. And to frighten us so badly as she did. That just isn't proper. And she showed no concern for us whatsoever."

"If she had let you know ahead of time, it could hardly be eloping, and that seems to be what she wanted to do. She did leave a note for you not to worry, remember? You can hardly say she didn't consider you at all."

"You surely don't think that little ridiculous note would keep a mother from worrying? Just wait until you have daughters of your own. Then you will understand what you don't seem to understand now."

"But I do understand, Mother." Bonnie also understood that to continue in this course was useless. Her mother was not to be consoled, placated, or appeased on any condition. "Listen," Bonnie continued, "let's plan a nice reception for them when they get home and invite all our acquaintances and make it look perfectly natural. After all, people get married all the time. And especially in June. It will all look as though it were fully planned."

"I'll think about that later. First I have to adjust to the shock."

"OK. Now you just go to the beauty parlor and relax a little while I get on with this painting. See you."

When Bonnie recovered her paint brush from the lid of the can, she discovered that it was beginning to stiffen. She hurriedly pried open the lid, plunged in the brush, and forced it against the inside of the can, manipulating the handle to soften the bristles. Then she stirred the paint remaining in the pan and poured in some more. The roller required little encouragement to prove itself pliable, and she began once more to cover the wall. However, she moved as a robot, her eyes unseeing, the roller strokes going in every direction. Her heart, as well as her mind, was somewhere on a highway in Maryland heading for Washington.

Yes, it was easy to understand why Sylvia had chosen the course she did. In fact, considering her impulsive disposition, it was probably to be expected. But poor Hal. Steady and sterling, he had never let Bonnie down.

Who else in all the world would have taken her back after that ridiculous fiasco with George Morrow? Stayed with her until she once more told him the end had come. And then still didn't completely drop out of the picture, even though the reason for her refusal he couldn't entirely comprehend. Always there, dating Sylvia occasionally, for real interest in her or only to be available in case this new romance of Bonnie's fell through also? Perhaps a little of both. And then, when Bonnie was finally and eternally married to Buz, knowing there was no more hope of his ever having her, he just naturally succumbed to Sylvia's attentions when she was left void of her dreams and drifting. Had Bonnie herself somehow driven him to this rash act by appearing, as he understood it, "too good for him"? Should she entertain a nagging suspicion of guilt that she was somehow to blame?

Nonsense. It had been evident at the first meeting of Hal and Sylvia a couple years ago that each was attracted to the other. And that while he was dating Bonnie! Any remorse was short-lived, for she knew her first allegiance was to God, that she had attempted to encourage Hal to come into the same relationship with Him that she enjoyed, and he had refused.

Yet a feeling of apprehension for him not unrelated to pity remained. Did he know how headstrong his enchanting tornado of vivacity really was? Oddly enough, her own thoughts seemed to resound with a portentous note.

"God, speed them on their way," she prayed. "Bless this marriage and bring good out of it according to Your own will. To that end I commit them both to You."

Hers was the only benediction spoken over the young newlyweds, and it was to be many years before there was any indication it bore fruit.

Meanwhile, James Lake bent lovingly over his wife,

still riveted to the phone bench completely lost in reverie, kissed her forehead, and headed for the door. With his hand on the knob, he turned back to her with a wink. "Now you see, we didn't lose a daughter today at all. We gained a son."

A *far cry*, she mused as the door closed behind him, *from the irate father who had vowed just twelve hours before to kill another young man for making off with his daughter.* Perhaps it was just as well; she drew a little strength from his optimism.

Now she was left entirely alone with her thoughts. The first thing she would need to do was to return to the kitchen and make a fresh pot of coffee. She was seized with the desire to take a very long sleep of complete oblivion and then awaken to learn it had all been a nightmare. But even as weary as she was, she knew this was a dream that would stalk her relentlessly upon awakening so she might as well cope with it now and make the necessary adjustment. She filled the pot with fresh coffee and cold water and plugged it in. And then she remembered.

The police! Should she phone them to say the search should be cancelled? Should she just forget it, knowing they wouldn't do anything for awhile anyway and would probably just ignore it? But yet, it was on the record and some day the truth would be out. What should she do? Why, oh why hadn't she listened to James and Bonnie when they told her not to call them in the first place? Now, no matter what she did—maybe Bonnie had had a point after all when she said to commit it to the Lord, whatever that meant. Wasn't God someone who was supposed to look after people, and hadn't she learned that Sylvia was at least alive and well? Why had she acted so rashly and not waited at least another hour or so? Well, there was no point in crucifying herself any further. She would go ahead and phone them and be done with it.

"Nick? This is Avonelle Lake again. Uh, we have heard from Sylvia. She is quite all right. She—well, she went off on a little overnight trip with some friends. That's all. Thanks ever so much." She thought Nick had started to reply, but she didn't wait to hear it. She didn't know what he would think when he heard that click in his ears, but she couldn't care about that.

Now then, the coffee wouldn't be quite finished yet—She walked to the front room and looked out the window. A couple of children were riding tricycles on the walk three floors below. The bushes which had seemed so secretive in the middle of the night now waved softly in a sunny breeze. Several people were sunning on the porches on the apartment building across the street. The peaceful scene contrasted too sharply with the turmoil Avonelle felt in her breast, and she turned from the window to pace aimlessly out to the dining room.

What have I done? she remonstrated with herself. *Where have I gone wrong? How in the world did I deserve this? I took Bonnie from a life of misery in Europe, gave her everything I had to give her, loved her every bit as much as I would my own flesh and blood, would have even died for her, and she turns around and tells me I'm a sinner. Then I take Sylvia out of the hospital where she had been placed after she was found neglected in that basement and give her beautiful clothes for her lovely figure.* Avonelle suddenly discovered she was wringing her hands. *Come now,* she said to herself, *let's not have any melodramatics. Let's take this calm and easy. There must be something I left out. Somewhere I went wrong. What was it that I did? Or didn't do?*

She poured another cup of coffee. *And then there's Perry. Found a few hours old wrapped in newspapers and stuffed into a garbage can. Then a succession of unsuccessful foster homes until he was finally awarded to us. At least the* girls had the gumption to get themselves jobs by the time they were his age. Bonnie sold tickets in a theater and Sylvia was so proud to pass her life-saving test. But Perry wouldn't even take the course.

Somewhere I went wrong, failed as a mother, she thought. *Just when I tried so hard to do always the right thing and present a respectable appearance. Now, what will people ever think? I believe I'd better go out—get out of the house—do something—keep my mind busy. Go over to Bonnie's? What kind of a sermon would I get there? I guess I'll just go into town.*

She got off the streetcar on Seventh Avenue and strolled leisurely, looking at the displays in the department store windows. *Those sheath dresses are so narrow around the hemline it must be like having your knees tied together to try to walk in them,* she thought. *Yet if you had a slender figure, they would be very smart and becoming.* She knew she would qualify in that category.

At once she began to search for a coffee shop. As there was no scarcity of such shops in the area, she was soon asking for a cup as she gazed absently out the window of one of them, watching the endless stream of humanity pass by. It occurred to her that it must be near noon, and all the offices in downtown Pittsburgh must have emptied of their employees as they poured out for lunch. She was fortunate to have been ahead of the rush, or she would never have gotten a table. She hoped that none of her acquaintances would see her there as they passed. Perhaps she should turn to face the other direction. The back of the head is not as recognizable as the face. Furthermore, she would have to stay in here for the next forty-five minutes in order not to risk running into someone out on the sidewalk.

She knew she looked a sight. There were dark circles under her eyes, and her hands were shaking terribly by this time. It didn't occur to her that the amount of coffee she was imbibing added to her weariness. The more she shook, the more she felt she should drink to steady herself. And in the dark muddling of her exhausted mind, she felt as though the weight would never be lifted from her shoulders. She simply could not face conversation with anyone today. She would just drink coffee until the noon rush hour was over.

When at length the tide of hot, hurrying bodies had subsided, and only the usual summer afternoon shoppers were left milling around from one display window to another, she ventured outside into the bright sunlight, looked both up and down the street, saw no one she recognized, and proceeded on her way. She wasn't sure exactly what her way should be, except that the steps leading up to Mellon Square beckoned to her from the next block, and she felt she would have a measure of seclusion there. She climbed the stairs and made her way to one of the stone benches under the shade of a tall shrub.

The sun had moved sufficiently that a ray shot directly into her eyes between the branches of the sheltering shrub. She blinked and jerked her head quickly to avoid the glare. As she did so, she caught sight of someone walking up the stairs. Something about the newcomer looked very familiar. It couldn't be—oh, no, of all people, it *was* Rose Cvetovich. If there was anyone she didn't want to see at that moment, it was Rose. Her husband would know—maybe if she looked the other way. But if she did, the sun shone directly into her eyes. She might still have time to get up and move quickly in the other direction. But that would probably only call attention to herself. Maybe if she just said nothing about her problem, just "Hello, and how are you?" But how could she pull that off? When Rose and Nick both got home that evening, Nick would say, "You know who called today to report someone missing?" And even if

Avonelle didn't mention it, it would soon be out that Sylvia was married and Rose would be able to add it up. After all, it would be quite obvious. Oh, if *only* she hadn't made that foolish call to the police.

Strangely enough, at that moment Avonelle fully perceived that Sylvia was now an adult married woman about to return from a honeymoon and set up housekeeping in a home provided for her by her lawfully married husband. Until then, Avonelle, in a clouded daze of shock, had thought vaguely only of Sylvia's having been spirited away on a clandestine, somehow immoral lark, bringing disgrace on the family's good name. This new perception entered her consciousness as a breath of fresh air, and she was even able to respond almost cheerily to Rose's gusty, "Hi, there! I certainly wasn't expecting to find you here. Why didn't you call, and we could have come downtown together?"

"Hi, Rose. I came away in somewhat of a hurry and didn't take time to call." Knowing how bad she looked, she thought she might jump the gun on Rose and make up an excuse for her appearance before Rose asked. "I have been a little under the weather lately. Little cold or sinus. When I saw what a lovely, sunshiny day it is, I thought maybe a change of scenery and a little basking in the sun might help. How have you been? It must be a couple months since we really talked. Of course, you were at Bonnie's wedding, but that is no place for visiting." To lend credence to her words, she took a tissue from her purse and blew her nose daintily. The ruse wasn't necessary; her nose was already red and raw from a night of sniffling.

"Avonelle, doll, you look like you haven't slept in a week. I think you had better stop off at the doctor's on your way home and then go to bed. Here, let me go with you."

"Oh, no, don't do that. I'll be quite all right. I think

just a little rest will fix me up fine."

"How is Bonnie getting on with her new home? She had such a lovely wedding. I'm so glad to see the young folks happy. Now, my Ramona is finding it isn't all the peaches and cream she thought it was going to be. There are some nights her man doesn't get home until eleven, twelve o'clock, and she sits there waiting with a cold supper wondering when he's ever going to show up. And babies crying for their daddy, and her pregnant again so soon. At this rate, there will be twenty of them in twenty years. I'd say he's home often enough, wouldn't you?" She stopped chattering long enough to raise her eyebrows with a knowing, gleeful wink. "Oh, but you didn't tell me how Bonnie is getting on."

How could I, thought Avonelle. She usually enjoyed Rose's company, but today, especially when she had started right off on the subject of their children's marriages, Avonelle felt it was just too much. She would try to make some excuse to get away. But if she did that, Rose would insist on accompanying her to see that she got to the doctor. Maybe a frontal approach would be more effective.

"Bonnie is extremely happy with her new husband and their new home. They are in the process of decorating it right now. She is painting today, and I probably would have helped her if it weren't that I think the paint wouldn't help this nasal irritation. Are you and Nick making any special plans for the summer?"

"We thought we would go up to Niagara Falls later on. Perhaps August. Funny thing, but living as close as we do, we've never seen it. I guess we'll have to go on a second honeymoon. Right?"

I've done it again, thought Avonelle ruefully. Wasn't there any way she could change the subject?

"Sure. That's a great idea. James and I thought we might take a motor trip through New England. We haven't been up there for several years. Only I believe this time I'd rather wait until the leaves change in the fall. New England is most beautiful at that time of year."

"Sounds wonderful to me. And especially now that you have only one child left in school to have to worry about. You could probably put him up with friends — or Bonnie — while you go, and really enjoy yourselves. Just the two of you. By the way, is Sylvia working again this summer? Is she going to college, or what will she do now that she's graduated?"

There it was. Sylvia. Avonelle knew sooner or later the subject would get around to Sylvia. She might as well bring it all out in the open and be done with it. Because Rose was sure to find out about Sylvia's marriage, and then explaining why she hadn't said anything today would be impossible.

Taking a deep breath, she said simply, but with an attempt at lightheartedness, "Sylvia's married. She and Hal Gregersen. They got married this week." That sounded a little better than yesterday.

"You don't say! Isn't he the fellow who was always hanging around, sort of seeing both the girls? Never could make up his mind between them. Seemed like a decent sort." Then she stopped abruptly, turned deliberately toward Avonelle, and searched piercingly into her eyes. "Wasn't this rather sudden? I mean, only two weeks ago at Bonnie's wedding there was nothing said about it. No ring. No announcement." Then a short pause. Suddenly her eyes lit up as though a hidden switch had been flipped. "Avonelle — this is what is bothering you, isn't it? Eloped, huh? Well, well. Now isn't that exciting. So romantic! You know Nick and I eloped, too. My mother nearly took a stroke. But we couldn't be happier. Just wait, you'll see. Sometimes those marriages work out better than the ones in which they've been engaged for years."

Her friend didn't reply. She seemed to be part of the stone that she was sitting on, while her eyes gazed vacantly into the fountain's spray.

"Is it you don't approve of Sylvia's choice? He seemed nice enough from what I heard of him."

"Oh, no, it's not that at all. It's just that, well, she could have *told* us. I mean she could have had a nice wedding. We could have made plans. As it was, she frightened us half to death just disappearing as she did. And she's so young. Some day she'll wish she had gone on to college. It's just not the thing to do anymore. It will look as though she *had* to and then what will people think?" Once she opened her mouth, she said far more than she had ever meant to.

"Oh, nonsense! People will think no such thing. But you'll feel better in no time." Rose reached in her purse and brought out a cigarette. "Want one?"

Avonelle looked at it with a loathesome expression. She had been taught that ladies of breeding did not use tobacco.

"Come on. Everyone smokes these days. Just try it. You'll find it relaxes you and wonder how you ever got along without them. Let me show you."

Rose flipped her lighter, put the cigarette delicately between her lips, and drew in a long breath. Then she exhaled a puff of smoke and handed the cigarette to Avonelle. Avonelle hesitated, then gingerly reached for it, placed it between her lips as though afraid it would burn, and drew a long breath. Then she doubled up gagging.

"You can't — cough — enjoy that — cough — surely!"

"Sure. Just try it again. It takes awhile sometimes. Some people take to them right off. Others have to develop a taste for it. But it will be worth it. Just try it long enough to find out."

The next drag didn't induce quite as severe a reaction.

By the fourth, Avonelle didn't cough once. She couldn't say she enjoyed it, but by the time only the stub was left, she somehow felt as though she had accomplished something. Surprisingly, she did feel a trifle relaxed. Sylvia's hasty marriage didn't seem nearly as catastrophic.

18

"I'm putting you up in an apartment only until I'm in a position to install you in a castle befitting royalty, Your Majesty," Buz had made a solemn promise to his bride on their honeymoon.

It had been only a year until he was able to begin his search for a suitable piece of land. But the setting he had in mind required many more weeks to locate. There were areas within the fringes of the city limits that afforded the old towering trees he envisioned, but no stream seemed readily forthcoming. Then one day, while inspecting the construction of a design he had drawn up for a client on Mount Royal Boulevard in the new subdivision out in Allison Park, he was stepping backward to gain a better perspective. Breaking through the shrubs bordering the rear of the property, he felt his footing give way beneath him and tumbled down an embankment. Thoroughly nonplused and not a little embarrassed, he collected himself from around the gnarled old trunk that broke his fall and discovered but for it he would have plunged into a twenty-foot ravine. How foolish of him not to realize the edge of that lot bordered on such a canyon! He had broken his own cardinal rule never to create a design for a lot until thoroughly familiar with its entire topography. He had merely supposed the bordering hedge of shrubbery separated that lot from the one adjacent.

Dusting off his pants, and assuring the assembled work crew as he regained their altitude he was in no way injured, he completed the inspection and returned to his downtown office. Chagrin permitted him no respite from the memory, and in time embarrassment resolved into curiosity. What lay beyond that gully? Hastening the necessity of his next inspection, he once more made his way out to Allison Park and stepped through the shrubs, albeit more carefully than the previous time. Discovering a small torrent pouring relentlessly through the floor of the ravine, he made his way down the embankment, scanning the opposite wall. A carpet of decaying deciduous leaves softened his footfalls as he picked his path over an occasional fallen branch. To his delight, he discovered the stream cascaded abruptly and in a series of miniature falls from a much higher level, winding around a low knoll. Clambering across the stream and up the far embankment, he reached the top of the knoll to discover a secluded area shaded with oaks, maples, and elms and outlined on three sides by the water course. *What a veritable Shangri-La,* he told himself breathlessly. If one could gain access from the jut of land unbroken by the stream, he could be almost marooned in his own secluded world.

Not daring to risk Bonnie's disappointment should he be unable to acquire the little knob of woods, he sought the owner who, not considering the property suitable for building, had set a nominal price and drew up the closing. One more task remained before he took Bonnie in for her approval. Hiring a grader and a load of gravel, he prepared an entrance from the only accessible approach. And when all was ready he took her to survey the site of her castle.

Words failed as she flung her arms about his neck and wept with joy at the sight of it. "If you give me very many surprises like this one," she finally managed to stammer, "you will live here as a widower, for my heart won't stand too much of this excitement!"

A squirrel scampered up an oak a few feet from them, scolding insistently at the invasion of his domain, and crickets chirped underfoot. An invigorating, delicious breeze wafted through the stately old trees, swaying the graceful blue-tipped skirts of the solitary spruce positioned to grace their front yard. Clasping her hands and sniffing the aromatic woodland scents, she sighed dreamily, "It must have a name. We will call it Windy Knoll."

Buz found it necessary to make one revision in his original plans. To fit the contour of the little knoll, he would have to design a multi-level floor plan. No problem was posed when he reversed the living area and the bedrooms, for then the living room merely appeared to be sunken from the level of the dining area, and a wrought iron stairway led up to the bedroom level. The lower floor for the living area lent itself to the rising of the high arched ceiling under which nestled a little balcony under amber skylights. In reality, the revision worked out so perfectly it appeared the house originally had been designed for just such a location.

The interior courtyard was Bonnie's chief delight, and she took on it's design as her personal project. A shallow pond was its central feature, and she chose for its inhabitants the most brilliant goldfish with red-fringed fins that she could find. Two miniature stone benches nestled among tiger lilies and Norfolk Island pine trees. She left standing the stately old elm that for decades had stretched heavenward from the very spot now within the enclosure. And under its branches, she was to spend many a contented hour with her Bible or a piece of good literature. When bad weather enforced the closing of the courtyard's plate glass doors, she was to find her seclusion in the balcony overlooking the living area, basking under the golden beams of a winter sun through the amber panels.

Her greatest pride lay in the massive, carved, oaken double doors with large iron rings for pulls. They once had graced a medieval castle in Spain. Buz had discovered them relocated on the entrance to an old church he had been commissioned to remodel. Happily the new design could not incorporate the ancient art pieces, and the building committee was only glad of an opportunity to be rid of them when Buz offered a fair price.

The one task that remained to be completed when they moved in was the terracing of the land's natural contour. Old railroad ties were in abundance when tracks were uprooted in the city's redevelopment, and Buz availed himself of a truckload. They were yet to be laid in cascading terraces from the flagstone walk that encircled the back of the house down to the point where the ravine started its final steep plunge. A variety of natural woodland wild flowers as well as hardy perennials to be interspersed among them were planned for the following spring.

As the two walked hand in hand through the ornate entrance to their dream home, Buz whispered, "Welcome home, my beloved." Bonnie thought she could experience no greater joy on earth. It was the first time she had ever lived in a house, with the exception of the old mansion on Arch Street, since demolished in the North Side's redevelopment. Even then she had been confined to an apartment. Now not only was the entire house her own, but also it was the most elegant creation she had ever dreamed in her wildest of reveries.

And her one remaining wish was also to be fulfilled, for they had succeeded in completing their home before the birth of their first child. With the utmost of loving care, she had supervised the construction of the little nursery just off the master bedroom on the second level, above the living room area. She had chosen white for the walls, the carpeting, and ornate French furnishings.

The flowers in the drapes and the skirt around the little bassinet were both pink and blue. "That way," she told Buz, "no one will guess whether we have ordered a boy or a girl."

And if she had thought her joy full upon moving into their magnificent home, it knew no bounds when a tiny pink-swathed bundle was laid into her welcoming arms just a few weeks later. She traced the outline of the rosebud lips and each delicate little ear with a trembling finger, counted all the miniature toes and fingers, and cupped the tiny bald head within one hand.

"She's beautiful." Buz swelled with pride upon his first sight of the product of his love.

"She is, but I'm afraid she is going to resemble me," responded the little mother.

"That's what I mean—I said she's beautiful."

"Well, let's not name her 'Bonnie' then, as my mother did me to signify beauty."

"No, I'd like to give all our childen Bible names."

"Then how about Joanna, or Judith? Perhaps Ruth. Those names all have character."

"Miriam. I like Miriam best of all."

"Very well, then. But I'm glad she didn't come accompanied by a twin brother. You'd probably insist on *Moses* for him!

"She isn't big enough for a grand name like Miriam yet. I shall call her Mimi," Bonnie announced when Buz led the new mother and infant into the dream house and they laid the tiny bundle in the bassinet prepared for her. The little one opened one small eyelid, stretched, and settled herself comfortably in her own special little bed at Windy Knoll. To the overjoyed parents she appeared to know she was at last home, nestled in the security of their love and devotion.

Gazing fondly down at the baby daughter cradled in

her arms as she rocked her to sleep, Bonnie could not evade the tormenting query that had struck her the first time Mimi was placed in her arms. Had she once been laid in the arms of the mother who had given birth to her? Had that mother thrilled to her sight and the realization of a new little life entrusted to her loving care? Had she fondled her and gently rested her head upon her shoulder and rocked her back and forth as she herself was now doing with her own daughter? Once more Bonnie was seized with a compelling urgency to try to find some answers.

It had been more than two years since she had last contacted the Salvation Army. They had promised to notify her if ever there were news to impart, but had never done so. Perhaps if she accomplished nothing else, a new inquiry could motivate them to renewed effort. A fresh horror struck her. In the excitement of her marriage and the diligence of settling down to the life of a housewife, she never had thought to notify them of her name change, and the address she had given when she placed her initial inquiry was that of the Child Evangelism Fellowship, housed in a building that no longer existed. In fact, Arch Street wasn't even there anymore; it had been lifted brick by brick, and the entire area had met destruction by the blows of the wrecking ball to be reborn as Allegheny Center. The agency may have attempted to contact her but had been unable to do so.

With renewed hope she flew to the phone, her fingers fumbling until she had to make a second attempt to dial.

"Yes, Mrs. Rockwell. You say that your name at the time was Lake? If you will hold the phone, I will connect you with the Missing Persons Bureau."

Bonnie's heart pounded in her throat.

"If you will give me a few moments," the second voice replied, "I will see what I can find. It seems to me there were some developments in that case."

The suspense was almost unendurable until the voice returned.

"Yes, Mrs. Rockwell, I'm happy to inform you we may have some leads. We have been able to make contact with the last remaining attendant of a now defunct orphanage in Reims. This lady, though elderly now, vaguely recalls a youngster who might answer to your description. If you will give us a little more time, we may be able to make a more definite identification."

Bonnie did not know whether to laugh or cry. She could at least dare to be optimistic; yet reason told her that in the time they had had, surely if there were anything concrete to be learned they should have done so by now. She resigned herself to another long wait.

Fortunately her darling Buz, being as family-oriented as his "plain folk" ancestry instilled in him, was in total sympathy with her need to discover her heritage. She had never mentioned her search to her adoptive mother, for she was positive that such a need was simply beyond Avonelle's perception.

Time had healed the breach between mother and daughter, and although Bonnie never permitted a situation to develop in which Avonelle had the slightest occasion to take offense, she yet made every possible attempt to indicate how much her personal faith and church life meant to her and to her marriage. In time Avonelle had come to respect Buz's talents as an architect, and eventually she began to accept him as a son. The acceptance was complete when he and Bonnie presented her with a granddaughter.

Not that it was the first time she had been made a grandmother, for Sylvia and Hal claimed that honor. Harold Gregersen, Junior, made his appearance less than a year from the eventful day his parents eloped.

"We shall call him 'Harry' to make the distinction

between him and his proud papa," announced the latter over the phone. "And he's going to be dark like his mother."

Dark he was. Not only did he have his mother's coloring, but also he bore his mother's features. When he was six months old he won a baby contest in a nationally known magazine. Nor did the subsequent months rob him of any pulchritude. As a frolicking toddler he appeared destined to be an extremely handsome adult. The Lakes had bidden him a tearful farewell when the family left Pittsburgh, for Hal soon received the promotion for which he had strived so diligently. But contrary to Sylvia's dreams of a southern location with access to the beach, Paramount Plastics had seen fit to elevate him to manager of the branch office they opened in Burlington, Vermont.

"Man alive!" Sylvia had written their first summer there. "It's so cold up here you have to heat the swimming pools in the middle of August. And you need an electric blanket in July." Even though Lake Champlain was at their doorstep, she longed for a warmer climate.

Now, anticipating long-awaited news from the Salvation Army, Bonnie was faced with the prospect of helping her mother entertain Sylvia and her little family. She was thankful for an activity to keep her mind occupied; otherwise, she felt she simply could not endure the delay until she received further word. But the Gregersens' visit developed into nothing more than an extension of the letters' complaints.

"For Pete's sake, Bonnie, I know you tried to tell me what a compound you have here at Windy Knoll, but I guess there are no words to describe it. That's what it is when you have an architect for a husband. But if it's the privacy of this out-of-the-way spot you want, you can find that in Vermont, without a palace to put on it. I don't believe one out of a hundred people you meet on the street even knows you are standing in front of him. And so far as making friends in the community is concerned, forget it."

That same wild sweep of the hand again. *She'd find a way to punctuate her speeches if she had a baby in each arm and both feet were tied,* thought her sister.

"If your ancestors didn't come over on the Mayflower, serve with the Green Mountain Boys under Ethan Allen, or help Benedict Arnold capture Fort Ticonderoga from the British, you are just persona non grata. They tell me the first thing you should do is join one or several of their little afternoon clubs if you want to socialize with them. What I'd like to know is, how do you get into the clubs in the first place? And can you imagine how stimulating the conversation would be among a group of prim New England matrons in their stiff, proper parlors?"

Bonnie could sympathize with one who preferred socializing nightly with dashing young swains. She longed to hear one encouraging word about the life Sylvia shared with Hal and their son. It appeared pleasant enough to her. Many a young wife would have given her right arm for the tender solicitation her sister received from her attentive husband.

"When they do have a get-together—oh, yes, I thought I would let you know, we do attend one of those picturesque little white steepled churches; it's good for boosting your acceptance in the community, you know—when there is a potluck dinner or some such, if you don't like *fish*"—the word was inflected with the relish that might have been inspired by stewed snails—"you might as well figure on going hungry."

"Sounds like a good deal to me," ventured Buz. "If I were up there I'd go out on that lake myself to try my luck."

"Well, I'm sure Hal would welcome your company. I

318

certainly haven't the patience to sit out there in a boat all day with him. And imagine, if you possibly can, what ill fortune you're into if you don't care for maple syrup on pancakes. And you haven't a chance if you can't stomach cheddar cheese or are sick of potatoes."

"That's the way she goes on all the time when she's at our house too," confided Avonelle to Bonnie aside. Avonelle herself had by this time become a chain smoker. Her voice's lovely modulation was flattening to a dull monotone, and the deftly applied makeup no longer was sufficient to erase her sallow complexion and tattle-telling wrinkles.

Bonnie ached for both her mother and sister. Nor was her pity abated at the sight of her brother-in-law, patiently mute at his wife's exaggerated ramblings of dissatisfaction. Although she enjoyed their company and delighted in little Harry's beguiling charm, Bonnie was relieved when the visit came to an end.

At last she was free to contact the Salvation Army once more. "No, Mrs. Rockwell," the same voice replied, "we do not yet have anything concrete, but we are in contact with the former matron of the orphanage, and we expect to have some information before too long. We will be sure to let you know."

Several months passed in which there was no ring of the phone, no exciting piece of mail from the Army headquarters. Bonnie's anticipation alternately grew and slackened as she reasoned first that the delay meant the information was being carefully double-checked and documented, and later that she would surely have heard had there been specific news.

19

It seemed no time at all until the three years of the fledgling architect's apprenticeship were fulfilled, and the Rockwells used the required examination for Buz's registration as an occasion to take a pleasant jaunt to visit the elder Rockwells in Harrisburg and acquaint them with their granddaughter. Baby Mimi proved to be an excellent traveler, having gone to sleep immediately upon their leaving Pittsburgh and not waking for a bottle until the little family had nearly reached their destination. Once again Bonnie relished the spectacular views afforded by the sunkissed valleys and mountain ranges as they crossed the southern portion of their beloved state, and the sight of the new grandparents thrilling to their first view of the little one warmed the heart in her travel-cramped body.

Aunt Gwen, an engaging teenager, practiced her emerging maternal instincts as she bathed and dressed her niece and proudly showed her off to her circle of envious friends. And the niece charmed them all with a beguiling smile and her first awkward attempts to crawl. Then all three generations visited the "plain folk" relatives while Buz labored the long hours over the examination.

He was exhausted but exuberant when at last it was completed. He had no fears of not passing it, feeling he had probably done well. And indeed, when he received his score, his optimism was not unfounded. But his pride in such an accomplishment paled beside that with which he returned to Pittsburgh bearing a stamp reading, "Registered Architect Nathaniel G. Rockwell." This he was to use from then on to legally bind all his contracts.

His old buddy, Steve Cameron, had taken the exam with him, and likewise had received the coveted stamp. And it was time for the third member of their anticipated firm to reappear to see the culmination of their plans. In the North Side Allegheny Center they rented office space for the time being and painted "Cameron, DeSantis, and Rockwell, Architects" over the door. Later they would design and build their own unique facilities.

The years flew with wings of ease as Buz's fame as an architect spread beyond the confines of western Pennsylvania. First it was the residence of an oil magnate in Texas who was introduced to his talents through contacts in the city. Next it was a new courthouse for a tiny county seat in Maryland, an elementary school in Ohio, a chain of motels throughout the southeast, and a modern shopping plaza in Indiana. In time, requests for his services far exceeded the time he could give to them. He and his partners were hard put to choose which to accept and which to refuse.

It followed as a matter of course that he should take his wife with him and combine business trips with pleasure as he surveyed sites, investigated local building codes and availability of contractors, and conferred with clients. And Bonnie took as much delight in viewing other states as he found in the opportunities to grant her the privilege. But the broader her travels took her, the more convinced she became that her own state—with its many varieties of scenery, its majestic forests, its wild and turbulent waterways, and its own Grand Canyon—was among the loveliest of the lovely.

It was a token of the metal of which the two were made that the more they found themselves blessed materially, the more they delighted in returning of themselves to the Giver of all good gifts, at whose hand they received in such abundance. Buz was soon elected to the office of deacon in their little church on the North Side, and at length Bonnie felt herself to be sufficiently mature in the faith that when so led of the Holy Spirit, she was willing to teach others. Her first assignment was a Sunday school class of toddlers the age of her own little Mimi. Meeting the challenge of a handful of inquisitive squirmers, she became readily available for any task requested of her. And she and Buz were ascertained to be God's choice of successors when the Courtneys announced they intended to relinquish their position as counselors to the college and career group.

"It's time for us to step down," they stated simply one evening at Windy Knoll. "God has prepared our prodigies well, and we feel totally confident of your competence to guide the next crop of eager young disciples."

"I'm not sure we share your confidence," Buz answered for both of them, "but with the Lord's help we will do our best."

Still, they didn't feel they were doing enough to communicate the Savior's love to others. The Holy Spirit had opened opportunities, and Bonnie had never failed to utilize every one to lend a helping hand or a listening ear. But still she prayed for a greater sense of real ministry. The answer arrived in a little booklet placed in their hands. It explained the procedure for home Bible study groups and that such a group did not require the teachings of one exceptionally knowledgeable in the Word, but rather an exploration by all assembled was sufficient. It recommended that opportunity for prayer should follow the study. The choice of whom to invite posed a real problem, for the book suggested neighbors. It was only then that the Rockwells recognized the comfortable seclusion of their Windy Knoll had effectively isolated them from the neighbors they would have to befriend if they were to witness to them of the Savior. The first project, therefore, would be to become acquainted with the neighbors.

The Cartrights were a likely starting place, for Buz had planned their dwelling when he discovered the knoll. At least they knew the Rockwells' names. With some fresh-baked dinner rolls in hand, Bonnie rang the lovely chime at their elegant front door.

"Hello, Mrs. Cartright," she greeted cordially, "I wanted to say hello with this little token and invite you over for a cup of coffee sometime soon."

Mrs. Cartright looked suspiciously at the proffered rolls, hesitated a moment, and then replied somewhat less than cordially, "Thank you. Perhaps I may in the future. But it is difficult to find time for everything one could wish to do. You know, my husband is vice president of a well-established bank, and we must do an awful lot of entertaining. But I may have a free morning some time."

The door was shut before Bonnie could say more. Refusing to admit discouragement, she turned her attention down the street. Mount Royal Boulevard was extensive enough that surely someone along the way could be found interested in a home Bible study. Then she remembered Lindy Colbeck's parents. They were likely prospects that she should have thought of first.

Lindy was a year older than Mimi and shared her skating class. When Lindy's mother learned that another pupil lived close by, she suggested sharing the driving. On rainy afternoons she invited Mimi to play indoors with Lindy. Here was a young mother who had offered friendship, and Bonnie hadn't even recognized it! A phone call would do it this time.

"Mrs. Colbeck? Buz and I are inviting you to a little get-together at Windy Knoll on Monday evenings. We plan to have a time of fellowship over coffee and look into God's Word together to learn some of the things He has said to us. Can we count on you and your husband?"

"Well, we already have our own church, but it was thoughtful of you to ask."

"I only mean a little neighborhood group unrelated to any particular church. We won't stick to any denominational creed; we'll just see what the Bible says for ourselves and make our own interpretation."

"I don't know whether Jeff would be interested in anything like that or not. How many others do you have planning to come?"

Bonnie hesitated only momentarily. "I'm not sure yet. We are only beginning, and I don't know how many we may gain along the way."

"You say it starts next Monday? I'll talk it over with Jeff and let you know later."

She sounded so doubtful that Bonnie's enthusiasm began to wane. *Too soon to give up yet*, she challenged herself. But she could see that the initial step would be to enlist the support of some of the Christians in the church. That way there would be a group to invite others to.

"Meredith? I haven't talked to you for some time. How are you getting along?"

"Great, just great. Mimi must be getting so big now I wouldn't recognize her."

"No doubt you're right. Listen, could you come out on Monday nights for a Bible study group? We're trying to get one started, and so far it's no go. We need a few stalwarts for backup."

"I'll give it a thought, but don't count on me. I never know what might come up."

To her consternation Bonnie received a similar reply

from each of the old gang she phoned. All had plans or were too tired in the evening. It appeared no one shared her burden for contacting the lost sheep. With a heavy heart she turned her attention once more up Mount Royal Boulevard.

She and Buz planned a barbecue to take place on the terraces behind the house, and invited everyone on the boulevard for three blocks each direction. Two couples attended and one responded with a return invitation. It seemed impossible even to become acquainted with their neighbors, not to mention interesting them in a Bible study. Clearly there would have to be some other tactics employed. But she was now far enough along in her second pregnancy that further attention to the project had to be shelved for awhile.

"This one is to be Timothy," Buz informed her just before she went to the hospital. "You may name all the next ten, but·I always had a special place in my heart for the young man who entered the ministry because of his mother's and grandmother's careful nurturing in the faith. I wish the same for my son."

"My dear! What will you do if it turns out to be another little girl?"

"Name her Lois or Eunice, I guess. But I don't think it will be. Somehow I have a feeling in my bones this is to be a fine son."

Bonnie had never considered that men were given to premonitions, but she bided her time in silence. And she was sure Buz was no more thrilled than she when he received his wish.

But her greatest delight came when they carried the cuddly mite home and laid him in the bassinet. For having at last the opportunity to explore his son closely, Buz inspected every tiny part. First he straightened out one little leg in his huge hand and observed, "That ought to send many a football flying." Then he took a miniature hand and opened out all the fingers. And Buz's forefinger played at the corner of the tiny mouth, trying to coax the hint of a smile into it. Next he opened the delicate little mouth, exclaiming in mock horror, "What! No teeth yet! How are you going to gnaw on sirloins and T-bones?" And then Bonnie read into the relieved expression on his face the true meaning in his exploration. She understood now that he had secretly feared all along that his son would be born with his physical imperfections. Unconcealed pride emanated from the glow on his face when he ascertained for himself that this son, created of his seed and born in his own image, bore no trace of a cleft palate.

The great delight Buz found in his son more than compensated for the extra difficulties Bonnie had had with this pregnancy, for she had been plagued with morning sickness for six months, suffered intermittent periods of depression, and developed a backache for the last three months. Before it was over, she had vowed this child was the last one for her. But seeing her husband hurry home each evening as soon as he could leave his work, bound up the stairs two at a time, and play with his baby son soon erased all the unpleasant memories. She felt her bliss was now complete.

It was not long after Timothy's birth that Nancy phoned one sunny afternoon. Her Gilbert had long since been transferred to the pastorate of a much larger church many miles distant in Lock Haven, and it was no longer an hour's drive from Pittsburgh for the two to visit. Nancy had not returned to the city for three years, and their only contact with each other was either by mail or phone.

"We have some happy news," Plucky Lucky bubbled. "It's been a long wait, but we have made up for lost time. We are now the pride-smitten parents of not one, but two beautiful babies. And guess what—"

Bonnie could interject only a quick, excited squeal.

"—we decided to use Bible names, too. Joel for the boy and Joy for the girl. Joel means 'Jehovah his God,' and Joy was Gilbert's idea. He said we should reflect both their belonging to the Lord and my usual disposition (bless him for that piece of flattery) in the choice."

"But, Nancy, Joy isn't a name in the Bible."

"Well, it certainly is a name that's biblical. You will find only twenty references to Joel and one hundred sixty-four to joy. That doesn't even count the variations like joyful, and joyous, et cetera."

"Oh, for Pete's sake, Nancy, if that doesn't sound just like you! Tell me, do they have your red hair?"

"Joel does, but Joy will resemble her father. Gilbert says we'll be equally divided now, two temperamental ones against two placid ones, not to mention any names. But this time, one of the temperamental ones will be on his side."

"These men! I believe Buz feels he will have a little masculine support too. Although it's not that he doesn't idolize Mimi."

When Sylvia arrived for a Christmas visit that year, the winter gave promise of being mild, and for once they felt they could risk travel in December. But no sooner had they arrived in Pittsburgh than a blizzard hit all of New England. Freezing cold set in with a death grasp, and all but necessary travel came to a standstill. It was the middle of January before the Gregersens attempted the return trip.

The little family spent a few days with the Lakes and then repaired to Windy Knoll. Apart from occasional lament from Hal that he had to be away from the office for so long, they appeared to be relatively contented. At last Sylvia seemed to have made peace with her environment, and Bonnie noted with relief that the complaints were at least less. Her major grief seemed to center around the effect that bringing up her childen in New England was having upon them.

Harry, as handsome as every prediction made for him, had entered school that year and begun to acquire the drawl attributable to that corner of the country.

"Man alive," his mother snorted, "he puts *r*'s on words where they do not belong and removes them where they do. Would you believe, I am now 'Mummer.' All dressed up for a Thanksgiving Day parade! He went to a birthday pahty at which they served bananer cake, and his prize for winning some little game was a bazooker. He came home and reported that the huntahs predict a plentiful supply of deah this wintah. So he was going to take his bazooker into the woods and frighten away the deah so that the huntahs couldn't shoot them. I told him if the deah could heah the way he was talking, they would drop dead from mortification, anyway. Then he assured me that since they are New England deah, they would consider his dialect perfectly normal; they would more likely flip over Pennsylvanier Dutch." Sylvia shrugged. Her palms thrown upward into the air bore a marked resemblance to the same expression Bonnie had seen from her sister many times before. Not even maturity and a family to care for appeared to have had any settling effect upon the old restlessness. Sylvia seemed doomed to a state that was half adult, half child.

And her own family had been increased by one since the previous visit. Jennifer bore her father's Nordic features and showed early signs of inheriting his height. But the coloring was Sylvia's. Dark hair already fell into ringlets, resulting in an interesting effect, even though the combined features did not bid fair to result in any great beauty. She was a sober, pensive child, apt to cry and not particularly receptive to others. Whenever Mimi attempted to amuse her, she would flee to the safety of her father's knee and peer around it periodically to see whether it was safe to reappear. Harry coddled her reticence by playing the role of protective big brother to perfection. He seemed to thrive on the status he enjoyed as the elder of the two.

Buz permitted Hal to accompany him on more than one tour of inspection of a building site. And when, by reason of the new baby at Windy Knoll and Sylvia's presence with her two youngsters, Bonnie would not be able to accompany him on a previously scheduled trip to Atlanta, he generously invited his brother-in-law to do so. Always on the lookout for an opportunity to witness to Hal of his faith, he finally realized it on the plane.

"I will confess," Hal confided as he drew a cigarette from his breast pocket, "these takeoffs and landings make me a bit edgy. Here, relax yourself a bit." He offered a cigarette to Buz.

"No, thanks, I have no need of them." Ah, the opportunity he had been waiting for! "When my Maker is ready for me to stand before Him, I will be ready for Him. In the meantime, I'm certain of His care and oversight. Nothing will happen to me that is not within His permissive will for me. And I want nothing else. Tell me, how is it with you? Would you be ready should this plane not stay up?"

"Ready? You can't mean a fellow can prepare for such an event!"

"I certainly do. At least the preparation is within a man's list of options. Whether he takes advantage of the privilege is entirely up to him."

"Ah, yes; it seems I have heard something similar to that in the distant past. If my memory serves me correctly, I believe one certain young lady tried to get me to—er—'take advantage' of some such golden opportunity at one time. The answer then was the same as now: I'm satisfied with things as they are."

"That answer may be sufficient when things are going

329

well and a man feels he has his destiny in his own control. But what happens when trouble strikes — when old age sets in and there is nothing left — when death overtakes and the end arrives? What then?"

"Why, I'll die as I lived. I'm not a coward to run for cover when the bullets start flying."

"In sin? With no hope for eternity?"

Hal flicked the ashes off the end of the cigarette. Scratching his head and assuming an air of total self-reliance, he replied coolly, "Man, I couldn't care less about a few sins. I figure I'm no worse than the next guy. That big Judge up there can't consign us all to perdition."

Buz dropped his head as he stated quietly, "But He's made it plain that those who don't believe are already condemned."

"Baloney!"

Buz suspected the smoke from Hal's cigarette did not accidentally find its way into his face. With a heavy heart he began to cast about for a different topic of conversation.

"Pardon me, sir. May I hear again what you were saying about sin?"

Buz had scarcely taken note of the gentleman on his left. Now he turned to gain a full view of the dark complexion, prominent nose and heavy brows. The English, though heavy with a foreign accent, was definitely Oxford.

"Why, certainly, I merely said that when one lives his life entirely according to his own dictates, without regard for God's claims upon it, and unheeding of sin's presence in it, there will surely come a time of reckoning, whether in this life or the life to come, in which that one could well wish that he had weighed his options more carefully."

"Exactly! So I have been aware all along. But I have

searched all my life for the option that will lead to the ultimate good, and I must confess, I have been unable to find it.

"You see, I am a Hindu, born a member of the privileged Brahmin caste. I have made many pilgrimages to holy places, six times bathed in the sacred Ganges. I fast weekly and bring every desire and activity into subjection in the practice of Yoga, while repeating the name of the god Vishnu for hours at a time, but nirvana remains as elusive as ever. There is no release, no respite from the evils of our existence, no severing of the soul from the consequences of our own ceaseless activity. No promise that the next existence won't be more morbid than this.

"I thought I would find enlightenment at the university, but my fellow students seemed to be as searching and despairing as I. Then upon my return to India, I happened upon an acquaintance from the little village in which we had lived as boys, who was also searching. He said he had been in contact with a chap educated in an American mission school. The fellow told him he could find peace if he talked to the people of the mission, but he was never able to locate the place. And so I wonder, do the Americans know where peace is to be found? I go to the American officials in the embassy in New Delhi, and they tell me peace doesn't exist. So I think when I make a business trip to America, maybe now I can learn where peace is to be found. I have not yet discovered anyone who can tell me."

"My friend, you have at last asked the right person. I can't give you peace, but I certainly can point you to the One who can. Jesus Christ is Himself the Prince of Peace. There is none to be found apart from Him."

"Jesus Christ, you say? Is He not the God of the Christians in whose Name wars have been fought, destruction wreaked, and whole nations plundered?"

"Such things might have been enacted in His Name, but never at His command. His Kingdom is not of this world; He reigns in the hearts of men. And He truly reigns only when men give Him Lordship. Those who don't act in accordance with His principles are simply not acting under His direction, no matter what justification they might lay to their deeds.

"But the soul who sincerely seeks Him finds Him, for He rewards those who diligently seek Him. And He gives His peace to those who seek—not the kind the world speaks of, but a peace that passes all earthly understanding—a *soul* peace that stills the anguishing restlessness that motivates your search."

"Tell me, sir, how can I find this peace?"

Pulling his New Testament out of his breast pocket, Buz opened it to the fourteenth chapter of John.

"This Book, my friend, is the message God, the Creator of all things, left for His creatures on earth. It tells us He sent His only Son, Jesus, to die for our sins so that, when we avail ourselves of His sacrifice, we can live eternally. Not in some other body, as an animal or a member of a lower caste, but as ourselves. However, after we leave this life through death we will receive a new body, which will resemble us but is no longer subject to decay. If you will check this twenty-seventh verse here you will see Jesus promised to give us the kind of peace you are looking for."

The Indian read with intense interest the verse Buz already had quoted in part in the conversation.

"And how does His sacrifice do me any good?"

"We are told in the book of Colossians that we are redeemed from paying the price for our own sin through His shed blood. And by it we can be forgiven those sins and have new life."

"Then tell me how I can have this myself."

Buz quickly instructed his new friend in the sinner's

prayer and pressed his own New Testament into his hand. "Here, friend, read it for yourself. You are welcome to my copy."

The Indian gratefully accepted the proffered gift and spent the remainder of the flight reading it.

Throughout the entire conversation between Buz and the Indian gentleman, Hal turned his attention to the passengers across the aisle, although Buz was positive the words could not have escaped his ears. It wasn't until they had disembarked from the plane that Hal finally commented, "Well, Reverend Rockwell, I see you finally preached to someone who would swallow the line."

Though smarting from the retort, Buz rejoiced that he had had the privilege of leading the seeker to the object of his search. He now experienced a clearer meaning of the apostle Paul's words to Timothy, his son in the faith, as Paul had advised him to be ready in season, out of season; to reprove, rebuke, exhort— He, Buz, had been ready at the right moment. He had been present, at hand, and had known the joy of leading a wandering soul to its Savior. Having experienced the elation of assisting in a new-birth process, he determined more than ever to renew attempts to open an outreach in their home. He and Bonnie would have to concentrate their efforts and work until they saw their vision realized. And speaking of Timothy— Buz was anxious to return to his own beloved son.

Shortly a weather forecast was made for a thawing trend throughout New England, and the Gregersens returned home. With mixed emotions Bonnie bade her sister farewell. How she longed for the message of salvation to penetrate Sylvia's flighty exterior, and how she ached for Hal, who had closed his heart to the healing balm that could spell the difference in his own home and life.

She wasn't sure what awakened her. An icicle breaking loose and falling from the eaves, clattering on the ground below; perhaps the mournful blast of a distant train whistle, the chimes from the grandfather clock in the entrance hall. A sense of foreboding chilled the marrow in her bones as she sat up, straining to hear a repetition of the sound. There was no sound. The children! Timothy, of course; some sixth sense told her she must go to Timothy. Silently Bonnie stole out of bed, anxious not to awaken her husband. She didn't flip a switch until she entered the nursery. Then she lit the little lamp with two lambs at the base near the crib. Reaching down to caress his soft little body, her heart stood still. She knew instinctively that something was wrong.

"Buz!" she screamed, "Buz, come quick." She dashed back to the bed to shake her husband. "Oh, Buz," she was sobbing by now. "Something is wrong with Timothy."

She half pulled her groggy husband from the covers before rushing back to the nursery. She had lifted the little one and shaken him by the time his father arrived. Seeing no response, she ran a finger down his throat. Finding no obstruction, she turned him upside down and massaged his rib cage.

"He—he isn't breathing." Her voice ended in a hysterical scream. Buz reached for the tiny bundle and turned on the overhead light. Holding the baby to catch the strongest light on his little face, he said simply, "I will phone for an ambulance." Laying Timothy back in his mother's arms, he hurried from the room.

Shakily Bonnie made her way to the rocker. Cradling the baby's back in one hand and supporting his drooping head with the other, she held him upright, hoping he would receive more air. It seemed an eternity before they heard the siren's wail from their gravel drive. Fortunately, the driver had had no difficulty finding the secluded little spot.

"I will stay here with Mimi until we can get your mother."

"No, just get her up. You must come with me."

Buz had the still-sleeping little girl in his arms by the time the emergency crew arrived at the door. With each of the children wrapped in heavy blankets, the little family entered the waiting vehicle.

A medic took the baby immediately and attempted to revive him with oxygen. The parents froze at the look of consternation on the attendant's intent face. A shot seemed to produce no more response than the oxygen was gaining.

Buz rested Mimi upon his knees while enfolding Bonnie in his strong arms. She buried her head in her hands and wept.

Her worst fears had come to pass. She did have a terrible hereditary disease that she had passed on unbeknownst to her beloved son. Something dreadful had happened to him, and it was all her fault. She should have obeyed the voice of her convictions and not had any children. Mimi probably carried the genes and she would pass it on to her children. Bonnie simply must never have any more babies. It was a terrible thing to bring children into the world when you did not know what dreadful afflictions may be lurking in the genetic makeup, ready to spring forth indiscriminately in innocent victims. The remorse of Bonnie's soul was exceeded only by her fears for her son's survival.

It seemed an aeon before the ambulance screeched to a halt before the brightly lit, big, swinging door of the emergency entrance. The grieving family could only clamber down from the back of the vehicle and follow mutely behind the attendant, who carried one of their dearest ahead of them. A nurse met them inside and took the little one behind closed doors. Father, mother, and sister found seats in the deserted waiting room and prepared for a nerve-searing vigil, too numb to formulate their prayers into words.

They started at every move made through the hall, half rose each time the door opened. But the white uniformed professionals who passed in and out ventured no move in their direction. Stern of countenance and firm-lipped, they moved silently down the hall and returned seemingly unmindful of the anxious parents weeping in the waiting room.

After one final age, a solemn but kindly doctor stepped toward them. Buz rose, placed the sleeping Mimi on the chair he had vacated, and helped his wife to her feet.

"I'm very sorry. But let me assure you there was nothing you have done to precipitate this and nothing is known by medical science that can be of any remedy. Sudden infant death syndrome strikes without warning approximately three times in every one thousand live births. Its cause is unknown, and there is no treatment. We have used every possible means to try to revive him, but there has been no response. I am terribly sorry."

Bonnie heard no more beyond the word "death." She sank into Buz's arms, and but for his strength and quick action, would have fallen to the floor. She would not have cared. A nurse phoned for a taxi and lifted Mimi into it as Buz gently led his distraught wife out into the cold and they made the return trip to an empty house. Their son had lived for four months, one week, and three days.

Refusing the sleeping pill the nurse had slipped into Buz's hand, Bonnie went into the nursery and spent the remainder of the night weeping uncontrollably in the little rocker. Buz stayed by her side until, convinced she was unaware of his presence, he slipped away to mourn alone.

With the first streaks of dawn, he phoned his mother-in-law, who arrived immediately. It was unseeing, tear-swollen eyes that Bonnie turned likewise upon her. Feeling an unwelcome intrusion upon her daughter's grief, she turned her attention to Mimi, who was yet to be told her brother was no more.

"Now as soon as Mimi awakes, please call me. I will tell her," Buz instructed his mother-in-law. He preferred his little daughter be informed in the manner befitting Christians.

When Miriam finally awakened, he took her upon his lap, smoothed back the tangled hair, and brushing a speck of "sleep" from her dewy eyes he said in a low, gentle voice, "Jesus has taken little Timothy to His home in heaven, where he will be very happy among the angels."

"Oh, can I go to see him sometime?"

"Only when Jesus comes for you, too. Timothy is in a land from which we do not return in this life. But we will certainly see him again when we go to be where he is."

"When will that be?"

Buz paused to brush a tear from his own eye before replying, "For you I hope that will be a very, very long time."

"Then if we have to wait a long time, we will miss him, won't we?"

"Terribly." Buz could say no more. He carried Mimi to her waiting grandmother and fled to the seclusion of his own room.

Meredith arrived later in the morning and learned likewise that Bonnie was inconsolable. She attempted to play with Mimi, but the child sat morosely in the playroom, afflicted with the gloom that settled over the household.

Avonelle prepared meals of which she, Meredith, and

Mimi partook. Bonnie refused to indicate she heard the summons to the table and ignored a tray placed by her side. Buz courteously thanked the ladies when he declined the plate offered him.

Meredith phoned Irene Fisher Anderson, who had been Drew's wife for several years, and together the two friends tidied up Windy Knoll, although little was in need of doing. As the shadows of the late afternoon lengthened into darkness, they took their leave of the sorrowing family, promising to return the next day.

Avonelle tucked Mimi into bed and retired to the guest room. Buz returned once more to the nursery, took Bonnie by the hand, and led her into their room. She offered no resistance as he gently removed her clothing and replaced it with her pink nightie. But when he produced the sleeping pill, she brushed it to the floor, sobbed convulsively, and threw herself distraught onto the bed. Enfolding her in his arms, he settled himself beside her, and prayed for the mercy of sleep to give respite from the pain.

Bonnie lay still for several hours until her muscles longed for release from the tension. Then she began to toss and turn. Buz had mercifully sunken into a light sleep, only to be awakened intermittently by his wife's agonizing thrashing. After another long period of disturbing unease, she finally also drifted into a subconscious doze that temporarily drowned out the anguish of her soul. Suddenly she was once more the tiny person of her dream, the dream that had been long forgotten over the blissful years. Dampness was assailing her small face, she was grasping wildly with her little arms, and waves of disconsolation swept over her in stifling torrents. She felt as though a hand were squeezing her throat, and she struggled to free herself of the strangulating grasp. Again the voice called with an urgency that rose to a frantic scream, "Marya . . . Marya . . . Marya." And with one frenzied effort to release herself from the stranglehold upon her throat, she awakened to realize she was crying out, "Timothy . . . Timothy . . . Timothy." Buz's loving arm was around her instantly, as he made a pitiable effort to soothe her. But as she lay there sheltered within the strength of his love, she relived the dream. And as she painstakingly thought over each detail, the anguish of her mother heart identified with the anguish she heard in the voice of her dream. She understood for the first time that it must be the voice of a mother. Could it have been *her* mother?

20

For all that Bonnie was aware of her son's funeral, she might as well have stayed in her room. For it was in there that she had shut herself, secluding herself in body, soul, and spirit from the ministrations of her friends and loved ones. Refusing all food and others' attempts to console her, she permitted none but her beloved Buz to enter, and she was only distantly aware of him.

The pastor called, but when attempt was made to summon her, she turned her face to the wall and refused to reply.

Avonelle had packed a bag and did not leave the house after her children had returned from the hospital with the dreadful news. Meredith had taken a short leave from her job to be near her friend. Nancy left her own little ones with her mother-in-law to take her place at the side of her former "almost roommate," and Sylvia arrived alone from Vermont, not bringing her family again so close upon their return from their last visit.

Tossing about on her bed, Bonnie heard their hushed voices outside the door like the murmurings of a distant multitude. Vaguely aware that others were about, she conceived them as no more than nameless wraiths. And when at last they entered her innermost sanctuary and urged a new dress upon her and gently led her down the wrought iron stairway, out the door, and into a waiting limousine, she offered no resistance, nor did she comprehend where she was other than that unthinkable word "funeral," from which her soul shrank as from the abyss itself.

No matter that Luanne was once again in the city and sang as feelingly as ever she did, nor that the new minister, Pastor Rogers, spoke with so much assurance that the little one was safe in the presence of the One who had given him life and who had simply changed his place of abode from this careworn world to a shining land of eternal bliss. Bonnie heard not a word and perceived no one, save the hands that led her out to a cemetery where her precious one was placed into a gaping hole in the ground. Collapsing into her husband's arms, she knew nothing more until she awakened upon her bed in her room at Windy Knoll.

She did not know Nancy had offered to take Mimi home with her to play with Joel and Joy while Bonnie had time to adjust to her loss, nor that the others thought it better to leave Mimi with her mother, hoping the reminder that she yet had a child would help to shake her from the nonresponsive state into which she once more was sinking. Each time her mother saw her, her thoughts raced back to more than twenty years ago when she fought to bring this same one to a normal life.

Bonnie did not know when Sylvia and Nancy left or that Meredith had returned to her job, except the murmurings outside the door died away and she was left in solitary silence. Nor did it seem to matter that Avonelle took Mimi in to her twice each day and hoped for some sign of delight to see her forgotten daughter.

When at last Bonnie ventured from her room and began to eat her meals at the table with the family, Mimi attempted to gain her mother's attention, for the child, not comprehending why her baby brother should no longer be with them, was at a further loss to understand why her mother didn't seem to want her anymore, either.

"Don't you love me anymore, Mommie? I love you." Mimi would query, tugging at her mother's hand.

"Yes, Baby, of course I love you." But the voice was far away and the eyes unseeing.

Buz took his wife for drives in the evenings, hoping to divert her attention and find an avenue of communication. But she would return not knowing where she had been, hardly aware she had left the house.

The only place to which she gave any thought of going was the cemetery. And it was not long before she drove out to it each afternoon the weather permitted, and there she wept over the little grave until no more tears could come.

In time she would sit in the little balcony overlooking the living room, but it was into space that she stared rather than onto the pages she had so loved to read. Having sat until she tired of the inactivity, she would rise and make her way into the silent nursery. Passing around the room, she would open the drawers in the little dresser, mercifully emptied by her friends' loving hands of the tiny garments they once contained. She would switch on the little lamp by whose light she had discerned the terrible truth, and sit for a few moments in the rocker where last she had held the still little body. Then flinging herself across the empty crib, she would weep great wrenching sobs that rocked her entire body, and from the depths of her wretchedness would come forth in agonizing gasps, "Timothy, oh, Timothy— Timothy, Timothy."

But strangely the voice that came back to her ears echoed through the buried recesses of her innermost subconsciousness, crying, "Marya, Marya, Marya!" In bewilderment she would return to the balcony.

Then one day she cast a final glance about the room, reached for the phone, and requested that Goodwill come to relieve it of its furnishings. That very afternoon, a truck backed up to the carved oak doors and carried off all the lovely white pieces. Bonnie closed the door of the empty room and never opened it again.

The next morning Avonelle sat down beside her on the lovely, airy, floral printed little sofa, nestled beneath the balcony's potted palms.

"Honey," she began, "you are the one who has tried to tell me for several years now that God is very real to you, that you have a relationship with Him that some of us don't know anything about. Would you tell me, where is it now?"

"Well, I—I—of course, I am His child and my life is different from what it once was. The Lord has given me a joy I didn't—" she began from habit, but the voice trailed off and the vacant look returned to the soft brown eyes.

"Where is the joy now? Isn't it good for times like this? Are you telling me this religion only works when everything is going well and you would be happy anyway? This Lord you speak of ignores people when trouble comes, and you have to shift for yourself in it?"

For answer Bonnie got up and returned to her room. In the midst of her numbing grief she had strangely given little thought to her Lord, as she had given none to anyone else. Now she was brought to realize she must consider what part God plays in the tragic events of our lives. She seated herself in the lounge chair by the sunny window and looked out upon the scene below. Down by the massive oaken doors she discovered the first daffodils of the newly awakening springtime. And peeping here and there around the flagstones of the walk that circled the house were a few brave little crocuses. The first birds to return from their southern sojourn were chattering from the branches of the ancient elms. Ordinarily the sight would have brought a quickening of her pulse and a lift to her spirit. But now she had some serious reflecting to do before she would ever again be free to enjoy anything.

Where had God been when Timothy was snatched so suddenly away? Could He have prevented that terrible attack that snuffed out the life of her precious babe, stayed it with a word or the touch of a finger, but chose not to? Was He angry with her for some unrecognized disobedience, or did He merely choose individuals arbitrarily on whom to inflict some awful pain, just to remind us all that we are indeed only human and He omnipotent?

The more she reflected, the more her turmoil grew. Forgetting that she had refused to talk to Pastor Rogers on the several occasions when he had called repeatedly, she began to feel her questions could not be answered. And with the despair that settled insidiously over her spirit, there crept lingering wisps of doubt that became forerunners of the first twinges of bitterness. And as a seed, the twinges grew until shortly she declared to herself that if God thought no more of her than to permit this tragedy, then she would just take care of herself from here on in; she could probably do a better job of it than He had done.

With that resolve, she determined to dry her eyes and face the world once more, although with a flint that would prevent her from ever being vulnerable again.

The first task upon which she must set her attention was outfitting Mimi for her spring ice show. Mimi and Lindy Colbeck were to be fairies in the annual production at the Ice Palace. Their costumes were to be pink, with sequin-spangled satin swirled round and round with yards of ruffled organdy. Mrs. Colbeck and Bonnie shopped together for the pattern and materials, although the former intended to create her daughter's costume herself and the latter sought the practiced expertise of Avonelle to fashion Mimi's. With leotards to complete the outfits, the two youngsters looked like enchanting figurines atop Swiss music boxes.

"Perhaps we had better have portraits made before the program," Mrs. Colbeck reasoned. "Who knows what shape those costumes may be in by the time that hectic evening is over!"

"I hope it isn't all that bad, but you are probably right. We shall have the portraits made beforehand."

Lindy posed while the photographer chose for Mimi the classic stance, her chubby little fingers lifting the edges of the ruffled costume. The child looked her most beguiling with her thin brown locks pulled to each side and tied with pink bows. Bonnie ordered an eight by ten enlargement in color and purchased an ornate, pearlized frame crafted in gold.

The program went off every bit as well as hoped for by the myriads of doting mothers holding their breath. Only once did one tiny moppet trip and pull several others down with her. The step that drew the most "oohs" and "ahs" was the waltz jump. Several of the youngsters could manage scarcely more than a long step; but many reflected the hard hours of work devoted lovingly to them by Miss Mathilde, and executed high, graceful leaps, not the least of which was Miriam Rockwell. Bonnie thrilled to the ease with which she seemed to float in the air and land without wavering on one foot. In the short time Mimi had been studying she had taken to the art as naturally as flowers open their petals to the sun, and Bonnie could now witness the form which once had prompted Miss Mathilde to comment the child gave evidence of natural talent. Where she had ever received it Bonnie could only muse. Certainly not from her ungainly father. And she herself felt as graceful as a duck on wheels.

At last Easter dawned, and as so often happens in

Pennsylvania, the Rockwells awoke that morning to a fresh unexpected snowfall, following a few weeks of comparative warmth and springlike atmosphere. Bonnie had taken care to outfit Mimi in the frilliest swath of chiffon ruffles and lace she could find. The disappointed child refused to don her winter coat over the swirl of crinolines, until Bonnie had to threaten her with not being permitted to wear the frock if she would not comply. With some difficulty, they succeeded in trapping the voluminous layers under the little red coat, and they set out, albeit a trifle late, for Sunday school.

Bonnie herself could not have cared less what she wore for the holiday, for indeed it was the first time since Timothy's death she had ventured inside the church. Having determined to handle the affairs of her own life, she felt no need of the inspiration and guidance she might have found within the sacred walls. It was upon nearly deaf ears that the words of the blessed story fell as she sat in that Easter worship service. She had heard the same words many times before, and always thrilled to the hope their message conveyed. Now, however, the thought of the angel seated upon the stone which had once sealed the body of the Lord Jesus stirred no excitement, no response in her own soul, that because He lives we too shall live eternally. He who conquered death conquered for all mankind.

"Why seek ye the living among the dead?" Pastor Rogers was reading. "He is not here, but is risen."

Bonnie looked at her watch and sketched a couple of silly pictures on a pad she found in her purse to entertain her small daughter. She heard the final "amen" with pronounced relief, thankful that her mother had invited them for dinner after church. She was not in the mood for cooking, and it would be lovely to spend a day with her parents and Perry again. She had not been back to the apartment since just before Timothy's death, and if

the excuse for a pleasant visit were not sufficient entice-
ment, she felt the need to face up to and put behind her
the occasion on which she could entertain the slightest
memory that the last time she had been there Timothy
had been alive and well. Each succeeding visit after this
one would become easier. She must overcome this one
hurdle.

Avonelle had prepared her usual lovely meal, although this time it featured the traditional baked ham
with gaily colored eggs encircling the platter. The family
ate heartily and made attempt at a light mood. However,
Bonnie noted with a rather heavy heart that her dear
father's fringe above his ears was somewhat grayer than
she had noticed before, and the lines about his forehead
seemed deeper. He maintained his unruffled composure,
but moved as one who, viewing life from the vantage
point of the second half of it, has developed patient
indulgence toward it as one would a trying child.

Perry had never achieved any more than slight proportions, and his face retained the boyish features of the
days when he had taunted his dark-haired sister mer-
cilessly. It was rare that he sat down with his parents to a
meal, for he moved with the restlessness of youth not
able to find its way. Upon his graduation from high
school, he had intended to enroll at one of the local
universities, but he was never sure which course he
wished to pursue. And he had delayed submitting his
application until it was too late to matriculate for the
current term. Listlessly, he sat about the house watching
television or sleeping until his father prevailed upon him
to find a job. The only employment he had been able to
locate without any experience was that of delivering pre-
scriptions for a downtown pharmacy. The hours were
odd, and when he wasn't actually on the job, he was as
apt as not to be killing time aimlessly, dawdling around
the streets over which he drove on his duty shift. By the

time another college term had rolled around, he had completely relinquished any idea of entering the ivy-covered halls, and neither had he applied himself with any diligence to establishing himself more securely in the work-a-day world.

Avonelle aroused the greatest pain in her daughter's eyes. For the lovely voice was now lower and rasping. If a stranger did not see her speaking, he might mistake her for a man. And much too often, Bonnie feared, she was wracked with a spasm of coughing that seemed as though it would nearly tear her lungs out. She seemed never to be without a cigarette in her hand. The once lovely skin was dark colored and spotted, and no amount of skillful makeup disguised the lines furrowing even deeper about her mouth and eyes. And the hand that held the endless cups of coffee shook more vigorously as the years passed. Sometimes she spilled much of it before it reached her lips.

Bonnie longed to reach out to them all as she surveyed them seated around the table. They hadn't listened when she tried to tell them of the Savior's love. Each had been self-sufficient, and now they were a product of their insufficiency. Some remnant of buried faith reminded Bonnie that God could have supplied the foundation for their lives. They might have developed goals, direction, a sense of purpose, and health in body, soul, and spirit. But they would not. Having assumed command, they had lost it. And yet as Bonnie lamented over them, she realized she now had little to offer instead.

"I got a letter from Sylvia yesterday." Bonnie roused from her musings to realize her mother was talking. "She wrote she is expecting again in the early fall. She must have already been pregnant when she was here last, but probably didn't know it yet. In fact, now that I think of it, it seemed to me at the time she wasn't looking too well and seemed tired. But then, I just chalked it up to her discontent. Although I can't for the life of me understand why she isn't happy with Hal. He seems so good to her."

"And he does right well with his business, also," added James. "He's come a long way for all the longer he's been at it. Not many office managers at his age."

"Mother—" Bonnie hesitated. "I believe Sylvia would be a little discontented no matter whom she married or where she lived. You know, she was always looking around for new excitement. Never dated the same fellow more than a few times and then it was on to someone else. Now that she's restricted to one permanently, she's bound to grow bored and restless."

"I can only hope it's permanent. I guess that is what worries me about her expecting another child. I wonder what kind of security those children find in their home. Not that both Sylvia and Hal aren't good to them, but Harry and Jennifer are getting old enough now to understand the things Sylvia says, and it's bound to have an effect on them."

"There you go again, Mom." Perry rose to make his departure. "Always worrying about Sylvia, and I've told you a hundred times that old gal can take care of herself. Just think how many times she's taken care of *me* in the past."

"Did a pretty good job of it," James said, and chuckled. "Although I must say, you did a fair piece of taking care of yourself. Not to mention the other end of it that Sylvia got. Buz, you should have heard those two about eight or ten years ago."

"I can just imagine," was the reply. "From what I've seen of Sylvia, I would not doubt she could handle any little brother. Although, I hope you don't misunderstand me; I find her perfectly charming myself."

"She sure is. She could charm the rattles off a snake." Perry had reached the door.

"Do you expect to be late?" his mother asked.

"Don't wait up for me." And he was gone.

Avonelle shook her head. Bonnie hoped her brother's instructions did not mean he was taking to staying out to all hours.

"Buz," proposed Mr. Lake, "shall we make ourselves comfortable in the other room while the girls clear the table?"

As the two men withdrew from the dining room, Avonelle reached rather shakily for the coffee pot. It filled her cup only half full.

"It seems every time I go for another cup, that thing is empty."

Avonelle contented herself with the half cup of coffee, but lit a cigarette.

"Mother, it's probably empty because you have drunk it all. Are you sure you're not taking more than is good for you?"

"Good for me? Why, if I didn't keep myself fueled on coffee I would stop navigating altogether. I never can get my day started right until I've finished off the first half potful. And if that Perry doesn't get himself settled down soon, it'll take the whole pot to get me in shape. That boy is going on twenty-four years old and still doesn't know girls exist. I would have thought he would find himself a wife by this time and set himself up in his own place with a good job. But no, he's satisfied with running delivery service to the little old ladies who can't get out to the drugstore. And the times he's on call during the night, it worries me half to death with him out there driving all over the city without a shred of protection. I suppose you saw where the fellow was murdered up on Mount Washington just last week. Some thugs got him as he left a tavern at two in the morning."

"Of course, Mother, but you have to remember he *was* at the tavern and you don't expect much good to come of that kind of night life. Perry isn't frequenting dives—or is he?"

"Well, I'm not exactly sure. That's something else. I don't know what he is up to all these times he's out without our having any idea what he is doing."

"Well, if I know Perry, he hasn't the gumption to get into much trouble."

"You're probably right there. Which is another point I'm trying to make. It seems that no matter how hard I tried to do right by you children, you are the only one I can really depend on to keep your head about yourself. Sylvia worries me to no end with her rantings. You never can tell how seriously to take them. But I fear sometimes she may yet do something drastic. I'm not sure what it would be. I just have that gut-level feeling I had better be prepared."

Avonelle rose to carry the coffee pot to the kitchen to refill it. Bonnie began to stack the plates and followed her. The two worked in silence until all had been cleared from the table. Then Bonnie poured the detergent into the sink and began to wash the dishes. At last Avonelle spoke again as she picked up the dish towel.

"I don't know where I've gone wrong. I always tried to teach my children to do the right thing, and I expected them to learn to be stable, industrious, and mature. But I see we really aren't any better off than any of the other people I know. It seems that most of my friends' children are getting divorced, into drugs, graduating from college and wanting to run around Europe rather than settle down in a respectable job, or else just plain hitting the road and no one ever knows what becomes of them. For the most part I've done no better than their parents." Avonelle crushed her cigarette into a saucer and dropped the butt into the wastebasket.

"Mother—" Bonnie hesitated before continuing. She had vowed never to open the rift between herself and her mother again. And now, the worst of it was, she hadn't much consolation to offer her. But she would make the attempt. "Mother, could it be you have always tried to do for yourself what only Jesus can do for a person?"

Bonnie waited nervously for her mother's next words. The die had been cast. Would she accept what her daughter had asked, or would there be another scene? Would Bonnie regret she had had the nerve to bring up the touchy subject again?

Laying down the dish towel, Avonelle rested the palm of her hand on the counter top. The other hand she propped on her hip. Giving her daughter a long, slow, thoughtful gaze while Bonnie waited breathlessly, she asked quietly, "And aren't you doing the same yourself?"

Time applied its healing balm. As shock gave way to bitterness, a clearer perspective from the vantage point of distance dispelled the bitterness. With the edge off her grief, a dull acceptance began to take root in Bonnie's heart, and as she learned to accept that which was irrevocable, she released a portion of her spirit to go one step farther and make the first faltering attempts to accept it as coming from God's hand. She was not yet ready to equate her son's death as an expression of His love. She was, however, at last willing to welcome Pastor Rogers to an evening call at Windy Knoll.

Pastor Rogers was an older man than Pastor Thomas had been. He had had more time to develop a more kindly spirit, if at all possible, than his predecessor. Bonnie soon learned that it was more than years that had helped to shape his godly character, for he related how he and his dear wife had lost not one, but three small children from one cause or another. And lastly, God had seen fit to call home his companion. His present wife he had married later in life. Bonnie sat silently as he talked, not so much listening to his words as searching for traces of bitterness. If such had ever existed, there was surely none discernible in him now.

"There are some experiences in life," he said gently, "in which we can't grasp God's purposes immediately; understanding only comes with time. And there are other situations for which we never know the reason in this life. But that is the opportunity for us to exercise faith, for it is faith that believes God is working out His purposes and will work all things together for good even when we cannot see the evidence. If we saw every detail of His workings now withheld from us, we would be walking by sight and not by faith."

Bonnie wasn't sure she was ready to be concerned about whether she was exercising any faith.

"It is extremely difficult," the kindly voice continued, "to view the passing of one so tiny as anything that could be for our good. And perhaps it is not for our good; it may just as likely be for his. Who is to say what evils may have befallen Timothy later in life, what hidden disabilities could have surfaced later, bringing a grief greater than that which you know at his passing. There are many questions. Our part is to believe our loving Father knows what is best for all concerned and that His actions are prompted only by divine, eternal love that transcends all other loves."

At the moment Bonnie could relate only to the love she had for her infant son. The pastor's words registered at a subconscious level. She did not retain them on any level at which she gave them serious consideration. Instead, she began to reflect on the challenge with which her mother had presented her on the balcony several weeks before.

Where is it now? The question flooded her first awakening thoughts in the morning, hammered away at her soul all the day long, and was her final thought as she dropped off to sleep at night. In time its incessant clamoring began to demand an answer—her own answer, compiled out of the depths of her innermost psyche, jarring the foundations upon which she had built her faith. Where was that faith? Had it ever been real? If so, where did it go? What did it amount to now?

Honesty demanded she admit to its former reality. She could not have maintained a phantom of exhilaration for the years in which she had experienced the joy of the Lord. Reason demanded that she acknowledge the reality of her experience and that she was now estranged from the fellowship she had once enjoyed with her Maker. On whose part the estrangement had been initiated, she was not able to discern. Was it not the Maker who had reclaimed the tiny creature and she, the instrument by which the creation had been wondrously wrought, who must stand aggrieved in mute agony?

To be sure, her mother had reason to question whether the experience of which she had spoken so glowingly was as genuine as she had professed. But Bonnie was no longer certain there was any consolation to be offered in it, or whether there was longer any incentive for her mother to seek for it.

In such inner turmoil she continued to make her daily treks to the cemetery. *Where is it now?* rattled the motor as she switched off the ignition. *Where is it now?* crunched from beneath her feet as she picked her way down the gravel walk inside the big iron gates. *Where is it now?* whispered to her from the first new blades of grass peeping their way up through the sod over the tiny grave.

And then the urgency of the question resolved into a calm, quiet confidence as she stood there, looking down at the spot where they had laid him. "Why seek ye the living among the dead? He is not here, he is risen," she heard distinctly.

She looked about her, startled, yet she saw no one.

Oh, yes, she remembered the words of the Easter story. She had not heard a voice; she had heard only a memory—a memory of life.

In the first dim perceptions of that moment she sensed the stirrings of a conviction. Timothy was indeed living, clouded from her earthly eyes for a season, but vibrant and shining in the land of eternal bliss. And she knew also that some day she would be reunited with him, never to grieve again. Upon the strength of that conviction she resolved never again to wend her way to a plot of ground upon this earth's surface in the hope of feeling herself close to her departed flesh. For he was not there; he was living.

Exuberantly Bonnie packed for an overnight trip to a little community in West Virginia. The Pleasant Valley Neighborhood Church had finally been completed after years of planning, fund raising, and community effort. It was the realization of a dream that had taken seed in the hearts of visionary men many years previously.

The church was octagonal, in earth tones reflecting man's humanity and that of the Son of God. But His divinity was revealed in the crown gracing His brow in the stained glass window through which the eastern sun filtered behind the dais. And the cross atop the steeple bore evidence of the meeting between man's reach for the divine and God's condescension to humanity.

It was a day to be remembered by the members of the community for as long as that generation should last, and as long as there remained tongue to relate the day's glories to the next generation and the next. It was a homecoming of all who could claim their roots in that neck of God's creation, who had departed for one reason or another to make their dwellings elsewhere. It was a day of celebration for all who remained and had built the edifice with their own blood, sweat, and tears. It was a day to welcome back every pastor who had once proclaimed the good news from the sacred desk in the temporary structure. And it was a day for inviting the architect who had been chosen with care to design an edifice to embody and demonstrate the vision of a generation of hardy saints.

Bonnie had chosen a new dress with the carefree delight her small daughter knew at such an occasion. It was not often that she was permitted to share so visibly in her husband's success. She determined to look her very best for him as she took her place at his side for the banquet following the dedicatory service, and she felt she had never known so much pride as she did when he rose to express his sentiments as the creator of the epitome of others' dreams.

His success had afforded Buz a demeanor of confidence and self-assurance that set him apart from lesser men. His inherent artistry had refined a sensitive spirit to the extent that others felt awe in his presence. The current hirsute styles permitted the grooming of a well-trimmed mustache, which effectively concealed the ugly scar and lent its own distinction to the impressive bearing manifested in his features. His wife beamed with pride as he delivered his entire speech unfalteringly and was greeted with a standing ovation from the assembled company. And he pulled her to her feet to receive his ovation with him.

But tears stung her eyes as she felt her unworthiness to share in his moment of triumph, for he had quietly accepted the passing of his beloved son as from the hand of a God who knew and understood all things better than he and, though grieved beyond words, submitted to a higher will than his. In the midst of her self-pity and despair, she had been unable to comfort her magnificent husband in his own hour of grief. She, who so willingly shared in his moment of glory, had deserted him in his hour of pain. And he in his own wretchedness had had to reach out to still her own ache. Now she forced the smile to stay upon her face as the remorse and ugly tears threatened to erase it. She was thankful for the seclusion of the motel room when the ordeal was over and she could bury her tear-stained face upon his shoulder and beg for forgiveness.

Shocked that she should even mention it, he once again sought to soothe and caress away the grief in which she was engulfed. But she determined ere she left that little room that she would seek until she found some avenue of peace upon which she could come to terms with herself and the Almighty.

And so it was that she sought out the pastor, whom she had so often shut out.

"Sister Rockwell," he greeted her as she settled herself into the familiar leather-covered chair of the office, "I have prayed for the day when you would seek the balm in Gilead, for Jeremiah, the weeping prophet, tells us that we shall find ourselves restored when we seek the Lord with all our heart."

"Pastor Rogers—" The tissue in Bonnie's hand became knotted beyond use. "I must have an answer. Please, can you tell me why?"

"Bonnie, you are asking me why you lost that which was dearer to you than your own life. I do not know, any more than I know why I lost my own precious little ones, other than the immediate cause, that is. What you are really desiring is an explanation that will satisfy your preconceived ideas of just how God works, what you can expect of Him next, and whether it is worth your while to go on trusting Him."

Bonnie stifled an exclamation of shock. How did the pastor know just exactly what had been in her mind? And then she remembered his own three babes. He had been through all this before her, not once but three times. Now she realized he had arrived at his own state of peace and acceptance by going the same route she now was taking. He had apparently experienced the same bitterness and disillusionment that she knew. Yet somehow he had arrived at some consolation that had given him the strength not only to survive, but to triumph.

Her initial confession was the most difficult, for she had never fully admitted it, even to herself. "Pastor, I've been angry with God; I'm angry that He took my little Timothy from me, and I don't understand why He wanted to bring me such grief."

She stopped. There wasn't much more she could say. How could she explain all that had passed through her mind these past weeks?

"Bonnie, you aren't the first Christian to be angry at God. What do you feel now?"

She looked down at her hands. "I don't know. I miss the fellowship I used to enjoy with my Heavenly Father, but I don't know whether I can have that peace again. I don't know whether our relationship can be restored. I can't shake this bitterness. It's taken over my thoughts. I don't want it anymore, but I can't find relief from it.

"I know now I can't live on my own," she continued. "I want to trust Him. I want what I used to have. I don't know how to get God back. I don't know whether He'll have me back."

"You never lost Him, Bonnie. He's been with you even in your rebellion. First Peter one tells us our inheritance is incorruptible, reserved in heaven for us. We are kept by God's power. He never leaves us.

"That same passage goes on to tell us that trials do have a purpose, to purify our faith as fire purifies gold. Because the Lord Jesus has not yet returned, death still holds its grip on this world. Even believers are not immune to tragedy. But because we have the assurance of

His love, we can face this life knowing our circumstances are not in vain. We'll never in this age understand every reason why. Yet if we can believe He died because He loved us enough that He wanted an eternal relationship with Him, then I think we can believe He desires nothing more than the best for each of us. Do you believe that, Bonnie?"

His eyes did not miss her struggle. It was many long moments before she could look into those eyes and say, "Yes. If He died for me, He must love me, too. I guess I trusted Him to save me from eternal damnation, but I didn't completely entrust my life and the lives of my family into His care, even if that meant separation from them. But I want to now."

"Then why don't you now?"

Together they bowed their heads.

"Father, I'm sorry I've been angry at You. I believe You can forgive me, and I ask for Your forgiveness. I also believe that You love me, and I want to surrender to You my entire life—my possessions, my talents, my health—and my family too, Lord. I know that we are all safer in Your care than in mine." Bonnie found it difficult to continue. "Father, even as I pray now, I feel as if I'm holding back. Please, Lord, honor this decision of my will. And continue to work in my life until it is fully accomplished. In Your Name I ask this. Amen."

Her minister continued, "Father, You have heard this request. Seal it now for eternity, and renew a right spirit within Bonnie. We ask You to shine forth in her life once more. In Your holy name, Amen."

A weight as of a ton of iron slipped from Bonnie's shoulders, and her heartstrings were loosed to vibrate again as the harp in the hands of a skillful player. Grasping the pastor's hand in a wordless farewell, she turned and fled out the door and to the seclusion of her own auto. "Thank you, Jesus," she breathed over the steering wheel. And she headed for Oakland to pick up Mimi. But before she arrived at the Shadyside Apartments, she had had time to make some momentous decisions. First, she was going to make up to her little daughter what she had deprived her in the long weeks and months she had wallowed in self-pity instead of being thankful she still had one child. Second, she was going to live a victorious life before her mother so that, even though she had miserably failed her test so far, her mother could not mistake the all-sufficiency provided in Jesus and could know beyond a shadow of doubt that what her daughter had professed all along was valid. And, last, but most important, she was going to start being worthy of the magnificent husband the Lord had given her. She would be the helpmate he deserved and begin to minister to his needs as she had expected him to minister to hers. Then perhaps together they would attempt once more to open their home in an outreach to their neighbors.

21

The noted architect, Nathaniel G. Rockwell, was at that moment in Denver. A congregation of believers there, having read in a religious periodical of the Pleasant Valley Community Church under construction in West Virginia, had desired a similar structure for their own worship. Upon receipt of a letter from the chairman of the building committee, the designer of the soon-to-become-famous edifice boarded a plane for the distant city at his earliest convenience. He had prevailed upon his semi-reclusive young wife to accompany him, thinking the change of scenery would instill fresh vigor into her languishing spirit. She had demurred, however, preferring the solitude of her own company as she had sought for a pinion with which she could mesh the grievous details of her life with a larger scheme of things she could not yet understand or perceive.

And now as her path led out route 28 and toward the little hillock bursting forth with the first hints of early summer, she vowed that never again would her love travel alone on any journey upon which he desired her company. She had failed him this time, as she had on several other recent occasions, but from this moment and henceforth, she would grace his side with her cheeriest self. And while traveling she would look for opportunities to witness to others of their shared faith in a God of love and compassion. She would renew her determination to practice the gift of helps, which she had temporarily forgotten, and at every presented opportunity she would extend the hand of love to anyone in need of it.

For starters she would begin immediately to present her husband with meals prepared lovingly with more diligence than she had shown heretofore. Not that Buz had ever complained about the fare which she set before him. With his courtesy, breeding, and profound adoration for her, she reflected ruefully, he would probably make a gallant effort to devour sauteed bird beaks if she deigned to serve them. But it didn't take too much insight to realize that anyone who had grown up as he had, accustomed to tantalizing relishes, pickled vegetables, and luscious pastries, could not help missing them when the supply was terminated. Why had it never occurred to her before to write to Mom Rockwell and ask for some of her fabulous recipes? Surely, with even her limited skills, she should be able to manage the superb *bot boi*, that rich stew of chicken with vegetables and tantalizing squares of egg noodles smothered in broth that must cause Buz homesickness just at the memory. And she would arrange a few days of the summer vacation time to spend in Harrisburg taking some firsthand lessons. Bonnie was repulsed by her eight years of thoughtlessness and wondered how she could forgive herself.

That would do for a beginning. Her next project would be to learn more of what Buz actually included in his work. She loved to listen to his glowing accounts of the magnificent creations that now studded much of southwestern Pennsylvania and many localities of other states as well. And she had on many occasions happily driven to an outlying construction site with him for inspection. But when he talked of section modulous, voussoirs, squinches, fenestration, and pediment, she would pretend to understand what he meant and then promptly forget it. She determined now to stop at the library at her earliest convenience, check out some books on modern architecture, and learn the definitions behind the terms he used. She might even attempt an occasional suggestion, not that she hoped his genius would stoop to listening to her, but only so he could be assured of her whole-hearted involvement with him in his profession.

And as soon as he returned from this trip, together they would once more explore the possibilities of developing an outreach in their immediate community. Her mind began turning over some possibilities. It was obvious from their previous attempts that there must be a nucleus of believers to form the backbone for a group to which others could be invited. Upon reflection, she decided Meredith was her most likely prospect. True, Meredith had sounded evasive and noncommittal on Bonnie's first attempt. But then she had been the energetic career girl, single and unattached to any commitment save the church and the middle-aged attorney for whom she labored with secretarial skills among the best in the city.

A year previously, the attorney's wife had lost her bout with cancer, and the courtly gentleman gradually discovered he employed not only the most efficient girl Friday money could entice, but also a lovely, gracious lady who could just as readily turn her skills to homemaking with the same warmth and good humor with which she graced his office. The wedding was now scheduled to take place in just a couple weeks, and Bonnie was to attend her old friend as Meredith had once taken her place at Bonnie's side as she had repeated her vows.

It's a wonder she would even ask me, Bonnie mused, *as crabby as I've been lately. She probably only did so out of duty to return the honor, and she probably wished she didn't have to cast such gloom upon her happy occasion. Well, I'll just show her, the Lord helping me, she can be as happy to have me in her wedding party as anyone else. In fact, I'll just phone her as soon as she gets home from work to tell her that the errant sheep has returned to the fold, and I will don my most beaming smile as I go down the aisle.*

The wedding was not to be elaborate, as the bride-to-be considered a conservative affair more in keeping with the groom's second marriage, his station in life, and her being somewhat older than the age of the starry-eyed young things who usually opted for the elegant panoplies.

"After all," she had snickered merrily, "having passed my thirtieth birthday, I'm somewhat over the hill for such frivolities. Whoever would have thought I'd ever make it at all? If there's hope for me, no one should despair."

"You make it sound as though you were a hopeless case," Bonnie replied sternly, "and you know very well you just had to wait a little longer than most to find someone who could measure up to you." *And,* she added to herself, *you did pretty well at that; the wait was worth it.* For Meredith was now to become the mistress of an elegant Tudor mansion furnished with Queen Anne and Regency pieces that rested upon luxurious Persian carpets. Carved ivories and exquisite figurines in Miessen and Dresden china graced the hand-carved mantelpieces of oak and the delicate inlaid tables of the parlors and drawing room. Intricately designed Belgian lace curtains hung from the graceful mullioned windows, and the magnificent crystal chandeliers had once adorned one of the stately old houses in Britain. Meredith need have no qualms about keeping the showplace in tiptop condition, for a live-in maid occupied the third-floor suite. Meredith's chief concern was how she was to occupy her time, as J. McCallister Langworthy did not intend his wife to work as a secretary in anyone's office, least of all his.

To Bonnie the best part of it all was that this fabulous residence soon to house her dear friend was only a few blocks down Mount Royal Boulevard from her own Windy Knoll. If she could blow a spark down the street from the fires of her own enthusiasm for reaching her neighbors, and set off a conflagration in the hearts of Meredith and her soon-to-be husband, the Langworthys might be able to witness to the neighbors on their end of the boulevard while the Rockwells reached the rest. Bonnie became excited at the prospect.

At that point she turned down the gravel drive leading into Windy Knoll.

"Something must be funny, Mommie." Mimi was looking at her mother expectantly. "You are laughing."

"Oh, I'm not really laughing ha, ha. I'm just smiling at the thought of something very exciting, darling." A stab of conscience smote Bonnie as she realized there was more in the child's simple words than what she had heard. Bonnie interpreted distinctly that Mimi was pleased to see a smile on her mother's face again.

"Look, baby." Bonnie gathered her small daughter into her arms as she turned off the motor. "Mimi—" she hesitated, choked with the admission she must make. "Mimi, baby, Mommie has been neglecting you terribly. Instead of being thankful I still had my darling little girl, I have been too busy feeling sorry for myself because Jesus found it best to take our little Timothy back to heaven to be with Him. I know now I was wrong to grieve that way over him, because he is much better off with Jesus than he would ever have been with us anyway. And Jesus always knows the best thing to do for us. So we should be happy that Timothy is happy now and never will know the sad things we encounter in this world. And with him all taken care of, I'm going to try to make up to you what you have missed from your Mommie all this time. We are going to do nice things together, maybe like play games, go to the park, and visit the zoo. How would you like to go to the zoo?"

"Oh, I would love to. The zoo where you can pet the baby animals. Can we go today?"

"It is a trifle late today. But I promise you, we will go as soon as it opens tomorrow, and we can stay just as long as you like."

The child's joy bubbled over the next morning when she and her mother made their way through the little gate marked "Children's Zoo." The gentle baby llama was the first to greet her, and she threw her arms around his long neck and buried her face in his soft thick fur. She squealed with delight when his rough tongue licked her cheek. When she dabbed with her hand to wipe off its wetness, he escaped her near strangling embrace; then her attention was arrested by a parade of ducklings. And off she went on the chase after them. She stroked woolly lambs, long-horned goats, a tiny, spotted fawn, and all the guinea pigs and rabbits she was successful in catching, and she slipped her fingers between the bars on a small cage housing two baby jaguars. After all, one couldn't properly appreciate their spotted little bodies unless she could feel their sleek coats. Inside Noah's Ark she watched in fascination as entire colonies of mice scampered about, hiding in miniature hollow logs and scampering into litter nests. Finding the baby groundhog too sleepy to respond to her raps on the glass, she hurried on to the little barn. There she thrilled to the sight of an attendant's feeding a tiny squirrel, inverted in one hand, from a doll's bottle. The squirrel just barely nestled in that one hand with his miniature tail trailing down over the attendant's wrist.

"Look, Mommie," she squealed excitedly, "his nose is square like a box. It isn't pointed like the squirrels' noses that we have around our house."

"Give him time. His nose will lengthen out soon enough and then he will be able to crack nuts in his powerful jaws."

"Then we'll come back tomorrow and see how much longer his nose is."

"Tomorrow will be a mite too soon to see any difference, but we could come back next week and visit him again."

"Next week and the next and the next and—"

"All right, baby, we'll come every week and watch him grow up into a big squirrel."

And come they did. Bonnie was glad summer had just begun, for the two of them had the entire season to enjoy together. They explored all the parks, and Mimi learned the names of many of the trees and shrubs. They went for swims every nice day they didn't have another activity scheduled. The little one developed into an excellent swimmer even though her Aunt Sylvia was not around to instruct her. And they spent many happy hours in the library perusing the colorfully illustrated children's books. Mimi's favorite story soon became "The Ugly Duckling."

"I'm going to grow up to be beautiful just like that ugly little duck," the child remarked every time she leafed through the story's pages.

"But you already are beautiful," her mother encouraged.

"No, Mommie, Daddy says I'm beautiful because I look like you, but I heard some ladies at the ice show say I wasn't as pretty as Lindy. I don't think Lindy's all that pretty anyway; so if I'm not that pretty, I'm not very beautiful at all."

"Now, darling, you are just as beautiful as you act. And you are a very lovely young lady. Mommie is proud of you."

"Just the same, I'm going to be beautiful when I grow up."

"I'm sure you are. And a person is always prettier when she has Jesus in her heart, for then His character shows through her."

"Is that the reason you're prettier now than you used to be?"

Bonnie was taken aback with the child's last astute statement. The immediate past was probably all Mimi remembered of her mother's disposition. How embittered she must have appeared to her adored daughter! She determined to strive even harder to erase the memory.

Seeing how his two most cherished women so enjoyed their outings together, Buz decreed that from now on a cleaning lady was to take the brunt off the hours Bonnie labored in the home, freeing her to spend even more time in leisurely pursuits.

"After all," he reasoned, "we are well enough situated now that you should not have to labor like a charwoman. You do not engage yourself in clubs or tennis matches as do other ladies of ease, but you are investing your time in the prospect of reaping greater dividends; and you may as well enjoy some of the privileges of those who are so stationed in life as we can now feel ourselves to be."

Bonnie's heart welled once again with pride in her beloved husband's accomplishments. How honored she was that he had chosen her, a nameless waif cast off as refuse following a cruel, horrible war, and established her as mistress of an architectural masterpiece, showered affection upon her, and permitted her to share in the glories he received for his brilliant creativity! She was humbled by her blessings and vowed to pay greater diligence in showing gratitude.

The daily jaunts with Mimi continued. But the child's favorite haunt remained the zoo. Not confining herself to the children's section, she had discovered to her immense delight that some mothers among the big cats in the main house were proudly displaying the cubs to which they had given birth in the spring. And she stood for long periods watching the newcomers' antics. Twin leopards, somewhat lighter in color than their mother but no bigger than an ordinary house cat, apparently were deemed in need of grooming by the solicitous parent. Her tongue was as large as the entire side of the offspring, and one unsuspecting tiny fellow, attempting to pass in front of his mother, found himself stopped dead in his tracks as she licked one swipe in the opposite direction from which he was moving.

"Now that's a giant washcloth!" Mimi giggled. "I'm glad you don't use that kind on me."

"Dear, it would take more than that to hold you still."

In front of the lion cage Mimi danced up and down in glee. The twin lions, being somewhat larger than the leopards, proved to be more of a handful for their mother, although the term should more properly be expressed as *mouthful*. One mischievous young one bit the end of her tail. The harder she pulled to release it from his grip, the more tenaciously he hung on. She then resorted to closing her powerful jaws over his rump with a sternness that spoke volumes. When the recalcitrant offspring at last gave up the sport, his brother immediately engaged in the tail pulling. And when the weary mother finally succeeded in discouraging his antics, the first resumed the game. A crowd always gathered to watch the performance and dispersed chuckling only when the youngsters' attention was drawn from their mother's tail to other diversions.

Mimi looked forward to the antics each week and could scarcely contain her disappointment when, by the end of the summer, the youngsters were placed elsewhere or shipped to distant zoos. She then began to spend more time in the children's zoo again, and her vigilance was rewarded when she discovered a family of albino rats. The mother was a lovely creature of fur white as snow, with pink feet, nose, and eyes. How solicitously she stroked each tiny baby with a paw and groomed them constantly with her tongue! Mimi exclaimed in fresh glee and declared that you just wouldn't suspect that motherly thing of being a rat.

"Please, Mommie, may I have one in a cage at home? I would like to have a family of baby rats."

Bonnie shuddered. "Beautiful or not, darling, people do not keep rats around at home. But I'll tell you what we'll do. People do keep hamsters, and they have lots of babies. We'll get a pair and you can watch them. It may be just what you need to keep the memories of our happy trips to the zoo alive after the weather gets bad and we won't get out so much."

Bonnie was true to her word. The next day Mimi spent forty-five minutes at a pet shop making her selection. Her hamsters were to have just the right shade of coloring. They must have delightful long whiskers that would twitch back and forth as they explored her arms and pockets, and they must enjoy being held. The squirmier ones were vetoed immediately. At last she proudly bore a small box forth from the store while her mother lugged a brand new cage.

"I shall call them Sleeping Beauty and Prince Charming, Beauty and Prince for short."

"I'm sure those names are just fine," Bonnie agreed, "but they sound more like horses to me."

"Well—" Mimi reflected for a moment, "they won't sound like horses when they run."

"And I sincerely hope they do all their running in their cage. I wouldn't want them gnawing holes through the partitions."

And so it was that Beauty and Prince took up their abode at Windy Knoll.

When the new Mr. and Mrs. J. McCallister Langworthy returned from their European honeymoon, Mr. and Mrs. Nathaniel G. Rockwell hosted a neighborhood reception for them at Windy Knoll. All the area acquaintances of each couple were on the guest list, and for a neighborhood mixer it appeared to be a success. People who had lived near each other for years learned some of their neighbors' names and discovered that most were the type of people they would like to have next door.

Bonnie engaged a caterer who served the most delectable smorgasbord many vowed they had ever set teeth into. A local ensemble provided entertainment, and the bridal couple showed slides of sites they had visited in Europe. It was midnight before the last reluctant guest took his departure, declaring his genuine enjoyment of the evening. And there were not a few declarations of intention to stage a repeat performance sans a bride and groom.

"We don't really have to have a special occasion such as a wedding to turn out for a good time," was the consensus. "We simply must do it again."

Bonnie and Buz could barely restrain their tongues from crying, "No, a Bible study would do just as well." But prudence forced them to bide their time, even though their sincerest desire was to bring their neighbors together again for that purpose. The remainder of the summer they spent quietly seeking to strengthen the friendships they had inaugurated on that fabulous evening. Three couples returned the invitation with a private backyard barbecue or indoor dinner, which the Rockwells accepted eagerly. Others they spoke to as occasion provided. And when the summer was ended and the frenzied activities of the season had quieted, the Rockwells and the Langworthys began to invite the residents of Mount Royal Boulevard to Windy Knoll for a Monday evening sharing in God's Word. One by one the invitations were rejected. Only Lindy Colbeck's parents made any attempt to join the Langworthys and Rockwells, and that was only halfhearted. They were just as likely to be absent as present on the designated evening.

The pitiful little number was reinforced by the addition of one couple. When business affairs became so demanding that Buz and his partners were spending more than a profitable amount of time with their bookwork, Buz proposed hiring a financial consultant to handle it for them. It would be a simple matter to turn all receipts and accounts over to a firm whose specialty it was to deal with that aspect of the business, thereby freeing the three architects to concentrate on designing. Remembering his old pal Drew Anderson, who was still with the firm that had engaged him upon his graduation, Buz suggested he be approached for the position. His proposal was met with hearty agreement, and negotiations proceeded accordingly.

With the Andersons and Rockwells in closer contact, the former occasionally lent their support to the Monday evening group. But still the little circle did not grow, although they earnestly prayed and besought the Lord to interest others in the venture. The faithful ones alternated between an optimism born of belief that they were following the Lord's leading in the attempt to reach their neighbors, and discouragement when it appeared that absolutely no one was concerned with the salvation of his soul. They had begun to believe that though the plan was God-ordained, the timing was not right. Perhaps they should wait awhile.

Mimi confirmed the latter when she returned one autumn afternoon from playing with Lindy.

"Are we crazy people, Mommie?" she asked, wide-eyed with wonderment.

"Are we crazy people?" Bonnie repeated the question,

attempting to grasp its meaning. "Well, I guess you could say we are to some extent. Your Daddy has quite a sense of humor, if that is what you—do you mean crazy ha! ha! or crazy like—" Bonnie's words trailed off as she twirled her finger in a circle at her ear. She grew serious when she discerned the look of consternation on her small daughter's countenance.

"I mean crazy like a way that isn't very nice. Lindy and I were playing behind the hedge between their house and the Brisbains' when I heard Lindy's mother and Mrs. Brisbain talking. I don't think Mrs. Brisbain knew Lindy and I were there. She said, 'Can you just imagine sane, sensible people like those Rockwells thinking we need a Bible study in this neighborhood! They say he's supposed to be a brilliant architect, but if he thinks people here need his kind of religion, he's crazier than I think he is.' She said a whole lot more than that, but I can't remember it. I really didn't know what all she said other than that we are crazy. Are we, Mommie?"

The child's eyes looked troubled and fearful.

"Darling, we are told in the Bible that God chooses foolish things to make wise people confused, because He wants people to serve Him who believe in a simple way the things He says. When we get our human wisdom mixed up with God's ways, we can't see His ways clearly. That is the reason we have to accept them with simplicity. Of course, people who feel they know everything and have a good enough life already, can't understand that. That is the reason we look crazy to them, but in reality, they are the ones who are confused. We must keep on praying for them and try to tell them somehow that they need to know the Lord, too."

"Oh! I'm so glad my Daddy isn't crazy. I thought from what Mrs. Brisbain said that he must be."

When Bonnie related the conversation to the little

group on the following Monday evening, it was agreed among them that they would continue to meet for prayer for the neighbors, but that for the time being, they would cease to invite them out. Perhaps by spring the Lord would move their friends to the point of being more amenable.

The engaging of Drew Anderson as financial consultant motivated the architectural firm to realize their original plan to construct their own office building. Buz was at last free to indulge himself in complete fantasy in its creation, for this was a design that did not have to be sold. His partners bought it enthusiastically, remarking that its distinction was befitting its function as the facility of the master designer. It was to be circular, of black stucco studded with trillions of seashells. The roof would spiral downward like a giant shell with fluted edge. But not just any seashells would do for so imaginative an undertaking. Cameron, DeSantis, and Rockwell spared no expense in flying in an assortment of colorful, small cowries from the Philippines for the background, whereas the larger, elegantly patterned Textile cone from Australia's Great Barrier Reef and six-inch coral-hued St. James scallop from the Mediterranean were to be arranged throughout in a harmonic symmetrical design.

And while the three artists were in an expansive mood, they decided to build a large office complex for sale or rent. It was the first project they undertook to construct for themselves, expecting financial gain from the building itself. If the venture proved to be successful, they might turn their energies toward a giant shopping mall. Excitement ran high through the firm. It was an excellent time to realize some of the wealth to be gained from the burgeoning commerce.

As Buz was on a project in Michigan when the contractor was selected, the contract was made by his two partners. A suitable site was chosen in the rapidly developing area around North Hills, and construction was speedily underway.

Beauty and Prince had been part of the Rockwell household for just a little over three weeks when Mimi squealed excitedly, "She's building a nest. Soon we'll have lots and lots of babies."

Bonnie hastened to purchase another cage to house the father-to-be before he could cause damage within the little family, and shortly Mimi's wait was rewarded.

"Look, Mommie! There must be dozens of them!" Mimi could scarcely contain her delight as she danced up and down.

"I think one dozen is more like it, but we must wait awhile to count them. If we disturb them now, Beauty might eat them."

"Oh! How horrible! I wouldn't eat my babies."

"I should hope not!" Bonnie laughed. "But you have to remember that Beauty is only a small animal, and she doesn't want to be disturbed. She will take very good care of all her babies if we leave her alone until they get a little bigger. And then you can watch them scamper about and play all you wish."

It was later that same day that the news came from Vermont of the birth of Veronica. When Avonelle received Hal's phone call, she hastened to Windy Knoll to inform the newcomer's aunt in person.

"She only weighed five pounds and nine ounces, Hal said, and Sylvia did not get along very well. He thought of phoning while she was in delivery, but thought better of it since there would be nothing we could do except worry anyway. And he says little Veronica is going to be another Sylvia. You know, it upsets me the way he said that; I don't believe he was entirely happy to think there would be another Sylvia in the house. I do worry about that situation up there."

"Sylvia has made her own bed; she will now have to lie in it," philosophized Bonnie. "But I do pray all the time she will somehow get her feet down to earth and mature a little. Let me fix a pot of coffee. It's a little early yet for dinner, and Buz said he would be late tonight anyway. You must phone Dad and tell him to come out when he gets off work."

"I already have; I knew what you would say about it and took the liberty to do so already. But, Bonnie, you can skip the coffee. You see, I've been realizing lately that I have expected caffeine and nicotine to do for me what I see the Lord is doing for you. You didn't know it, but I have watched you ever since that long ago night when you burst in, starry-eyed and bubbly, to tell us you had found the Lord. You know, I didn't pay any attention at the time to what I thought was silly babbling, but I began to realize you had found something that was genuine. Your life took such a complete turn around with your making a completely different set of friends and all. And then you went and married a man I thought wasn't half as good as Hal. Well, it didn't take me long to find out what you had got for yourself, and I knew you would never have made such a wonderful marriage if it hadn't been for the way you were living for the Lord, as you put it.

"I was about ready to admit my folly and blindness when Timothy was snatched from you. Then when I saw how you reacted to that, I said to myself, see, there wasn't anything to it after all. But now I see how radiantly you have recovered from the grief and are going to go on and trust God anyway. There is nothing more I can say. I have watched you all these years now, and I have to admit that even though you have stumbled, you are still ringing true blue. It takes something supernatural for that."

Bonnie's eyes had filled with tears as her mother was speaking. They spilled over down her cheeks. Avonelle's eyes likewise began to overflow. Bonnie reached for her mother's hand, but Avonelle gathered her daughter into her arms and pressed Bonnie's head against her shoulder.

"I looked in the mirror and I loathed what I saw," she continued. "Wrinkles and sallow skin far beyond my years. I realized those cigarettes hadn't helped me one bit. I reached for another cup of coffee, and I wanted to spit it out. It would only make my nerves worse than ever. So I dumped it. I'm not saying I won't drink it at all anymore, but I'm certainly not going to depend on it for stamina, for I can see that isn't where you get yours.

"Then when Hal called, my heart just went out to my poor daughter up there. And deep down inside I knew that there wasn't any hope for her, either, apart from what God can do for her. And I am not in any shape to lead her that way. So on the way over here, I determined that with God's help, I'm going to put my own life in His hands, and join you in praying for Sylvia—and for Perry and James, too."

Their tears mingled as Avonelle asked, "Will you forgive me for the way I have treated you? I know I brought you much grief, practically kicking you out of the house when you had done nothing to merit such a reaction. Oh, Bonnie, you just don't know how I have grieved over my acting that way and how I have wished I could take back the angry words. I would do anything to make it up—"

"Please never mention it again," Bonnie stammered between sniffs. "I believe now as I did then that it was all in God's plan that I should make a move on my own, and you certainly never kicked me out. I went of my own volition. What's past is past. I'm so happy for you now—I can hardly contain it. Are you aware that Luke tells us in Scripture there is joy in the presence of the angels over one sinner that repents? Honestly, Mother, I don't know how I can stand getting a new niece and a new mother all on the same day! You know, you have become a new creation."

"That was what you were trying to tell me all the while, wasn't it? Now I would know it without your even having to say it, for I feel it. How could I have waited so long?"

"Mother, dear, this isn't a day for remorse for what is gone. It's a time for great rejoicing for what is before. The Lord has been merciful to keep you until you would get right with Him, and the best is yet to come. If you wish, we will agree together for Sylvia's salvation. God says there is power in united prayer. And we can start right now."

"By all means; let's do so."

Bonnie shared her small daughter's delight in the hamster babies. In a few days they felt it safe enough to count them.

"Fourteen!" Mimi exclaimed. "Aren't you glad there weren't fourteen of me?"

"No, dear, I wouldn't mind if they were all just like you." Bonnie looked down adoringly at her little girl.

A thought had been germinating in her mind for some time now. When Timothy was born, she had been so miserable that she vowed never to have another baby. But now that her memory was of an empty crib rather than her own misery, she was beginning to think differently of that vow. And with the blessed event in the hamster cage and the news from Vermont, it seemed to be the season for babies. Her arms ached for a tiny bundle to nestle within them. And here was her precious little daughter having to lavish her affection on animals instead of a brother or sister. That situation must be remedied. Now was as good a time to start as ever.

Mother and daughter watched day by day as the baby hamsters grew fur and struggled together in the nest. At mealtime Beauty was fairly smothered under the pummeling she received from her brood. Each miniature mouth opened in its pursuit of food, and the tiny balls of fur shoved and kicked each other to gain a position that would be productive. They formed one solid cluster of movement as they wriggled and squirmed like the seething of a minute, turbulent sea.

One day as she stood watching their ceaseless movement, Bonnie was suddenly seized with faint vertigo. Deep in her subconscious she was gripped with the sensation of being rocked and pummeled herself until she began to sway on her feet. Transported as in a trance back into her old, familiar dream, she instinctively started to reach upward in a grasping motion, then realized what she was doing and, feeling foolish, brought her arm back down to her side. But she knew in that fleeting, subconscious moment she was not grasping for a rope in her dream, for she was not as she had thought, drowning in water. She was being jostled violently by hundreds of human bodies as real and tangible as her own. Whose were they? And for what was she grasping?

22

As surely as the tide recedes only to witness the resurgence of new billows, the decade that had dawned with the uniting of two hearts in the ecstacy of young love was about to fade into an eternity that exists only in memory.

It had been a decade of unprecedented turbulence in the world of human affairs. Angry young people had burned administration buildings on college campuses and insisted on the right to shape their own courses of study. Youths of a differing ideology had immolated the communities in which they lived and carried on their trading. A president, a respected leader of the black community, and a presidential aspirant had met violent death at the hands of misguided assassins. A power shortage had brought the nation's largest, most populous city to a complete standstill.

A vocal group from a foreign shore had paved the route to a new decline in morality and to the practice of a heathen religion whose insidious influence had once been removed by a vast ocean. The nation's young men were being sent to a foreign soil to forfeit their lives in a losing cause, while on the other side of the world God's chosen people had reclaimed a strategic portion of their ancient homeland in a lightning attack that lasted for six days. Planes were hijacked and their passengers taken hostage at the hands of fanatical political extremists.

A weary, bruised, and buffeted world looked to the dawn of a new decade in the hope that some semblance of sanity would arise from the ashes of past mistakes and that a new order could be shaped from increased enlightenment.

And while uncontrolled forces raged and fomented without, peace and tranquility prevailed within Windy Knoll's serene walls. Seven winters had clothed the cozy little hillock in their white mantles, and as many generations of squirrels had gamboled in the limbs of the stately elms and oaks that crowned it. Six summers had smiled their sunshine upon the secluded nook while the climatis threaded its way among the tiles of the roof on the sprawling, palatial residence of its young architect and his family.

He and his wife surveyed their lives with great contentment, secure in each other's love and the stable establishment of the firm of which he was a partner. His fame as an architect had ever grown until there was scarcely a state from which he did not receive a request for his services. And many were the commissions he accepted in a far distant city where he raised monuments to his creative genius. It was whispered in voices hushed in awe behind the closed doors of numerous envious fellow architects that the spirit of Frank Lloyd Wright lived on in the dreams and aspirations of this one who harbored his visionary ideals in his breast. And Mount Royal Boulevard was plagued with an endless stream of traffic slowing to catch a glimpse through the trees of the grandeur of the masterpiece which housed its designer.

The little girl within its spacious walls had grown and flourished as seed in the warm earth watered by gentle rains. She was fast becoming an accomplished skater with the ease and agility of a graceful doe. Having mastered the difficult sit spin, she spent many golden hours perfecting the loop jump. The hint of greatness that

Miss Mathilde had first detected in her protégé was showing promise of fruition.

Miriam's love for animals, which had been kindled at an early age, was now exhibited in a hutch that housed a rabbit family, a chattering, whistling mynah bird as sleek and glistening as the bituminous coal mined under the rolling hills of Pennsylvania, and a noble Great Dane that never left her side except when she boarded the bus that carried her to school. And every day promptly at three-thirty he waited at the end of the gravel lane to escort her back to the threshhold of her happy home.

The only flaw was the absence of a brother or sister for Mimi. For try as she would, Bonnie could discover no indication that there was ever to be one. A trip to a specialist in Boston and consultation with a team of doctors at Johns Hopkins University offered no respite from the fear that there would never be another fine, beautiful son such as Timothy had been. How Bonnie longed to delight her adored husband with the joy of another perfect little replica of himself, a son to accompany him on the white water rafting he had once so loved and had forsaken under the pressure of business, a son whose brush-laden hand he might guide in the artistic strokes of his own genius, a son with whom he could trek the fields and streams of his own youth, reliving golden memories of a carefree idyllic childhood. But for all the devotion he lavished on Mimi, another daughter would be no less welcome. After the first year of fruitless attempt, Bonnie's disappointment turned to abject despair. She and her beloved husband were getting no younger.

As the Rockwells anticipated the celebration of their tenth wedding anniversary, they planned a second honeymoon in Hawaii. They had visited every state on the continent in the course of business, contrary to the practices of Steve Cameron and Mike DeSantis, Buz's partners in business, who often indulged in European tours or Caribbean cruises. Now, however, Buz and Bonnie cherished the dream of relaxing on a sun-drenched beach, listening to the crashing of the surf, and searching for starfish among rings of coral. They sent for travel brochures as excitedly as children searching the pages of the Christmas catalog. And they made hotel reservations many months in advance.

"This is the one at which we must stay," Bonnie pointed excitedly to a brochure picture of a hotel buried beneath elaborate hanging gardens. "We can imagine we are in ancient Babylon. And look at the sparkling beach directly beneath it. It certainly will be a far cry from the terrible storm that's blowing tonight." She pulled her sweater more snugly about her, nestled closer to her husband, and mused dreamily for some moments before adding, "I must purchase some new bathing suits. After we get there I'll find some of those brilliant muumuus for myself and the gaily designed shirts for you. We might as well get with the aloha spirit."

"That we must, my darling. And I shall lade your lovely neck with the most fragrant jasmine leis ever."

"And when the sun dips low over the distant horizon, we shall gather with the natives to dance to the strum of guitars accompanied by the rustling of the wind high in the palm branches."

"I may try a little surfing. That might even beat white water rafting."

"And I will learn now what a juicy mango and papaya taste like straight off the tree. My mouth is already watering. Darling—do you suppose that either Mauna Loa or Kilauea might be accommodating enough to erupt just for us while we are there?"

"My dear Mrs. Rockwell, there is a miniature volcano any place where you are."

Bonnie's mouth curved into a fake pout. "My dear Mr.

Rockwell, would you mind explaining just what you meant by your last remark?"

His reply was interrupted by the ringing of the door-bell.

"Now who can that be at this hour of night and in this dastardly blizzard?" he puzzled. "Never mind, just sit still; I'll get it."

Striding to the great oaken doors, he flipped on the outside light, lifted the iron latch and flung open the door on his right. There, to his amazement, stood a woman holding a young child, with a boy of about nine or ten at her side. A younger child peered timidly from behind them. Their coats were pulled together about their necks to ward off the penetrating chill, toboggan caps fit snugly about the children's heads, and a scarf concealed all but the mother's face. They were snow-covered and obviously shivering. An array of large, bulging pieces of luggage was assembled around them. Wonderingly, Buz squinted in the dim light, trying to ascertain whether they were of his acquaintance. A blast of wind blew snow in through the open door as the young woman indicated she wished to step inside.

"H-hello," Buz began hesitantly, thinking they must have lost their way. "Were you looking for someone?"

"Looking for someone! Buz Rockwell, don't you know your own sister-in-law?" Sylvia strode indignantly into the hall. "Here we are, worn out and frozen, and I'm beginning to wonder whether we are to be turned away from my own sister's door."

She removed her headscarf, shaking the snow from it and her hair about her shoulders, set the little one on the floor, and proceeded to drag in the luggage. Buz hastened to lift each piece inside as Bonnie appeared. The latter was momentarily rooted immobile in the little foyer as she surveyed the situation. Why hadn't she noticed before how long Sylvia's hair was becoming? It had been several months since she had last seen her, but that growth had required many years without trimming. The heavy, raven tresses must be nearly reaching their owner's knees. Parted in the middle, they cascaded straight down her shoulders and nearly blanketed the slight frame. Gone was the soft deep curl Bonnie had once envied. The weight must be pulling it straight, she reasoned. The witch-like effect stirred a faint recollection of a dark-haired woman on an old television program that portrayed a family of extremely weird and eccentric people. *Your own flesh and—well, your own sister, anyway!* Bonnie scolded herself for the uncomplimentary comparison.

"What a surprise!" she exclaimed aloud. "If I had known you were coming, I would have prepared the guest rooms. I'm afraid you are going to find them somewhat dusty. They haven't been opened for weeks. Here let me take your things. It certainly was a terrible day to be traveling. You must be nearly frozen."

"Nonsense! This would only be an average summer day in Vermont!"

Sylvia unbuttoned her ankle-length coat that resembled a Cossack field marshall's uniform and revealed a miniskirt a trifle too mini. Above her tall boots her legs were bare. No wonder she didn't care for New England winters, Bonnie thought with disgust, if those were all the clothes she wore.

Harry already had removed his jacket and was attempting to assist Jennifer with her leggings.

"I can't believe this little toddler is Veronica." Bonnie scooped the baby into her arms. "They grow up fast when you don't see them often. But she is just as much a doll as I remember her to be. Come into the kitchen while I make some sandwiches. Did you just arrive, or have you been to Mother's first?"

"Yes and no. This is the first place I have stopped. We

just got off the plane a short while ago and took a cab out here. I thought we should come here where you have more room until I can get myself situated. I'll call Mom later and let her know we're here."

"I really wish you had let me know you were coming," Bonnie mumbled, rummaging in the refrigerator. "I'm afraid the cupboard is rather bare. How about cold tongue? I believe there is enough left for a few sandwiches. By the way—" Bonnie straightened from her exploration of the lower shelves and looked at her sister quizzically, "where is Hal?"

"Hal? Oh, him." Sylvia dismissed the name with a wave of her hand. "He didn't come."

"Oh, really. His folks will be rather disappointed when they hear that. But I suppose it was hard for him to get away just now."

"Tell me what's new on the home front. The family still the same?"

"Mother and Dad are both very well, although the winter is taking its toll on Dad. He seems to have the flu every couple weeks. And would you believe, Mom tells me Perry finally discovered there are girls around. She hasn't met the one he's been seeing lately; he never brings her home. And he is still driving that delivery service for the pharmacy."

"At his speed I would hate to see someone in distress needing a drug in a hurry. The patient would die before he ever reached the scene."

"Sylvia, I don't believe you are ever going to change." Her sister shook her head in mock horror. "Although I must add, there may be truth in what you say."

"I hate to make a nuisance of myself, but Jennifer and Veronica won't take very well to the cold tongue. Perhaps if you have just a bowl of cereal they could fill the empty space in the tummy and then get to bed. It is getting late for them, and they have had a rather hard day."

"Of course, I should have thought of it myself." But Veronica was already whimpering her need for a comfortable bed and was uninterested in food of any kind.

"I really don't know where she will sleep—"

"I was thinking of the crib. Since I may be here for some time, I thought perhaps you might move the crib out of the nursery and into a guest room where she will be near me. That is, if you don't mind."

"The crib isn't there anymore."

"Oh!" Sylvia was momentarily taken aback. "Then I guess she will just have to sleep with me. Although you do have plenty of empty rooms, all those you built for the family that didn't materialize."

Bonnie winced. That was just like the old Sylvia to bring her three beautiful children and flaunt them in Bonnie's face. Would she ever learn not to be cruel?

"Well, come along, and I'll find some linens and make up something for you to put the girls into."

Buz was already occupying himself with moving Sylvia's luggage into the guest rooms and completed the job as Bonnie carefully smoothed the last spread over a bed. Sylvia deftly buttoned the girls into their pajamas and braced herself for wails of opposition to the unfamiliar quarters. However, the little ones were sufficiently exhausted to offer no resistance and seemed grateful for the soft covers' comforting warmth. The adults slipped back to the kitchen to resume making sandwiches.

"Well, Sylvia." Buz was setting cups and spoons on the table. "I wouldn't have thought the business of household utensils so pressing at this time of year that the hubby couldn't have gotten away to come along."

"The business is pressing at any time of year." Sylvia emitted a low snort. "Would you believe we had a stopover of four hours in New York! And me with these three kids to entertain. I've never been so wild in all my life. We drank all the coffee and milk in the snack shop, read all the magazines in the newsstand, scrutinized the objets d'art in all the international gift shops, purchased one fuzzy mouse, a pair of ivory elephants from India, a miniature boomerang from Australia, and a package of safety pins, because the sight of a turbaned Arab in the men's room frightened Harry so badly he got his zipper stuck and broke it trying to undo it. Whee-ew! I'd hate to have to make that trip alone again with this crew."

"I can't imagine why you ever tried it. Surely you could have scheduled a visit at a time when Hal would be able to come with you."

"And then we were fully five miles from the gate for the next flight. I know now why flying takes so little time compared with the older modes of transportation: You walk so much of the distance there is little left for flying. And with Veronica screaming in my arms and Harry continually losing Jennifer's hand in the crowd! We nearly lost her three times. Once a bearded thing in a long robe with beads said, 'Hey, lady, this your kid?' I mumbled something like, yeah, seems to me I started out with her, thanks, and he tried to let go her hand after bringing her back to us. But she hung on and would have gone off with him if Harry hadn't been there to take her in tow.

"As if that wasn't enough, Veronica threw up all over the place in the plane and Jennifer dumped her meal tray onto the floor. I'll bet that hostess was never so glad to get off duty as she was when she hit ground in Pittsburgh this evening. Then after the mess was all cleaned up and things sort of settled down to normal, Veronica was so restless I gave her the only handy thing I could find available to entertain her. You know that furry mouse? Well, a fat lady was in the seat across the aisle, and she took one look at the mouse, screamed, and fainted."

Sylvia stopped her recitation long enough to throw her hands into the air and dramatize the scene, make a second sandwich, and sugar a cup of coffee. The Rockwells did not reply, for they were burdened by an uncanny foreboding of an ill wind blowing. Silence reigned for several moments until it was broken by Sylvia resuming her performance.

"Of course, no one else on the plane had seen the mouse and couldn't imagine why the woman fainted. So panic broke out, and people started asking, has there been an accident? Are we going to crash? Did something go wrong? One young thing started crying and said, 'I knew when I said goodbye to Roberto that I would never see him again.' Well, the stewardesses quickly got the old dame revived and assured everyone that all was well. Needless to say, I hid the mouse in my purse. And I doubt any of the crew was more thankful to hit Pittsburgh than I was."

"Have you phoned Hal yet to tell him that you really did make it all right? You're welcome to use the phone here."

"No thank you. Let him guess. It's his turn to do some guessing, anyway."

Harry had laid his head on the table and gone to sleep.

"I must get the bed made up in the room next to the girls." Bonnie got up. "If you will excuse me, poor Harry looks as if he's had a bad day."

"Yes, he has, poor thing. I'm glad I won't have to drag them through this again. Glad for them and myself both. Not to mention the stewardesses."

Both women rose to attend to the project at hand, Sylvia to arouse Harry and propel him toward the bedroom, and Bonnie to look for linens.

Several minutes later, with the task accomplished, they returned to the kitchen, where Buz had removed the remnants of the repast. Only the coffee remained.

"Ordinarily I wouldn't drink this much of the stuff this late at night." Sylvia refilled her cup. "But this time a shot of adrenalin couldn't keep me awake. I feel as though I've been dismembered and glued back together again. I tell you, that's the last trip I'll ever make like that!"

"Well, how are you going to get back?"

"Get back?" Sylvia's inflection indicated the question was incredible. She paused with her cup poised in midair, her eyebrows raised enigmatically. Then taking an unhurried sip, she set the cup down deliberately and dabbed at the corners of her pursed, sensuous lips with the napkin. With a slight shrug of the shoulders, she dismissed the thought with a nonchalant flourish. Her voice was light, flippant.

"I'm not going back."

"Not going back!" the Rockwells echoed together.

"No, I'm tired of marriage. It's a dead-end street." The dark, exotic eyes flashed with a thousand brilliant facets as the speaker paused, enjoying the arresting consternation her exaggerated air produced in her audience.

"I'm tired of his preoccupation with his work; I'm tired of Vermont—sick and tired of it; I'm tired of the dull old routine that makes every day the same. I'm going to lick my finger, turn a new page, and start on a different story. I thought you might need a secretary in your office. Or if you don't, there's probably someone somewhere who does. I'm going to do my own thing."

She rose and dropped the slightest hint of a sarcastic curtsey toward her astounded listeners.

"Meet the new Miz Sylvia Gregersen."

23

The pleasure Bonnie had known in planning her second honeymoon paled in the ensuing months as her grief for her sister and her family grew. Her initial shock over Sylvia's action first resolved into pity for Hal. Although no power on earth could ever make her regret she had married Buz instead of Hal, she still could not escape the nagging torment that Hal would never have met Sylvia if it had not been for her. And even though she tried to console herself with the reminder that Hal had been in full possession of his own will when he chose to marry Sylvia, she yet could not avoid the fact that she had, in a remote sense, set the stage when she introduced them and then refused Hal herself.

In her clearer moments, Bonnie reasoned that she had had absolutely nothing to do with Sylvia's infatuation for the new swim coach at the high school and then his final rejection of Sylvia that drove the bereft girl to take drastic action. But the fact remained that Sylvia had Hal to fall back on because of Bonnie. And dear, loveable, steady, dependable Hal, whose only crime had been being too predictable for an excitement-craving, impetuous wife, had certainly done nothing to deserve the treatment he had received at the hands of the Lake girls other than offer his heart and hand to each of them in turn. Bonnie wept many a silent tear on behalf of her brother-in-law.

The next problem had been to help Sylvia establish herself again in Pittsburgh. The Rockwells resisted attempting to talk Sylvia into returning to her husband because they knew any such attempt would only result in Sylvia's increased determination not to do so. Therefore, the best solution seemed to be to help her get as well situated as possible and then hope she would one day realize the best she could do was not as satisfactory as returning to her home and husband.

The first project, accordingly, was to help her find employment. Having never worked in any capacity other than that of lifeguard, she was disadvantaged at the outset. The only position available was that of waitress in a downtown hotel. Within two weeks it was evident she didn't have the temperament to attend to the wishes of others. Bonnie agreed to watch the children until she could find a place of her own. But when Sylvia returned from the hotel and refused to attend to their needs because she had "been running after people all day," her sister and brother-in-law recognized that a change was necessary. And even though a competent secretary had long been employed in the architecture firm, Buz made room for her in his office and instructed the older employee to find work she could do. On more than one occasion he observed a pained expression on Phyllis's face as she apparently found Sylvia to be more a hindrance than a help.

Bonnie's greatest grief was realized in the children. Harry, growing increasingly handsome with each passing year, was a sensitive, quiet child who missed his father intensely. Having never been given to much vocal expression, he retreated farther and farther into his own counsel as the weeks passed, and his wish to see his father was not granted. Bonnie was certain she heard sobs from the room he occupied as she passed by the door late on many a night. But never a word fell from his lips. He developed the habit of sitting before the television set for hours at a time, seemingly looking through the screen and not comprehending the action. He made no effort to find any friends, though his aunt suggested he could most surely find other boys his age if he would go down the street a few doors.

As for Jennifer, the loss of her father prompted temper tantrums. Always moody and pensive, she now exhibited her displeasure over the separation in uncooperative behavior and sulking. When in time her sense of loss diminished and she appeared nearly to have forgotten her father, the misbehavior continued, much to her mother's despair. Unfortunately, it never occurred to Sylvia that to reunite the family would remedy the difficulties.

When it seemed to Bonnie that the burden upon the children must be more than their fragile constitutions could bear, she found their problems only multiplied. For Sylvia first enrolled them in the school nearest Windy Knoll in Allison Park. As slowly as they were making an adjustment, they had each only begun to feel acclimated to the new situation when Sylvia succeeded in finding an apartment near her parents' home in Oakland and uprooted them once more, this time so late in the term that neither made full recovery. They struggled helplessly and despairingly on toward the end, but with grades plunging to failure. As it was only Jennifer's second year, the teacher recommended that the grade be repeated, and the frustrated child was to find herself humiliatingly back in the same grade again for the following term, and already tall for her age, head and shoulders above her classmates.

The bubbly Veronica was the child least to suffer from her parents' separation, because she was too young to miss her father for long. Indeed it seemed all too soon he was completely forgotten by his tow-headed girlish replica of himself. Always she had been a happy baby, seeming not to be affected by the friction that crackled around her. And now she found herself the happy recipient of voluminous attention showered upon her by her paternal grandparents. For despite the fact Sylvia had first vowed not to permit her parents-in-law to visit their grandchildren, she soon learned they could be very convenient in freeing her from her maternal duties. And the time the children spent in the elder Gregersen home increased considerably. Having shown promise of favoring her mother at birth, Veronica soon lost her fringe of dark hair, her button nose straightened, and she gradually acquired her father's features. The close resemblance to the elder Gregersens' son, in addition to her happy, outgoing personality, endeared her to her grandparents so that she did not lack for the attention she did not receive from her own parents.

Grandfather Gregersen fortunately recognized the source of Harry's introversion and, in spite of the child's resemblance to his mother, whom the older couple found it difficult to forgive, resolved to treat him kindly for his own sake. The elderly gentleman found many an occasion to entertain the young one, taking him fishing and teaching him to play chess. And never did he complain about the exorbitant telephone bill when he permitted Harry to call his father every couple of weeks. Harry began to look forward to the regular conversations and his disposition improved considerably.

But try as they would, the Gregersens were not able to heal the open wound that festered in Jennifer's little soul. It was many weeks before she could be left in their home without a crying session when her mother departed. Very gradually her grandparents won her trust, but no amount of love and attention would erase the disruptive behavior. Sylvia learned she had a problem much larger than she had expected.

Bonnie and Buz had lent every assistance possible to the little family, ignoring their own needs and pleasures selflessly and affectionately. And when Sylvia finally established herself in her own apartment with the attention of both her parents and Hal's, it began to look as though they could carry through their plans for the trip to Hawaii. The old excitement returned, and Bonnie was making some shopping trips in preparation. On one such occasion she stopped in the office of Cameron, DeSantis, and Rockwell with her arms burdened under myriads of parcels and she laughingly displayed the flourescent green bathing trunks she had purchased for her husband, and he gravely handed her a sheaf of mail.

"Bonnie, my love, I've wanted to mention this to you, and perhaps now that you are here and can witness for yourself the volume of offers for commissions I have received, it is the best time to do so. You see, these are all very attractive offers, ones I hate very much to turn down. A court house in Arizona, a shopping plaza in upstate New York, a college dormitory in Florida. They require immediate attention. If I accept them, it means the trip to Hawaii will have to be postponed. I thought maybe—"

"Of course, you will accept them. Just because it is to be an anniversary trip, it doesn't have to occur right over the exact date. How about postponing it until Christmas? I think it would be lovely to be in Hawaii at a time when it is winter here anyway. Why go to a sunny place while we are having summer and then stay home in the winter?"

"But I know how you've looked forward to this so much, and it seemed for awhile we wouldn't be able to get away because of Sylvia. And now that we are free, I haven't the heart to expect you to give it up again."

"But I wouldn't be giving it up. I will just have a little longer to look forward to it. I insist that you accept those contracts, and I don't want to hear any more about it, Mr. Rockwell. But you needn't think you'll get out of wearing these swimming trunks just because it's postponed. They will still be waiting for you come Christmas. In fact, I might just go and find myself a red one to match. Look out, Hawaii! Here come the Rockwells."

"Hawaii will never be the same again, I'm sure. But you certainly are a great sport. What would I do without an understanding wife like you?" He folded her in his arms and expressed his appreciation with an extended kiss.

It was one of those days when October's bright, blue weather was never more glorious. A few pure white wisps of cloud floated lazily about, while gentle, warm breezes caressed the earth. The leaves were firing wooded areas with golds, scarlets, and rust while milkweed pods burst forth with miniature silken parachutes. Chrysanthemums crowned flower beds with brilliant glory, and here and there one brave rose held forth, defying frost and the threat of coming winter. Katydids chirruped about Windy Knoll's terraces. All nature seemed glad to be alive.

Bonnie, hustling ecstatically about her kitchen, had never been more grateful for the gift of life, had never felt more vibrant, more optimistic, more so at peace with herself and the world—more grateful for the abundance of blessings that were hers. This was a very special day, one that called for the finest in culinary skills and the most glittering brilliance of silver candelabra to grace a festive occasion. This was the moment she had anticipated for several years, had wept for, prayed, and agonized over. The miracle had taken place, and she could now greet her beloved husband with assurance that their joy was to be complete.

It had been a rather uneventful summer, she mused, as she peeled potatoes and sauteed mushrooms. There had been an occasional business trip with Buz as he surveyed the sites upon which his designs were being raised. However, most of the trips had exhibited nothing worthy of note, with the exception of the private residence in Watertown, New York. It was constructed of the native white stone with which she noticed many of the city's buildings had been erected, giving the area an aura of grand opulence reminiscent of a bygone era. The trips became wearying, and she was happy enough to return to the comfort of her own peaceful retreat.

Toward the end of the summer, she and Buz had taken Mimi, Sylvia, Harry, and Jennifer to Disneyworld in Florida. But the holiday atmosphere of the little party had failed to penetrate her spirits. She found that riding the little conveyance through the attractions made her feel nauseous. Even the smooth-sailing vessels that crept along waterways with scarcely a ripple didn't fail to make her feel like leaning over the side of the boat for relief. *Getting old before my time,* she had scolded herself disgustedly. *Can't even take a little bit of amusement.* Just reading the warning sign at Space Mountain about not riding that super roller coaster if you were crippled, had heart trouble, or were pregnant had made her dizzy. But she never suspected she fit any of the categories.

It wasn't until she had been home for several weeks and still found herself feeling as though she were racing at high speed several hundred feet up in the air that she began to get suspicious. At first she dismissed the thought as incredible, impossible now after all this time. But when her symptoms worsened instead of abating, she waited anxiously for one more sign before making an appointment with the doctor she had not had to call for too long. She had not dared to breathe her suspicions to Buz, for fear of disappointing that patient darling once again. But this had been the day when her doctor happily assured her she need question no longer. She planned the most extravagant feast she was capable of preparing to delight her husband before breaking the wonderful news, for not only was all nature alive on this day. A new little creation was taking form within her with a life of its own, one that might happily be a handsome, stalwart son to grace his father's old age, one who would stand in the stead of the cherished one who had departed this life so abruptly, one who would live on and grow to manhood and be a delight and source of pride to both his parents.

She wondered whether she could now make that long-awaited trip to Hawaii after all. Maybe it would have to be postponed indefinitely. But what was a mild disappointment like that compared with the delirious excitement that awaited them later on? At the very least she would have to forego that red bathing suit!

An exhilarating memory rushed in on her happiness, causing her to nearly cut her finger in dropping the knife she was using, so startling was its suddenness. The nursery, of course! After the years of pain that closed door had represented to her, she could now fling it wide open, pull back the drapes to admit the glorious sunlight, and hear the walls echo with the crying of a babe again. Yes, she would delight in even the cries. Timothy had ceased to cry. But she would not think of that again. She would get a can of paint. This time it really would be blue, for she cherished a deep, instinctive feeling that blue would be the appropriate color. And how exciting it would be to refurnish it. She was glad she had disposed of the former furnishings, for choosing all new would be so much fun, even more so than the first time. They made such cute little nursery rhyme plaques and hanging mobiles now with which to adorn a nursery.

The school bus stopped and Miriam alighted as Bonnie prepared to place the Bavarian china upon the lace table cover. Bonnie hesitated as the child entered the door. Should she divulge the secret to her daughter and enlist her cooperation in preparing a special feast for her father? Upon reflection she determined Buz should be the first to know and therefore shooed Mimi out of the way before she would begin to ask questions.

In the buffet drawer she found both gold and pale pink candles. Which should she choose to cast their mellow glow over the Rock Island lobster tails? But, of course, it shouldn't be pink. And she didn't have any blue. The gold was most appropriate anyway, as either a boy or girl would be a golden child to them. She paused to rearrange the bronze mums she had placed in a silver compote. Yes, the gold candles would definitely enhance the varied hues of the floral centerpiece. The crystal goblets looked slightly cloudy. There was still time to restore their gleam with some hot, soapy water, she calculated with a quick glance at the clock. She needn't expect Buz for another hour at least.

Carrying the goblets quickly to the sink, she was startled to hear a car in the drive. Few people ever sought out their hidden nook unless they intended a real visit. Her mother, or Sylvia? Was she to have unexpected company on this most special of occasions? Perhaps the caller would not stay long. Placing the goblets on the counter, she started for the huge, oaken doors. Ere she reached them Buz had stepped inside, his face drawn and gray as an overcast sky before a great storm. Wordlessly he stood for a moment before her, a picture of excruciating agony and despair. Hanging his head, he made no move to enfold her in his arms as was his usual custom upon his return.

Alarmed, she cried, "Buz, darling, are you ill? Has something happened? What is it?" Her voice rose shrilly with each unanswered question. Fear gripped her heart as he only shook his head and struggled to stifle great, convulsive, silent sobs.

After what seemed an eternity, she led him to the sofa where he sank with the weight of a crushed life, and cradled his head in his hands.

He appeared to struggle with several attempts at speech while she reached for him compulsively, encircling him in her arm encouragingly.

At last his voice broke forth, low and distinct, with a finality like that of the tomb: "I'm bankrupt. We must lose everything I have worked for."

"B-but—what—"

With the dread admission his tongue was loosed, and he poured forth his agony in a hollow voice she had never heard before.

"You see, we have this—it's what you call a reserve account—from which we draw our operating expenses. Pay our salaries, build our own office and the big one in North Hills, finance business trips—Unfortunately, it is also the funds from which DeSantis and Cameron drew to make all those European tours." His voice stopped and he mused bitterly a moment before continuing as though to himself. "I always wondered about those extravagant trips." Clenching his fist, he smacked it into the other palm while pursing his lower lip. "I knew I should have kept a closer watch on it. That's what I hired Drew for. He got us all into this. Should have warned us it was coming. Why does he think he was one of the best-paid accountants in the city?" Buz's tone raised, and his voice started shaking as he got up off the sofa and paced twice around the room before shaking his head resignedly and reseating himself beside his wife. She watched him, stricken and helpless as he vented his anger in movement.

"I still don't understand the reserve account, darling." Bonnie spoke calmly, trying to force a steadiness into her words she didn't feel.

"It's overdrawn. We have simply taken too much out.

A little too extravagant on our own office and the North Hills project, well, that's a different matter. Worse, in fact." The muscles working his jaw tightened while his eyes squinted to narrow slits. "Whenever the boys put in for expense money, Drew just signed over the check, apparently without considering whether it could be covered. So the bank called in the loan. They can foreclose on everything. We got the news this morning about ten o'clock and spent the rest of the day haggling over what to do about it.

"As if our problems aren't bad enough, those contractors the guys hired for the North Hills place must not know a hammer from a screw driver. The foundation is cracking, letting in water. We'll never find a buyer now. The most we can hope for is to rent the space long enough to get our investment back. Do you know how many years that will take?

"DeSantis and Cameron want to declare bankruptcy and slide out of it all easily. I prefer to do the honorable thing and pay off the loan. After all, I expect to maintain my reputation as a respectable architect. So we spent the rest of the day disagreeing about what move to make. I figured that if each of us pays our share, it shouldn't work too great havoc with anyone. But they won't go along with that. And so if I liquidate, I'm stuck for the whole bill. Like a quarter of a million. Of course, Sylvia will have to go. She really was excess baggage in the first place. That's another thing—" The anger mounted in his voice again. "Why didn't Anderson tell me when we took her on that hers was one salary the load wouldn't bear? There's also your weekly cleaning woman who will have to go. And as for the trip to Hawaii, well, that's over for good, for the present anyway."

"But I—" Bonnie's attempt to protest that she was more than willing to forego that luxury was lost in Buz's next torrent of lament.

"There's no way out. I have figured every possible way and if I'm to pay off that loan I'll have to sell Windy Knoll. I figure I can get about a hundred fifty thousand for it. Although that won't all be clear. We still owe on it; but I can make a nice profit over what I put into it. I just don't know how I can do this to you, but I really haven't any choice." He cupped his head in his palms again, and a despair settled over him so deeply Bonnie herself felt stifled and entombed.

It was then that she remembered the wonderful news she had waited so anxiously to impart to him. Fleetingly she wondered where her child would be born and whether there would be a dainty blue nursery to receive him. For that matter, any roof over his head at all seemed like a remote possibility. This certainly was not the time now to greet Buz with the news that additional expense was to be added to the family. In his distraught state he would probably feel even worse with that knowledge rather than elated as she had hoped. The news would just have to wait.

She felt herself begin to sway and feel slightly nauseous. But a commanding fear gripped her and helped to restore her equilibrium. Surely she wasn't going to suffer shock and miscarry? Not now, after all these years of hoping! No! It was as though a ramrod went directly up her spine. She had failed her cherished husband once. She would not fail him again. She had once looked to him to give her support when she should have been lending him her own. And she would not play the part of the immature child again to the point where she permitted herself to give in to lamenting and self-pity and lose his anticipated child. Beside that the finest house in the world paled. She would be strong and support Buz no matter what was required, even if she lived in a hovel.

Taking his hand again in hers, she replied softly, "Buz,

darling, no matter where we live, it will still be home so long as we are together. And nothing in all the earth can take from us what we have together. Actually Windy Knoll doesn't mean that much to me. You are my whole life, and wherever you are, I'll be happy."

"Aw, it's no use, Bonnie." He rose from the sofa and started for the door. "No words can repair the damage this day has brought." He walked as though iron chains rattled from his ankles as he dragged himself out of the room.

Bonnie stared mutely behind him and remained motionless until she heard the bedroom door slam moments later. Intuitively she understood he had entered a private sanctuary she neither should nor could penetrate.

Numbly she made her way back to the kitchen. Fortunately she hadn't started the lobster tails. But she would have to find something for Miriam to eat. And the child would have to be told that Daddy was not to be bothered tonight. Soon Mimi would have to learn that she was to leave her beloved home, the only one she had ever known.

Bonnie never knew how she got through that evening. She sat for a long time looking out the kitchen windows that opened onto the interior courtyard. She was able to catch the last rays of the sunset that filtered over the tops of the hills cradling the city below. When at last the golden streaks faded into gray and a dismal gloom descended over her sprawling mansion's roof and she could no longer make out the forms of the statuary and the courtyard fountain, she decided to look for a way to spend the night, though the hour was early. Thankfully the evening had been one of television specials that had absorbed the young girl's interest, and little explanation for the interior gloom in the household had been necessary. Bonnie called Mimi from the screen and tucked her into bed. Then she looked about for a means of making herself comfortable. Pausing outside the bedroom door, her hand halted over the knob. A deep intuition told her the knob was not to be turned. Searching in a linen closet, she withdrew a warm blanket and settled herself on the floral sofa in the little balcony she had loved so much. How many more times she could bask in the comfort this spot afforded her, she could not tell; but they would be few. She would make the most of it for now. Stretching out, she felt herself sink into the luxurious softness of the sofa. But it still seemed hard. She turned. After a few minutes she sat up for a while. Ages passed before she attempted to lie down again. But relaxation did not come. She tossed restlessly for half the night. And when fitful sleep finally overtook her in the wee small hours just before the dawn, she dreamed the dream again.

It was noon the next day before she fearfully ventured to knock on the closed door. There had been no word, no stirring from within. She began to be alarmed.

"Just leave me alone."

"Could I get you some coffee? Anything?"

"Nothing. I'm all right."

She would have to believe that. And turning, she resolved not to knock again until Buz opened the door of his own accord.

Once more she prepared a solitary supper for Mimi, explaining Daddy wasn't feeling very well, but that he would be all right. Then since the next day was Saturday, she suggested that perhaps Grandma Lake could come by and take her home with her for the weekend. When that proposition was greeted enthusiastically, she phoned her mother, who responded readily to the suggestion. As Avonelle had been given the dread news by phone during the day, she delayed not at all in loading Mimi and her overnight case into her car and whisking her away from the house of gloom. And Bonnie prepared to settle herself for another long night of dreariness.

Retreating to the seclusion of her beloved eyrie high under the second story beamed ceiling, she settled herself once more on the floral sofa.

Crises, crises, she mused. *My life seems to be nothing but a series of crises.* Then she immediately felt ashamed of her complaining when she remembered all the wonderful years she had spent at her husband's side. Her eyes fell on the Bible on the little table by the sofa. This was not the white one. That cherished keepsake several years ago had begun to show signs of wear, and she had secreted it away for safekeeping. Even if Mimi did not choose to carry it at her wedding, it was too sacred to Bonnie to wear the life out of it. So she had purchased several others and placed them in convenient locations about the house. This particular copy was the one she used in her daily devotions, as this dear balcony was her "closet." Now it occurred to her to wonder why she hadn't given consideration to what God would have to say about the crisis in which the Rockwells found themselves.

With the last rays of the early evening sun still creeping through the skylights overhead, she leafed at random through the pages. The word "trust" leaped at her, and she paused for the entire phrase: "Though He slay me, yet will I trust Him." Job, of course, that Old Testament pillar of unquestioning devotion. He had lost ten children, and she only one. He, all the wealth he had owned, and she would at least still have a roof overhead. Somewhere. His spouse was about as encouraging as the captain of the Titanic when he had relieved all hands of command and decreed "every man for himself." Her spouse was a solid rock of strength and support. But, then, she wondered, whom was she trying to convince? She had already settled once and for all that come what may, she would trust unswervingly in the goodness of a righteous Father. Nothing could ever be more devastating than the death of her beloved child, and she had survived—not unscathed, but ultimately victorious. Surely the loss of material possessions couldn't qualify in the same realm as real tragedy. She was reminded of the words of the gospel song, "Each victory will help you some other to win." With the strength she had gained in her first great trial, this one was much easier to tackle. With that resolved, she would now go on to determine just where they stood in relation to God's intent in that matter.

Was it possible He was not pleased with the lavish display of wealth about them when much of the world lived in squalor and starvation? But that was an old, moot question kicked around for years. Jesus Himself had said we would always have the poor with us, and she couldn't share her riches with starving Africans or Asians if she wished to. She couldn't believe that they were being punished for having undue pride or being thankless. She never let a day go by without returning thanks for her life's abundance. Perhaps He wanted to teach them some lessons. If that were the case, He would just have to show them what those lessons were to be. At this point, she had not the faintest idea. After some time of meditating and soul-searching, she felt no farther ahead with her quest than she had when she began. Clearly she must not be on the right track.

Starting at the end of the Bible, she began leafing backward. She didn't favor random searching for guidance, but at this point, there seemed to be nothing else to do. Her eye caught a red pencil underline that she had placed on some forgotten occasion. "In every thing give thanks," she had underscored. That wasn't an impossible command, she reasoned. At least, it didn't say *for* every thing give thanks. She couldn't at the moment be thankful for her husband's financial straits; but she certainly could be thankful that God had His hand on the situation, and by faith she could believe He would control it and never permit it to become more than they could bear.

"All things work together for good" marched across her memory slate, as a herd of deer leaping gracefully but forcefully across a highway at dusk. That was the answer! Why had it taken so long to come into view? God had probably not specifically ordained Drew Anderson to bungle his job as financial consultant to the architecture firm. Human error was involved. And her own dear husband had blindly permitted the bungling to proceed without being detected, as had the other two partners. After all, were they not all in it together? But now that the worst had befallen them, God certainly would not forsake them; rather He had promised He would make all things work together for good. What things besides the financial predicament she could not at the moment guess. But if she could see what they were, she would once again be walking by sight and not by faith. And the faith walk was God's way. She would simply believe extenuating factors would be brought into play in such a manner that good would come of the whole catastrophe.

That determined, the next matter at hand was to pray for Buz. She had no idea what all had transpired in his mind during the twenty-four hours he had been closeted away. Was he submerged in bitterness, in self-recrimination, despair? Or was he too reaching out for a pinion, something on which to buoy up his faith in a sovereign God, formulating a code of determination that no matter what, he would trust Him? Remembering her resolve to support him, she prayed, "Sustain him, Father. Give him the faith to believe that you will see him through."

How much longer she sat in silent, fervent prayer,

seeking for strength to flow from the heavenly throne to revitalize the sagging spirits of her loved one, she did not know. But at length she was aware of a familiar, though muffled, sound. Was it Buz's razor? In a few moments, the evidence strode out of the door, clean-shaven and freshly dressed.

"I was thinking—" He towered above her, choosing not to sit down, "have to get a hold on myself. Quit blaming Anderson for his stupidity. Forgive him if that is what's called for. Although I don't think I can quit kicking myself for being so blind to what he was doing. And I have to reason out the next step. I thought that if we could go to that little park over there on the North Side where we—"

"Divulged your glorious dream," she finished for him.

"Yes, that's right. When I had the world by the tail and figured I could dish it up to you on a silver platter. I thought maybe something of the promise and anticipation that I knew then might somehow filter back—if you know what I mean."

"Of course, I do. I think it's a wonderful idea," his wife exclaimed, jumping up excitedly. *He doesn't know the half of it,* she told herself, *but this will give me the opportunity to tell him.*

They wended their way in silence down route 28, into the city and over several blocks to the little park behind the planetarium. Parking by the curb, they walked hand in hand down the path until they located the bench nearest the spot where they had sat long ago. The evening was balmy, surprisingly warm for the lateness of the season. The sun was low in the western sky. In just a short time it would be casting its long, golden farewell to the day. A couple planes circled slowly overhead, scarcely seeming to move, awaiting their clearance to land.

"Darling, do you remember that time eleven years

ago, the night you fashioned the chewing gum cathedral? It was very much like this evening. And it must have been very nearly the same date, although I don't remember exactly. Just think how many fabulous creations you have made since then, in something far more durable than gum. You have a record that is the envy of many in your profession."

"Yes, and that's one of the reasons I don't want to declare bankruptcy. If I were to do so, I would not be able to create for a year, for you must give up your profession for that long in such a case. Cameron and DeSantis either are crazy or don't care. I must keep producing. And in time I will once again stand upon my own feet."

"But you are standing on your own feet, dear, and I am proud of you."

His strong arm had stolen around her and pulled her close.

"A couple verses from Isaiah keep coming to me. 'For my thoughts are not your thoughts, neither are your ways my ways, saith the Lord. For as the heavens are higher than the earth, so are my ways higher than your ways, and my thoughts than your thoughts.' This situation calls for active, positive faith, not just some blind, negative submission to a vague Sovereign will."

"Now that sounds like the Nathaniel Rockwell who introduced himself to me eleven years ago in this same spot. We will trust our God together to work out His plan for us, even in this." She kissed him, and they sat in silence a few more minutes before he spoke again with the stress gone from his voice.

"Cohen Associates assured me when I left there that I would be welcomed back at any time I chose. So I shall reassociate myself with them until I can see my way clear to go on my own again. In fact, it would be no crime if I just remained with them indefinitely, and I have a very attractive way to supplement the income. I hadn't mentioned it, but my old alma mater, Carnegie-Mellon, as it is now known, has been after me to do some teaching for them on a part-time basis. I believe I'll just take them up on it. Being back among the young folks with their energy and enthusiasm would be stimulating.

"And I've been thinking, I was out in Bridgeville a couple weeks ago looking over the site for a new city building. That's that little burg about five miles south of the city, in case you can't place it. I happened to notice a lovely little house up for sale — small, but neat, and reasonably well kept. Had a nice backyard with lilac bushes spilling over the fence. If I can get Windy Knoll sold before the bank forecloses on it, which I doubt I will have any trouble doing, I should be able to satisfy them for the moment and still have enough left over to buy that little place. At least we can be comfortable."

"It sounds wonderful to me. And our son will have a yard to play in."

"Our what?"

"I said our son, darling. I have a feeling that's what it will be. I meant to tell you as soon as I found out for sure. But since I didn't, I'm telling you now. You are about to become a father again, Buz Rockwell."

The father-to-be sat stunned and speechless for several moments.

"You're sure it's not a — a mistake? Not a false alarm?"

"Dr. Kaufmann had no doubt."

He patted her tummy gleefully.

"Is he kicking yet?"

"It's not time yet for that; but I believe he's making his presence known already. He must be going to be a lively little rascal."

A small flock of swallows arched over their heads and toward the hills to which clung Schenley Park. No doubt they would be joined by other small flocks, roosting there for the night before resuming their southerly flight.

"Buz—" Bonnie nodded in their direction. "By the time they return our baby will be here."

The couple lapsed into a prolonged silence as the last rays of the sun faded into oblivion. And still they sat until the air grew chilly, and millers and moths fluttered about the street lights.

The whole city became ablaze with lights. The Rockwells looked across the Monongahela to the necklace of gleaming jewels strung along Grandview Avenue cresting the ridge of Mount Washington. The illuminated cable car of the Duquesne Incline was making its steep ascent up the slope of the mount. Over in the Triangle across the Allegheny the dome of the Koppers Building glowed a ghostly blue, the Gulf Building flashed the weather prediction in orange from its limestone pyramid skyline, and the Grant Building signaled P-i-t-t-s-b-u-r-g-h in blinking Morse code.

"Come," Buz broke the stillness at last. "It's getting late and we must be thinking about tomorrow. I'm going to have a lot of work to do to get ready for a move."

"Yes, dear, tomorrow will be coming. There will be a new baby, a new home, and even a new dream. This isn't the end. It is the beginning."

Nathaniel Rockwell took his wife into his arms as they rose from the bench. After a poignant embrace and prolonged, communing kiss, they turned to walk in the direction in which the sun had set. At the door of their auto, they paused to look back toward the east. In just a few hours the sun would be rising.

411

Part 3

24

In retrospect, Bonnie and Buz recognized that the years spent in Bridgeville were the best of their lives. They verified from their own blessed experience the scriptural axiom that a person's life does not consist in the abundance of things he possesses. For after all, one can only live in a dwelling, be it mansion or hovel. The quality of that living is generated from within oneself, rather than from external circumstances.

They had moved their elegant furnishings from Windy Knoll without so much as one backward glance. And, recovering their spirits on the drive to their new home, they had entered its welcoming shelter with an optimism born of faith in the security of their love and companionship rather than in spacious walls. They arranged and rearranged in order to fit so much into so small a space. And being almost as handy with hammer and saw as he was with T-square and drawing board, Buz knocked out the wall between the tiny, old-fashioned kitchen and the small dining room, modernized the former with labor-saving built-ins, and connected the same to the dining area with a breakfast nook. Bonnie was nearly ecstatic over the transformation.

Once again she welcomed the opportunity to utilize vivid colors to enrich her surroundings. She discovered to her delight that there was a much wider selection of hues than there had been when she had first turned a drab little honeymoon apartment into glowing warmth. She carried home many sample cards and spent days choosing exactly coordinating shades to complement her furnishings. She lightened the old woodwork, but splashed daringly on the walls. Then she hung her cherished original oil paintings in their gilt frames, tastefully displayed her few exquisite pieces of Meissen porcelain and chose the center of the mantel for her favorite framed photograph.

Lifting it carefully from its excelsior packing, she paused to dwell lovingly on each detail: large brown eyes peering beguilingly from under silken lashes on the innocent baby face framed with the pale locks pulled back and tied above the ears with pink bows. If Mimi had been endowed with no more beauty than Bonnie herself possessed, she certainly more than compensated for it in charm. It was the frilly, sequin-spangled little pink costume that arrested Bonnie's attention, however. It might have been the physical weariness resulting from the strenuous redecorating, in addition to her pregnancy, that played havoc with her imagination. Or was it really a faint awakening of a long-buried memory that placed herself within that gold frame? The excitement of donning the costume, going to the studio, and posing before the camera stirred within her breast. Was she momentarily reliving a long-ago experience or the more recent one when Miriam was three and one-half years old?

Her most exciting project was the fashioning of a nursery from a little nook at the head of the stairs, probably once a sewing room. A trip to a second-hand shop produced a crib in excellent condition except for the happy need of refinishing. Never more lovingly were brush and blue lacquer applied to maple railings, nor fat, brown teddy bear decals mounted on a head panel. Bonnie hesitated about sanding off the teeth marks across the top of the side rail where some former occupant had experimented with his first little pearls. She finally decided against the desecration. Those tiny indentations symbolized a silent commitment to faith she made with herself, that her baby should live until he too would cut his teeth. And she longingly anticipated the time some new scars would be chewed alongside the old.

When the labors of many long weeks were completed, Bonnie and Buz surveyed their handiwork with satisfaction. What they lacked in space, they more than made up in taste and comfort.

"I do believe that if we were really pinched, you could set yourself up in the decorating business, my dear," Buz complimented his wife.

"Well, that's an idea. You build 'em, I'll decorate 'em. That ought to make a super team."

"I fear I may have some more building to do right at home before too long. That old front porch will have to be replaced in time. I have an idea for an enclosed porch on the back, and unfortunately I don't trust the roof too far. We'll be lucky if raindrops don't start falling on our heads." Buz sought to embrace his wife, but she was becoming increasingly difficult to reach around. He placed his hands on her shoulders and leaned exaggeratedly to plant a kiss on her lips as they both giggled like children trying to keep a secret before Christmas.

The couple were delighted with the friendliness they discovered among their new neighbors. Edith and Ted Corbin, who lived immediately on one side of them, had hastened to welcome them to the neighborhood before the moving van had pulled away. They in turn introduced the Rockwells to most of the other couples on the block. Occasionally one or another stopped by to take stock of the transformation taking place under Buz's skillful hands and Bonnie's ever active paint brush.

"Most spruced up that place has ever been," they

commented. And when all was completed, most of the neighborhood descended unexpectedly upon them for a grand housewarming party. Bonnie had paled in mortification when the doorbell rang to announce the commencement of the festivities, for she was inelegantly attired in faded stretch pants and one of Buz's cast off sloppy T-shirts. But she hastily excused herself to don her most presentable maternity frock. A touch of lipstick worked wonders, but no trick in all the world could compensate for her hair.

"Never mind," Buz whispered, with a light kiss on the back of her neck, "their eyes won't get past the watermelon you're carrying out front, anyway."

"I know; that's what I'm afraid of." But she jauntily skipped down the steps with her head held high to graciously accept her new friends' good wishes.

She was greeted with an assortment of fancy cookies, sweet breads, and cheese balls temptingly arranged on her dining room table. Miraculously, Edith had managed to unearth her punch bowl from the back of a cupboard and already had pink ice swans floating gracefully on a pond of green punch.

Doris Cooper, the vivacious one of the lot, proposed a game of charades. It proved to be so hilarious the players exhausted themselves with laughter. But it was Bonnie herself who threw them into their final uproarious agony. Borrowing from a well-known television commercial, she pantomimed, "I can't believe I ate the whole thing."

They were shaky fingers that undid the lovely ribbon on a gift box. But when an elegant silver tea service was revealed under the tissue paper, voices shaken with emotion attempted to express the Rockwells' appreciation for so generous a gift. And then all glasses were filled and raised for a toast to the health and happiness of the new neighbors in their new home. The entire atmosphere was one of congeniality and genuine good-will, and everyone assembled seemed to totally enjoy the evening's fellowship.

Buz waited until an opportune moment when the farewells began to make the speech he had formulated in his mind at the beginning of the evening.

"Folks, this has been one of the most wonderful occasions for Bonnie and me in our life together. And I offer our most heartfelt thanks. We've had such a great time I'm going to ask each and every one of you to drop back in again same time next week. Bonnie and I are Christians, and we like to study God's Word, the Bible. So if any of you would care to join us next week, we'll look into it together and see if we can discover what it might have to say to us. It will all be very informal, and all opinions are welcome. We'll get out the coffeepot and have an evening of fellowship."

The Coopers hurried out the door, the Lucases and Braskos nodded, several others murmured something like, "Thanks, we'll think about it," and the Corbins replied, "We just might do that." It was the Forsythes who remained after the others had made their departure.

"You don't know how great this is to us," Jenny Forsythe exclaimed. "You see, we've been Christians for several years, and for some time now we have been praying that somehow we would be able to get a home Bible study started in the neighborhood. You can bet we will be right here. We might even alternate having it in our home."

The first meeting proved to be a nominal success. True to their word, the Forsythes arrived with Bibles tucked eagerly under their arms. The Corbins were the only others in attendance, and then only because Bonnie had prevailed so insistently that Edith found it too difficult to refuse. However, the enthusiasm with which the Forsythes and Rockwells delved into the sacred writings was infectious, and the Corbins found themselves involved in the discussion in spite of themselves. And the forthcoming week found them all assembled once again. It was only three more weeks until Edith and Ted began to understand God's claims upon their lives.

"And this is his commandment, that we should believe on the name of his Son Jesus Christ, and love one another, as he gave us commandment. And he that keepeth his commandments dwelleth in him, and he in him. And hereby we know that he abideth in us, by the Spirit which he hath given us," Buz read from 1 John 3. "It is wonderful to have the assurance of God's abiding with us. The guesswork has been taken right out of it. By His Spirit we can know we are right with Him."

"I certainly never heard anything like that before." Ted's words were hesitant, contemplative. "I always thought that about the best you could do was to give to a few charities here and there, be respectable, and hope for the best. But I didn't think you could ever *know* until you got to the other side."

"Since you can know right here and now and make preparation before you get to the other side, don't you think it's a good idea to do so?"

"I sure do; but how do you go about it?"

"The writer Luke tells about a man a couple of thousand years ago who didn't have any problem with that question. He just beat on his chest and cried, 'Lord, be merciful to me, a sinner.' And Jesus said that he went home justified, just as if he had never sinned. You see, we prepare for eternity by recognizing the sin in our lives and dealing with it here and now. That man's simple prayer is just as efficacious today as it was then: 'Lord, have mercy; I'm a sinner.' "

"That's good enough for me. How about you, Edith?" Ted reached for his wife's hand.

"Of course, hon. I think I've been wanting to do this for a long time, but didn't know quite what I was after."

The simple prayer they prayed together with bowed heads and glistening eyes was no more profound than that of the publican of long ago, but the transformation in their lives was.

And the very next week showed that the new babes in Christ were eager to spread the sunshine of God's love abroad upon others. For upon the Corbins' urgent insistence the little group expanded to include the Coopers, the Lucases, and the Braskos. And the three couples already within the heavenly fold dared to trust that the three new ones would not be long in entering.

Bonnie especially could scarcely contain her excitement. How wonderful, she exclaimed to no one in particular, that new babes should be born into God's family at just the same time one was about to be born into her own. Her time of waiting was nearly over, after what had seemed like an eternity. And with a weight gain of thirty-five pounds, she was increasingly more miserable each slowly passing day. She wondered whether she would have the strength to carry in her arms what must be a small elephant. And that little one would arrive in a neighborhood in which God was working His miracles, changing lives and claiming them for His own. Surely no one could ask for more.

Her joy over the awakening in the neighborhood, however, was clouded by one perplexity. She had noticed ever since her arrival on this pleasant little street that the bungalow adjacent to her own happy abode, on the other side from the Corbins, gave an aura of pending gloom. On many occasions the shades were pulled, and the only sign of stirring Bonnie ever observed was the weekly arrival of a young woman somewhere near her own age. Edith had once volunteered the information over morning coffee that the bungalow was inhabited by one cranky old woman, and that her daughter came in once a week, cleaned the house, and carried in groceries.

"That's about all anyone knows of them, and the rest of the neighborhood has nothing to do with them. The old lady has kept to herself all the time she has lived there." Edith dismissed the subject with a nonchalant shrug.

Even as Bonnie mused on the subject, she realized that with the faint stirrings of pain in her lower back, she too would have to dismiss it for the time being.

Her waiting came to an end on a rainy, dismal, gray afternoon early in the spring. Low visibility and poor driving conditions, plus the little one's haste to enter the world, called for a close race to the hospital, barely won by the excited parents. But when the strong little lungs gave forth with a lusty yell, his father heard him long before he ever laid eyes on him, as did everyone else on that particular floor. The newcomer heralded his entry with a pronouncement that seemed to warn that the world would never be the same again.

Buz was fairly bursting when he bent to kiss his sleepy wife.

"May I remind you, my dear Mrs. Rockwell, that we agreed that all our children should bear Bible names, and furthermore that Nathaniel is, after all, a very distinguished Bible name."

"To be sure, Nathaniel is a Bible name, and Nathaniel it will be. However, may I remind you, my dear Mr. Rockwell, that this one was to be my turn to name. And I shall add Peter to it. Nathaniel Peter Rockwell. And Peter he will be called. Peter just seems to be so—so right, somehow. I can't really explain it. But it is as though something were left unfinished— something he can conclude. For the life of me I don't know what. As though—" she groped for words as Buz's brow furrowed in bewilderment. "It is as though some destiny has decreed that Peter should be his name."

"Very well, then, Peter it shall be."

And Peter's vigorous enthusiasm for life and his lusty yells became a steady portion of the Rockwells' life in Bridgeville. Bonnie was to discover that the little community of which they had become a part was actually a more wholesome area to rear the children than would have been the neighborhood around Windy Knoll. Whereas in that secluded residential area there was scarcely another child to play with Miriam, they discovered their shady little street now to be a haven for a host of small fry of all sizes and inclinations. There was never lack for activity in each other's backyards. And when they all tired of private amusements, an amply supplied public playground could be found only one block down the street. Bonnie was thankful many times over for the diversions to which Peter's energies could be channeled; otherwise, she did not know how they could ever have lived with him.

25

With the family complete and the home comfortable, the Rockwells had settled down to the steady business of living. High on their priorities remained the weekly Bible study. And they soon found themselves giving thanks to a gracious God who had seen fit to permit them to lose their elegant Windy Knoll in order that they might gain something of eternal value, for they experienced the joy of seeing their neighbors one by one come into the fellowship of the family of Christ. First it had been the Braskos.

"You know," Paul Brasko confided one night after they had attended the study for about a month, "I grew up in a religious home. But no one ever told me I needed to be saved, as you put it. I was led to believe that the church would take care of all of that for me. I can see now that I need to place my trust in a Person instead of an organization."

Happily his wife joined him in the transferral of his faith.

"It's like taking your money out of a bank going under and opening an account at Chase Manhattan," said he, a teller at Second National, with a beam spreading across his genial face.

It was not many weeks before Spud and Doris Cooper made an admission of their own. Merlin Forsythe had chosen 1 Corinthians 6 in which to lead the study.

" 'What? know ye not that your body is the temple of the Holy Ghost which is in you, which ye have of God, and ye are not your own? For ye are bought with a price: therefore glorify God in your body, and in your spirit, which are God's.'

"I think we are all tempted at times to lose sight of the fact that we are serving either one God or another. We read in the sixth chapter of Romans that we are servants to whomsoever we yield: 'whether of sin unto death, or of obedience unto righteousness.' And this portion in First Corinthians says we are bought and are supposed to 'glorify' God, who has title deed because of ownership. We all want to do our own thing, and then find ourselves in the warfare Paul spoke of when he said he found himself doing what he didn't want to do, and did not do the things he knew he should be doing. I think the crux of the matter lies in recognizing we really do not belong to ourselves. We either choose to serve the law of sin or we submit to the Lordship of Christ in our lives."

"I guess you might say that's my Waterloo," ventured Spud. "Actually I made some sort of 'commitment' when I was a young teenager. But the peer pressure got to me. It seemed that the things the gang did were more exciting than sitting around in some stuffy group of saints singing, *Holy, Holy, Holy, Lord God of Hosts.*' Before long I didn't make any distinction at all between the gang and myself. I just faded into the crowd and lost out spiritually. I realize now the old gang has dispersed, the things we did together were downright devilish, and I ended up impoverished in spirit. None of the material things I've been able to gain in this life and the position I have in the work-a-day world—not even my wife and family—have been able to make up for the vacuum left in my soul when I left God out so many years ago. And all because it is one thing to make a sort of commitment and something else to make good on it, submitting to new Ownership. I believe I'll just have to hang up a sign reading, 'Under New Management.' "

Doris Cooper smiled at her husband through tear-blurred eyes as he spoke.

"I'm afraid I'll have to make the same kind of admission. I was brought up to be a Christian, in the fullest sense of the word. But I took myself out of the Lord's will by marrying Spud when I knew he was far from Him. It nearly broke my mother's heart, but she accepted Spud for himself and prayed that someday we would both come back to our senses and make things right. She is gone now, beyond knowing her prayers are to be answered. You know, I hope Jesus will tell her on one of the walks they take together up there."

At that, Tina Lucas began to weep convulsively. "Both my mother and father are gone, never knowing that it is possible to be saved. I often heard them talking about what would happen to them if there is life after death. They couldn't even be sure of that. But it did worry them that there was the possibility, and they didn't know how to do anything about it if there were. How I wish they could have been in a group such as this one where someone could have told them. I'm going to start living for God myself, but I know that means I'll never see either of them again. We won't be going to the same place—But then" she paused in speculation—"I guess there will be no comfort in the company of those who die without Him anyway." And her tears broke forth in fresh torrent.

"Well, you can be slobbery about it if you want," her husband sneered. "As for me, I'll take care of myself. None of that wishy-washy stuff for me."

The only fortunate aspect of Sonny Lucas's attitude toward his wife's conversion was that he did not forbid her to continue attending the meetings.

"Just as long as it's not some church where they'll take

your—my—money. As long as a few crazy neighbors want to meet together in their homes, you can go along with them, if you want to be that nutty. But you'll never give any of my money away. Leeches, all of them—all those religious freaks. Just after your money. They'll get none of mine."

He never attended a meeting again. Tina continued bravely alone, and endured a divided home without complaint.

If it could possibly be said Bonnie's joy was not complete through seeing her neighbors brought to know the Lord as a result of her joint witness with her husband, she sought further avenues of service in practicing the gift of helps. For she had not forgotten her vow made many years before, to show Christ's love in a practical way. What better way to tell her neighbors about Him than to drive their children to lessons when their cars were under repair, or to dust the house down the street when its mistress had to spend a couple weeks in the hospital. And she organized six of her new friends along with herself to each one day a week carry a hot meal to old Mr. Carpenter, who lived alone behind them on the next block. If she lived to be one hundred, she would not forget the tears of gratitude that crept into his eyes each week when her turn arrived. Taking care to learn his preference was plain, thinly sliced roast beef with gravy and mashed potatoes, she always made sure that was her offering to her own family on her appointed day for Mr. Carpenter so he could be extra pleased when she carried him his portion. There were six other days in the week in which she could indulge her family with pizza, tacos, french fries, and other modern whimsies not familiar to a gentleman who had developed his tastes nearly ninety years before.

But her sense of satisfaction received a smarting jolt every time she passed by the little bungalow next door or looked out her window. The shades were lifted some-what more often now that the summer sun beckoned to be invited in, but the little dwelling huddled under the same gloom Bonnie had observed ever since her arrival in Bridgeville.

"—one cranky old woman, and . . . her daughter . . . and the rest of the neighborhood has nothing to do with them. . . ." Bonnie could not evade the memory of her earlier conversation with Edith Corbin. She had dis-missed it at the time, as she was then preoccupied with Peter's pending birth. Now it hammered at her con-science like an ugly unpaid debt. Somewhere a creditor was demanding an accounting. Was she not placed in her particular spot on earth to minister Christ's love to others about her? And if it is not the well who need a physician, neither is it the neighbors who seem to have everything going well for them who are in need of the hand of friendship. Bonnie had lived next to the gloomy house for nearly eight months, had seen nothing of its occupant and had made no effort to do so. She could excuse herself no longer. Baking her most successful cookie recipe, she wrapped a plateful and watched for the daughter's next arrival.

It was questioning brown eyes that peered levelly into her own when the door was opened following her ring. Straight dark hair hung over the slight shoulders and framed a rather attractive face, which though peaceful nonetheless betrayed a weary patience with life.

"Yes?" The gentle voice was cautious.

"My name is Bonnie Rockwell, and I live next door. We moved into the neighborhood several months ago, and I have been trying to make the acquaintance of the folks around us. I just wanted to say hello and invite you over for coffee."

The cookies were accepted with slight hesitance. "I'm sure she will enjoy these, as she is very fond of cookies.

Her health is not strong, and she doesn't get out much, you know."

The speaker obviously assumed Bonnie understood the identity of the "she." Taking her cue accordingly, Bonnie hastened to add:

"So I understand. I wonder if I may have the privilege of speaking to her?"

"Oh, she has had a very bad day, and is not in a position to receive visitors. But I'm sure that if you would come back again when she is feeling better, she would probably be willing enough to see you."

Although the tone remained cordial, Bonnie sensed the visit was drawing to a close. She had not been invited inside, and the door was soon to be drawn. Casting about mentally for a gracious farewell which would reiterate her invitation for a return visit, her attention was riveted by the sight of Mimi watching her from behind the young woman. How, she wondered in amazement, had Mimi arrived here ahead of her? And why? How did she know these people? But the illusion was momentary. Closer observation disclosed this girl to be three or four years older than Mimi, but the resemblance was striking.

Noting the fleeting expression of shock which crossed Bonnie's face, the woman stated simply, "This is my daughter, Bronya."

"I'm glad to know you, Bronya. You are most welcome to come over to play with Mimi, my girl, when you are here visiting your grandmother. And please won't you—" she directed her words to the older one—"won't you come and bring your mother?"

"Yes, thank you, sometime I will."

The door was shut. It wasn't until Bonnie reached her own door she realized the only name she had learned in the encounter was that of Bronya. Bronya's mother had made no offer to introduce herself. And Bonnie still hadn't had the slightest glimpse of the old lady.

It was not to be long until Bronya made her presence known to Mimi. A week later baby Peter awoke from his nap fretful and restless on the first uncomfortable hot day of the early summer.

"Perhaps if you take him out for a little ride in the stroller, he will get settled," Bonnie had called to Mimi. But Peter didn't settle. He squalled when he was lowered into the stroller, and he screamed as Mimi started up the walk with him. She stopped before the bungalow to attempt to replace the rejected pacifier in his mouth, but he wailed only louder and knocked the pacifier to the ground with his wildly swinging little fists. The door of the bungalow opened and Bronya descended the steps haughtily.

"Please keep that noisy brat quiet," she demanded before she even reached the discouraged big sister. "My grandmother has a headache and that racket certainly isn't helping matters any."

When Mimi turned the stroller around and sought her mother's aid in comforting the distressful little one, Bonnie calculated that living on the quiet, shady street wasn't going to be all peaches and cream. A worm was to appear here and there among the peaches.

From then on Bonnie wasn't so sure she wanted to meet the crotchety old lady next door. And still she was nagged with the compulsion to do so. But how was she to go about it now? Clearly the cookie offering had flopped. And the daughter had so far made no effort to return the visit. Bonnie tried to simply dismiss the whole question from her mind.

She was looking out a front window some days later, trying to determine whether the sudden shower would blow over in a few minutes or whether it would probably last for the remainder of the day. The shower had scattered the neighborhood children and sent them scurrying to their homes. Thankful that Miriam was safely sheltered indoors and that she had done her shopping the previous day, she looked forward to a peaceful afternoon. Then her attention was drawn to movement at the house next door. Bronya's mother was leading her own mother out to her waiting car. Bronya followed closely behind.

Out in weather like this! she mused sympathetically. And especially one who seldom ever goes out. She did not recall ever seeing the old lady outside the house before. Her daughter must have come to take her to the doctor or to some other previous appointment; otherwise, they would surely not have stirred on such a day. She tried vainly to catch a better glimpse of the older one, but an umbrella was held closely over their heads, and as the car pulled away from the curb, the water-streaked windows prevented a clear view.

And poor Bronya, having to trudge along with them, fair weather or foul! Why, she could have stayed here and played with Mimi. Suddenly Bonnie had found her answer. She could meet Bronya's grandmother through her own daughter.

"Mimi," she called to her, "the next time Bronya comes to visit next door, let's just forget she spoke to you rudely, and you go out and ask her if she would like to play with you."

The following Tuesday the forthcoming invitation was accepted enthusiastically. Bronya appeared to appreciate the offered diversion, and soon the two girls made their way together over to the public playground. From that moment, they became the best of friends. Mimi began to look forward to Bronya's weekly visit, and Bronya lost no time in seeking out Mimi upon her arrival. They enjoyed the same activities in spite of the age difference. Bronya was most delighted when Bonnie drove both girls to the skating rink for an afternoon, and Mimi attempted to show Bronya how to do some figures.

"I would love to learn to skate myself," Bronya confided one enchanting afternoon, "but my mother can't afford to give me lessons. She has to go out and work to support us, and she can't manage any extras."

"What does she do? My mother doesn't go to work. She stays home with Peter and me."

"She cleans other people's houses. Of course, when she comes here on Tuesdays, she doesn't charge my grandmother anything. She does that on her days off. I wish I had a father to support us like you have. Then my mother could stay home and I could learn to skate."

"Don't you have a father?"

"Yes, I have one. But I never saw him. He went to the hospital just after I was born, and he has never gotten out."

"Oh, how terrible. Is he very sick?" Mimi's eyes widened in sympathy.

"Well, I guess he must be. They wouldn't keep him there if he weren't, would they?"

"No, I guess they wouldn't."

"Mother is taking night courses over at the business school. She hopes to get a job as a secretary when she is finished. But when my father had to go to the hospital, she wasn't trained to do anything, and she had to do whatever she could. She is almost finished with her course, and she thinks it might be possible for my father to come home before too long. If he does, she wants to go away from here and get a job."

"Won't your father get a job, also, if he comes home, I mean? And then you'll be able to take skating lessons. Maybe you could study with me. Wouldn't that be fun?"

"It certainly would." Bronya's reply was wistful. "I would also like to study piano. There are such wonderful things to do if you only could."

Miriam and Bronya made every possible use of the time they could be together, swinging at the playground, walking Peter around the block in his stroller, playing games, visiting the ice cream parlor. Occasionally they walked the long blocks to the swimming pool where merriment was always the order of the day as they splashed boisterously and tumbled down the water slide. The summer went all too quickly, and Bronya especially began to mourn the swift passing of the days.

A cool breeze and clouded sky induced the two indoors on the very last Tuesday of August. It was to the bungalow that they elected to go, where they spent the afternoon on the floor before the television with Bronya's mother bustling here and there with vacuum sweeper and mop while her grandmother knitted from a great, reclining chair.

"You must stay and have dinner with us this evening," Bronya invited sadly. "It will be the very last time we can see each other until Christmas vacation, at least. If not until next summer. I do hate to see school start next week. It means I won't be able to come here with Mother."

"Yes, I'm going to miss you too. The school term is always so long and summer so short. It never begins before it's about over."

Bronya's mother served a tempting meal of steak and french fries, admonishing the older woman to eat well as she didn't do much cooking for herself when she was alone. The two girls picked lightly over their plates, appetites diminished with the grief of their parting. They were nearly in tears when the dishes had been washed and Bronya and her mother made their way to the car.

"We could at least phone each other once in a while," suggested Bronya. "And maybe you could come over after school on the days when my mother is here and give her messages for me."

"That would be sort of fun. I'll look forward each

week to hearing your messages. Maybe that way it won't seem so long until next summer. 'Bye now."

Bronya was still calling her farewells out the window as the motor started and the car pulled away from the curb.

"Gracious! That must have been a miserable afternoon, judging by the looks of you! You didn't have a disagreement with Bronya, did you?" Bonnie viewed her daughter's downcast mien with apprehension, as the latter entered the front door and flopped dejectedly onto a chair.

"Why no! Don't you *understand,* this is the last time Bronya will be here for a whole year." Mimi spoke with deliberation, as though she were the parent addressing a simple-minded child. "And if that isn't bad enough, she says that when her father gets out of the hospital, she might leave for good. They will go away some place."

"Oh? I didn't realize her father was in the hospital."

"Sure he is. He has been ever since she was a tiny baby. She never saw him. But they think he will come home before too long. They are not sure when."

A puzzled expression clouded Bonnie's face. "She didn't say why he is there, did she? Or just which hospital? She didn't by any chance mention something like State Institution or Western Psychiatric, did she?" Bonnie couldn't remember any types of cases in which people would be hospitalized for nearly twelve years other than severe disability or—or mental illness.

"No, she didn't. And do you know what else? Her grandmother seems kind of—well, you know—funny. The way she talks—I can hardly understand what she says. And do you know what she called me? *Little Stefiania.* Imagine that! I said, 'No, my name is Mimi. Mi-mi.' That seems simple enough to say. But she wouldn't say it. Sometimes you just can't do anything with people." She shook her head resignedly. Bonnie hoped she wasn't seeing a mirror image of herself.

"And do you know what else she did? She's really weird. As soon as I walked in the door she waved her hand across herself and over her face. I thought she had another of her headaches. Bronya told me once she has them all the time. But she didn't seem sick then. She looked at me as if I had stepped out of some monster movie. Mother, I don't look that bad, do I?"

"You don't look bad at all. There's nothing wrong with the way you look. Perhaps she really did not feel well."

"But she kept on looking at me—funny like—the whole time I was there. Every time I looked at her, there she was looking at me with that funny look in her face. And she shook her head all the time. She was weird." Mimi punctuated her words with a slight shudder. "She gave me the creeps."

"Did Bronya ever tell you what her last name is?"

"Last name? No. She's just Bronya. She didn't need a last name."

"I just wondered. Do you know whether her grandmother is her mother's mother or her father's mother?"

"She's just her grandmother. I don't know who's mother she is."

I guess you can't expect much information from a nine-year-old, Bonnie reminded herself. *And here I intended to make the old lady's acquaintance through the children, but the whole summer has slipped by. What's your excuse now, Mrs. Rockwell?*

Aloud she bade the child shower and don her pajamas. "You have to start back to school, also, and will have to get into the habit of going to bed earlier so you can get up earlier."

"—don't have anything to do with them . . . keeps to herself and never goes out." Once more Edith Corbin's words seared themselves onto her memory. Why must she be forever haunted with the problem of one old lady whom she had never been able to meet? Obviously the lady wasn't interested in meeting her or she could at least have gone half way. But perhaps Bonnie was beginning to get the picture. If what Mimi said was true, was it possible Edith was mistaken about the relationship between the mother and daughter? Perhaps it was Bronya's father who was son to the old lady. And were the shades drawn also in his hospital room—? And what of Bronya? No, she didn't seem to be afflicted. Mental illness may run in families, but it doesn't necessarily strike every member. At last she could begin to understand Edith's reticence to talk about them.

It was probably just as well if Bonnie dropped the whole subject. Bronya would not be back before the end of a school term, which hadn't even begun as yet. With the lady shut up in her own house, there would be no reason to think about her at all. She would concentrate on witnessing to the people whom she could reach.

Summer rapidly faded into fall. Life in the Rockwell household settled into the routine of school hours, homework, lessons, and the two evening courses Buz was teaching at Carnegie-Mellon, in addition to many long hours of work during the day. Peter, who was growing into the proportions of a half-pint quarterback while they watched, kept all his wakeful hours in a turmoil until Bonnie would sink into the nearest chair or sofa in sheer exhaustion. If she couldn't keep up with him when he was only crawling, what would it be like when he walked? Clearly, the pieces of Meissen porcelain would have to go back into storage. And there didn't seem to be a toy that could hold his attention for any longer than it took him to dismantle it.

Buz was of little help when he was home, for he had overloaded his own schedule with an abundance of commissions from clients desperately trying to get their buildings under roof before the winter set in. If he had any reserve energy by the end of the day, it was exerted on his ever-present sketch pad. He wearily anticipated a slackening of pace during the winter months when he might be able to romp with and enjoy this son whom he had desired for so long.

Bonnie felt the old, familiar melancholy descending over her spirits as she watched the last blossom wither, took up some begonias to pot for the winter, removed the awnings over the windows, felt the dryness in the air, and shivered in the evening chill. Once more she knew it would get worse before it got any better. Winter was not her favorite season.

Depressed, she watched the leaves color and begin to fall. The lovely little street that drew its pleasantness from its shade in the heat of the summer turned from friend to foe as the trees bared their branches against the brilliant azure autumn sky. And the rustling beneath the footsteps on the walk signalled the task most distasteful to her. As Buz was much too occupied to concern himself with it, she reluctantly picked up the rake and headed for the front lawn.

After several minutes of steady stretching and pulling, she decided the chore wasn't so arduous after all. The air was clear, invigorating, and just warm enough to be pleasant. She soon removed the sweater she had needed before exercising. And she began to feel rejuvenated, stimulated. Some cobwebs were shaken loose inside her head, and she began to feel relaxed, at peace, almost giddy. Why had she considered the opportunity to engage in meaningful occupation out in such a congenial atmosphere so distasteful? Her own stretch of real estate fronting the street began to appear too short. She would soon run out of leaves. I'll just find some more, she told herself.

A backward glance revealed that Ted Corbin was

ahead of her on the yard detail. But, of course, there was the bungalow adjacent on the other side. And Bronya's grandmother would probably appreciate a neighborly hand. Bonnie wondered how else she would get her leaves raked unless her daughter managed the chore on the day she devoted to her mother. But first Bonnie must dash back inside for some leaf bags.

The dash proved to be rather extended as she found Peter had awakened early from his nap and required attention. But what better occupation could she find for him than sitting by her in the lovely sunshine as she raked? With his sweater and little cap on, he squealed excitedly while she brought out the stroller. Maneuvering it down the steps she went back for him and steered the stroller toward the pile of leaves she had waiting to be bagged. It was then she became aware that someone was in the adjacent yard already at work on the leaves. Bronya's mother must have emerged from the bungalow while Bonnie had been inside tending to Peter.

But this was not the day of the weekly visit. And a closer scrutiny revealed that the one wielding the rake in the nearby yard was not as young as Bronya's mother. The jacket styled to be worn loosely was stretched across a broad back, and the movements were cumbersome, those of someone much older. Surely not Bronya's grandmother? But then, a lovely day such as this was alluring enough to coax out all but the most feeble. The old lady probably had learned long ago the sunshine and fresh air, coupled with mild exercise, would chase whatever aches or ills may be lurking about. Here was the chance for which Bonnie had waited many a month. She would just rake her way closer and say Hello casually.

Her own leaves filled two bags, which she tied and leaned against a tree while Peter kicked, jabbered, and continually threw down his toys. She had retrieved them for him until she realized that he was playing games with her, and she left them lie where he dropped them. His happy jabbering changed to scolding, which increased in volume the more she ignored him. Never mind, he was outdoors, and his voice couldn't carry far. Let him exercise his lungs.

Gratifyingly she observed her area of work to be drawing closer to that of the lady nearby. They were now only a matter of a few feet apart. As soon as the other looked up, she would speak. Bonnie noticed the woman had no bags for the two small piles she had assembled. She would just take one of her own and offer to fill it herself. The woman turned as Bonnie approached and looked her full in the face. Time stood still as Bonnie caught her breath and froze in her tracks. She had known many years ago on the street of the city that that face was to be etched forever upon her memory, and that no matter where on the surface of the earth she would encounter the same woman again, she would recognize her. But surely she had to be mistaken. Her mind must be playing tricks on her. And then the woman's mouth parted the myriad of tiny, wrinkled lines playing across her countenance. She was speaking. "Could you please keep your child from being so noisy?" Or had she said "annoying?" It was difficult to tell with that heavy, foreign accent. But of her identity there could be no mistake. This was indeed George Morrow's mother!

Revulsion swept over Bonnie. A long buried past crept unbidden into her memory, and she felt again the sting of the revelation this woman had once opened to her. She relived the shame of the knowledge that she had kept the company of a married man. And she suffered once more the despair and uncertainty of being unemployed. A wave of nausea swept over her, bringing crimson to her cheeks and heat to her forehead in spite of the security she had known for most of the intervening years

439

at the side of her beloved Buz. Flustered, she murmured something like, "Of course, I'm sorry." And dashing to the stroller she pushed the astonished child up to the porch so quickly he closed his own mouth in fright. Snatching him up, she sped inside and sank onto the sofa. After several moments she collected herself enough to realize she must certainly have overreacted. Why shouldn't it be George's mother? She had to be somewhere in this world. It was only coincidence that she was next door.

A fine introduction I've made to her, Bonnie thought ruefully, *after the honest attempt I've made at it.* But on second thought, she decided it was probably just as well. She was not sure she was enthusiastic about developing a friendship with this particular neighbor now that she knew her identity.

A moment's reflection caused her to realize the younger woman could not be Mrs. Morrow's daughter, for George had stated clearly that he was an only child. And yet if Bronya were truly the older woman's grand-daughter, there remained only one relationship for her mother. She had to be George's wife. What was it his mother had called her? Could she ever really forget that it was *Shirley?* And Bronya, of course, was the child whose birth had detained her father when the date for the conservatory had been broken. Bonnie was now gratified for their sakes that George had discharged his family responsibilities at that time in preference to see-ing her. Undoubtedly there had been no more children, as George had left the family circle shortly thereafter.

He had spent those long years in the hospital, Shirley had informed her daughter. Yes, indeed, he had been in the "hospital" a long time, and unless he was granted an early parole, he had a stretch yet to go. Bonnie vaguely remembered reading, following his trial, that he had received two consecutive sentences, one for each place of employment where he had practiced his underhanded craft. The sentences totalled eighteen years. How touching that Shirley had shielded her little girl from the harsh reality of the penitentiary.

Furthermore, Shirley must be a rather remarkable person to remain loyal to the mother of a man who had betrayed and disgraced her. It was more than Bonnie felt she herself could have done. She must not think ill of either woman, no matter how deeply she herself had been hurt. But neither was she sure she desired a friendly relationship with them. A chapter had been closed on her life many years ago, and she did not wish to reopen it.

26

"You've just got to take them!" Sylvia was screaming nearly hysterically. "Keep them here for a while until he gives up and goes back north. He doesn't know where you live, and there's no way in all the world he can find them."

"Listen, Sylvia, talk sense. You can't possibly hide a twelve-year-old boy and two little girls. If he couldn't find our home address in the phone book, it certainly would be no problem to look up the architecture office of Cohen Associates. Now will you pull yourself together and try to think through this thing reasonably?"

It always was like Sylvia to go off the deep end. Perhaps her swimming proficiency gave her too much confidence!

"But he wouldn't think to actually *look* here. And if he phoned, you could always say you didn't know—"

"There are no untruthful statements made over the phone in this house. Now, if you will just be rational for a minute, you will realize that hiding the children is not the answer. If he is serious about gaining custody, he will take it all properly through the courts, and you will have to be prepared to battle on his field. By the way—" Bonnie laid aside the magazine with which she had been relaxing when Sylvia burst agitatedly through the door, and peered intently at her younger sister. "On what grounds is he going to ask for it? Is he going to try to claim you are incompetent or what?"

"He said he simply wanted the companionship of his children. You know how men are these days. There was a time when it was automatically taken for granted that a mother was more suited to raise the children. Men didn't even want to be bothered with them. Now they get these freaky ideas, and they don't even have to have grounds."

"And the courts are becoming increasingly more sympathetic with them. You may have more of a fight on your hands than you bargained for. But why now?"

Sylvia picked up the corner of the afghan which adorned the back of the sofa and nervously twisted one corner of it into a ball.

"He said he has been trying for months to get transferred back into this area so he can see them once or twice a week, and he would have let it go at that. But there is no way Paramount Plastics is going to give him anything here. It seems that company is finding competition a little stiffer than when they first started out, and they are having to curtail here and there. So he decided to take the children up there. I suppose some joker in the office put that into his head if he didn't have enough smarts to think it up for himself." The characteristic pout was playing at the corners of Sylvia's sensuous mouth again.

Bonnie longed to be able to take this scatter-brained sister of hers into her arms and soothe away the spectre that was stalking her. But the threat Sylvia faced was too formidable to be dispelled by mere sympathy. Poor Sylvia! When one's major asset is physical beauty, it serves one poorly where shrewdness and integrity are more powerful weapons. And compounding it all was the obstinacy with which she refused to commit her life and problems to an all-sufficient, loving heavenly Father.

"Perhaps some kind of compromise? Maybe if you just

reasoned with him, he might be agreeable to having the children for certain months of the year. Like the summer, for instance. They would probably love spending summers in Vermont. People of means choose to do so when their summer residences are farther south. It can't be all that bad a place." Bonnie was not forgetting Sylvia's aversion to the north.

"Reason with him?" The voice rose shrilly. "Not very well when I've already stopped on my way here to have the phone disconnected. And if you won't help out your sister when she needs it, I'll just go immediately and find another apartment—with no forwarding address."

"Sylvia!" Bonnie couldn't disguise her despair. "Please try to be sensible. The more foolishly you act, the less chance you will have in court. Can't you listen to reason just this once?"

"Just this once? So I'm unreasonable, am I? Well, thanks a lot. It isn't your children someone is trying to steal. You can afford to tell me not to worry. You with that adoring husband who would cut off both his hands for you. Some people just don't understand a thing."

With a shrug of hopelessness, more for Bonnie than for herself, Sylvia rose determinedly, slammed the door, and headed for her car. Bonnie watched her regretfully as she revved up the motor and peeled out with a raucous squealing of rubber.

Bonnie's heart ached for the handsome, shy, and withdrawn Harry who undoubtedly needed the guidance and companionship of a father. The worst of it was that the child was entering the years when a father's influence was decidedly most important. And thinking of that particular child's father once more evoked the twinge of regret. What had Hal done to deserve all this? And how large a part did she play in bringing him to grief? Bonnie had long ago tried to still that persistent voice that nagged with the pain of others' torment, but always there seemed to be new reasons to revive the concern. None the least of which were also Jennifer and Veronica.

The moody, sulking behavior that Jennifer had first manifested upon her parents' separation was only intensified with the passing years, until she had become completely unmanageable. Always the child herself, Sylvia never had been able to apply the firm wisdom by which it might once have been possible to remold the little one's disposition. And the baby Veronica, spoiled at her grandparents' hands, evidenced signs of developing no more depth than Sylvia herself had managed. Bonnie couldn't help thinking that all three children would profit greatly from the counsel and care of their father. She shuddered at the fear that suddenly surfaced, that she might have to testify at a hearing. Testify against her own beloved sister? Or go against her own convictions to the detriment of three young lives caught up in and confounded by the Great Twentieth-Century American Tragedy?

Heavy of heart, she turned from the door, only to be immediately recalled to it by the sounds from outside. If she were pained over the plight of her sister's children, her own little one seemed not to cease to cause agitation and small crises. What was he up to now? It was the voice of Mrs. Morrow next door that she heard scolding angrily.

"Leave those flowers alone. Go back home, you naughty little rascal." It had been ever thus from the time Peter first toddled down off his own front porch. He had grown rapidly and robust, and his zest for life and venturesome disposition led him and his parents into more trials than they had been aware of bargaining for. Unfortunately, of all the flowers that grew in lovely plots along the street, Mrs. Morrow's were the only ones sufficiently enticing to Peter that he systematically uprooted each one.

Bonnie hastened to her angry neighbor to apologize once more.

"I know Peter is very trying to you. I do try to keep him inside our own yard, but he always seems to keep one jump ahead of me." Mentally she added that he probably wouldn't seem as annoying to a person who wasn't so easily aggravated. But this old woman always had a headache or some such ailment. She was more in view recently than she had been the first couple years the Rockwells had lived beside her. But Bonnie wasn't sure her more numerous appearances were because she felt fit for longer periods between the headaches or whether she was determined to keep her eye on the antics of the young one next door, even if it killed her.

Bonnie recalled that the first real conversation she had ever had with Mrs. Morrow was a result of Peter's obsession with throwing his toys over the backyard fence. Unhappily it was necessary for the older woman to retrieve them, for her yard was enclosed completely and latched shut at the gate. The first couple of times she replaced the balls and plastic riding horsie, she appeared to take it in stride. By the third time, she called to Bonnie to please restrain her son's aim, or she would let the toys lie where they landed. Bonnie had hurried apologetically to the fence and promised to keep a better eye on Peter's behavior.

"What did you say his name is?" Mrs. Morrow had queried quickly.

When Bonnie replied the child's name was Peter, she recognized what Miriam had been trying to tell her about Mrs. Morrow's odd behavior the first time she had seen her, for the peculiar old lady made the sign of the cross. Bonnie wondered whether she had also, upon the first occasion, lifted her eyes heavenward in a momentary pained supplication, as she did when she heard the boy's name. The younger woman shook her head as she had slowly walked away. Maybe her first assumption had been correct—mental problems in that family in addition to the prison sentence.

Relations were somewhat smoothed between the two neighbors that summer because Bronya once again made the weekly visit with her mother. She had scurried immediately upon her arrival to seek Mimi and renew their acquaintance. The two chatted eagerly at great length to fill in the details of the previous nine months when they had not seen each other.

Bronya had begun to grow tall and evidenced some signs of the beginnings of the awkward years when all her parts didn't seem to coordinate. But the features remained the same, enough like Mimi to cause Bonnie to muse on the quirk of fate that decreed George Morrow's daughter should look enough like her own that she supposed there should have been no difference if she had married him and borne his child.

It was the name that caused Mimi to take notice.

"It's so different," she had observed one day at the rink. "Where did your mother hear of it?"

"Oh, it wasn't my mother. My father named me. For his mother. You see, the name is really Polish. That is the reason you don't hear of many Americans having it. I rather like having a different name. It makes me sort of—stand out, you might say. I like to pretend that I could be a skater like you, or a great prima ballerina." Bronya clasped her hands and sighed. "Bronya Morawski. The great Bronya Morawski. Doesn't it sound romantic, arty? I often pretend I see it in the newspapers and on television. That really is our name, you know. Bronya Janina Morawski. Sometimes I wish they had called me Janina. I would have liked Nina for short. It would be like your 'Mimi' for Miriam."

"Yes, I suppose it is. My mother tells me I was given a Bible name. I don't believe 'Nina' is in the Bible, is it?"

"Oh, it must be in there somewhere. The Bible has everything in it, doesn't it?"

"I guess so. It has Peter and Timothy. That was my little brother that died, you know."

"I wish I had had little brothers and sisters. Mom and I have been alone as long as I can remember. It would be so nice to have playmates right at home."

"It isn't always nice. Sometimes Peter is a real bother."

"I know. Grandmother tells me Peter pulls one of his pranks everytime she has a headache. And *that* is most of the time."

"Why does she always have those headaches? My grandmother doesn't have them. She's nice."

"I'm not sure; but she says it really is her back. Her back makes her head ache. Did you ever hear anything so silly?"

The two girls giggled and skated over to the wall for a breather.

The truce bought with Mimi and Bronya's friendship was broken when Bronya returned to school in the fall. Nor was it reinstated the following summer, for by then Bronya was maturing rapidly and was disinclined to divert herself with the younger child's company. Often she simply elected not to accompany her mother on the weekly visits, and when she did appear she made herself useful inside the house.

Aside from the occasions when Mrs. Morrow sallied forth to scold Peter, and an infrequent digging about in her flower bed on the lovelier days, Bonnie saw nothing of that fretful soul. Shirley arrived on days other than Tuesdays to take her out in the car. And, furthermore, those trips gradually became more frequent.

So did Peter's aggravations.

In his fourth summer he discovered the lid of Mrs. Morrow's garbage can made an excellent shield with which to fend off blows by imaginary foes. The final foe, however, dealt a death blow to at least the shield, as a ton of steel rolled over it where he left it lie in the street. Of course, in replacing it Buz had to purchase a new can and all, but not before a dog entered the Morrow yard through the open gate and left garbage all over the place.

Mrs. Morrow's front porch for some reason proved to be the most inviting location for stirring mud pies following a summer shower, and her rugs airing on the line strung from the back porch made wonderful magic carpets for imaginary journeys. Bonnie wondered wearily how one small boy could think of so many things to get into in a place where he was not supposed to be at all. But it seemed impossible to restrain him short of chaining him. Threats and paddlings were of no avail, and a latched gate seemed only to heighten the challenge.

But the worst was yet to be. Peter was four when Buz at last determined the repair on the roof could be delayed no longer. Workmen were in the process of tarring it when Peter, entranced with the "painting" of his roof, observed the arrival of Shirley Morrow, surveyed the battered condition of her old car, and decided to be helpful. His deed had long since been accomplished by the time Shirley discovered her auto, smeared on all sides with the black, sticky goo. Fortunately Buz arrived just in time to hear the wails of anguish that arose from her lips when she discovered the uncommissioned paint job.

"I was only trying to help, Daddy," Buz's young son lamented the lack of appreciation of his benevolence.

"That's fine, son. Because you'll have plenty of 'helping' to do now to remove that mess."

By the time the cleanup was completed, Buz had expended three hours of hard labor, most of a can of gasoline intended for the lawn mower, and enough water with suds to fill a swimming pool. Needless to say, his resulting humor at the close of what had already been a difficult day left something to be desired.

Attempting gently to soothe an irritated husband, Bonnie remembered ruefully the time she had been so thankful George Morrow was out of her life forever, or so she had thought. Now it seemed that if not he, at least his family were an inescapable part of it. By what quirk of fate must she find herself unwillingly enmeshed in their lives?

27

Bonnie didn't mind feeling so miserable when she paused to think of how many reasons she had for feeling good. Peter had somehow miraculously survived his reckless early years of riding his tricycle down the porch steps, climbing to the highest, flimsiest branches on the very top of the apple tree in the backyard, plunging into the deep end of the swimming pool, and chasing Mimi's Great Dane across the street a split second before a car reached the same spot. Even the scar under his left eye—from riding his sled into a fire hydrant—scarcely showed anymore. And now that he had finally entered school, his mother hoped both her neighbor and she would find a little more peace. She enjoyed the days now when he was safely corraled at a desk and she could get her work done in the mornings and relax a little. And relax was just what she needed to do now, she decided with her umpteenth sneeze.

Miriam was turning into a studious, charming teenager who thrived on junior high school, made friends easily, and continually improved her skating technique. Mimi's instructors assured Bonnie repeatedly that her daughter was endowed with a natural grace and talent that could take her a long way, though Bonnie wondered where she had ever acquired it.

Even Sylvia's youngsters caused Bonnie less concern than they once had. Sylvia had been spared the distress of a hearing a few years back, for she had finally recognized the necessity of facing her estranged husband to work out an agreement between them. Christmas vacation and two months of the summer for him; they were hers with no strings attached the rest of the year. After the second summer, Harry calmly announced he chose to live permanently with his father and that he felt he was old enough to merit respect for his own preference in the matter. Oddly enough, Sylvia capitulated without an argument, and Bonnie suspected that somewhere beneath her irresponsible exterior there nagged the fear that she really wasn't qualified to guide a maturing boy into commendable manhood.

As for Jennifer and Veronica, a few years' added growth had worked wonders with their dispositions. They had elected to spend the entire summer in New England simply because they had learned to love the area. But when the school term began they had readily enough returned to Pittsburgh and their mother's apartment without complaint. Bonnie sighed as she reached for another tissue and settled herself more comfortably among the pillows. Her ache for that family could end if only they would give place to God in their lives.

There were Perry and her own beloved father, also, still outside the fold of eternal salvation. She never failed to pray daily for all of them, nor to return thanks for the marvel of grace that her mother had become. Some of Avonelle's youthfulness had returned, her voice once again resonated the musical cadences of a woodland brook, and her love for her Savior radiated from her as the sun gleaming on a golden beach.

Bonnie had even learned to welcome the onset of winter, for she had observed with the passing of the years that no matter how severe and desolate it became, spring always burst forth again in all its glory. "While the earth remaineth, seedtime and harvest, and cold and heat, and summer and winter, and day and night shall not cease." *Even though the changing of the seasons usually precipitates a cold for me,* she thought as she sneezed once again. The only problem was, this one was a little worse than usual. When she no longer had the strength to stand on her feet, she had capitulated, fortified herself with aspirin and nasal spray, and headed upstairs to bed. She should have several hours in which she could sleep peacefully before the children returned from school. But she had only begun to doze when she was disturbed by the slamming of a car door down on the street below.

She couldn't guess what prompted her curiosity to propel her out of bed and over to the window, as she heard numerous cars during the course of a day without their evoking so much as the lift of an eyebrow. But she was arrested on the spot by the sight that greeted her from the walk next door, for whom should she see emerging from the car but George Morrow! Or perhaps one might conclude, the shell of George Morrow, for though this gaunt, bent figure bore little resemblance to the dashing, distinctive young man she had known, it could be no other. The massive sea of golden waves that once had crowned the arrogant head was now sparse and snow white. The once broad, ramrod shoulders were now stooped. With the head bent, she could not determine what expression might be read in the face, or whether it was lined by stress and middle age.

The most difficult sight of all to comprehend was that of Shirley, taking his arm protectively and leading him into the house. Was the girl completely nuts to stick with such a despicable character? Welcome him back? She must be as far off base as he was. Maybe she had been fully cognizant of his defrauding, even encouraged him in it. Bonnie had always thought well of her until this moment.

Then there was Bronya following them. Why wasn't she in school? But of course, this would be a very special occasion, meeting her father for the first time in her memory. How many years had it been? Sixteen? Seventeen? She might have even graduated from high school last spring. Bonnie had failed to take notice. And George must have been paroled early, she hoped on good behavior.

Bonnie shuddered as she turned from the window. She had expected—indeed intended—never to see his face again. Well, actually she hadn't even yet, and she didn't plan to. But as she settled herself back under the covers, a vision of his mother flashed before her, a memory of how she had looked many years before on the city street. Why, she had looked as old then as she did now. How old must she be? Very old, or had she aged terribly while still relatively young?

Bonnie remembered Mrs. Morrow's eagerness to see her son, clouded by a fleeting expression of hurt as George had abruptly pulled Bonnie away. Bonnie had ignored the older woman's pain at the time under the acuteness of her own. If Mrs. Morrow were that hurt by a moment of rudeness, how great must have been her anguish when she watched her son sentenced to incarceration for the best years of his life? Then Bonnie knew the place to which Shirley had driven her one time every month was not to a doctor, but to a prison. Bonnie immediately repented of her ill feelings. No wonder the woman's head ached, and she was rather cranky. And what might be her deepest feelings to Peter, beyond her annoyance at his pranks? Was she noting that he, at least, was young and innocent—and his mother still enjoyed his company at home?

Bonnie determined to make some attempt to visit the old lady and make amends for her un-christian attitude. She began to pray that a natural opportunity would present itself, rather than a contrived one in which her neighbor could be suspicious of her motives. She didn't have long to await her answer. The following Tuesday, a taxi drew up to the Morrow house and carried away its mistress. No Shirley this time, Bonnie observed through the window, and it was unlikely Mrs. Morrow could well afford a taxi. Then it dawned on her that that was her perfect opportunity.

The following day found her on her neighbor's doorstep.

"Mrs. Rockwell, do come in and sit down." Mrs. Morrow had never sounded so amiable. Was she lonely or just feeling particularly well?

"Thank you, I will. I have come to inquire about your health. I hope these colder days aren't taking their toll."

"I am quite fine, thank you. Right at the moment, anyway. Here, take this chair by the window where it will be sunny and pleasant for you." She seated herself cumbersomely on the sofa by an inside wall. "I don't usually sit there, as I can't take the light when I have one of my headaches. My eyes feel like they're going to burn right out of my head."

Bonnie had to strain to catch all of the lady's words, so heavy was the foreign accent.

"And when you don't have a headache, you do enjoy getting out in the fresh air, don't you? Perhaps we could drive out to one of the parks and take advantage of what remaining decent weather we have before winter sets in."

Mrs. Morrow gazed for a moment in Bonnie's face before replying, the wrinkles playing about the corners of her mouth as she worked it nervously. The younger woman believed she detected a look of amazed gratitude on the older one's face.

"How lovely that would be. I have no way of getting out now with Shirley gone. I certainly am going to miss that girl." A wave of pain replaced the last expression on the careworn face. "But it is all for the better. We have waited a long time for this day."

"I'm sure you have." Did Mrs. Morrow assume her neighbor knew the circumstances surrounding her son, or did she simply intend no explanation regardless of whether she did or not?

After a moment's silence, Mrs. Morrow continued on the former subject.

"To tell you the truth, whether I feel like taking that drive will depend on how my back is. Sometimes it doesn't want to hold the rest of me up. Then it pulls up into my neck—you know, the muscles or ligaments or whatever it is you have in your back, tighten and draw until the top of my head feels as if it's being pulled down into my brain. It is then that I often feel a good ball bat well-placed would be a mercy."

"Horrors!" Bonnie tried to sound as sympathetic as she felt. "Do you know what caused your trouble?"

Once more the other eyed her pensively before speaking.

"I don't often talk of it. Yes, I know all right. Could I ever forget?"

She closed her eyes and tilted her head back. Then with a slow shaking of it, she began quietly: "It was in the Nazi concentration camp. They had conceived this foolhardy idea of building a bridge across some river. Only it wasn't to be a real bridge. They thought that if enough stones were dropped into the water to form a sort of bed across it—well, I don't exactly know how they intended to engineer it because they apparently realized it wasn't going to be practical and gave up the project anyway. But not before the damage was done.

"We had to get out at four in the morning in freezing temperatures and row out into the middle of the channel and drop these huge stones overboard. They must have weighed fifty to a hundred pounds. It was more than I or the other women could manage. And the spray from the water when they dropped! In no time at all we would be drenched to the skin. Then our clothes—we had only thin cotton dresses on our backs—turned to ice. Our hands would become so numb we couldn't get a hold on the stones."

She stopped her narrative, silent in nightmarish memories. Suddenly every wrinkle, every line on that etched, wretched face came into sharp focus. For every line Bonnie saw a hundred-pound stone dropped over the side of a rowboat and felt the spray of icy water drenching her to the skin and freezing her thin, tattered dress to her body.

"If we were lucky," the voice was stronger, as though with relief that the dread spectre had been exhumed to be laid the more comfortably to rest, "we were assigned the task of hewing the rock out of the quarry and loading it onto the wagon to be hauled to the boats. At least, there was no water to drench us."

"I daresay your back has given you not a moment's peace since."

"When I first got to this country after we were liberated, I went to chiropractors, osteopaths, any kind of a doctor I could hope might help. Once they even offered surgery, but no real hope along with it. There was no guarantee I wouldn't be worse off than before. I finally quit spending money and determined to do as they said I would have to do—learn to live with it. If you call that living."

"I am so sorry." Bonnie feared the words sounded superficial, and was nearly ashamed to voice them; yet what else could she say when words were inadequate? "Let's plan for an excursion tomorrow about this same time. And then if you don't feel up to it, we can always postpone it for another time."

"I'm sure that will be fine."

And fine it turned out to be. The weather favored them with a mild, clear day, and the two women breathed deeply of the invigorating air as they strolled over graveled paths and rested for awhile on a bench by a rippling fountain.

"I don't know how I can thank you for the pleasant afternoon," Mrs. Morrow spoke warmly as the car drew up before her door.

"You needn't. I enjoy having a companion when I get the urge to take a little exercise. I do wish you would let me know when you have to go shopping or wherever. Chances are I'll have to be going out around that time too, and I might as well drop you off on the way."

It was so simple, this arrangement whereby Bonnie found herself involved with this old lady's errands. It was not long before she filled the place Shirley had once occupied. And as she looked after the needs of the bereft woman, Bonnie felt for the first time her long ago dedication to practicing the gift of helps was only now fully realized. The satisfaction it gave her heightened the joy she found in her ministry.

It was one blustery, wintry day while carrying the mail inside for her ailing friend that she observed the name of the addressee on an envelope: "Mrs. Stefania Morrow."

"Is something wrong?" The anxious words indicated the puzzled frown on Bonnie's face.

"Oh, nothing, really. It's just that—well, didn't Miriam tell me once that Bronya said she had been named for her grandmother? And that her second name was—"

"Janina. That's correct. Bronya Janina." That seemed to be the end of it so far as Mrs. Morrow was concerned.

"Well, I see here your name is Stefania. That's a very interesting name. Would you pronounce it in Polish?"

Bonnie hoped to encourage her to continue talking.

" 'Stef-AHN-ya' we would say. You would say Stephanie. Yes, I always felt it to be an elegant name. Some people don't like their names, but I was rather proud of mine."

"It sounds lovely when you pronounce it correctly. But how is it then Bronya could be named for her grandmother?"

Bonnie observed again the meditating expression that seemed to indicate Mrs. Morrow was trying to decide whether to divulge some information. The older woman pursed her lips and turned her gaze out the window for a moment. Then she dropped it to the letter in her hand. Bonnie held her breath for what seemed like ages. Then Mrs. Morrow spoke.

"I am not her grandmother. I am her great aunt." Bonnie's hearing had never been so alert; she couldn't have mistaken the words she heard. What shattering revelation was to come now?

"George's mother was my twin sister. It was on that day in September of 1939 when the Germans invaded our beloved fatherland. George was six years old then. He had been playing in the lawn in front of the house, attracted by the booms and explosions of the invasion, not really understanding each fresh bang brought death and bloodshed—until his mother walked out the door to call him in because the battle was coming closer. A large shell caught her squarely where she stood and she disintegrated before George's eyes. Then he understood. He learned a lesson he never forgot. I shall always believe the horror of that moment was partly to blame for—"

Bonnie had no need of her finishing the statement. She also could believe what the other would have said if her voice had not trailed off into silence.

"What did George do then?" she nudged gently.

"He ran across town to me, screaming hysterically.

Some children don't quite comprehend the finality of death when they only see a parent laid out in a coffin, there but not responding. With George it was 'now she is here, now she isn't.' He never had any difficulty with it. He even—" the poor woman shuddered and visibly forced herself to continue. "—he even picked up her shoe and brought it with him. To show me how it was in case I couldn't grasp it, I guess."

Bonnie felt nauseated.

"And you've—you've had him ever since?"

"Yes—and he's all I have left in the world. I took him in and kept him until he met Shirley. She has been good to him."

That's an understatement, thought Bonnie. Aloud she prodded some more.

"What of his father? Had he no hand in his upbringing?"

"He was never seen again from that day." She gave a sniff of utter contempt. "German, he was. Hans Schmidt. He and my sister met while they were students at the university in Salzburg. He was practicing law in Warsaw at the time of the invasion. But whereas the Nazis killed off all the national professional people in Poland, they left the German inhabitants alone, including him. He joined them and became one of those despicable fifth columnists." She was spitting out her words with a venom Bonnie hadn't thought possible with her depleted strength.

"He would have brought terrible disgrace on my poor sister; but mercifully she was killed on the first day of the blitz and never knew the shame under which she would otherwise have lived."

Bonnie recoiled from a horror so great that having your twin sister blown to bits in a German blitz would be a mercy.

Then she thought of the six-year-old George, witnessing the tragic event, never knowing what became of his father, a traitor to his adopted country and a disgrace to his family. Suddenly it dawned on her that George would even have accompanied his aunt to that concentration camp of which she had spoken. She was gripped with the chilling memory of the terrible stories she had read, of the deprivation and starvation that were the scourge of those vile places. Hadn't a chunk of coarsebread and thin cabbage soup often been their only sustenance?

Bonnie now understood his later preoccupation with good food, and his need to increase his income to provide it! Shirley had known and understood, even if she did not condone it. Who was she, Bonnie, to judge— she who but for some unfathomable miracle of God's amazing grace would have spent her youth completely abandoned in a dismal foundling home in Reims, France, and who knows what then? A streetwalker trying to eke out a miserable living? Would his sin be greater than hers?

What would *I have been, anyway,* she wondered, tossing on her pillow that night. Every time she did doze off she would awaken abruptly in a cold sweat, dreaming of a blonde, curly-haired youngster poking about in some rubble. Once she even felt herself being jostled about in her own old, familiar nightmare that surfaced periodically when she was in the midst of a crisis. But oddly enough, this time the voice that hysterically called out was silent.

It's probably these old box springs that need to be replaced, she told herself, *and every time Buz turns over I'm rocked in the cradle of the deep. I'll have to see about shopping for some new bedding.* With the approach of daylight, she determined to make another investigation.

It was evident that the Salvation Army had gone about as far as was humanly possible in attempting to learn her true identity and place her with her natural family. However since her mother no longer volunteered at the Red Cross there would be no repercussions if she were to try there. After all, they might have access to records that the Salvation Army did not have. Someone of her own family might have filed an inquiry with them that by some miracle could be matched with her own. And as a final safeguard, in the remote chance that some of Avonelle's old acquaintances at the office might hurry to her with any tales, Bonnie could use Buz's middle name. Hadn't he told her once his name was then to become hers? Even if Avonelle were to see "Mrs. Bonnie Gibson" spelled out in black and white, she would never in a million years suspect it was her own daughter.

The old excitement returned as she donned a fresh blouse and slacks and made her way to Fourth Avenue.

"And beyond the fact that you have been traced as far back as the orphanage in Reims, and that you were listed as among some refugees from Hungary, you know nothing?" The interviewer was courteous and obviously desired to be helpful.

"That is correct. And, as I said, the matron there is now deceased. There is nothing to be gained from retracing that route. I was hopeful someone may have been inquiring for me, and there would be some data on file that would match up with a lost girl from Hungary. I must have been born somewhere near the beginning of the war, as I was around the age of six when it was over. The age and the country are all I know."

"We have people still making such inquiries after all these years. Although, the number is negligible to what it was in the years immediately following the end of the war. There is right here in this city a gentleman from Hungary looking for a brother. Someone from Romania is looking for cousins and a sister, and a lady comes in every few months to check up on whether we have received any news of her daughter, but she is listed as being

462

from Austria. Of course, your data will be cross-referenced with information from all over the country. The entire world, in fact. We will do our best. Good luck, Mrs. Gibson."

28

"We're going to start thinking about that second honeymoon trip to Hawaii for our twentieth anniversary. I know we have about three years yet, but it won't detract anything from it to be looking forward.to it." Buz was changing from his business suit for the evening's Bible study. "We probably could go now; but I figure if we give it a little more time, I will be able to get more put away for it. You know, so we can do it right while we're at it. No skimping. That debt is just about liquidated. Our breath will be our own again. And then we will celebrate. Might come back home by way of Europe and make a few stops along the way. Paris, London, Rome— the works. How does that sound?"

"Need you ask? You know there's nothing I could like better." Bonnie made no attempt to disguise the excitement in her voice. Nor could she smother the sparkle in her eyes. In truth, her eyes still sparkled just looking at her husband.

How very fortunate I am, she mused, *when I chose to accept the ugly duckling the other girls rejected. Now their husbands are paunchy, balding and—well, just look at Buz.* She surveyed him appreciatively from head to toe.

Success had worked its wonders with the talented architect. Taking care to keep in shape, he was straight as a ramrod and trim in the middle as a twenty-year-old athlete. The streaks of silver, just beginning to highlight his sideburns, only enhanced the appearance of distinction that his self-respect, secure in the knowledge of his success,. had embellished. Even his short stature was obscured by the dignity of his bearing as he drew himself up to his full height. Bonnie had never been able to resist measuring him against all their old friends from past years as they had seen them from time to time. It was usually the latter who were found wanting.

Of the Walker three, only Reginald maintained the youthful physique and dashing appearance of the fun-loving young brothers. Bonnie assumed it was because he had the good fortune of a petite wife who regimented her own diet and grooming to maintain her professional image as a performer, and probably exerted considerable influence in the same areas over her husband. Ron, the theology professor, showed evidence that he spent too much of his time presiding at his desk. Apparently the walk from his apartment on campus to the classroom was too short to discourage the thickness creeping about his middle, and his dark brown waves had nearly all waved good-bye. The most talented of the three, Royle seemed to have molded himself to the stereotyped artist, now sporting enormous wire-rimmed spectacles and long, straight hair. Having never married, he had long ago made his home in New York City's Greenwich Village and made his fortune sketching illustrations for a famous fashion magazine. Rarely if ever seen by his old circle of friends, he was reported by the favored few to have become as eccentric as his life-style suggested.

Dave Fisher, slight of frame to begin with, had continued expanding with the years, though horizontally rather than vertically. And he was doing well to coax a few hairs up over an ever widening part. He, with his wife, had found greener pastures in a famous clinic in the midwest, and they rarely were seen in Pittsburgh.

Of the girls, Ruth Konovich appeared to have suffered the least satisfying life of any of the old gang. Having married in Florida at the completion of her airline training, she transferred to Chicago with her husband. But her long hours airborne had not contributed to a compatible marriage, and it was soon dissolved. Finally she resettled in Pittsburgh at a desk job, youthfulness gone and hard lines developing around the firm set of her once lovely lips. The dark locks of silken hair rapidly turned to silver, the once shapely figure became stooped, and her clothing, though smart and stylish, seemed ill-fitting.

Drew and Irene Fisher Anderson remained as they had established themselves in Pittsburgh, reared three children, and managed to retain some youthfulness themselves, either because of or in spite of it. However, after the architecture firm dissolved, they were rarely seen by their old circle of friends.

Dr. and Mrs. Courtney had remained stalwart pillars in the Emmanuel Tabernacle and were beginning to age gracefully. He had presented a striking, dignified, proud appearance as he escorted a tall, elegant, and radiantly beautiful Lisa down the aisle to be joined in marriage with a young surgeon.

Nancy and Gilbert, with their delightful twins, had long since followed God's call to minister among the Hispanics in Southern California and had not been in Pennsylvania for a number of years. When last seen thereabouts, it was evident that under Nancy's diligent adherence to good health practices, Gilbert had been the only one among their acquaintances who, having begun heavier, had ended lighter. Plucky Lucky and Bonnie still corresponded regularly, and the former's letters never ceased to exude the aura of bubbling exuberance with which their author had faced all of life.

Yes, Bonnie thought, as Buz stooped to tie his shoelaces, *I'll take him any day over the whole lot of all who were available when I made my choice.*

The Bible study that evening was going to be a very special occasion. Though Sylvia, after much prevailing upon by her mother and sister and a considerable amount of prayer, had now attended intermittently for a number of months, it was only for this gathering that James Lake had ever succumbed to his wife's coaxing. And the womenfolk and Buz hoped desperately that Perry would deign to put in an appearance. But, as usual, a finger could not be definitely placed upon the younger man. His parents had long despaired that he would ever become stabilized, marry, and put down roots.

If it weren't gratifying enough to anticipate her own family's attendance, Bonnie had reason to hope that her neighbor would also appear. She had often invited Mrs. Morrow to avail herself of their fellowship, but whether for ill health or shyness, or both, the reclusive friend always declined. Now she had given a half promise, based on the state of her back when it would be time to assemble. Bonnie flew down the stairs at the first ring of the bell and eagerly threw open the door to welcome the old lady.

"I'm so glad you've come." Bonnie tried not to sound overly enthusiastic. "Come right in. I believe this chair over by the mantle would probably be the most comfortable for you."

The older woman's eyes took in every detail of the colorful, restful room appreciatively. "How elegant, but cozy your home is. Just what I would expect of you, my dear."

"Why, thank you. How silly of me to forget this is the first time you've been in." Bonnie was leading Mrs. Morrow to the seat by the mantle as she talked.

Suddenly the other woman stopped, her eyes arrested by Mimi's portrait on the mantle. For a long moment she gazed transfixed, agitatedly fingering the rosary she held in her hand. It was then that Bonnie's attention was drawn to it. *Should I tell her,* she wondered, *we don't use that when we pray?* Her better judgment decided against it.

It was her own dear parents with Sylvia who arrived next. And wonder of all wonders Perry, looking somewhat reluctant, brought up the rear. Introductions were scarcely completed when the usual group of neighbors and old friends had assembled, and all must be repeated. The little living and dining rooms were strained to capacity by the time all were seated, and Buz had difficulty finding a spot where he could be seen and heard by everyone from which to read the Holy Word.

"Our study tonight is going to be taken from the first chapter of Ephesians, verses three to seven," he began earnestly. "Blessed be the God and Father of our Lord Jesus Christ, who hath blessed us with all spiritual blessings in heavenly places in Christ: according as he hath chosen us in him before the foundation of the world, that we should be holy and without blame before him in love: having predestinated us unto the adoption of children by Jesus Christ to himself, according to the good pleasure of his will, to the praise of the glory of his grace, wherein he hath made us accepted in the beloved. In whom we have redemption through his blood, the forgiveness of sins, according to the riches of his grace."

Strange how every word comes out distinctly when he is reading the Bible, thought his proud wife. *Or is it because I know so well what his next word is going to be?*

And then James Lake interrupted him.

"I just don't see how you all can profess to serve a God who is as choosy as that. Don't you say that He accepts everyone who comes to Him, and then you turn around and say that He just predestines *some*—adopting them just as we chose only certain children to adopt ourselves. We certainly didn't adopt every kid born that year."

It was Bonnie who replied slowly.

"Dad, I don't remember it, but you have told me how I screamed in terror the first time I saw you. But you returned to the orphanage and brought me some little toy a couple times until I could get used to you. Gradually you broke down my fear and strangeness until when I finally accepted you, I couldn't be wrenched away from you. I could have remained fearful, refused your attentions, and perhaps jeopardized forever the opportunity you were offering. But I didn't. It is so in the Christian realm. Actually, God chooses everyone, but of all those to whom He offers, only those who receive His overtures are adopted. And you are being chosen when you are given the opportunity."

"Yes, but if you are going to make that comparison, let me remind you that you were in very desperate circumstances. You would probably have welcomed anything."

"Exactly. The very condition lost mankind is in without God. The only trouble is, most of us choose to continue in a wretched condition. We don't avail ourselves of the opportunity to be adopted when it is given to us. Let me repeat, you are being chosen when you are given the opportunity, as you are right now."

Silence reigned in the rooms for several seconds as many bowed their heads in prayer. Bonnie noted the intent expression on the face of Mrs. Morrow and the tear that glistened in her eye as she earnestly fingered one after the other of the beads of her rosary. And then James spoke quietly.

"All right, I see it now. What I have been fighting all these years, I see, is answered by comparing a heavenly Father with what I myself am here on earth. When He adopts, I'll sign the papers myself."

Avonelle threw her arms about her husband and wept joyfully upon his neck, while Buz instructed him in the two-millenia-old sinners' prayer. And then when he lifted his face, beaming in the relief of forgiven sin, he turned to his own son.

"How about you, too, Perry? You need this as well as I. Only you are fortunate in that you don't have to waste most of your life before you find it. There certainly isn't any better time than now."

Perry shifted his feet and dropped his eyes. He looked as though he were wishing he was any place but there at that moment.

"I don't know, Dad. Actually, I have plenty of time. I'll do it someday. But not just yet."

Buz felt inclined to press the issue, but seeing the bland look upon his brother-in-law's face, thought better of it. He couldn't, however, shake the conviction that underneath the stolid expression a real battle was being waged. Surely the Lord was dealing with the boy. Dare Perry refuse to accept? Buz could only pray that the Holy Spirit's persistence would wear down his procrastination before Perry was beyond the point at which he could listen.

Bonnie turned quietly to Sylvia and attempted to press her for a commitment.

"Oh, I guess I will sometime, too," the darker one replied rather flippantly. "But if Perry's got time yet, so have I."

The meeting then continued with its usual give-and-take of ideas and sharing of the past week's experiences. With mixed emotions the Rockwells stood at the door to bid their guests farewell. They rejoiced that James had at last found his way into the fold, but their hearts were heavy for his other children.

One by one each worshiper filed out until at last Mrs. Morrow rose to make her exit. Bonnie happened to be looking in her direction when the older lady attempted to raise herself out of the easy chair; and for a moment it looked as though she wasn't going to make it. Bonnie, rushing to her aid, offered her arm. Solid of build that she was, she pulled heavily, attempting to steady herself. *Her back again*, thought Bonnie. But Mrs. Morrow seemed not to be able to lift her feet. With a slow, shuffling step she dragged on Bonnie's arm across the floor.

"I'm sorry the meeting was so long. You must be very cramped," Bonnie offered solicitously.

"Oh, no, not at all. I enjoyed every minute of it. This—this has been like this for I guess several weeks now. I didn't think much about it at first. Thought I was tired or something. But it is getting worse. The bottoms of my feet are numb and sometimes I just can't pick them up."

They had reached the door and Bonnie continued out with her and down the steps and across the walk.

"Several weeks? You never mentioned it; I didn't realize."

"Oh, I didn't want to concern you with it. I'm sure it will pass. You know, I can't expect much at my age and what with all that back trouble I've had all these years."

"Nonsense. It isn't something that you just let pass. You shall go to see the doctor tomorrow."

But the doctor listened for a couple minutes and sent them to a neurologist. Before the day was over, Mrs. Morrow was admitted to the hospital for tests. Bonnie drove her back home to make preparation before entering.

"Now, dear, if you will just run up to the nightstand by my bed and get the prayer book lying there. And make sure you get my rosary into my bag. I can't go without that."

"Of course not. And we'll stop on the way and find you several pretty nighties. We'll make the doctors take notice."

"Of a crumpled-up has-been like me! One more

471

thing. I feel as if I'm being very demanding, but will you please see that they don't take off my locket." She cupped her hand protectively around a gold pendant hanging from a fragile gold chain. On its face was a delicate miniature of an old-fashioned lady surrounded by exquisite filigree. Bonnie suddenly realized she had seen that necklace on the woman every time she had spoken with her. Apparently she never removed it. Stefiania had never once spoken of having had a husband, but a tiny, plain gold band on the left hand bore evidence. Was it his picture she guarded so lovingly?

"I'll do my best. But I can't promise they will listen."

"But I just can't bear to part with it. I fear that if they take it, I'll never get it back."

"Please don't worry about it. I'm sure they would put it in a safe place; but I will speak to them."

Bonnie spent as much of the next two days with her neighbor as she could spare from her duties at home. She listened sympathetically as Mrs. Morrow told of the long needle that had been inserted repeatedly up and down the muscles of her legs. And she watched as a nurse brought a rubber ball for her to squeeze in her hands. Stefiania began to tire of the constant aggravations. But not a word fell from the lips of the attendants concerning the suspicions that prompted their examinations.

"Are you related to her?" the nurse asked Bonnie at the end of the second day.

"No, but I do look after her. She has no one else."

"Well, then, Dr. Johnson would probably want you present tomorrow when he gives her the results of the tests, and then she will be released."

Bonnie arrived early the next morning so as not to miss the conference. She too was exhausted by that time and wondered how she could get herself into such a position just by practicing the gift of helps. Was it worth all this? Surely she had enough to do to look after her own family.

"We don't know what causes these things, although we are trying to gather some information and do some research." The doctor was speaking gently, but impersonally. "At this point we can only say there seems to be some evidence that it can be initiated by an injury to the back. Not always, but it has been known to result in those with injuries. The prognosis, of course, is not good. It is a gradual deterioration that can lead only downward. At this time there is no cure. The particular type you have is known as amyotropic lateral sclerosis, a form of nerve deterioration leading to the atrophy of muscles. It is very rare, but no less devastating for its rarity. Fortunately, there is little or no pain connected with it—other than what you already had before the onset of the disease. The only pain you will know is that of the spirit as you find your body responds less and less to your commands. Now the first thing we will do is provide you with a walker. When that is no longer sufficient, we may try some braces. Usually it is a wheelchair before the end comes. Pardon me if I'm blunt, but it is better that you know the facts. You may not have much time. The average is six months to three years, although we have a patient right now who has been afflicted for ten years. She is not what you would call good, but she is managing."

The doctor appeared to be finished. But he read and answered the unworded question in both the women's eyes.

"The end is usually easy. I know of one patient who was sitting in a chair talking when her head just dropped over on her chest. Now if you will wait a moment, I'll have a walker brought around for you. You will have to adjust to life as you now find it. There is nothing we can do for you except help you live with it."

Until you die with it, Bonnie thought ruefully. She had her work cut out for her now, as Stefiania certainly would not be able to afford a nursing home. Maybe Bonnie could locate George and Shirley and summon them back here when things got worse. In the meantime, her neighbor would probably be able to get along well enough with the walker.

She settled the lady comfortably in her home, after ascertaining that the refrigerator was well stocked with food and that clean clothes were available. She had flopped wearily on her own sofa when the phone rang.

"Bonnie!" Avonelle's voice was high pitched and strained. "I've tried all morning to get you. I was getting frantic wondering where on earth—well, it's Perry. Oh, Bonnie, he was *killed* last night!" The anguish in her voice wrenched Bonnie's spirit as nothing had since the death of her own tiny son.

"Say no more. I'll be right over." Numbly she fumbled in her purse again for the car key. Were the crises in her life never to end?

"Now tell me all about it," she resumed as she hurried into the apartment twenty minutes later.

"He was delivering a prescription to an address out in Dormont. Somewhere around one this morning. The fellow who hit him claims, of course, that he had the green light, but whatever else Perry might have been, he wasn't a careless driver. And the other fellow definitely was drunk. And Bonnie, you know Perry wasn't even saved."

The daughter could only reach out in mute agony as her mother doubled over in grief.

"Your father and I had to go to the hospital to identify him. I would have called you, but I figured you might as well finish the night's sleep. Then I couldn't get you later. Don't ever let me have to go through that again. You watch them pull back the sheet and then—" Avonelle's body was shaken with a paroxysm of grief.

"His face was only half there, but the hair—I knew it

had to be Perry with the strawberry blonde curls. Oh, my poor boy. What have I done wrong?"

"Nothing, Mother." Bonnie was surprised at the calmness in her voice. She certainly wasn't feeling calm. Somehow she had to help these two parents get through this terrible day—Avonelle, and James who sat in his favorite chair, silent and unseeing.

She never did know how they got through the day. Buz left the office to accompany them to the funeral home, fortunately having been alerted hours before his scheduled departure for Kansas City. Together they chose the casket, bought a new suit, and purchased a cemetery lot.

And, not surprisingly, Bonnie dreamed the dream again that night. This time the voice resembled Avonelle's, rising with intensity with each repetition of the name, "Marya." When it reached a frenzied pitch that seemed to emanate from right next to her ear, she awoke in a cold sweat. Unable to steady herself enough to sleep again, she tossed until she awakened Buz. Together they made their way downstairs for a cup of coffee.

The next day, she forced herself to look for a suitable dress in which to receive friends at the funeral parlor. And taking several out on approval, she carried them to Avonelle. But the latter only looked at them blankly and shook her head. Bonnie had to choose herself and hope that when her mother's spirits revived she wouldn't dislike her choice.

With dark circles under their eyes and an unsteady step, the two women, with Sylvia and James, made their way into the parlor to face a closed casket. Bonnie was thankful for Pastor Rogers's encouraging words, but she knew that all the words in the world wouldn't atone for the unforgiven sin with which Perry had died. Had he had any time at all to reach out for mercy before the moment of impact? They would never know in this life.

Bonnie couldn't help being amazed at the number of old friends and acquaintances who came to pay their respects. It seemed that the entire congregation of their church on the North Side appeared, as well as business associates of Buz's, her parents' neighbors, the men with whom James worked at the steel mill, everyone it seemed with whom they had ever remotely had contact. It was too bad it takes a death to make you realize just how great is the army of well-wishers that a person has in this life.

When it seemed that the room was packed to capacity, Sylvia suddenly dashed out from the crowd and flung herself prostrate before the coffin, weeping convulsively. Fortunately only those who were closest took any notice, but they seemed ill at ease, uncertain what to do.

Oh, no, Bonnie groaned inwardly. *Not any theatrics here, Sylvia. It might be just like you, but this isn't the place for it.* But she was rooted to the spot, incapable of making a move toward the distraught girl. Sylvia had planted herself squarely on both knees and cradling her face in her hands, leaned forward until her head nearly scraped the floor. Gratefully, Bonnie watched the pastor make his way toward her, drop beside her, and gently nudge her shoulder. There the two remained several moments in quiet conversation. Eventually, they rose; Sylvia retreated to a settee against the wall, and sat quietly until visiting hours were over, and all the callers had departed.

When only the family remained, she gathered them about her while she stated simply, through shining eyes, "I have asked Jesus into my heart. I see now just how fragile life is. Perry waited too long; I dare not."

"Oh, thank God," her mother breathed with an embrace. And when she released her, James enfolded her in his own arms.

"I'll grieve throughout this life for my boy, but I'm thankful if his passing has brought at least you to this point."

"Really, it wasn't only that. I've been thinking about it for a long time. When I see how truly happy Bonnie and Buz are, and I know it is only because Christ is in their lives, and then I look at my own wretched life, I've known for some time I was at a dead end until I made things right. I only fear that if I had taken the step last Monday night, it might have encouraged Perry, and although the same thing would probably have happened, we could be assured he is in heaven."

With great effort James replied, "We can only leave that in God's hands."

The three women were sitting around the table in Avonelle's cheerful kitchen on the evening following the funeral, writing acknowledgments. Bonnie glanced with amazement at her sober sister diligently checking addresses in the phone book. She was sure this must be the longest period of time Sylvia had ever sat still in one place. Impishly she couldn't resist comparing her with the Gadarene demoniac recorded in the fifth chapter of the book of Mark, who, when the devils that once possessed him had entered the swine and driven them to their deaths in the sea, had himself sat clothed and in his right mind. That seemed to describe this once flighty woman for the moment. But Bonnie was sure her tempestuous sister had a long way to go. Her prayers for her weren't ended—perhaps they should be only starting.

Avonelle wiped a tear as she wrote "Perry C. Lake," on another card inscribed with "The family of . . . ." Then, laying down her pen, she fixed her gaze somewhere over the heads of her two daughters and nowhere in particular. Her voice was hollow, distant.

"I keep trying to remind myself that I didn't give him birth; that since I only had him for a while to bring up, I shouldn't feel as bad as though he had been a part of me. But it doesn't work. He was every bit mine, just as much as though he were the product of my body. I remember that wretched little soul with the forlorn look on his face who was handed to me that day. He was so accustomed to being just passed around that he hadn't learned yet what it was to be really loved and have a stable home. But by the time he knew, he had become so much a part of me I forgot I hadn't given him birth."

"Even those who are born to us are only on loan. They are never really ours." Bonnie hoped Avonelle remembered she was speaking from her own grievous experience, she who had produced a son of her own body, flesh of her flesh, and blood of her blood, and then saw him snatched from her after so little a time. She longed to remind her mother that at least Avonelle had been privileged to witness her son's growth to manhood, and Bonnie had been denied even that consolation, but this did not seem to be the time. Avonelle was faced also with the dread of never seeing her son again, whereas Bonnie anticipated the moment when she would be reunited with Timothy for eternity.

But Bonnie understood for the first time something she had never before been able to comprehend. Avonelle's maternal instincts and affection for her adopted children were every bit as tenacious as her own for her natural children. And now Bonnie knew why her mother would have felt threatened had she mentioned looking for her natural parents. Avonelle would see no need for Bonnie ever to look for more than she herself had provided.

When flight 181 originating in Pittsburgh landed at Burlington, Vermont, two days after the funeral, Sylvia escorted her two daughters down the ramp. She had tormented herself during the entire flight with an unsuccessful attempt to stifle the memories of that nightmarish trip she had made on a wintry day several years ago. What a fool she had been then, and now she had all the rest of her life to regret it. When the plane touched down on a sunny, summer afternoon, she breathed silently. *Well, Hal Gregersen, here comes the world's most colossal fool.*

From the time she started to pack, she had debated over the best way to approach her estranged husband. Go straight to the house and just let him find her sitting there when he left work in the afternoon? Make an appointment with him through his secretary for lunch? Or check in at a hotel and phone him herself to ask for a date that evening? None of the possibilities really sat well. At best it was going to be a gamble.

She did take a room in a hotel to freshen up. She was not fooled about her youthful beauty's slipping away. She understood all too well that what looks remained required diligence and careful attention. At least she had cut that luxurious fall of raven hair about three years back when she complained of frequent headaches and the doctor advised her to take the weight off her head. Now she had taken care before she left Pittsburgh to visit a beautician and have her locks snipped into the neatest blow-dry style possible with the amount of curls that still wanted to do their own thing. With a final dab of lipstick, a fresh resolution to bolster her apprehensive spirits, and an admonition to the girls to stay put until she returned, she phoned for a taxi.

The receptionist at the office of Paramount Plastics informed her Mr. Gregersen already had an appointment for lunch, but that he would see her for a few minutes in his office.

"Well, if it isn't *Miz* Sylvia Gregersen!" Hal's tone was sarcastic as she seated herself unbidden in a chair opposite the desk. "Something concerning the children, I presume?"

"Certainly in a way it does, but it is more specifically

about you and me, Hal. I know I've been a stupid fool, and I don't blame you for hating me" (she astounded herself that she had ever come to the place where she would admit it), "but I have given my heart to Jesus. You know, I'm now a Christian like the Rockwells and Mom—and now Dad, also. I believe I've really learned my lesson and I would like to come back home and behave myself."

She fidgeted nervously for what seemed like an eternity while he regarded her very aloofly. Then pushing his chair back for emphasis, he replied deliberately and coldly: "That's a switch. First Bonnie couldn't have me because she was a Christian, and now you want to come back because you are."

"I agree it sounds rather confusing, but please believe me, I mean every word of it. Couldn't you give me just one chance to try again? I promise you I'll do everything in my power to try to make it up to you."

"My dear Mrs. Gregersen—" he was talking condescendingly as though she were a child. "I guess I must inform you I have sold the house, disposed of everything except a few pieces that I've moved into the apartment where Harry and I hang our hats, and—" he stopped as though to savor the pained look on her face and emphasize his final words—"I've filed for divorce. Grounds? Separation, of course. What do you expect after seven years?"

"We could get a new house, buy some furniture, and start all over again. In the meantime the girls and I could move into your apartment to wait—"

"There isn't room."

"Not even for your daughters?"

Again that cold, calculating look.

"Does that mean you are giving me custody?"

"That wasn't what I had in mind. I mean, with us back together again there won't be need of custody—

Please?" Sylvia's voice began to sound pleading.

Hal rose from his chair, shook his head cynically, pursed his lips, and pulling back his coat, hooked his thumbs in his belt.

"No."

It was spoken with a finality that the simplest of souls could comprehend.

Stiffly she arose, and her voice was choked.

"I'll be in the Downtowner in case you'd like to call."

There was no answer. Numbed, Sylvia somehow found the door. Back in the hotel room she sent Jennifer and Veronica to the dining room while she sat in semi-shock for the remainder of the afternoon. By the time the shadows began to stretch lengthwise she had cleared the cobwebs sufficiently from her mind that she could begin to plan her next step with rationality.

Somehow she would have to try to win Hal back—maybe through the children. She knew it was a wild idea, but just possibly she *could* give him custody, and then when she had visiting rights, she could go to the apartment and hang around enough to let him know she wasn't the same old, flippant, selfish Sylvia. Yes, somehow, some way, with the Lord's help, she would win him back.

29

It was several months later when Bonnie was taking Mrs. Morrow to be fitted for braces that the latter brought up the subject. She had become the most enthusiastic supporter of the weekly Bible study. There she sat throughout each session fingering every bead of her rosary, and listening intently to every word that was uttered. She gave her most rapt attention, sometimes with a tear in her eye, to the latest guests to find salvation and who were very eager to express their joy and gratitude in the Lord.

"Bonnie," Stefiania drew her attention as she nosed the wheels onto the Boulevard of the Allies, "tell me one thing: how is it that you and the people who attend your evening study can feel so confident about your sins' being forgiven? I have tried these forty years to find forgiveness, but I guess my crime was too great, and God can't bother with me now. I say the rosary over and over again, all ten Hail Marys, and the five Our Fathers. I have placed candles before the Blessed Virgin, and I go to confession regularly for absolution, but none of it seems to get me anywhere. I guess what I have done can't be forgiven in this life."

"Nonsense! Don't you know that the apostle Paul claimed to be the greatest sinner? And you know how God turned him around and began to use him. Now, if a fiend like what he had been could be used in writing down the tenets of our faith—which I would think was one of the most important assignments any human being ever had—it makes it difficult for any of us to think we are past being forgiven."

"Yes, but was he guilty of murder, also?"

"Have you forgotten that the reason he was on the road to Damascus when he had his conversion experience was that he was even then transporting official documents to condemn Christians to death? Whether or not he drew the sword or lit the fire under the stake, he was as much a murderer as those who did so." Bonnie suddenly peered keenly at her neighbor. "Murder, did you say?"

"Yes. Murder. That's what I am—a murderess. I can hardly bear to speak of it, but I feel that I must do *something* to find peace about it. I have not mentioned it to a soul except the priest, but I haven't much time in this world and I wish to be able to rest in peace when I go."

"I can understand your desire for that; but I can't imagine why you would think of yourself as a murderess."

"Because I am one." Visibly forcing her mouth to open and form some words, she took a deep breath and began rather haltingly.

"It was in the concentration camp. You know, when you're there and the world is upside down, you get stripped of every shred of dignity and self-respect you ever had. And you do things you would not do under ordinary circumstances. But here I am justifying myself, and I know I can't do that. I'll try to give you just the facts.

"Really, it began before I ever was taken to that—that despicable place. It was in the early months of the war. Once the Nazis felt they had pretty well wiped out Poland, the soldiers roamed the streets, intent on any mischief they could imagine. They thought that they could—well—being victors and all, they now took the spoils, what was left of the rubble and the wretched Poles who remained.

"I was hurrying down the street to the university to try to get my husband's papers, although if I'd known then what I know now, that wouldn't have been necessary. The Germans even closed the university after the war. And I can't imagine they gave much thought to the papers that were there. Well, anyway, I never made it."

She stopped speaking, seemingly to gather courage to continue.

"And so you were out on the street." Bonnie couldn't bear to miss the rest of the narration.

"Yes, the worst place to be, because those soldiers didn't care where it was. They were going to take what they wanted, no matter what. First he grabbed me from behind—mind you, I was very fleet footed and could have gotten away from him if I'd even known he was coming—and then threw me down on the street. And those awful eyes looking right through me. I hate to say it, but over the years every time I've looked at George, I've seen that horrid character again. The mountain of blonde hair, and steely eyes like lights in the night. You know George and that soldier are both Germans. I had to keep reminding myself that George was George, and not a German soldier. But I can see that man yet if I close my eyes, sneering down at me, leering with those wicked eyes, and ripping off what little clothes I managed to have on my back."

Is this one more torment that this poor woman has had to live through? Bonnie asked herself. To be reminded of that ignominious scene every time she gazed on the only person she had to call her own in the world? And how much had George read revulsion in her expression, directed not at him, but probably not realizing that it wasn't. Surely it was not without its effect on him, though his aunt willed it or not. The web of tragedy seemed only to tighten around these people the more she knew about them.

"He carried a bayonet, the kind of a gun with a sword on the end of it. If I had resisted, he most certainly would have used it. And I wouldn't have been the first Polish woman to meet that fate." Bitterness darkened Mrs. Morrow's face. "For myself I wouldn't have cared. In fact, it would have been a blessing. I didn't know what had become of my poor Peter." (She cupped the locket again in her hand.) "But I felt deep in my heart I would never see him again. So although I would have been contented enough to meet death at that vile man's hand, I felt that I had to live for that—that other one." She had dropped her voice to a whisper.

Bonnie sympathized once more as she brought into focus the remorse Stefiania must have known to learn that the nephew for whom she had sacrificed so much would then turn out the wrong way. She began to wonder whether she could ever condemn anyone for anything again. Unfortunately, the two had reached the out-patient clinic, and the conversation must be dropped for a while. Bonnie had never waited so restlessly for anyone; she still hadn't heard the important part of the story. She even feared Mrs. Morrow would not care to resume the subject when she returned from her fitting, and that she might never know what it was that made the old lady feel so guilty.

But she needn't have worried. After she had helped the woman laboriously climb into the car with her cumbersome new braces, the latter leaned back and closed her eyes.

"Now, then, to get on with it. Let's see now, where was I? Oh, yes, I didn't fight it, and my poor Peter died never knowing I was to bear another man's son. I nearly died in delivery, and I hoped desperately the little fellow

485

wouldn't survive either without proper care. The doctors were all at the front, you know. But there was a midwife down the street who managed to pull us both through. She told me I had a fine, beautiful son, but I couldn't bear to look at him. I cared for him as best I could without really seeing him—you understand when I looked at him I would see his father. And he was a little past two when we were taken to that awful camp. I could barely manage to find enough rags to cover his thin little body, and I knew he would only starve to death anyway if he didn't freeze first. So I tried to think of a way to dispose of him.

"It wasn't hard. They came every morning and called out a list of numbers. The Jewish people, you understand. 'To be located elsewhere,' they told us. But rumors had spread, and we all knew they were going to the gas chamber. So one day as I watched the wretched, condemned people file out as their numbers were called, I waited until a young woman passed and thrust the baby into her arms. She looked startled for a moment, and then my purpose dawned on her. She turned her glazed eyes to me for only a second, nodded, and grasped the baby. I only hope it was quick and painless."

A sob wrenched itself loose from her pitiful frame, and Bonnie tried to think of something consoling to say. But by the time anything came to mind, the elder one was continuing.

"I have often thought what a comfort and help to me that one might have been in later years. After all, he was my son—my only son—and surely with time and an ocean between here and the scene of his conception, I could have forgotten some of it. But at the time I doubted whether I myself would survive the camp. Hundreds died of disease, filth, and starvation every day, even if they weren't sent to the gas chamber. Anyway, I've had these many years to feel not only guilt, but grief.

Oh, Bonnie, it's almost more than I can bear!"

"I'm sure it certainly is," Bonnie murmured. She paused for a moment. "But the good thing about it is you don't have to bear it yourself. You can just turn it all over to Jesus. He said we are to cast our care upon Him, because He cares for us. You do believe that, don't you?"

"I just don't know any more what to believe."

They had reached the house by that time, and after leading Stefiania up her steps and seeing her comfortably seated in her favorite chair, Bonnie reached for the little New Testament she always carried in her purse. Flipping quickly through the pages, she turned to the book of Romans.

"I'll tell you what, you read here, and every place it says 'whosoever' or 'thou' or such pronouns, put your own name in it."

"I'm not that good at reading in English." Mrs. Morrow's small laugh was from embarrassment.

"Please just try it. You might do better than you think you can."

"All right." Her eyes dropped to the lines Bonnie was pointing out with her finger. "That if—Stefiania—shall con-confess with thy—her—mouth the Lord Jesus and shalt believe in thine—her—heart that God hath raised him from the dead, thou—Stefiania—shall be saved." Bonnie's finger skipped a few lines. "For who—Stefiania—shall call upon the name of the Lord shall be saved. What do you mean, 'saved'?"

"That is what you are looking for. Saved from the judgment to come and freedom from the guilt of sin in this life. What did that passage say to you?"

"Why, it says—it says—" she fell silent a few moments as she studied the passage. "If you confess, you are—s-saved."

"And have you confessed?"

"Over and over again. I have kissed the feet of the

Virgin and said every 'Hail Mary' more times than—"

Bonnie leaned over to grasp the older woman's hand as she interrupted. "First Timothy two, five tells us Jesus Christ is the only mediator between God and man. And in Romans we read that Jesus is able also to save those that come to God *by Him,* and that He ever lives to make intercession for them. Mrs. Morrow, do you believe this?"

"I-I—"

"If we throw out this wonderful promise, we have to throw out all the rest of God's Word. We haven't anything on which to stand. Else how would you know what to believe and what to throw out?"

Mrs. Morrow's eyes widened as illumination gradually penetrated her understanding. Hesitantly she asked, "Believe. Is that all?"

"That is what God has promised. And we are told in Scripture at least three times that He cannot lie."

"Then I believe."

No bells rang, no lightning branded the cloudless sky, and there were no earthquakes in the eastern United States. But from that day forward a glow began to emanate from the war-wearied, misery-inscribed face, a delight to Bonnie and a tribute to the transforming power of the Lord Jesus Christ. It was as though an uncomfortable, tight-fitting garment fell from the tired shoulders of the guilt-laden sufferer, and she began to relax and enjoy the caressing assurances of forgiveness from Him to whom she had petitioned for so long. As she experienced His forgiveness and began to forgive herself, she felt a quickening in her body that relaxed the tension of damaged muscles; and although she continued to lose tone and mobility, the pain with which she had lived for forty years began to subside. Eventually the headaches ceased altogether, and she came to realize the truth of the doctors' prediction that though gradually becoming debilitated, the only distress she would know was that of the mind as the body would not respond to her bidding.

But the more she felt her physical powers slipping from her, the more her neighbor offered her aid. Bonnie was thankful Miriam was capable of assuming many of her own household tasks, for her energies were needed next door. And thankfully, even Peter found more profitable ways to channel his own boundless supply as he began to mature. Thus, life in the two households settled more or less into a steady routine as the months wended their way into eternity.

The one grief that marred the scene of domestic contentment was the inexorable fact of Mrs. Morrow's relentless deterioration. If ever Bonnie felt inclined to become impatient with her voluntary servitude, a nervous check of the calendar dispelled any such thoughts. Surely it would not be long. Three years, they had said, was the average. In no time, it seemed, two had evaporated. Of course, it could be longer, but the most superficial of examinations of the afflicted body would dispel any hope. Bonnie began to entertain some concern as to what she could expect next. When the old lady actually became confined to a wheelchair, which could not be far in the distance, how could she manage the two households then? Or even the lady herself?

Bonnie had never known the exact state of the Morrow financial affairs. However, she did not need to ask to recognize that Stefania had brought nothing with her when she entered this country following her liberation. And most of George's adult years had been spent in prison. There was no hope of an income that would permit admittance to a nursing home. Perhaps the only hope lay in George himself. Or Shirley, as the case would be. How was Bonnie to find out where they could be located? She feared the subject would bring distress to her charge, not for their own sakes, but for hers. Should

Mrs. Morrow ever suspect that Bonnie wondered how she would be able to manage when the end was near, Stefiania would fret herself sick that Bonnie should be so imposed upon. Bonnie would simply have to exercise discretion.

It was not many days before she received the answer. Carrying in the mail one morning she noticed an envelope with a foreign stamp. Curious, she opened it, as that simple act was becoming difficult for the limp hands, and held it out for the invalid.

"I see it is from Shirley and George. Do they send good news?"

A quick scan was all that she was obliged to wait for before receiving her answer.

"Yes, in a way, you would say it was good. Perhaps. You see, in this country, George has a record. An unfortunate one, that is. It is impossible for him to find decent employment. But that record really is under a false name, you remember. He hoped his father might be found, although heaven only knows where or if that's possible. But the most likely chances are he would be in Germany if he is still living. Therefore, as soon as George was released from his parole, he left for Germany in the hope of finding him, reestablishing himself as his Polish-born German son with the name of George Schmidt, and making a new life for himself, leaving his old record on the other side of the world. I only hope for his sake he is successful. This—" she waved the paper in the air, "—this simply informs me that he has arrived safely and leaves no forwarding address, as he doesn't know where his search will take him."

"I see." Bonnie knew it was a weak reply, and she had no way of knowing what the tone of her voice would convey to her hearer. For she didn't know whether her disinterest in the saga of George Morrow Schmidt, or her concern about what she was to do with his invalid aunt, was the greater. At least one thing was certain. She, Bonnie Rockwell, of no more connection than that of a mere neighbor, and that through her family's personal misfortune, was to have the sole responsibility for this woman until her end. To cast her upon the charity of the welfare system was unthinkable.

As though she read her thoughts, which Bonnie hoped fervently she could not do, Stefania mused softly, "George is gone. That little one that I so cruelly disposed of—he is gone also. But God has seen my emptiness, and He has given me you. How good He is to this worthless creature." And with that, her head dropped on her chest.

With pulse pounding at her temples, Bonnie flew to her side. Hadn't they said she could just be sitting there and her head drop over? Surely not right now. Not this soon. Not this unexpectedly. No, Lord, please—not like this! With wildly trembling hand, Bonnie lifted the still chin. A faint smile fluttered across the worn face. Thank heaven she was still there! She had only temporarily bowed under the weight of tears. Gently Bonnie reached for a tissue and wiped them away.

Bonnie was thankful Buz came home that evening in a light mood. She needed something to dispel the heaviness of the strain that day had brought.

"Guess what, Honey!" He was whistling when he walked in the door. "There is to be an international building and trade show at Geneva, Switzerland, next summer. And who, would you like to make a wild guess, is the choice of representative to be sent by Cohen Associates? Good girl! You guessed it on first try. And do you know what else? All expenses are to be paid for representative and wife included! How does that sound? Two second honeymoons in the same year. Too good to be true."

He grabbed her like the eighteen-year-old for which

she still had the figure, and spun her around until she began to be dizzy.

"If I weren't familiar with the reputation for honesty enjoyed by N. G. Rockwell, Architect, I would fear that spirits had been imbibed in the office just before quitting time. Yes, Mr. Representative, it sounds too good to be true."

This wasn't the time to tell him that maybe it *was* too good to be true, that she was for some inscrutable reason saddled with an invalid neighbor until—until—when would the end come? Soon enough to release her from nursing duties that could prevent her making the coveted trip?

Stepping backward so as to take his full measure, she surveyed him with pride shining in her eyes.

"I surely picked the cream of the crop when I plucked you off the tree. Now just how do you propose getting in two second honeymoons in one year?"

"Oh, we'll plan the Hawaii trip for sometime in the fall, as I believe we were going to do the last time. In the meantime, we'll live it up in Europe in the middle of June. Incidentally—" he studied her closely for the effect. "—I'm beginning to see my way clear to leave this humble abode and build for ourselves again. Something to our liking, although probably not as spacious as Windy Knoll. After all, my dear Mrs. Rockwell, we're settling into middle age and we needn't expect any more family."

"How about grandchildren?" An impish gleam played in the corner of Bonnie's eye.

"Have it your way. Uh, one more thing. I'm also in a position now where I can choose to leave the firm and go into private practice again. Actually, I have sufficient reputation I could probably resettle elsewhere. Do you have any particular hankering for a change of scenery? South Carolina? The midwest? How about Florida where there seems to be development all the time?"

"Why—why I hadn't given it a thought. But I really have nothing against Pittsburgh. My folks are here, and now that I'm the only one around, I hate to leave them. They'll be needing us as they get on in years. Also, we have so many friends— But, please don't rush me with so much at once. I can only handle one excitement at a time."

30

Tears of fury burned Bonnie's eyes as she sped along the interstate. By what irony of fate must she endure yet this disappointment? She had seen it coming ever since Mrs. Morrow's condition had worsened until she was confined to a wheelchair. There was nothing to do then but take her right into the Rockwell home, procure a hospital bed that they placed in a corner of the dining room, and wait on her hand and foot. With some assistance she was still able to make her laborious way into the chair in the morning, where she sat before the television set or by the window during the day, and then return to the bed for the night. But she was obviously failing daily. Of late even her voice was weak. Bonnie often had to strain to catch the feeble words. It would not be long now.

She and Buz had at least been able to go out for dinner and a concert on the actual date of their twentieth anniversary. But the time of the Geneva trade fair crept on far too rapidly, and knowing the end for Mrs. Morrow must inevitably come soon, regardless of outside circumstances, she had kept an agitated eye on both the calendar and the patient. For a while she had entertained the idea of leaving the latter in the care of Miriam who, having graduated from high school several weeks previously, might have sufficed in a real emergency. But somehow her young shoulders didn't seem broad enough for so great a responsibility. Who could tell just when the real crisis might come?

Bonnie remembered the commencement with pride. The tall, young woman looking so much like herself at that age, yet possessing a distinct physical grace and a self-confident poise that modern girls seemed to have in abundance, yet she herself had lacked so sadly.

"Miriam Rockwell, with high honors," the superintendent had intoned as Mimi stepped lithely across the stage, tossing her long, straight brown hair. It seemed like only yesterday that Bonnie had been in the same position—and so much had taken place in her life since then. Only there had been no honors for her. Mimi must have inherited her brains from her father.

Miriam had sat with the invalid on this day long enough that Bonnie could make the trip to the airport, the one in which she had kissed Buz goodbye and then hurried to a window in a futile attempt to see the jet begin its hop to New York where Buz would make connections for the flight to Switzerland.

Buz's regret had been as deep as her own when he realized she could not accompany him. But his great love for her was founded upon the character that had been shaped in her submission to God; and in spite of his disappointment, he was constrained to be proud of her selfless ministration to one so desperately in need.

It wasn't fair, she told herself vehemently, foot heavy on the accelerator. All she had wanted was to serve the Lord in some manner. When she wasn't "called" into any "full-time service" as her friends had been, why didn't she just leave it at that? This idea of trying to be helpful in order to show Christ's love had more often than not just gotten her into inconvenience, to say the least. And now to miss out on such a coveted trip was inconceivable. She wasn't sure she could even be gracious to the old lady when she got back home.

"*Inasmuch as ye have done it unto the least of these . . . ye have done it unto Me,*" beat itself unbidden into some hidden recess of her mind. *Yes, I know, Lord. But You see Switzerland all the time. You know every snow-capped peak and every beautiful lake. I don't. Couldn't You have taken pity just this once?* "*Pure religion and undefiled before God and the Father is this, To visit the fatherless and widows in their affliction, and to keep himself unspotted from the world.*" The words seemed to well up from nowhere. *Sure, I know about keeping myself unspotted, and all that. That's easy. But do I have to look after the old ladies just to show that I have pure religion?*

In spite of the conviction that seared its way into her heart, Bonnie was not in a much better mood as she pulled the car up before the house and switched off the motor. Seeing her patient comfortable by the window, and Mimi engrossed in a magazine, she dismissed her daughter from nurse duty and made an honest attempt to wipe the frown from her face. Knowing her manner was still too brusque, she hated herself for not acting in a more Christian demeanor; but this disappointment was almost more than she could cope with. Clearly she needed a few more rough edges polished off before she could hope to bear the image of Christ. Her one redeeming feature was that she and Buz had carefully concealed from Mrs. Morrow the fact that Bonnie had been invited on the trip also. They had known her resulting remorse would have been an unfair burden to impose in what must surely be her last days.

"Bonnie, dear," the weak voice from the wheelchair was barely audible, "it grieves me to see you so sad, but take heart; he'll come back."

So! She recognized Bonnie's irritation but misinterpreted its source. Perhaps it was just as well. Bonnie looked at her callously, not trusting herself to speak.

"Maybe it would be some consolation to you to remind yourself how fortunate you are that he will soon return. I would give all the world if my husband could have done so. But he went away and never came back."

The feeble hand stole up to the chain about the neck and enclosed the tiny gold case that hung on it, the locket around which Bonnie had to work every time she bathed her patient. She supposed there was nothing to do but bury it with her when the time came. Suddenly Bonnie was alerted to the significance of the gesture.

"Your locket has your husband's picture in it, doesn't it?"

"Yes, my dear Peter. I would have lost it in that loathsome prison but for my hair. They ordered us to take off everything until we stood there naked, more embarrassed than I'd ever been in my life. But they never thought about the two heavy braids I had wound about my head in those days. I had plaited the chain right in and hidden the locket with my wedding band under one braid before I went past the guards."

"Then he had gone away before you entered the prison?"

"Oh, yes, he went out the first day of that dreadful invasion and enlisted, along with all the other loyal sons of Poland. As he was a professor at the University of Warsaw, he was immediately commissioned an officer. He came by just to say hello only twice while the fighting still raged in the city. Before the month was over Poland had capitulated to Germany and the fighting ceased. It soon started again, however, and oddly enough, it was the Soviet Army that had moved in and resumed fire. Thousands of our gallant men were herded onto cattle cars and carried away to Russia. I received one letter telling me Peter had been taken to some rest house in Kozelsk Winter Resort. I wrote many times to the address given, but never received a reply. Years later I learned the address was a concentration camp at

Kozelsk. Many of the brave Poles were eventually released from there, but the officers were never seen alive again. Their bodies were finally discovered in a common grave in 1943 in the Katyn Forest near Smolensk. Their hands had been tied behind their backs and each had been shot through the head."

The voice was by now little more than a whisper, and the weary head dropped to the chest again. But Bonnie didn't panic this time. Of course, the poor soul had expended her frail strength on the emotion she poured into that painful memory.

"Here, let me help you back into bed. I fear you've exhausted yourself."

It was becoming increasingly difficult for Bonnie to manage even so shrunken a body, for the afflicted one was losing strength by the day, and Bonnie had to bear her entire weight. She was beginning to wonder whether her own strength would hold out. And now with Buz gone, she wouldn't even have his help. She might just have to leave the poor woman in her bed. But after this last narration she didn't see how she could feel imposed upon again. How had Stefiania smiled even as much as she had?

"You are so good to me," she murmured as Bonnie tucked the cover around her.

In reply, Bonnie bent to kiss the pale cheek.

Strange, she mused as she turned her steps to the kitchen to prepare dinner, *I was never terribly interested in history as such.* But she who was Stefiania Morawski in another life was stepping forth from the pages in living color. For the first time Bonnie connected real flesh and blood with the dates and atrocities she had read about in school those many years gone by. Unfortunately, Stefiania's tragedy was multiplied by the millions whose lives had been touched—or ended—by that terrible conflict.

She would like to have thought the world was past such savagery, that history never repeated itself, that each generation learned from the sins of the forefathers. But the television and newspapers denied any such illusions. In fact, the most recent years had witnessed a slaughter and oppression only dissimilar in scope and magnitude. And when a person was tortured or killed, did it make any difference whether the perpetrator was a demonic demagogue from Germany or a demented dictator in Africa? The victim was as dead that way as he was had he met his fate at the hands of Communism in Southeast Asia, as witnessed by the decade that had just barely slipped into history. And if political ideologies were not sufficient to account for the deaths of uncountable numbers, Islam must now rear its ugly head again.

"For we know that the whole creation groaneth and travaileth in pain together until now," slipped into Bonnie's mind. It wasn't for lack of a better name that Christ was spoken of as the Prince of Peace. And the root of all the turmoil and travail could be summarized in one word: sin. The sin that had sent Christ to die the ultimate death, the death by which a tragic world could be reconciled to God.

Thank You, Father, she breathed silently. *Because of that sacrifice we can be assured the evils of this world will eventually end.*

The following day dawned with the promise of transparent skies and cool breezes to drive out the early summer heat that settled oppressively over the area. *A perfect day to be out in God's great outdoors,* thought Bonnie as she prepared breakfast. But on what pretext could she devise a trip? The addresses, of course, if she could find them. She would surprise Buz when he returned with the information that she had already inspected the possible sites for their new home. Having determined they

499

would relocate in the vicinity, he had alerted himself immediately to available lots; and just days before his departure excitedly told her of two prospects. Now if she could find that little slip of paper. Right inside the top drawer of his desk, of course.

The next problem was what to do with the invalid. But on second thought, what better way for her to spend some time than to enjoy the trip with her? With Miriam's help she could probably maneuver her into the car.

"I hate to complain and add all that to the burden I already am to you," the frail little soul fretted, "but it is terribly distressing not to be able to use my hands."

"I'm sure it is, but don't trouble yourself so far as I'm concerned. I really don't mind doing your hair at all." Especially for all the more there is of it, Bonnie could have added. Stefiania would never hide so much as a chain in her thin locks now, to say nothing of the pendant.

She chose what she felt was the elder one's prettiest dress and brushed a touch of rouge across the pale cheeks, feeling an inner compulsion to make this a festive occasion. There was the dread possibility it may be her friend's last outing. But perish such thoughts for the moment; relax and enjoy it.

Taking the wheelchair down the steps without Buz's strong arms supporting it was somewhat frightening, but mother and daughter succeeded without mishap. Miriam chose to accompany the two women, and with Peter occupied with a previously arranged activity with his friends, the three set out in high spirits.

Bonnie searched for quite a while before locating the first address. Making what she thought was the correct turn, she wound her way quite a distance from the main thoroughfare before finally arriving at a dead end.

"Well, so much for that." Her patience was wearing

thin. And there was no way to return except by the way she had gone in. The whole little jaunt had taken forty-five minutes.

Choosing very carefully, she made another turn. It was not long before the road led her straight in the back entrance to a shopping mall under construction. The dry dust from the newly-scraped earth clouded the windshield until it was necessary to pull into a service station and have it cleaned.

"This wasn't exactly what I had in mind when I anticipated a pleasant drive." Her happy, hopeful resolve was beginning to fade by the time she finally came upon the site. But it revived immediately at the beauty she beheld. For they were, as she had expected, off the beaten path, away from the noise and bustle of the highway, and at a distance from the nearest neighbors. Pussy willows lined the edge of the lot, and cattails waved from the creek bank several yards away. A weeping willow swept gracefully over what would be the back yard, and old-fashioned rambler roses sprawled over the remains of a rusting fence. The fence could be removed, and the roses recuperated.

"Oh, Mom, please take this place. I *love* it." Mimi's effervescence seemed to go with her age.

"Yes, it is lovely." Bonnie's eye had been well-trained under the tutelage of an architect, and she quickly envisioned a lovely recreation of an English country cottage, although of much more spacious proportions. A rustic chimney would go up that side over there— But her reverie ended abruptly. As much trouble as she had had in locating this faraway place, it would be next to impossible for anyone else to do so. Anyone who might be in need of encouragement, a word of prayer, just an ear for listening. She remembered Windy Knoll's isolation too vividly. Great for recluses, but entirely unpractical for sharing Christ with others. Clearly this place would not do.

501

It was a considerable drive to the other address, but she located it as though she had always known where it was. Only a block from a major artery, it was surrounded by dwellings. Here and there Bonnie could catch a glimpse of a wading pool in a back yard. And children were riding bicycles and tricycles on the walks. Children who were part of families, young families who needed to hear of the Christ who had died for them, families who should be encouraged to go to Sunday school, perhaps some who would be interested in home Bible studies.

"We'll take this one." She said it quietly, without visible emotion.

And then they looked for a sandwich shop. They had been driving for a long time.

The monotony of the next few days was broken by a visit from Sylvia. Her sister took her in her arms when she met her at the airport and wept tears of gratitude over the once proud, glamorous girl. Beauty remained in abundance, but a deeper, more refined type of beauty, the type that is refined as by fire.

Sylvia had given Hal custody of the girls according to the plan she had formulated in her mind. Taking an apartment nearby, she visited and phoned almost to the point of making a nuisance of herself. She prepared lovely dinners and invited the entire family to her apartment. And she remembered every one of Hal's birthdays, and Father's Days, and offered not-so-subtle reminders on wedding anniversaries. But she had never won him back. He remained distantly polite and totally disinterested. Bonnie ached for them both as she feared Hal's hurts had been too deep for the wound ever to close apart from the healing power of the Lord Jesus Christ. But Hal would not seek that source of balm.

Realizing the girls were profiting by the nurture of both parents, Sylvia made no move to change the arrangement. And as she made that sacrifice with the benefit of others in mind, it was a means by which she could at last reach out of her own small shell and begin to blossom into the trophy of grace that the heavenly Father had in mind for her when he rescued her from her downward path. Reaching adulthood by now, the girls were ready to venture out on their own, and Harry was already engaged to a lovely local girl.

"Clothed and in her right mind," Bonnie had once bemused herself about her sister. But it went far further than that now. There was a settled composure in place of the old flightiness, and a serenity borne of sorrow and suffering.

Nine days had sped by astonishingly, and unbelievably Bonnie had not fretted over remaining behind as she had thought she would when Buz went to Europe. Tomorrow was the grand day when her dear one would return and she could at least hear all about it. She was singing as she carried in the morning mail.

"How lovely," she exclaimed over the picture postcard of Lake Lucerne. Another day and Buz would have arrived home ahead of it. Turning over the card she read: "Dearest—sat on the bank last night and watched the huge, gorgeous moon come up over this lake. Need I tell you my thoughts were across the ocean, wrapping my heart around you, if not my arms. See you soon. Love, Buz."

She felt giddy, like a young bride again.

"From your husband, I would guess?" The voice was so weak it scarcely carried across the room from the hospital bed. It was the third day Stefania had made no attempt to rise from it.

"Yes, he has been to Lake Lucerne. Here, would you like to see the picture?"

Holding the card before the wrinkled face, she observed tears making their way into the corners of the eyes.

"Ah, yes, my Peter and I—we used to go to Lake Lucerne. Paris, Geneva, Rome. We would drive over for vacations, and sometimes it was an engagement of the Warsaw Ballet. You see, I was a ballerina—" Bonnie knew the tear-brimmed eyes were not seeing her, but another life, another world, one that had disappeared forever on one day in September, 1939. Helpless to think of anything to say, she brushed away the tears with her finger.

The feeble hands reached up to the chain about the neck and fumbled helplessly with the old ancient locket a few moments before dropping in despair.

"Please, Bonnie, dear, would you undo the clasp and open it so that I can get one good last look?"

Bonnie's fingers trembled, and she had to lift Stefiania's head forward in order to pull the chain around to where she could reach the clasp. Gently she laid the head back upon the pillow and cranked the head-end of the bed up a trifle so the patient could gain a better view. Suddenly Bonnie's fingers seemed to work no better than the paralyzed ones. Inserting her thumbnail into the cleft between the two faces of the case, she nearly broke it before she could pry apart the ancient catch. And then there in her hand she met the clear, steady, penetrating gaze of an intellectual peering at her intently from a sensitive, youthful face crowned with thin, light hair in the style of the thirties. Turning the trinket so his wife could see it clearly, Bonnie caught sight of the inside of the cover. There, startlingly, was Mimi, as though right out of the picture on the mantle.

"W-what—w-w-who—?"

"My daughter." It was nothing more than a whisper, the fainter for the reverence with which it was spoken.

"But you said George was your only remaining—"

"I said nothing of her, for I couldn't bear to. Though I am forced to think of her every time I look at your Mimi. That picture of her on your mantle could be a copy of what this one had been. Of course, I had to cut away the rest of it with the little pink tutu to fit it into the locket."

"Then she was a ballerina?"

"She might have been, although she had only begun to study. I sometimes liked to look at that picture of Miriam and pretend I was seeing my little Stefiania again after all these years. For that is just the way she looked when I—" the voice choked and paused for a moment, "—when I last saw her."

The feeble hand made its way up to the emotion-strained face and covered it, while Bonnie stood mutely, completely stripped of words at yet another of these tragic recollections. Then taking the hand in her own, she found her voice again.

"The *blitzkrieg*—it was then that you last saw her?"

"Oh, no, she was only newborn at that time. It was as much to see her as me that her father made those visits at home after he enlisted in the armed forces. He picked her up in his arms and held her tight. I believe he knew he was never to see her again. It was later, in Hungary, where we had fled following Poland's fall, and where the little one of which I had told you was born. We had known comparative peace there, but they somehow caught up with us. My father had been Jewish, you see. That made me one of the stigmatized ones. They rounded us up with some Jewish sympathizers and a multitude of others on one flimsy pretext or another. They were herding us like cattle into one of those infamous trains to be taken to the concentration camp in Austria. The babe was in one arm and three-year-old little Stefiania I had firmly in the other hand; George was by my other side, trying to keep up as well as he could. It was terrible—black of night and a cold drizzle of rain drenching us to the skin." (She subconsciously pulled the cover up tight about herself, although the room was very warm.) "She—she was just—just pulled from my grasp by the struggling of the crowds about her. I never saw my child again."

Bonnie took both the withered hands in her own and stroked them gently. They seemed so cold. She also noticed a rattle in the weakened throat; it obviously was extremely difficult for the bereaved old mother to speak of the subject which she had never trusted herself to voice before.

"I searched and searched for her. Many times I went to the Red Cross hoping they would have some news of her. Just a few years ago they thought they had found her, but that lead turned out to be a girl listed as coming from Hungary, and I was inquiring for one from Austria, as that was the country from which I had been liberated and made my departure for the States. You see, I never did know what became of my daughter. But as she had been in the crowds being herded into that train, I assumed she would have been swept up with them and arrived in Austria also. If she ever survived the trip. But when I think of how kind you have been to me, and my own daughter couldn't have done more for me, I feel as though I can slip away as peacefully as though I had found her. You certainly have in a great measure replaced her. There's no way in this life I can reward you, but I'm sure the good Lord will not overlook your kindness. I will at least leave you my most cherished possession. Keep the locket to remember me by."

"I accept it with gratitude, although I need no other reminder than the memory of you."

Stefiania withdrew her hands from Bonnie's and seemed to clutch at the covers once again.

"You know, Bonnie, dear, so many times when I can't

506

sleep at night I go over and over that dreadful scene in my mind—how I called and called to her, and I hear her pitiful little voice screaming for her mother, but she is carried farther and farther away from me, and I can't reach her." Mrs. Morrow's left hand pulled the covers into a little wad over her chest, while the right arm began a feeble, though somewhat wild tossing in the air. "Sometimes I dream that I am pushing my way through the crowd and reaching and reaching for her little hand, but I never find it. I always just wake up in a sweat and tears. And then I lie there in the still of the night and tell myself if it hadn't been for that child of rape I lost soon after, I would have been carrying Stefiania, and she would not have been lost. As it was, I lost them both."

Suddenly the floor started swaying beneath Bonnie's feet as the significance of what she heard penetrated her dazed consciousness. A portentous pounding in her temples started her mind swirling. In a flash her discovery of the already existing marriage of the man she planned to marry, the estrangement from her mother, the death of her beloved Timothy, and her husband's bankruptcy paraded before her bewildered memory as one sustained agonizing sequence. She felt again the turbulence of the pulsating waves of her own dream, and it seemed that she was about to be overcome by it.

Struggling to keep her voice uttering what her heart wanted to say, she stammered, "Mrs. Morrow, did you call your daughter by Stefiania?"

She had to bend over the still form on the bed, and press her ear to the mouth laboring to form the words between gasps for breath.

"No, no. To avoid confusion in the family, we called her by a second name.

"Her other name—you see, it was during that terrible fighting—shells exploding all around. Russian shells, they were this time, however,—as it was on the night of

507

the seventeenth of September when they entered upon the ruins that the Germans had left. We were crammed into basements, public buildings, any place where we could hope to find some shelter from the destruction. I was in the basement of the library of the university, as we had lived near there. That was when my pains began." She paused for breath. "We had just a few belongings we had brought with us, not knowing whether we would ever find our homes again. I had my rosary, and I prayed all night to the Holy Virgin, Queen of Poland. I prayed, 'Blessed Mother, you know how it is to bear a little one, and you know how it felt to see that precious One die. Now if you will just spare my little one and let it live through birth and this bombing attack, I will call it by your name' " Stefania made a desperate effort to breathe deeply. But she could only gulp air in vain. "And that was how it was that I gave my little daughter her second name, Marya."

A lifetime of torment and longing welled into one agonized throb as Bonnie threw herself upon the old lady, and with every quivering fiber of her being poured into the one word, she half sobbed, half screamed, "Mother!"

But when she found the strength to pull herself from the old woman, her mother did not reply, for all that was left upon earth of the one who had been Stefania Morawski was a radiant smile that transformed the tragedy-scarred face. She had slipped peacefully into the presence of the Lord she loved so dearly.